The
Divorcées

The Divorcées

· · · · · · · · ·

ROWAN BEAIRD

FLATIRON
BOOKS
NEW YORK

THE DIVORCÉES. Copyright © 2024 by Rowan Beaird. All rights reserved. Printed in the United States of America. For information, address Flatiron Books, 120 Broadway, New York, NY 10271.

www.flatironbooks.com

Library of Congress Cataloging-in-Publication Data

Names: Beaird, Rowan, author.
Title: The divorcées / Rowan Beaird.
Description: First edition. | New York : Flatiron Books, 2024.
Identifiers: LCCN 2023029115 | ISBN 9781250896582 (hardcover) |
    ISBN 9781250896599 (ebook)
Subjects: LCGFT: Novels.
Classification: LCC PS3602.E2424 D58 2024 | DDC 813/.6—dc23/eng/20231016
LC record available at https://lccn.loc.gov/2023029115)

Our books may be purchased in bulk for promotional, educational, or business use. Please contact your local bookseller or the Macmillan Corporate and Premium Sales Department at 1-800-221-7945, extension 5442, or by email at MacmillanSpecialMarkets@macmillan.com.

First Edition: 2024

10 9 8 7 6 5 4 3 2 1

For my mother, my first reader

There are pitfalls on every side. There is, for example, the constant danger that the girls will go wild.

—Robert Wernick, "Last of the Divorce Ranches"
Saturday Evening Post, July 17, 1965

The
Divorcées

. . . .

When she can't fall asleep, Lois decides what she will wear to the casino. In the drowsy glow of her bedside lamp, she stares at the slack shapes of her shirts and dresses spaced out wide as the teeth of a comb.

In the narrow closet that mirrors every other girl's at the ranch, she tugs at hems and cuffs. Rubs a belt buckle. The casino is different from how it appeared to her a month before, when she was first led through its polished glass doors—its glamour rubbed off like lipstick. She pictures the low ceilings where cigarette smoke clouds, the long tables furred with green felt. The gamblers crushed against roulette wheels are sweaty and swollen, their cheeks stippled with burst capillaries. Makeup gums the women's eyelids. She imagines the waitresses cutting cleanly across the carpet patterned in fleur-de-lis circled with ivy, each print the size of her hand. She really looked at the carpet for the first time several days before. A mashed cocktail olive nudged her heel and she began to see how the frenetic, repeating pattern could camouflage all manner of refuse. This is how the casino comes to her now, coated with cigarette ash and slivers of orange peel, stained with spit and spilled gin.

She unfolds a pair of stiff blue jeans, thinking of how the denim would brush against the leather seat she'll sit in at the bar tomorrow evening. The angle at which she'll watch for the supervisors, ensuring they click into their standard circuit as she orders no more than one drink, ready to sound the alarm if they deviate. She traces her route to the ladies' room, to the third stall from the door. To where Greer will empty the chips into her purse.

Wind rattles the open window of her bedroom, and she needs to use both palms to jam it shut. She looks out to the desert dark, unsure if she's able to actually see the line of mountains in the distance or if she just knows they're there. The other girls are still at the Highlands, where someone is probably playing a Perry Como record just to annoy the cowboys, who want

Hank Williams or no music at all. Though the bar is no more than five miles away, it's as if the girls are in another country, another time. If she told them what she and Greer were planning, they would never understand, even if they've hungered for the same freedom. Her own appetite is greater. Lois knows this now.

She turns back to the room. The few items she traveled with, her books, her makeup, have worn into the same groove as the blue vase and daisy curtains, so that it all feels of herself. Her eyes scan the stretch of empty wall by the door, waiting for the lizard that skitters across the plaster. Its body is light as paper, something she could crumple in her hand.

Rolling her shoulders back, she unhooks hangers, bringing items of clothing into the light. This is what she must focus on. Choosing from the clothing that she packed six weeks ago in Lake Forest, ignoring the yellow plaid and lavender polka-dot dresses that make her look like some plain, innocent housewife who just arrived on the train. The absurd shirt she'd been talked into at Parker's with the sweep of fringe, the one that everyone told her would make her look like a real westerner, but that actually makes her look like a caricature, someone too easily remembered. The stiff, glossy boots that pinch her toes but make her taller. The navy heels with accordion bows at their ankle buckles. The linen shirts, their flax a soft braille.

She removes a green cocktail dress and lays it on her unmade bed. She'd bought it for a Christmas party last December, but it had seemed too severe when the evening came, its color like the mold that kept blooming on the bathroom ceiling no matter how often their maid bleached it. It's a dress a mistress would wear. A thief of one thing or another. For the casino, it feels right.

It calms her, to brush her hands across its silk. To think not of this girl standing in a frail nightgown, but of who she will be tomorrow, and the day after.

One

· · · ·

6 Weeks Earlier

The train smells like sweat, warm and sour. Once they entered Nevada, passengers could no longer keep the windows open, the desert wind whipping in red sand that coated their eyes and throats. "The summer's first dust storm," the conductor said. Now no one can stay clean. The air is fetid as a marsh and makes everything swell: the wooden banisters, the liver-colored seats, the pale face of the ticket taker. Everything ripens and splits, while outside the passengers' windows the desert is hard as glass.

When Lois first boarded the train in Chicago two days ago, everyone looked ready for church, starched and ironed. A man in a navy suit and fedora gallantly swung her luggage into her compartment. She passed women who looked just like the Onwentsia Club matrons who snubbed her mother every time she asked about joining. Only after marrying Lawrence had Lois been allowed inside. In the dining car, the conversations around her were loud and joyous and she felt giddy from the shared feeling of escape, ordering two desserts with dinner—a temporary extravagance, undoubtedly not the way her father imagined her spending his money. At night, she lay awake listening to the hoarse laughter of men smoking cigarettes in the corridor, awed by the fact that she could join them and no one would know. She'd never been this far from home.

But in the heat, she is sullen and claustrophobic like everyone else, the sugared rush flattening to a familiar restlessness. When they first closed the windows, Lois rubbed the smooth nose of her Ivory soap beneath her armpits every few hours, splashing them with sink water. Eventually she found it was no use. Everyone has given up on certain proprieties. In the dining cars, people barely speak. Children scratch at their stomachs and whine like overheated dogs. Even the women who serve meals stop making conversation, wordlessly filling water glasses and handing out limp sandwiches. Lois sees one slip an ice cube into the cup of her bra.

In her compartment, Lois dreams of the shower in her house and its cool, mint-green tile. *We'll have to rip this out,* Lawrence said. *It won't ever look clean.* Lois told him that didn't make sense. Color didn't make something dirty. In her fevered state she finds herself saying this again and again, even though he's nowhere near.

An hour or so from the station, everyone becomes nearly manic with relief. Passengers stop by other compartments to chat, making promises to have dinner together in Reno. A man outside Lois's compartment explains to two others how best to count cards.

"And prepare yourself for the women," he says, his voice dropping to a loud whisper. "At the casinos, it's all chorus girls and divorcées."

Lois draws closed the curtains for the windows that open to the corridor, muffling the men. She blackens Betty Grable's lips with a ballpoint pen on the cover of a *Silver Screen* magazine. Plucks her eyebrows until the skin puffs in irritation. Outside the window, the desert looks bleached and barren, more like a backdrop for a film set than anything else, and she imagines reaching her hand out and, with one push, tipping it to the ground. It's nothing like the lush lawns of Lake Forest, sparrows perched in the boxwoods.

There is a rapping on the glass of the compartment, and Lois sits up, re-buttoning her blouse so her bra doesn't show.

"Excuse me," a girl says, opening the door.

"Yes?" Lois says.

The girl steps inside the compartment, sliding the door shut behind her. She is around Lois's age, in her early twenties, with the sort of freshly scrubbed prettiness that will grow faint as she gets older, and has clearly just put on a clean swing dress and done her makeup. The line of her upper lip is a perfect half heart. The innocent pink of a carnation. Lois becomes conscious of her oily face and open suitcase, dirty underwear foaming at its corners.

"Are you Lois Saunders?" the girl asks. Her voice is Southern, careful and considered.

"Yes," Lois says, narrowing her eyes. "How do you—"

"I'm so sorry to bother you," the girl says, taking a seat at the edge of the leather bench. "I'm Mary Elizabeth Shores, I mean, Brown—Mary Elizabeth Brown from Lexington, and I'm going to the Golden Yarrow too. They told me we'd be traveling on the same train, and I finally got one of the ticket takers to tell me where your compartment was. I hope this isn't impolite."

Lois remembers the girl from that first day in the dining car, when she was trying to pick out who else was traveling for the same reason. A fact most would be trying to hide, knowing how it would mark them. She looked for girls who were alone. They had to look deeply sad or deeply happy, though neither described Lois's own emptiness, the crackle of a blank frame of film. Mary Elizabeth had been seated at the other end of the car, her sadness its own aura, quietly drinking a cup of tea. Her wealth was obvious in the weight of her silk blouse and tightly stitched cotton skirt, the studied choreography with which she moved her hands. Familiar to Lois as language. She knew her, and so had no interest in knowing her.

"You're getting divorced?" Lois asks.

"Well, yes." The girl glances at the door, confirming it's shut and no one can hear them. "I think everyone will be, at the ranch. I've honestly been looking forward to that aspect of it. Not being the one everyone's whispering about."

"I suppose that's true. Why are you getting divorced?"

"Oh." Mary Elizabeth's brow furrows. "There were difficulties, with my husband."

"Ah." It was forward of Lois to ask so quickly, and embarrassment flares in her stomach, the familiar feeling of saying the wrong thing.

"I thought we might find the driver together," Mary Elizabeth says, delicately skipping over the beat of silence. "Charlie, if I'm remembering right. I honestly didn't expect anyone else to be taking the train. I'm terrified of planes. I just don't understand how they stay up there." She laughs at her own foolishness, as if her fear could only be a joke.

"My father doesn't trust them either, so, here I am."

Lois would have preferred to fly. She thinks of the film *Five Came Back*, which her mother took her to see when she was nine years old. A chrome plane falling from the sky, the passengers awakening in the wet, seething dark of a jungle, their location untraceable. How even at that age Lois desired such an escape, no matter how violent the means. To open her eyes and find a different world.

"Well," Mary Elizabeth says, standing and pressing her palms flat against her dress. "I'm so glad to have met someone before arriving. I'll see you in an hour?"

Lois smiles and looks back down to her magazine, desperate to unbutton her blouse again in the still air of the compartment. But after Mary Elizabeth opens the door, she turns back to Lois, her skirt swishing.

"It's good to start with a friend. A bit like camp, isn't it?"

Lois nods, and Mary Elizabeth gives her a smile—as if they're in on a secret together—before she closes the door. Lois feels a small thrill at this. She's never been very close to any girl or woman aside from their housekeeper, Ela, and her mother, though her love burned in short, bright flares. As a child Lois was on her own too often, left to make up stories and imagine friends, like a large bulldog named Lacey, with whom she had tea every morning. Her mother always needed time to herself, their outings confined to when she would let Lois miss school so she'd have someone to go to the movies with in the afternoons, pulling Lois further away from her classmates, who were quick to sniff out any oddity. It will undoubtedly only be a matter of time until Mary Elizabeth senses this same strangeness; she'll find other friends, and Lois will once again be alone.

Perhaps this will be for the best, she tells herself. It's what she's accustomed to. When she told her father she was going to Reno for the six weeks needed to establish residency and be granted a divorce, she imagined renting a room in a hotel, eating a rare steak alone at a table draped in thick white cloth, men watching her as she lit a cigarette. A new romance to her solitude. But her father refused to pay unless she went to one of the state's famed ranches. He'd chosen a reputable institution that promised discretion and supervision for wealthy girls in her same position. *You need to be watched,* he said. *Look what kind of a mess you get into when you're left alone.*

The ticket takers begin to walk through the corridors, telling everyone to pack up their belongings. Lois tucks a fresh shirt into her waistband. No amount of powder can salvage her sweat-streaked face, but still, she brushes on some peach blush and flattens a flyaway with a glob of spit, attempting to become presentable. Her lips are colored a self-possessed burgundy. She's always thought she has a plain face, her skin made even paler by her black hair. Without lipstick and mascara, her features disappear, and so even when she's home alone she puts on makeup just to assure herself that they exist. She loves the process of it, the slow recovery of her face. At school, she did makeup for all of the plays, and when her classmates would look in the mirror afterward, it was one of the rare times she experienced warmth from any of them, flushes of gratitude that would hang in the air briefly, like a breath of perfume.

When they pull into the station, the corridor is teeming with people, more than Lois ever imagined could fit on the train. After checking her reflection in the window glass one last time, she lugs her bags down the corridor, each suitcase banging against her knees. No man offers his assistance.

Outside, Reno stretches before her, low-lying brick buildings and store signs rimmed with light bulbs, dead in the daylight. Men in cowboy hats lean out of car windows and others shepherd women into backseats as if they're lost lambs. Striped awnings billow in the desert breeze, and in the distance mountains rise. It's nothing like Chicago or New York, the only cities she's visited, with their austere gray skyscrapers, and its vast newness makes her heart trill.

Near the strip of idling motors, she sees Mary Elizabeth talking to a young man wrestling with her luggage. She takes a deep breath in. The red sand smells of the chalk in her old schoolroom and something else, something metallic and elemental, a note that catches in the back of her throat like blood.

Two

· · · ·

The driver, Charlie, is not handsome. He's young, with a wide face and too-full lips that are chapped and peeling. Lois feels a flicker of disappointment at this, the irritation of a cracked nail. She imagined someone rougher, older, like Robert Mitchum—the type of man who could kiss you so intensely you'd faint. Charlie does wear a cowboy hat, and after Mary Elizabeth comments on it he spends most of the car ride explaining the types of hats men wear in the West: Colorado cowboys wear ten-gallon hats, the high crown giving them insulation from the cold, whereas Nevada cowboys' hats aren't so exaggerated, needing a wide, flat brim to protect them from the sun. Mary Elizabeth listens politely, and Lois can't tell if she's actually interested or if Southern girls are simply better at feigning it.

Lois looks out the window as the buildings disappear behind them, giving way to ribbons of meadow and desert dirt, and she feels a sadness at leaving the city so quickly. The ranch is farther out in the country, twenty miles from the center of Reno—a selling point for her father, who told her she should learn to milk a cow. He'd purchased a meatpacking plant in Chicago just before she was born, always bringing home tripe and liver tightly wrapped in wax paper, pieces of meat that Ela would sigh over. *He can bring you a porterhouse, and he brings you entrails,* she would say to Lois's mother as they drank bitter coffee by the stove. They'd let Lois sit with them, and she would entertain with exaggerated tales of her school days. The more she made them laugh or gasp, the longer she was allowed to stay. Stories as currency.

They pass a pasture, two blond horses dipping their heads into a trough. Charlie waves at a man leaning against a fence post, his hat tipped back from his forehead.

"Either of you ridden before?" Charlie asks.

"We grew up with horses, and I've actually competed. Though in English style," Mary Elizabeth says.

"No kidding!" Charlie says.

"I never really placed or anything," Mary Elizabeth says demurely, looking down at her knees. She turns to Lois. "Do they have stables in Chicago?"

"Outside of the city they do. I live in a town farther north, along the lake."

Lois's parents never thought to take her riding. In the Polish neighborhood where her mother and father grew up, horses pulled carts of firewood and dirt-caked potatoes. They were bred for bulk. The words Lois's classmates used—*Appaloosa, Friesian, Saddlebred*—were incomprehensible, and when she asked to go to the stables, her father laughed as if it were a joke.

"Well, we have to go out on the trail together, then."

Lois smiles. It is so simple, not to correct Mary Elizabeth's assumption that she would have visited these stables. Lies have always come naturally to her, flowering from her hours alone, from watching too many films and reading too many of her mother's books. Only Ela and the occasional teacher would catch her in one, though she suspects her mother sensed every falsehood and was simply too amused to consider punishment.

"We've got very gentle horses," Charlie says. "Samson especially is one of the kindest horses I've ever come across in my life, stops when you so much as twitch at the reins. Though on the trails the heat can start to get brutal the closer we get to July."

"Will we be able to make calls when we get to the ranch? I'll need to tell my mother I've arrived safe and sound. I'm sure Lois will need to do the same," Mary Elizabeth says.

"Of course."

Grief shudders through Lois, and she rolls down the window, letting her fingertips fall over the blunted glass edge. It's been nearly seven years since her mother passed, during the last gasp of the war. When her father told Lois what was going to happen—the months remaining, the waves of radiation that would burn through her mother's body—Lois didn't fully absorb it, the words hitting some barrier an inch beneath her skin. She had understood that her mother would die, but she hadn't been able to imagine the complete absence that immediately followed, like a dark, dense shard of obsidian, absorbing all other light. This grief returns when she least expects it, sudden and surprising.

She knows this isn't how she'll miss Lawrence, though it's been just under two weeks since she last saw him. She's slept better without him lying next to her, even during the nights when she wakes in a tremor, restless with dreams she can't recall.

W ell, there she is," Charlie says, pointing over the steering wheel.

In the distance, a large white house rests beneath two maples, their branches shading the roof and long balcony that runs the length of the second story. Two cars gleam in the parking lot. It's plainer than Lois imagined, given what her father said about its well-established reputation—all simple lines, each window edged in forest-green. Perhaps that's part of the appeal for well-off girls used to much finer accommodations; the ranch offers them a novel existence—a reprieve or a punishment.

As they get closer, Lois sees the rope of a tire swing falling from a tree branch and the figures of two small girls. One is hugging the body of the tire, her legs dangling above the ground, and the other is slowly pulling the tire up and back. Soon the second girl drops her arms, and the tire swings like a pendulum. Lois didn't expect to see children at the ranch. It doesn't feel like a place where children should be, and for a moment she wonders if she's imagining them. When she was little, sometimes she felt she really could see the girls and dogs she'd conjure to play with her, the desire for companionship so potent that a silhouette would singe the air.

When they finally pull into the lot, the girls have retreated into the house. Charlie tells them he will bring their suitcases up to their rooms and that they should meet the owner, Rita, in the living room to sign the register. Lois is desperate for a shower, but before she can ask Charlie if she can go directly to her room, the front door opens. Out steps a tall, handsome woman, her hair brushed back into short curls threaded with gray. She wears jeans and a button-up whose sleeves are rolled to reveal tanned, freckled arms. A kerchief is knotted at her neck, and three small dachshunds trot at her heels.

"Welcome, welcome, welcome," the woman says, walking down the front steps, the dogs hopping alongside her, "to the Golden Yarrow."

Three

· · · · · ·

Rita does not stand still. Lois expects to sit for coffee, but instead Rita walks them from room to room, out to the pool and the pasture, pulling a carrot nub from the back pocket of her jeans and offering it up to one of the horses. The guests are napping in their rooms to escape the heat, but in the dining room Rita introduces them to the cook, a ruddy-faced woman named Anna whose hands are flaked with dough. Another woman emerges from the kitchen tearing at a cold chicken leg. With her height and muscled forearms, she seems more like a ranch hand than Charlie, and Lois tries to think if she's ever seen a grown woman eat not seated at a table.

"Bailey's my right-hand woman," Rita says, introducing her. "Organizes the trips to Pyramid Lake, the trips to town. Keeps an eye on things. I don't know what I'd do without her."

"Oh please, you'd do just fine," Bailey says, smiling. She has a broad, weather-beaten face. Lois guesses she's in her early thirties—wrinkles faint as leaf veins at the corners of her eyes.

Rita continues their tour at a brisk pace. Lois likes her swiftness, her sense of purpose.

The ranch is full of contradictions. In the living room, there are large cotton curtains printed with palm leaves and red plaid pillows, glossy rattan side tables and dark walnut colonial chairs. It is East and West, a New England cabin and a desert bungalow, but somehow—remarkably—it all sits in harmony, like Rita herself, with her seed-pearl earrings and navy bandanna. When they linger at the living room's threshold, Lois picks up a painted porcelain pheasant to test its weight, but when she sees Rita watching her, she gingerly sets it back down. Rita's owned the ranch for ten years. She tells them that she originally purchased it with her husband, a man she found much later in life than Mary Elizabeth or Lois had, but they separated after fourteen years of marriage and he's gone on to marry some woman who gets sick every time it rains. They live in Palm Springs now and he comes out every Christmas to see the children, bringing them oranges and sundresses that are always a size too small.

"You have children?" Mary Elizabeth asks.

"Yes, two daughters. Carol and Patty. God only knows where they are right now, but they know to stay out of everyone's way. They use the pool on Friday afternoons, so if you don't want to pretend to be a mermaid just don't leave the deck chairs."

Lois remembers her surprise at seeing the children and tells herself she was being prudish. There is nothing wrong with children living among soon-to-be divorcées in a ranch with horses and a pool ten yards long. Perhaps they'll learn something none of the ranch's guests had until after they were wed, and be better for it.

As Rita walks them back to the house she tells them the schedule, how most girls spend their days. With them included, there are five girls currently boarding at the ranch. All meals have set times, though no formal dress is expected, and Anna has a menu that she rotates through every six weeks, so they don't have to worry about lacking for variety. Cocktails are at five thirty. There are horseback rides and picnics, trips to the desert and trips to town. Lois is overwhelmed by the thought of being around others for seemingly every hour of the day.

"Now, when you go into town beware any reporters that start asking you too many questions about the place," Rita says, grabbing keys from the drawer of a rolltop desk. "Stringers, we call them. It happens every once in a while when you mention our name, because of our clientele. They're always trying to see if someone famous is staying here, or some name they know from the *Social Register*."

"*Has* anyone famous stayed here?" Lois asks Rita.

"Well, I wouldn't be very good at my job if I told you that, would I?"

"Of course," Lois says. "I'm sorry."

Rita bends over to pull up one of her dachshunds and cradles it under her arm. Her soft reprimand makes Lois hold her tongue between her teeth.

"Two final things before I let you go and freshen up," Rita says, pausing before the staircase, the dachshund wriggling in her arms. "First, these are your keys, but don't worry about locking your rooms. Obviously, it's perfectly safe here. And second, either I or Bailey will be your witness in court. In order to do that we need to see you once a day, because otherwise we can't testify that you've been here for the full six weeks. Now, I know that sounds simple enough, but you'd be surprised at how girls seem to disappear every once in a while. So, if you're going to disappear, make sure it's not for any longer than half a day. All right?"

"Yes," Lois says.

"Of *course,*" Mary Elizabeth says.

"Wonderful," Rita says, her eyes lingering on Lois for a second too long. Lois shifts on her feet, conscious of how loud it sounds when she swallows. "Well, up to your rooms!"

Upstairs, Lois turns on the shower and strips clean, throwing her clothes into a corner of the room. She never wants to put them on again, wishing she could take them deep into the desert and let the sun burn them up. The water is hot and steaming, and she stands beneath the showerhead until it becomes painful.

The room itself is small and lived-in, with heavy oak furniture and worn, daisy-speckled curtains that she never would have chosen. Sitting naked on the floor, she feels a shiver of unease at just how far she is from everything she's known, and turns to click open her suitcase. She packed it after Lawrence left to spend the night at his mother's—two tense days after she asked for a divorce. Two days after she'd gotten her period, the relief nearly erotic. Though she often had the house to herself, there was something new and deep in her aloneness that afternoon, and she felt almost unsteady with it, as if she'd swallowed an entire glass of gin. She didn't have to attune herself to Lawrence's imminent return. The sharp click of his key in the door that felt like a nick at her skin.

After watching his Bentley pull out of the driveway, she locked all the doors and put on the Columbia Playtime records she used to listen to as a child, singing along to tinny songs about ducks and posies. She fingered herself while slouched in Lawrence's leather desk chair, staring at a water stain on the ceiling and imagining Cary Grant kissing Ingrid Bergman in *Notorious.* Afterward, she ate sour cream with a spoon and smoked one of the cigars he kept in the cabinet above the refrigerator, always slightly too high for her natural reach. The smoke scorched the back of her throat and her mouth made the cigar too damp, so that threads of leaves clung to her tongue and lips. Still, she began to feel stronger. As if a spirit, not of someone dead but of someone yet to be, were passing through her.

She didn't finish packing for the ranch until the next morning, after she woke up on their living room sofa. Lipstick smeared against the yellow chintz. And it's not until now, in this small room in the middle of the desert, that she begins to think of what she left behind. She'd brought so little to Lawrence's after they married, desperate to begin anew, really just her clothes and her mother's books, which felt as elemental to her as the birthmark on her thigh or her two front teeth. Outside of a few that she packed for this trip, the books are all with Lawrence and will be until she can have them brought back to her father's house, just under a mile away. Returned to the same narrow shelves her mother always complained about, the spines packed so tightly it hurt your fingers to pinch one free. Lois's body shivers again, and she pulls a slip over her head.

She decides she'll feel better if she unpacks her things, and so she pulls out dresses and blouses, folding each into the room's cedar drawers, and lines up her lipsticks and compact on the vanity. At the bottom of the suitcase she finds the black opal necklace her mother wore whenever she threw a party, desperately courting neighbors who wanted little to do with their new money or their odd Polish name—Gorski, which Lois realizes she'll have to use again—and the envelope, wrapped in a silk scarf. Inside, she counts each of the twenty-dollar bills, making sure it's everything she left with, everything her father had given her in order to make it through the next six weeks and back home, now that she's dependent on him again.

Folding the paper seal, she tucks it beneath her mattress like a sin.

Four

· · · · ·

ownstairs, the other girls circle the dining room table. Lois hid from them during cocktail hour, but at the scraping of chairs across wood, the peal of set dishes below her, she knew she had to leave her room. Like the girls from school, they all have the fresh, clear skin that signifies not just money, but wealth—Lois's lesser lineage apparent in the bumps prickling her forehead, the thick hair on her forearms. The oldest at the table looks to be in her forties. They all look up at the click of Lois's heels on the polished floor.

"She emerges," Rita says.

"Yes, I'm alive," Lois says, so many people's attention making her jaw clench.

"Alive and a vision in floral." Rita presses her thumb and forefinger to her ear to twist at her pearl stud. "For those of you who haven't met her, this is Lois Saunders, from Chicago. Lois, this is, well, everyone."

Everyone smiles and murmurs hello, and Mary Elizabeth waves Lois to a chair by her side. On Lois's left is a thirty-something-year-old with vermilion lipstick whose dark brown hair is pulled into a ponytail. At the display of food before her, including a pork roast large enough to feed an army of men, Lois feels her stomach seize and rumble. She hopes no one hears.

"Did everyone see what George sent today? He even had it engraved."

Lois turns to a red-haired girl, likely just a few years older than her, holding up her wrist. A thin gold watch winds around the bone. The girl has a bow mouth and thick, fringed lashes, pretty in the way Lois thinks is too obvious.

"It's Cartier, if you're not familiar," she says. The other girls' strained smiles suggest this is not unusual. Only Mary Elizabeth coos.

"Very lovely," Rita says. "Lois and Mary Elizabeth, this is Dorothy."

Dorothy smiles smugly, and the other two girls briefly introduce themselves. The brunette at Lois's side is June and the older guest is Vera. As the table settles back into its normal rhythm, June passes Lois a bowl of puffed rolls.

"June is from Connecticut," Mary Elizabeth says.

Even in the heat, Mary Elizabeth's butter-colored gingham dress is still buttoned up to her wrists, and she nibbles at the bread like a rabbit. Her wineglass is filled with lemonade.

"Yes, though my cousin and I will be moving to Los Angeles after my stay," June says.

"Your cousin? Why would—" Lois begins, but Mary Elizabeth gently presses her elbow into Lois's armpit, to stop her from saying anything else. She doesn't know whether to be grateful or annoyed that Mary Elizabeth already senses her potential improprieties.

Lois turns her attention to her plate. As she eats, conversation hums around her. There are discussions of whether someone actually saw a snake that morning or if it was just a slither of desert grass, of a bartender who pours stiff drinks for the girl he wants to go home with, and how it's a good deal if you can fend him off. As Lois listens, she begins to see the faint threads tying the girls to one another, whether they are taut or tangled. Everyone ignores Vera, who is plump as a pincushion, and Bailey indulges Dorothy's continued preening. Each of the girls is clearly bound to Rita. They ask for her advice and opinions, telling her the rich, creamy top of every story, what so-and-so had said, what so-and-so had done, one of her dachshunds asleep on her lap, its nose a dark, wet cherry. There is a calmness to Rita, the inscrutable strength of a sphinx—she has suffered the girls' same trials and judgments and somehow emerged unscathed.

"So you're from Chicago?" June asks, and everyone but Rita and Bailey stops to listen, both deep in another conversation. "What does your family do?"

"Oh, my father's in business," Lois says, putting down her fork.

"What sort of business?" Vera asks.

Lois has been here before. Though her father, especially with his stinginess, had as much money as any of the Lake Forest families, it was new money made from something no one wanted to think about. They would look at Lois as if her hands were rusted with blood.

"Real estate," Lois says, and each of the girls nods approvingly. She realizes that out here in the desert, her lying is frictionless—all anyone knows is where her train has come from. "He owns properties across the city. Our family's been in the business for years."

"My family as well, though out East, obviously," June asks. "And what are your plans for after Reno? Old home or new home?"

"I'm sorry?"

"Mary Elizabeth's already told us she's old home, poor thing, but at least she has a lovely estate in Kentucky to go back to," Dorothy says, her tone as loud and unsubtle as her red hair. Lois imagines that, unlike the others, she married into her money. "Vera's the same—moving back into her mother's house in Boston. But I'm marrying George. New home."

"And I'm not in Boston year-round. In the summers, you know, well, in the summers we always go to this charming little—" Vera begins.

"Yes, we *know*, Vera, but we're talking about Lois," June interrupts, and Vera tucks back into herself. Lois imagines June as the head of her class, frustrated by everyone else's idiocy. "So, old home or new home?"

"Well, at first I'm going to have to live with my father," Lois says. "But then I was thinking of living somewhere on my own, perhaps somewhere in the city."

"On your own?" Mary Elizabeth asks, her brows knit together in a tight stitch.

"You can't possibly mean that. Even sad little secretaries have room-mates," June says.

Lois is surprised; she hadn't thought this to be something she should conceal, imagining that at least some of the girls at the ranch would share her desires. That they could act as a compass, charting a path forward through the fog swallowing the days ahead.

"I don't know where I'd even find a roommate," she says.

"I hate to say it, but you'd never marry again. Never. It's poisonous enough to be a divorcée. Only widows and certain *types* of girls live alone," Dorothy says.

"And Dorothy would know," June says, and Dorothy glares at her. There's a weighted pause, and Lois feels a surge of excitement—she's so used to tensions coursing below the surface, like water rushing through a house's hidden pipes.

"As if you could even—" Dorothy begins.

"Now, Anna, what a lovely dinner," Rita says, loud enough to silence the table.

Anna has begun to clear the dishes and stops to smile at Rita. All of the other girls chime in with their praise, Vera and Mary Elizabeth going so far as to clap their hands.

"Now, are you all going to the Highlands this evening?" Rita asks.

The girls nod, erupting into conversation. Dorothy and June disappear into the downstairs bathroom to wash out their mouths and brush their hair. Lois is exhausted, but her curiosity is pricked by the possibility of going out. She wonders if the clubs would be like in *Gilda*—brass bands curved in a half-moon, men with whisper-thin mustaches pouring drinks. How much crueler June and Dorothy would be when drunk. And no one there to tell Lois what to do, just like on the train.

"Are you joining us, Lois?" Bailey asks.

"Well, I know Lois's father wants her to stay close to the ranch," Rita interjects.

"My father?"

"Yes. I told him we'd take special care of you."

Lois's jaw judders open. She knows she wouldn't be here without her father's money, but she didn't imagine she'd feel his presence in this way, as if he were in the other room.

"We could play a few hands of gin rummy in the living room?" Rita offers.

Gin rummy was what Lawrence's mother played, her hands rivered with throbbing blue veins. Lois could never say no to her, bound by everything she was told to be as a wife. Always tamping down her instinct to run, the desires she never failed to act on as a child—sprinting across the shoreline's damp sand, scattering a flight of seagulls.

"What do you think?" Rita asks, and Lois knows what her answer has to be. The other girls are out the front door, consumed by the night's darkness, sudden as a curtain fall. Already out of Lois's reach.

S omewhere deep in the house, a telephone rings.

When Lois first hears it, she thinks she's back in Lake Forest. She reaches over to shove Lawrence awake so he can go downstairs to answer, and when she realizes the bed is empty her body seizes, as if she had grasped for a stair rail to keep from falling and found only air. But then she remembers where she is, and her head drops back to the pillow in relief.

The telephone rings again. Lois opens her eyes, trying to gauge what time it is by the deep, oceanic darkness outside her window. It's late at night or very early in the morning, not a time for someone to call unless something is wrong. She'd been woken at one by the girls returning, piqued by the roar of the car engine, by their muffled laughter as they filed out of the backseat. The ringing stops, only to start again a minute later, and Lois wonders why no one is answering. After two more rings, it ceases.

She lies in bed, now fully awake, surprised by how cold the night has become. As her eyes adjust to the darkness, the shapes of her room sharpen— her tall, narrow bureau, the vase of tightly rippled marigolds on her desk. Her throat is dry, and she rises to get the empty glass from her window ledge. When she bends to pick it up, she sees something out of the corner of her eye, someone short and slight disappearing beneath the house's front porch roof. She turns to scan the open lawn—imagining everything she feared as a child: hobgoblins with long, bony fingers; Gloria Holden's powdered face in *Dracula's Daughter*, which her mother let her see when she was seven, as if she were already grown—but there is no other sign of movement. When she crouches near her bedroom door, she hears nothing.

A coyote, perhaps. Or a jackrabbit. Something that has already slipped back beneath the dark. She places the empty glass on her bedside table, telling herself she's not actually thirsty, even as she swallows just to wet her throat.

Five

· · · ·

Lois wakes to harsh desert sunlight, which bleaches every surface in her room. The air is sharp with coffee and bacon fat. In the distance, the Sierras sit like sentinels. There's an unreality to the landscape, as if her window is simply a painting. She ties her black hair back and picks through her closet for something suitable to wear to her lawyer's, pulling out her high-necked navy dress with the wide buckle, frowning at a crease slicing the skirt.

Downstairs, she passes the study, its door yawning open. Inside, Rita is crouched next to a hunched-over Mary Elizabeth, her voice a calming purr. An intimate moment Lois feels she shouldn't have seen. Bailey is in the living room, as if waiting for her. Someone's game of solitaire patterns a side table, but everything else looks untouched, almost staged. The pillows are fluffed and angled, the face of the grandfather clock gleaming as if someone just polished the glass. Lois has the sudden urge to flip up the end of a carpet or tip over a figurine. Last night, she and Rita played only a single hand of cards in the living room before one of Rita's daughters called for her, crying about a swollen mosquito bite, and Lois once again found herself alone.

"You sleep all right?" Bailey asks. Her hair, which has the red undergleam of a deer's, is pulled into a short ponytail, and she only gestures at makeup, with a thin coat of mascara and lined brows.

"Oh yes. Well, the phone woke me up for a bit, but other than that—"

"I'm sorry about that." Bailey hooks her thumbs into the back pocket of her jeans. "Mary Elizabeth's husband got drunk and decided he needed to tell her everything she's ever done wrong, and then eventually he got so drunk that he needed to apologize for telling her everything she's ever done wrong."

"That's awful."

"Yes, well, girls don't usually come here because they have not-awful husbands."

"I suppose that's true," Lois says, though she knows no one but her would use that word to describe Lawrence, whom the neighbors would fawn over as he spent hours pulling out dandelions and pigweed alongside their gardener. *The only lawyer with a green thumb,* they'd sigh. As if gardening weren't just another exercise of control.

At breakfast, she watches Mary Elizabeth dribble milk into her coffee, her blond hair curling in the heat. She realizes that she looks a bit like she did when Lois first noticed her in the train car: a film over her eyes, some sense of distance, as if Lois were looking not at the flesh-and-blood Mary Elizabeth, but merely her reflection in a mirror.

"Are you going to see your lawyer today?" June asks.

"Later this morning," Lois says.

"I figured. No one ever puts on a dress during the day unless they're seeing their lawyer."

Lois looks around the table and realizes she's right. Only herself and Mary Elizabeth are in dresses. The rest of the girls are in thick blue jeans or trousers, western-style shirts with mother-of-pearl buttons or soft plaid button-ups, latticed with shades of yellow and rose. June and Vera have belts with filigreed silver buckles, Dorothy wears bangles dotted with turquoise. The clothing makes the girls sit differently, resting their elbows on the table and slumping ever so slightly into their chair backs, a foot dangling at their knees. It's not that they act like men, but like girls when no men are present.

Lois feels foolish in her dress, as if she'd shown up to an intimate dinner party wearing white satin gloves. She doesn't even own a pair of jeans.

"My advice is not to sleep with him," June says, after taking a sip of coffee. Her liner is half a shade darker than her lipstick, and Lois has to clench her fist to keep from blending the colors with her thumb.

"Who?" Lois asks.

"Your lawyer. Just think about all the clients who've slept with him before you. Their beds are a revolving door."

"Well, I wasn't planning on it."

"I don't think anyone really plans on that." June places her cup back down, and Lois can't tell if there's some joke she's missing.

T he waiting room of her lawyer's office reminds Lois of her pediatrician's. The frosted ceiling fixture emanates a similar white light, which her mother always said made her nauseous, sometimes telling Lois she'd wait for her in the car, even when Lois begged her to come inside. *I'll run into the street if you don't,* Lois would threaten. *No, you won't,* she'd retort, and she was right, though Lois came close: heel angled like a springboard on the curb, the warm roar of passing cars so near she could taste their exhaust. She hated her doctor. Hairs sprouted out of his nose and he rested his hand too close to her bottom whenever he listened to her lungs.

Lois's father had been the one to find her lawyer. She told him she wanted a divorce one rainy morning in late May, the ground soft and muddied. The thought of telling him made her feel as if a balloon were slowly inflating beneath her skin. It reminded her of being in the house as a child, waiting for her mother to tell him about her poor grades or how she had stolen their neighbor's cat, keeping it in her closet for nearly three days, feeding it drumsticks and shortbread. Her father told Lois that she'd been a fool to rush into this marriage and now she was a fool to leave it, that he was once again embarrassed to be her father, and then he sent her to her room. After an hour she was summoned, and without looking her in the eye he told her which train she would get on and who she should speak to in Reno. A colleague of a colleague had recommended a lawyer. When she returned, she would sleep in her old bedroom until she found some other naive man from Lake Forest to marry.

"I don't want to remarry," Lois said.

"You won't have a choice. I want you out of this house by the end of the year, and what else could you possibly do?"

His words did not shock her. Lois thought of how it had been, living there after her mother passed. The prickly silences at dinner. How her father would abruptly stalk across the floor of the living room and throw an entire newspaper in the fire, or leave monthly tallies of how much her clothing cost on her dresser.

When she made the decision to leave Lawrence—the day she found out she wasn't pregnant, seven weeks after he buried her diaphragm in the trash—her mind refused to think she would have to return to her childhood home. She hated being a wife, was terrified of becoming a mother, but she couldn't stomach the idea of once again being only a daughter. Each role an ill-fitting dress. Still, she didn't know what shape a life outside of Lake Forest could take. She could only see pulses from films: drunken evenings in grand ballrooms, strangers and strange cities, a lipstick mark left on a napkin, on someone's throat. Scenes electric with desire. Scenes too dramatic to be real. And then one she could not place: Lois peeling a sheet from her newspaper for a person seated across from her at a diner, their silence as comfortable as a warm bath.

"Miss Gorski?" a voice says, and Lois looks up to find an older man with a belly round like a fishbowl, his tie a thick silk. Young enough to have served in the war, though it is impossible to imagine him crouched in a trench, a carbine resting against his shoulder. She thinks of what June said, and the image of his naked body makes her queasy.

"Yes, I'm sorry, that's me," she says, rising from her chair. She has to get used to her maiden name again.

"Wonderful. You can call me Mr. Tarleton."

As he ushers her into his office, Mr. Tarleton speaks for too long about how the girls who stay at the Golden Yarrow are always a class above the rest, as if they're a grade of cattle. He recommended the ranch to Lois's father when he called, insisting the price was worth it.

"So, what exactly do I need to do for the divorce?" Lois asks when he pauses for breath.

"Ha, down to business, then?"

"Well, that's why I'm here."

Mr. Tarleton looks surly and opens a leather folder. Though Lois feels like she should apologize, she's never understood how to charm men. Her energy is too intense, saturated as a drop of ink.

"Did your father share with you the possible grounds for your divorce?" he asks, putting on a pair of gold wire glasses.

"No. He just told me what time my train left."

"Well, we're far past the times when you'd have to have proof of any sort of adultery, at least in Nevada. So if that's why you're here, don't worry. I had one woman last week who came with a folder full of photographs, all different women, all in the same hotel room. It was really extraordinary, like a casting call."

"My husband wasn't unfaithful."

"Well, then," he says, with the faint edge of disappointment. "There are eight remaining grounds for divorce in this state: impotency, desertion, conviction of a felony, drunkenness, neglect—economic neglect, which I gather isn't the case for you—insanity, living apart for three years, and extreme cruelty."

"All right," Lois says, her mouth becoming dry.

"So, what are your grounds?"

"Can you repeat them again?"

Mr. Tarleton pulls out a sheet of paper that has each reason typed in smudged letters, and looks at his wristwatch. Lois leans over the list, touching her fingertips to its edge. Everyone knew you could get a divorce in Reno. It was a rootless, shared understanding. Women at the salon whispered about fallen neighbors who traveled there, shaking their heads at the audacity of it as their ringlets set beneath milk-white domes. Lois read magazine stories of movie stars separating just by visiting the city's courthouse after six weeks. Maureen O'Hara, Myrna Loy. In Illinois she would need grounds she didn't have, and Lois thought in Nevada she could simply ask for it. She didn't realize she'd need to give a reason as to why she was asking.

"Had you been trying for a child?" Mr. Tarleton asks.

"Not really."

"All right. Sometimes I think women choose impotency just to twist the knife."

Lois turns back to the paper. There isn't a word to explain how Lawrence talked to her, almost as if she were his secretary, or how his constant questions about how she spent her time spurred her to conjure luncheons or hours of bridge. She was used to lying, but these endless, small falsehoods made the borders of her life feel porous, so that some days she couldn't recall what she'd actually done. How different it had been than what she imagined when he first tucked a lock of hair behind her ear: an acceptance of every part of her, a wanting as simple as salt. There isn't a word to explain how sex with him left her feeling more alone, or how guilty she felt, as he'd fought in the war and seen things she could never imagine, and how sometimes she tried to make him talk about it, asking him awful things, like what it smelled like or if they would bury their dead, and how, when there were so many. How he could be both indifferent to her and critical at the same time. How a child would bind her not just to him, but to who she was becoming. A girl with no story. An extra moving her mouth but not making a sound. She knew most girls had more desperate reasons, but this to her felt desperate.

"What do most girls say?" she asks.

"Well, that very much depends on their situation, but extreme cruelty is most common. It covers all manner of sins not otherwise listed."

She thinks of Lawrence's face when she'd opened her nightstand to find the diaphragm missing. His skin flushed and wet.

"Extreme cruelty," she says.

"Extreme cruelty," Mr. Tarleton repeats, writing down the words on his notepad.

Lois smooths out the top of her skirt and keeps swallowing, as if a splinter of chicken bone is piercing her throat.

"Now, the hearing itself will last all of five minutes," he continues. "Someone from the ranch will testify you've been a resident for six weeks and you'll swear you plan to stay in Nevada. Then you can be on the next train, plane, car, or riverboat out of here."

"So it doesn't matter that I've just sworn I'm going to stay?"

"No. No one cares. The judges know. The state changed its laws for a reason: without gambling and you young ladies arriving every week, we never would have recovered from the Depression. Everyone looks the other way. Now, in regards to financial support—"

"Lawrence said he'd take care of that. That there will be . . . funds." She hates that she'll have to accept this, but given how tightfisted her father is, she's not sure what other choice she has. She needs to figure out what this money will pay for: the rent for an apartment, the tally for a week of groceries. And more than that, what the true cost is of becoming a leper. Whether anyone will invite her into their homes, or if they'll always be whispering, the sounds vibrating against her ear like wind rolling off the lake.

"Do you have that in writing?" he asks.

"No."

"All right." He frowns.

"Is that a problem?"

"No, no, don't worry your pretty little head. I'll sort it out."

Other questions take shape in her mind, but Mr. Tarleton briskly continues with what he'll ask for in terms of money and property. When he's done, he leads her out of the office by placing his hand on the small of her back, and she thinks again of her doctor's large, warm palm.

Six

. . .

Over the next two days, Lois tries to fall in step with the Golden Yarrow's rhythm. Breakfast is always at eight, except on Sundays when they go to church. Horseback rides follow at ten, to Little Valley or Washoe Lake. Lunch is served promptly at one. Afterward, a handful of girls pile into Charlie's or Bailey's car to see their lawyers or shop, to get their hair done or nails painted, the colors always seeming to say so much, though they're all just different shades of red, peach, or pink. As divorcées, they have the run of downtown Reno; the clubs, the clothing stores, and the hotels were built around their wants and needs. They're back in time for cocktails and then Anna has dinner on the table at seven, and never exactly the same meal, as promised, serving platters of pork chops and fried brook trout, shirred batter encasing its skin; bowls of butter beans and bitter mustard greens; and always a pie with a crisp, lacquered crust.

I love to watch you eat. Like a little bird, Lawrence said on their second date, when Lois had been wary of satisfying her hunger, small shreds of lettuce stuck to the roof of her mouth. She felt she could never eat as much as she wanted in front of him, glutting herself with movie theater popcorn in the afternoons. Her body inelegant, devoid of muscle, just bone and a scrim of fat. *I'll be able to tell the second you're with child,* her mother-in-law would say, staring longingly at Lois's flat stomach.

At the ranch, she feels she must match the restrained appetites of the other girls, who all pick delicately at their plates. As if her hunger is yet another marker of her impoverished roots.

After dinner, Bailey drives whoever is up for it to the Highlands, a local bar in Carson City. "You take care of my girls, Bailey," Rita always says before they leave, sitting at the card table with her glass of amber port, one of her dachshunds asleep in her lap. Bailey the older sister and Rita the mother to everyone at the ranch. During the day, the girls often slip into Rita's study, and when they emerge, though it's obvious they've been crying, they always look calmer for it, as if they needed to break some dam. All the girls seem happy to become daughters again, especially after the anger of their own families, their threats of disownment.

Lois has not been invited into the study, which feels like a slight even though she plays cards with Rita every evening. Just like the first night, they're often interrupted by Rita's daughters, mewing about small injustices—itchy eyes and cold feet. Rita wearily inspects their sleepy, tender bodies and tucks them back into bed, and Lois feels her exhaustion in their card playing, in her responses to Lois's questions about how she came to own the ranch, as if Lois were just another small child who needs tending.

Some nights the other guests return a few hours later, other nights not until the sky softens to a cool lavender, the car door puncturing Lois's dreams. Though the next morning they're at the table the minute breakfast is served, always obedient to Rita's schedule.

On her third morning, Lois is pulled out on the trail. Mary Elizabeth asks her to join, and although Lois at first demurs, Rita insists. "You need some color in your skin. The sunshine out here will make you stronger." Lois acquiesces to impress her—to prove that she is also tough and capable—and Rita nods in approval.

Charlie has to help Lois onto the horse. The other girls watch with barely concealed amusement as he forces her feet into the stirrups; only Bailey and Mary Elizabeth pretend to look away, fiddling with their bridles. On-screen, Jane Russell had made it look simple enough, but Lois is unsteady in the saddle, gripping the reins so tightly her fingers pale. Though the girls say nothing, she knows what they must be thinking: that she's not one of them.

The desert is dotted with short, dry bushes the muted green of crocodiles. The mountains undulate in the distance. Lois is awed by their immensity, accustomed to Illinois' flat lawns and flat roads. The wildest place she's been is the woods outside of Chicago, where her mother would sometimes take her on Sunday drives, pulling alongside a stretch of forest just so they could open their lungs and yell. Though the hoarse strangle in her mother's voice frightened Lois, soon it would smooth to a wail, like a knot loosening, and Lois would join her in chorus. Afterward, her mother would turn to her, grinning, and Lois would lift with her same happiness, her mother's moods coloring her life like weather.

On the trail, the girls speak openly about their lives, as if the ranch gives them an immediate confidence, a shared sin. She learns that Vera has been at the ranch the longest, while the others arrived just a few days before Lois. Vera's husband cheated on her with their Irish maid—she came home early with their three children to find the girl wearing her house slippers and nothing else while coddling an egg—and she talks as incessantly as if she's just recovered her voice. June's "cousin" is actually a man she plans on marrying, a screenwriter seven years her junior. The term is some Reno slang. Her husband is a friend of her father's she thought she was in love with at sixteen. Dorothy's George has yet to leave his current wife, though just that morning he sent a bouquet of lilies tied with thin pink ribbon.

They all recall Lois's school days—Dorothy the flirt, June the valedictorian, Mary Elizabeth the sweetheart, Vera the bumbling hanger-on. Like Lois, they all still wear their wedding and engagement rings. She tells herself she might lose them otherwise, and aside from her mother's opal necklace, they're the most expensive things she owns.

"So, Lois, if you're not getting remarried, why are you getting divorced?" June asks.

"Oh . . . well." The girls haven't asked about Lawrence yet, and she isn't sure exactly how to explain him, to make them understand. "We just weren't right together," she tries. "Kind of like pieces from different ends of a puzzle."

Charlie gestures at a hawk coasting overhead. Mary Elizabeth rides beside him, the others trailing behind. There isn't a cloud in the sky, and Lois's body is warming. Her rose lipstick melts on her mouth.

"That can't be all of it, though. I'm sure your family is on the verge of disowning you, just like all of ours, and no one would choose that because of, well, dissimilarities."

"No, of course not." She can't say anything about not wanting a child. An unforgivable sin, even here. "He was also impotent. I obviously had no idea, when I married him."

"Oh, that's awful," June says.

"No wonder you left," Dorothy shouts from behind, clucking her tongue to urge her horse to catch up.

"The only thing that makes all of this tolerable is my children," Vera says. "Did I tell you all I got a letter from Helen the other day? She's the one from Santa Barbara who has children the same age as mine, almost down to the month, if you can believe it. She says she's doing quite well. I wish you all could have met her. She left just one day before Dorothy arrived, and—"

"So, given that, do you think they'll forgive you?" Dorothy interrupts, her white horse now clopping in rhythm beside them.

"Sorry?" Lois asks.

"Your family," June says.

"Oh no. Never. I think my father would rather I had died than get divorced." Lois meant this as a joke, but it's met with a beat of strained silence.

"I don't think mine will either," June continues. "But that's part of the appeal of Los Angeles. We can start over. I've realized I don't even have to tell people about the divorce if I don't want to."

"You're not going to tell anyone?" Vera asks, shocked. Lois is surprised she hadn't thought of this either: the possibility of withholding.

"There's nothing wrong with being a divorcée," Bailey interjects. "But if you act ashamed, people will shame you."

They pass a growth of low cacti that look like dead coral. Each arm riddled with quills.

"I just don't know if it's anyone's business," June says.

"Divorce is everyone's business," Dorothy says. "We're branded like those cattle on the next ranch over. Whether we want them to or not, they'll all know."

Every morning, the girls' eyes sweep across Lois's clothes, making her feel like she's back at school, conscious that although she made her mother take her to the right stores, she somehow bought the wrong things. She hates how easy it is to lapse back into these insecurities; in certain moments, she loathes the girls for it, and in others, she finds herself desperate to form a new pattern and find a point of connection, her body whirring as she tries to think of the right thing to say—a sharp, sophisticated line from a Joan

Crawford film. The girls can sense this, she knows, their looks snagging at the sweat stippling her armpits. Only Mary Elizabeth withholds judgment, though she thinks well of everyone, whether they're Bess Truman or Jean Harlow, or the ranchers they hear shooting at coyotes one evening.

Dorothy—forever preoccupied with appearances, the click of her pocket mirror opening as constant as breath—tells Lois it's time she purchased her Reno uniform, but there is no offer to take her shopping. Even if there was, Lois knows she shouldn't spend any of the money in her brown envelope on clothing. Her father won't send her another penny.

The only place she comes to love is the pool. Especially after nearly falling out of the saddle in dismount on that first trail ride, she stays close to the ranch in the afternoons. The constant presence of others is so unfamiliar that her body comes to crave moments of solitude. Though she feared Lake Michigan's murky depths in Lake Forest, she laps back and forth until her muscles become heavy. She decides her task at the ranch is to swim every day, to burn off the soft, flaccid skin at her thighs and upper arms until she is lean as a fish.

In her room, she begins to tally how much she thinks she'll need to live on her own, greasy pencil marks with her guesses at electricity bills, the cost of a carton of milk. Before going to sleep, she tries to conjure an apartment, but finds that fixtures from her old life keep repeating. The dark brass sconces from her father's dining room. Her and Lawrence's glossy eggshell stove. Like cavities she can't pull, bone deep and festering. It feels impossible to envision a place wholly her own. *Even sad little secretaries have roommates,* June had said, and she feels the threat of this pressing against her bedroom window glass. Like the figure she looks for every night, unable to brush aside the sense that someone is approaching.

Seven

· · · · · ·

Anna is making gołąbki for dinner. "She wanted to do something nice for you," Rita shares. Lois has eaten the dish once, when her mother first went to the hospital. Ela made it, the pale cabbage head bobbing in a vat of boiling water, meat browning in a skillet. Lois's mother hated Polish food, saying it reminded her of her grandmother's tiny hovel of an apartment in Portage Park, rancid with herring and vinegar. This drove Lois's father mad. Sometimes, when they were particularly angry with one another, he would bring home the kielbasa his mother always made for him as a child for Ela to fry up, and eat several of them at the dinner table without pausing for breath, as Lois's mother quietly speared the pale, wet cucumbers on her salad plate. This is how Lois first conceived of marriage: as a poorly played chess game no one ever seems to win.

But Lois can't tell Anna this. After nearly a week at the ranch, everyone can clearly see she's not fitting in, her solitude a flare shot up into the sky. The attention makes her uncomfortable. It reminds her of how her second-grade teacher's face thawed with pity at how the other girls ignored Lois. She urged them to play with Lois, which only made everything worse. *Teacher's little pet,* they chanted, and so Lois drew houses and rabbits instead of practicing cursive, hunted for tadpoles in the creek instead of going to school. She preferred the resulting anger: her teachers' mouths tight when her absences doubled, their rulers smiting her open palms.

Dorothy is helming the bar cart in the living room. She's pouring Cointreau into a silver cocktail shaker, her red hair pulled back with a ribbon. Mary Elizabeth is picking through records as Bing and Gary Crosby croon over the old gramophone, her neck swaying as if the weight of her head is too great to hold up. Her husband called again the night before, and Lois stayed up counting the rings. She's noticed that as the day goes on,

Mary Elizabeth's words begin to slip and smudge almost as if she's had too much to drink, though her glass is only ever filled with water or lemonade. Lois can't make sense of it. Rita is speaking to Bailey in the corner, two of her dachshunds gnawing at the ends of a bone at her feet, their teeth splitting the marrow. Lois overheard that Bailey originally came to the ranch as a guest and never left—her family disowning her after her divorce. It explains how attuned she is to the girls' needs and her tough, clay-red skin, as if she let the sun burn and blister her until she formed an impenetrable hide.

"Who wants a sidecar?" Dorothy calls out, lining up coupes along the bar top.

"You never use enough lemon," June says.

"I use as much lemon as I want to," Dorothy says, filling several glasses, the liquor a deep burnt orange. Over the past several days, June and Dorothy's dislike for one another has only become more apparent. From whispered remarks in the hallway, Lois knows that June thinks Dorothy is a gold digger who slept her way into the right cocktail parties in New York, and that her hair isn't even naturally that color, which she knows because she leaves a pink ring in the bathtub every time she showers. Dorothy thinks June is too old for her "cousin" and that he'll leave her for someone younger. They each have their meager alliances—Dorothy coddling Mary Elizabeth, June bearing Vera's company.

"Do you want one?" Dorothy asks, and Lois realizes that she's stopped in the middle of the carpet, lost in thought. The day before, she played solitaire during cocktail hour—a reprieve for everyone, she felt—but now there's no choice but to engage.

"Oh, I don't know," Lois says.

"Try one. Tell me if there's enough lemon," June commands. "You'll be my—what's the word for the person who kings would have taste their food? To make sure it wasn't poisoned?"

"A servant?" Dorothy offers.

"No, there's an actual word for it, I'm sure." June claps her palms against the arms of her chair and looks back to Lois. "Well?"

Dorothy offers her a glass and Lois takes a sip. June is right—there's not enough lemon. "It tastes fine," she says, and June rolls her eyes.

"Thank you, Lois," Dorothy says, and Lois is given another drink to pass to Vera, who rearranges herself on the couch so Lois can take a seat between her and June.

"So where was I?" June begins as Dorothy folds her legs atop a wicker armchair, pulling a plaid pillow onto her lap. "Oh yes, so instead of throwing them away, he would just leave these used tissues by the sink. As if there wasn't a wastepaper basket a foot away. He'd do that with everything. Candy wrappers on his desk, orange peels on the kitchen table. Our maid would practically trail behind him. You'd think it's because he's over sixty, but he's sharp as a tack."

"It's his mother's fault," Vera says. "Helen and I would always tell the other girls that if you don't teach children to pick up after themselves, they never will. Joe leaves his cigar butts on every side table, though, honestly, I wish I'd never nagged—" Lois takes a too-large sip of her drink, so that she has to wipe the corners of her mouth as the girls wait out Vera's monologue. Vera wears too much mascara, her lashes clumping like the peaks of a crown.

"Lois, isn't your father in real estate?" Mary Elizabeth asks once Vera's finished.

"Yes."

"You were telling me something about real estate, weren't you, Dorothy?" she asks. Her voice has its distant, evening dreaminess.

"Oh yes," Dorothy says. "George wants to move us to Chicago after we get married. He said there's a lot of opportunity there. And good people. Not like out East, exactly, but still."

"My father's traveled to Chicago, so I know a little about it," June says, shifting away from Dorothy in annoyance and addressing only Lois. "Do you know the McCormicks? You must, given your father."

"Of course," Lois lies, knowing there's no way to say anything else. "My father lunches with them regularly, and we all go to the same weddings."

"Oh good, well, we'll have to talk more, then," Dorothy says, taking Lois's empty coupe and standing to fix her another drink. Lois can feel the girls' perception of her shift ever so slightly, and is pleased. Normally she limits herself to one cocktail. *Only one drink tonight,* Lawrence would tell her when he invited over friends, knowing that if she had another her tongue would unknot and she'd talk too much about the last film she saw or her theory that their neighbor planned to poison her husband by putting arsenic in his plum charlotte, which was a joke, though Lawrence never found it funny.

She takes a sip of her new drink, the lemon now barely more than a drop. Leaning deeper into the cushions, she's not as conscious of how her upper arms rub against Vera and June as she was minutes before. She's never felt comfortable with other girls' bodies. The only friend Lois ever had was a girl in second grade who went along with every strange game Lois proposed—letting herself be locked in closets, not flinching when Lois cut off four inches of her milky hair—until her family moved to Iowa.

Lawrence thought this was a choice. That if she wanted to, she could be like all of the others. He was three years ahead of her at school, unaware of her reputation as an odd, quiet girl. They began dating the year after he returned from the war, after sitting in the same row at two Sunday matinees. She first noticed Lawrence's glossy blond hair, prettier than any man she'd known, and at first he seemed to find her so fascinating, listening to her go on about Joan Crawford winning the Oscar over Ingrid Bergman and how she couldn't sleep at night knowing her mother's body was beneath the ground. He told her she was honest and pure, and even though she did not feel like either of those things, she thought he understood her. And how romantic it was, that they met in the velvet dark of the theater, that he didn't care how his mother looked at Lois. Disappointment setting her jaw tight as a mousetrap.

But within a month of marrying, Lawrence admitted to her that he slept through most films; that he went to the theater just to escape his mother. He began to ask her why she didn't go to lunch with the other wives at his firm. *Pretend we're in a movie,* he would say before they went to a dinner party, but she wasn't sure how to, as no one was there to give her the lines.

W ho wants another?" Dorothy says, and Lois lifts her coupe to the light. It's empty again.

Dorothy brings the cocktail shaker over, and as she tips its mouth to Lois's glass, Lois finds herself wanting to reach out and grab her fingers, wondering if that's all it took to be at ease with the girls, to just follow every impulse. Each of Dorothy's digits is so perfectly straight, barely knotted at the joint, and her fingernails are a pale pink, like the inside of a mouth.

The girls have started to talk about the Highlands, the bar they frequent. Lois doesn't know who they're speaking about, but she laughs anyway at their impressions, at how their sentences overlap when they reach a story's crescendo, each desperate to be the one who finishes it. Tonight, maybe she'll find some way to join them. She could crawl out the bathroom window before the car roars down the road and swear Bailey to secrecy.

A bright *ping-ping* echoes across the room. Everyone turns to Rita, who is tapping a silver oyster fork against one of the empty coupes. When Lois shifts, she feels as if she's moving through water, her head and limbs suddenly light. She wonders where the fork came from. If they ever have oysters in the middle of the desert.

"There will be a last-minute addition to our Golden Yarrow family," Rita says. "She'll be arriving tonight, so let's all plan to give her a warm welcome at breakfast."

"Is it Ingrid Bergman?" Lois asks. "No, wait, she just got married to that shiny Italian man."

"How about Judy Garland?" Dorothy asks.

The girls are all tittering, hiding their smiles behind their coupes' etched glass.

"Or, wait, wait, is it Bette Davis?" Lois says, and then drops her forehead into her hand. "Wait, no, she's already divorced again, isn't she? Another divorce down, but maybe she's on to the next, I don't know, these divorces seem to become a habit, like smoking cigarettes. Can't have just one, right? That would be im— possible."

"I think this is the most Lois has ever talked," June says, and the girls laugh more.

"Or, wait, you can't tell us, right, Rita? You can't tell us anything," Lois says, and then pitches her voice to match Rita's precise New England cadence. "*I wouldn't be very good at my job if I told you that, would I?*"

Lois looks down at her empty glass, laughing until she realizes everyone around her has quieted. She looks up to find Rita's lips drawn together in something that is almost a smile, if she traced the lines, but that is most certainly not when she takes in her whole face. As if confirming that Lois is just what she thought—a foolish little girl.

"Are we all done?" Rita asks.

Lois nods, and she can feel the girls pull away from her, loyal to Rita above all else. Even Mary Elizabeth is silent, twisting one of her shirt's pearl buttons. Lois puts her coupe down on the side table, hating the color that she feels seeping up from her chest to her cheeks.

No one speaks of the new guest for the rest of the evening. At dinner, the gołąbki is served in a crimped casserole dish. The cabbage reminds Lois of how her fingers look when she sits too long in the bath. "How *fun*," June says when Rita tells everyone that Anna made the dish for Lois. Everything returns to how it was before, and soon the alcohol Lois drank evaporates, leaving only a hammering headache behind. Each girl takes such small bites of the gołąbki, the way you take a sip of milk to see if it has spoiled, talking louder than usual, as if that could distract everyone from all of the food left uneaten on their plates.

Eight

· · · · ·

That evening, Lois can't sleep. There's a lizard in her room, no bigger than a thumb, and she watches it skitter across the wall. Sometimes it's so still that for a moment she thinks she imagined it, that its outline is just a shadow. But then it moves again, almost as if to prove to her that it's flesh and blood.

The cold wind picks up, rattling the windowpanes. In a reflex of fear, her hand skims the other side of the bed and she thinks of Lawrence. She hasn't seen him since he left her to pack her suitcase, dressed in that sad, plum-colored sweater his mother bought him last Christmas, the one that fits too large at the shoulders. He asked her again if she would reconsider, though it felt more like a line he thought he should say than a genuine question. The anger had passed after that first evening—the tart rot of the spoiled apples on the counter, the front door she left open, as if they needed air. How resigned he became when she said she wasn't pregnant. That she'd make sure she never would be.

After they were married, Lawrence often seemed to see sex as a chore, a means to an end. Their first time was right after he proposed, and he emerged from it like a captain swept ashore after a shipwreck, tousled and slack-jawed, convinced he'd done something very wrong. He was the second man to have kissed her. The first was James Mosele, who entered the school's dressing room one night after everyone else had left, striding up to Lois and mashing his lips against her mouth. Even though she'd never looked at him before—he was thin, with stippled, sallow skin, and had cried once during Christmas Eve Mass—she found herself matching the urgent muscle of his tongue. She only pushed him away when he palmed her left breast, after which he stuttered an apology and stumbled out the door. They never spoke again.

Afterward, she thought of James when she touched herself: how his lips were slick, as if he'd rubbed them with Vaseline; the way he'd walked toward her so purposefully, without saying a word. But since nothing else ever came of it, she let her need match Lawrence's in the back of his Bentley, worried there wouldn't be another chance to have it met.

As he used her handkerchief to dry himself, Lawrence told her they shouldn't do it again until after they were married, and she always worried that he was repulsed by how quickly she'd given in to him. A well-bred girl would have resisted. She found it impossible to come unless she thought of James, or Cary Grant, or William Holden, which she worried she did too often, a hunger overtaking her on the living room sofa or in the bathtub. A brief, feverish release she only experienced with Lawrence if she pretended they were not themselves—that he was a piano teacher and she the mother of his student, that they were strangers seated in the same train car.

The lizard scurries up toward the ceiling and pauses at the molding. Lois hated the spiders and glistening centipedes that would invade her house in Lake Forest, demanding that Lawrence kill them, which he did with a weary pride. But there is something about the lizard, something about how impossibly still it becomes, that she doesn't mind.

Footsteps sound out across the hallway floorboards. Lois listens as the person walks down the staircase, the quick *clack-clack* of their steps suggesting haste. She looks at the clock on her bedside table. It's nearing one in the morning.

Headlights warm her room. A car has pulled into the driveway, but Lois doesn't hear the voices that always accompany Bailey's return: the hushed, drunken laughter, the sloshing of unsteady feet in the gravel. She gets out of her bed and walks toward the window.

A taxi idles by the front door, piping a small flume of exhaust into the night air. The driver opens the trunk and pulls out a single leather bag. There's a dull click, and a girl emerges from one of the back doors, though Lois can't see her face, only a long, straight sheet of hair, so light that it shines silver in the dark.

The new guest, Lois remembers. She speaks to the driver and slips something into his palm, taking the bag from him, though she must have more luggage—most of the girls come with at least two trunks. Lois can't tell exactly what she's wearing, but it looks to be a man's wool overcoat, the kind Lawrence would wear to the office, but finer somehow, softening at her shoulders and elbows.

The front door opens, spilling light out onto the steps. As the driver gives whoever is approaching a stiff wave—without Bailey here, it must be Rita—the girl steps toward the entryway. As she comes into the light, Lois inhales sharply. The girl is beautiful, with hard, high cheekbones and a square jaw, but across the side of her face that is turned toward Lois, blooming from the side of her mouth up toward the corner of her eye, is a bruise so severe that the colors of it pulse, even from this distance. Purple, umber, and an acrid, sickly green.

Lois watches as the girl disappears inside, and then she walks hurriedly over to the bedroom door, pressing her ear against the wood. She can barely make out the low murmur of voices, the creak of their shoes as they walk deeper into the house and away from the staircase. The girl must have been given one of the rooms on the first floor, close to Bailey. Lois moves to turn the doorknob, thinking she'll pretend she needs a glass of water from the kitchen, but how obvious that would seem to them. Her desire to take another look at the girl's face would be impossible to hide.

The house quiets and Lois tiptoes back to her bed, slipping beneath the wool blanket. She lies awake, listening as her heart slows to its normal rhythm, the steady thud of a metronome. Bailey and the others will be back soon, and she will be awake to hear them. As her eyes adjust back to the darkness, she looks for the lizard, but can't find where it's gone.

Nine

* * * * *

The next day, the guest does not leave her room. She doesn't come to breakfast, lunch, or dinner. Though no one says as much, everyone is waiting for her, their eyes darting upward at any *chirr* in the floor. Anna prepares trays of food, tottering past the table with a plate of dark bread and smoked salmon, food none of the girls has been served, and a single, proud lily peeking out of a silver vase.

There are rumors that she's a Vanderbilt or an Astor. At first there's talk of her actually being an actress, but at lunch Bailey lets slip that she isn't famous. June overhears the new guest tell the maid, Florence, that she doesn't need her room cleaned, and she swears her voice has a New York cadence. "*Definitely* an Upper East Sider," she says, and the girls speak about who they know from the *Social Register,* who they've been to parties with, how lovely Amy is and what she ordered for lunch at Barbetta, who Vincent married and whether or not she really is that pretty. These families are a realm of society above each of their own, but no one will admit this, and Lois can feel the girls sizing each other up, attempting casualness as they drop the names of acquaintances.

They worry that the new guest is hiding because she thinks too little of them. They wonder how fine of a rider she'll be and who she's divorcing. The only time they change the subject is when Rita approaches, accompanied by the patter of dachshund feet.

Lois listens to every word as she lines up domino tiles in neat, meaningless columns. Though most of it is nonsense, she waits for stories of the small glimpses girls have stolen in the hallway, the overheard words. The description of the hand that took the tray from Anna—how the guest's nails were unvarnished, with no rings on any finger. A silk dress thrown in the wastebasket, soiled with what looked like a gentle splatter of mud, as disposable as a tissue. The loud scraping Dorothy heard in the afternoon, as if the guest were dragging her bed across the floor.

No one at the ranch mentions the bruise, so Lois is certain she's the only one of the guests who's seen the new girl's face. This secret knowledge—the feeling of being connected to this stranger in a way no one else is—rests like a gold coin in her pocket. It makes her feel like the two of them have some understanding, some intimacy, that she is already keeping a secret for her. At dinner, she loses the threads of conversations, distracted by the possibility of the guest emerging, listening for the soft knock of footsteps against the hallway floor.

When Lois thinks of the bruise, her cheek begins to hum. Her sophomore year, she had to paint a bruise on a girl's cheek for a school play, but she could never get the dimension right; the skin always looked too matted, no matter how many hours Lois practiced on herself at home. When she thinks of the new guest, she imagines the scene: a scuffle in a penthouse; large arched windows, ivory chairs tipped over onto the floor. A man in a tuxedo shirt—the girl's husband—with rolled-up sleeves, the light from a fallen porcelain table lamp cutting across her face as he raises his fist. A steak pulled from the icebox, its marbled fat cooling her throbbing cheek. How she must have left the next morning in her gleaming wool coat, like the one Lauren Bacall wore in *To Have and Have Not,* bringing her hand to her face as she passed the doorman so as not to draw any comment.

Lois envies the simplicity of this scene, how it's clear and dramatic as a film, though she knows she shouldn't covet such pain. She's hungry for the way any audience would yell at the girl to leave, never questioning whether what the man did was that wrong, if he was really such a poor husband. Not with a bruise so severe that just by looking at it you felt a phantom punch.

s the new guest a princess?" one of Rita's daughters asks while wading into the pool.

It's Friday, two days since the new guest has arrived, and she has still not made an appearance. Lois has been at the ranch for over a week. Bailey is chaperoning, Lois relegated to her deck chair once Rita's daughters arrived in their matching gingham suits. The others are out on a trail ride, and the young girls pay Lois little attention. Patty and Carol, she remembers. Until now she has only seen them in the evenings, their honeyed hair tangled by preludes to sleep. They eat before the guests, and sometimes Lois finds their remnants on the dining room carpet: a colored pencil; a doll's slipper, no bigger than her thumbnail.

"You'll have to ask her when you meet her," Bailey says.

"I think she is," Carol, the youngest, says. "And she's in hiding from her wicked stepmother and a prince will come on a big white horse and save her."

Bailey smiles at Lois, shaking her head. Lois wonders how old they each are. She's nearing an age where all children begin to blur. It would be different if she were a mother, but even before Lawrence, the idea frightened her. Her own mother strained under the weight of just one child. There was a single photograph of her before marriage, before motherhood—her body louche against a doorway, her eyes clear as autumn.

"She's not really, though?" Lois asks Bailey, trying to affect a note of disinterest. "A princess, I mean."

"There is something a little regal about her. I wouldn't be surprised if she was a descendant of some Swiss viscount," Bailey says.

"The other girls can't stop talking about her."

"I know. Speculation as sport."

"Yes, they all think she's an Astor or something. In Lake Forest people are wealthy, but not like that. I don't know that much about those families unless they marry some movie star. So, I know the names, I suppose, but I wouldn't recognize anyone if they *were* from one of those families."

"I wouldn't really either, except for Cornelius Vanderbilt—you know he's lived around here, though he's a bit absurd. Owned the Lazy Me, which would send cowboys in Rolls-Royces to pick up their guests. I think he's on his fourth or fifth marriage himself. But other than him, nothing. I grew up on a big cattle ranch in California. A long way from New York." Bailey rubs away some of the mud licking the sides of her leather boots, her face placid. Lois realizes she's not going to tell her a thing about the new guest.

"When did you get divorced?"

"Six years ago, and I've been at the Golden Yarrow ever since. Obviously I knew about life on a ranch, so Rita offered to let me stay on. She knew I had nowhere else to go."

"That was kind of her."

"More than kind." Bailey looks at Lois. "Though we don't agree on every-thing, she's the best person I know. Because of Rita, I can say with certainty that there's a path for every girl who comes here. You just need one light to turn on to show you the way."

"Bailey! You have to be the sea witch and we have to be the mermaids and you have to chase us," Patty says, gripping the stone lip of the pool.

"Yes, yes, yes," Carol says, kicking over to where Patty's perched.

Patty doesn't pay her sister any attention, thumbing one of her bathing suit straps, which is starting to fall down the slope of her shoulder, the knot of muscle small as a crabapple.

"I didn't put my bathing suit on today," Bailey says. "But you know, Miss Lois has her suit on. Have you met Miss Lois?"

At that, Patty takes a big inhalation and plunges under the pool water. Carol laughs or screams, Lois can't tell, and follows suit. Beneath the water, their bodies smudge and ripple, their hair splaying out like brushstrokes of paint.

"Seems they aren't too impressed with me," Lois says.

"They have the attention span of goldfish," Bailey says. "Don't take it personally."

Ten

· · · ·

The third morning after the guest arrives, Anna burns her hand. She comes through the swinging door with pebbles of ice cradled in her palm, telling Rita she can't bring the new guest her tray.

Bailey goes to find gauze and cream, and Rita lifts the ice to take a look at the blistered line of red, the width of a cast-iron handle. Melt dribbles onto the carpet. June and Dorothy rise, but Rita tells them not to crowd, so they stay seated as Anna presses her lips together. She is tougher than anyone thought, with her flowered apron and the loose, wobbly skin at her chin. Lois looks longingly at the plate in front of her, the thick, rich orange of broken yolk wetting her toast. She knows she can't eat it. She can already see the look Rita would give her, as if she'd scraped the contents onto the floor, and Lois still craves her approval. Next to her, Mary Elizabeth kneads her napkin. Her knuckles are white as bone.

Bailey returns and disappears with Anna into the kitchen. Within a few minutes they emerge, Anna's hand wrapped in a clean strip of bandage. The girls murmur their condolences and Dorothy's bottom lip puffs to a concerned pout. Everything she does is slightly exaggerated: her two-fingered whistle to corral the girls into the backseat of the car, the hard smack of her lips after applying her poppy-colored lipstick.

"Well, that's enough excitement for the day, isn't it? Everyone, please steer clear of potholes and broken glass," Rita says, filling her coffee cup, and Lois has a sudden thought.

"You know, I can take the new guest her tray, if you like?"

Rita holds her gaze, and Lois remembers how she looked at her the first afternoon she arrived, with the faint tightening of suspicion. Lois thought perhaps she imagined it, but here it is again, impossible to ignore.

"Thank you, Lois, but that won't be necessary." Rita looks at Bailey, who disappears into the kitchen.

The girls return to their plates, and Lois serves herself another piece of toast, feigning indifference. Bailey walks past the table, balancing the tray on one of her large palms, and Mary Elizabeth lets out a shaky breath. Lois is surprised by how upset she is, as if she herself had been burned. She murmurs that Anna will be fine, and Mary Elizabeth gives her a grateful nod.

"Is the new guest sick, Rita?" June asks.

"What do you mean?"

"I assumed you couldn't have breakfast in your room, and she's had not just breakfast, but all of her meals taken to her. Is it because she's sick?" Lois admires how June never hesitates to push, always confident in her own authority.

Rita smiles at June, holding her coffee cup close to her chin. Lois has learned the power of this pause—how it makes the speaker question every word they've just said, weighing whether Rita would find them wanting. The grandfather clock chimes out its low, deep scale.

"You're all awfully concerned about the new guest. It's very sweet," Rita says, and Lois hears June's small exhale. "It's not standard practice to serve a guest a meal in their rooms, you're correct, but we decided to make an exception because of Miss Lang's situation."

Mary Elizabeth and Dorothy turn to one another, mouthing the last name: *Lang.* Vera clucks her tongue, mumbling about the Germanness of it, which Lois finds absurd. Her own memories of the war have become dreamlike: a black car pulling up to their neighbors' house; an image of a young boy dead on a beach, his leg bent beneath him so unnaturally on the sand, shown on a newsreel at the cinema; towers of newspapers on their dining room table. How much more immediate her mother's death felt, with faint streaks of her blood in the bathroom sink, her sour, ragged breath altering the house's chemistry.

"Now, is that all right with all of you? The exception we've decided to make? I don't want anyone to be upset by this," Rita says.

They all murmur their approval. Rita knows precisely how to make everyone feel as if they're part of a big, boisterous family, with her at the head of the table. These are the talents of a real mother, Lois thinks, knowing when to discipline and when to make your children feel they're your equal.

The girls drop their napkins on the table, soiled with grease and smudges of lipstick, and Bailey begins to stack the dishes. Mary Elizabeth offers to help, but Rita waves her away. Charlie is waiting for her at the stables. Lois thinks she'll get one of her books from her room and read on the front porch.

Vera and June ascend the staircase in front of her, their jeans bunching at the backs of their knees in a way that makes Lois never want to wear anything but skirts and dresses. June loops her arm through Vera's as if they're proceeding down an aisle and leans her dark head toward Vera's ear.

"What did Rita mean, *situation*?" she whispers.

The next day is the hottest it's been since Lois arrived. The heat wakes her early in the morning, clouding her room. Downstairs, ceiling fans sputter at full speed and curtains are drawn across any window that faces east. At breakfast, girls ask for ice in their coffee, and the bowl of pale, steaming grits is left untouched. Later everyone goes into town to escape into the cool air-conditioning of the movie theater. Lois stays, even though she would like nothing more than to see a film. These afternoons are the only hours she has to herself, when she doesn't have to weigh and measure every word.

In the heat, the house is a tightly latched jewelry box. She tries to make herself comfortable in several of the rooms: lying across one of the fainting couches, spreading her thighs apart beneath her skirt, and sitting upright in the cool, dry bathtub, though the porcelain soon warms under her skin.

When she realizes it's empty, she steals into Rita's study, feeling like a child slipping into the headmaster's office. There's a safe in the corner, and photographs tile the walls: Carol and Patty as plump toddlers in feathered lace, a stiff man in a Union uniform. An antique Springfield rifle looms above them, mounted on the plaster. Lois hovers over the desk, though there's not much there: an emerald glass paperweight, a ballpoint pen. Looking to the doorway, she quickly opens one of the top drawers, startled to find a nest of Tootsie Roll wrappers, their crinkled waxed paper bursting open like chrysanthemums. It makes her giddy, the idea of Rita unwrapping candy after candy late in the evening, mashing the taffy between her teeth. It's a picture so unlike what she presents to the girls. She sees a curve of green metal beneath the mound, and pushes the wrappers aside to find a small tin box. Inside is a key, though she does not know to what. She reburies it beneath the soft paper.

Afterward, she paces the hallway, swinging her arms back and forth in the stifling air, just to feel the breeze of her own movement. She sweats through her underwear, the cups of her bra softening. In the living room, the maid, Florence, finds her wiping her armpits with one of Rita's plaid throw pillows.

That morning, Rita told everyone not to spend any time in the sun. They'd burn in fifteen minutes in this heat or come down with sunstroke. Last year one of her guests vomited into the pool after a day spent on the trail; just bent over the side and retched as the other girls paddled frantically to the shallow end. Charlie had to pump the water out, hundreds of gallons. It took him a full afternoon to foam and scrub the walls clean. Still, Lois approaches the screen door, the blue beckoning.

A wasp batters against the mesh. When she looks beyond it, to the placid water and concrete, she finds something she did not expect: the new guest reclining in the hard desert sun.

She turns back to the darkness of the house, expecting Anna to have appeared behind her, shooing her away from the door as if she's a rabbit that found its way into a vegetable bed, but the room is empty. Her heartbeat drops to her stomach, pulsing at her belly button. The other girls will not return for hours.

She pads upstairs to put on her bathing suit.

When the door clicks open, the new guest does not turn her head. She's wearing a large white oxford, mostly unbuttoned, in the crisp cotton of a dress shirt. There's a sheen to the fabric, luminous as a pearl. Lois wears no cover-up, and her burgundy suit is hopelessly dated. The new guest's eyes are covered with a pair of tortoiseshell sunglasses, similar to the frames Mary Elizabeth sometimes wears, and beneath them Lois can see the bruise has changed. It's mercurial, shifting like a skein of clouds, the colors slightly faded to lavender and a lichen-green.

Lois knows it would be too bold to take the seat next to her, but she doesn't want to distance herself by sitting in a chair at the pool's opposite edge. She's been waiting for the guest to appear for three days, and now that she's here, the fear of saying the wrong thing is pointed as a fractured bone. She decides on the water.

To display her bravery, she dives right in, not slowly submerging her body up to her waist like she normally does. The water's cold is a shock, nearly religious—a feeling of being reborn. She swims to the edge and crests only to fill her lungs, kicking off the wall and swimming to the other end, picturing herself from the guest's vantage, her arms gracefully cutting through the water. She pushes herself harder, farther.

Though she imagines herself being watched, when she finally stops to rest, she's startled to find the guest looking at her—perched on the lip of her chair, her ankle balanced on her knee. From this low angle Lois can see she's not wearing a bathing suit. Between her thighs is a triangle of thin yellow underwear. She's watching Lois with a frank openness, and when their eyes meet, Lois's body is struck like a tuning fork.

Without thinking, she takes in a massive breath and plunges to the pool's bottom.

Her toes scrape against the stippled concrete. She opens her eyes— something she didn't know she could do until she was eleven, when Ela threw pennies into a community pool and she dove to fetch them, slipping beneath the surface as cleanly as a seal—and looks upward. Sunshine ribbons through the water, and at the pool's edge Lois can just make out the arch of the new guest's foot, though, like the bruise, the shape keeps shifting. Pressure builds in her chest, the tightness of held air. She wishes she could stay at the pool's bottom and just watch her, but instead she brings her body up to the sun.

"Were you trying to drown yourself?" the new guest asks.

Her voice is lower than Lois imagined, with a slight croak to each word, as if she's recovering from a cold. Lois wipes her eyes and shakes her head back and forth. She tries to take delicate, measured breaths, but her body needs great gasps.

"No, that's part of my routine."

"Really?"

"Yes."

"Quite a routine." The new guest leans back in her chair and closes her eyes.

Lois wrests herself out of the water. She wants to demonstrate an ease, but her labored breathing betrays her. A tremor lingers in her limbs. After reaching for her towel, she pats her face dry. Her makeup is running, rubs of peach and black sullying the cotton.

The new guest's face is bare. She unfolds a newspaper, one arm crossed above her head. To Lois's surprise, a heavy comma of blood wets her thumbnail, as if she'd been gnawing at the skin. She doesn't wear a wedding ring.

Lois looks back down at her thighs, trying not to stare. The sun bakes her neck and shoulders. She knows her skin will burn, can almost smell it, like the heady scent of a match catching flame. Wrapping herself in her towel, she stands in defeat, her feet unsteady in her leather slides, and walks over to the door. But when her fingers grip the handle, she remembers how she felt when the new guest emerged from the taxi's backseat—that sense of possibility, an opening—and she returns to the cluster of chairs.

"I almost drowned once, in Lake Michigan," Lois says, and the girl turns. "I got pulled out by a riptide. This old woman who was missing several of her bottom teeth saved me. She swam parallel and brought me back to shore. So, I really wasn't trying to drown myself—I know what drowning feels like, and even if I wanted to end things, I'd choose another way of doing it."

The new guest tilts her head, pushing up her sunglasses so they nestle in her hair like a crown. In the light, Lois can see the girl's eyes are a dark, deep green, like the pond in her father's backyard at the peak of summer.

"It's unusual to be missing your bottom teeth and not your top."

"I suppose," Lois says, trying to recall anyone else she's known with missing teeth.

"And how would you end things? If you had to choose."

"A gun. I'd want it to be quick." Lois is both surprised and calmed by the question, asked in the same manner as someone inquiring whether she preferred coffee or tea.

"Me too."

They continue to stare at one another, even as the moment of silence stretches. The girl's look is not one of judgment in the way Lois has experienced—not with the girls at the ranch or the countless others before that. There's no calculation, no appraisal of how Lois appears and sounds;

she's not looking at her dated bathing suit or trying to discern if her words carry the flat, nasal accent of Chicago's countergirls and waitresses. Instead, the girl seems to be watching her in the way Lois watches Marlene Dietrich in the first frames of a film, trying to decide what sort of character she'll be and whether or not to trust her.

"What's your name?" the new guest asks.

"I'm Lois. Lois Saunders, or, well, Gorski now."

"I'm Greer."

"Greer Lang, isn't it? Rita mentioned your last name at breakfast yesterday."

"That's my married name. I'm still using it, for now. It draws less attention, though don't mention that to any of the other girls."

"I would never tell them anything about you."

Greer smiles, the surprising warmth of which feels like syrup being poured down Lois's spine, and tips her sunglasses back over her eyes. She returns to her newspaper, giving it a shake to stiffen the pages. Lois waits to see if she'll say something else, but she continues to read, the smile lingering at the corners of her mouth.

In her room, Lois strips off her suit and lies on her bed, folding her hands over her belly button. Her limbs are becoming darker, a soft contrast to the skin of her breasts and stomach, which have the pallor of an uncooked chicken. She takes in deep breaths until her body quiets. The words each of them spoke loop through her head, Greer's so near to her she can see them printed on a page. *Me too.* And then she had smiled at her, genuinely and unreservedly, and not felt forced to prattle on with any polite chatter—her silence suggesting that their conversation was not ending, but ongoing, that they were somehow still talking, even now. Florence has cleaned Lois's room, lining up all of her shoes so that their heels are kissing. The air is woozy with pine oil. Lois stays there until the shadows begin to recede and the sound of a car door slamming wakes her, as if from a dream.

Eleven

· · · · · ·

Lois receives a letter from Ela the next morning. Ela refuses to talk on the telephone—she covers her ears every time the bell echoes through their hallway—and at the sight of her block letters Lois feels a pang of homesickness. Not for the house itself, but for Ela. She writes about how Lois's father isn't eating enough and how the gardener is cutting the grass too short, not the way Lois's mother liked it. She complains that the neighbor's calico keeps stealing into the kitchen. Yesterday, she found it gnawing on a beef plate on the counter, its paws pressed against the wax paper. She shares the name of a boardinghouse for young ladies downtown, telling Lois that she does not approve of her leaving home, but if she does, she heard from another housekeeper that this building was respectable. To Lois's surprise, Ela was the only person who did not try to convince her to stay with Lawrence.

In the past few days, Lois has thought less about after, but, alone in her bedroom, she counts the months until the end of the year. Just a little more than six. A boardinghouse is not what she imagined, but perhaps it's her best choice. Ela closes by telling Lois that Lawrence stopped by the house, disappearing into her father's study. Ela brought them coffee, but they stopped speaking when she entered, mumbling about the players the Cubs traded to the Dodgers while she poured them each a cup. *He needs to shave,* she writes.

Lois sits cross-legged on her bed, staring at the paper. She cuts her thumb on the envelope's edge and absentmindedly sucks at it, a note of iron on her tongue. Even though her father was grateful to Lawrence for marrying his daughter so that he could be left in peace, they were never close. They talked about baseball and Mayor Kennelly's reforms, but little else.

She folds the letter back up and slips it into a drawer. Lawrence must have gotten the papers. Perhaps there was some business to discuss. Though she's not sure why, worry worms through her, and she thinks of what Ela said after Lois told her she was seeking a divorce. *Serce nie kłamie. The heart sees farther than the head.*

G reer is not at breakfast. After the pool, she disappeared into her room again, and that evening Anna brought her a tray of steamed spinach and a thick slice of pot roast, a fresh bandage wrapped around Anna's palm. The girls watched in silence as she passed.

At the table, Vera consumes everyone's attention by talking about her children. It's the time of year they usually go to the Cape, and they don't understand why they're stuck inside their grandmother's house in Beacon Hill, playing with the same three puzzles and eating boiled mutton. Last night, they asked her why their grandmother calls her a fallen woman—if she, in fact, fell—and her voice catches while excusing herself from the table. June half-heartedly rises to follow, but Rita tells them all to leave her be, and so the girls briskly move on to the day's plans, attempting to strip the sadness from the room like a sheet. Dorothy has a hair appointment. June wants to buy a silver necklace at Hoot Newman's to replace a locket that's gone missing. Florence nearly dismantled the house looking for it.

That afternoon, Lois sits by the pool even though she's burnt from yesterday, her skin tender and freckled. Two large mydas flies, which Bailey promised are harmless, buzz around her feet. She waits for over an hour, until Mary Elizabeth and Bailey join her, an ungainly easel tucked under Bailey's arm. Mary Elizabeth has never been to the pool before, and even by the water she still wears a long-sleeved dress. Crescents puff beneath her eyes. Bailey has been more solicitous of Mary Elizabeth than any other guest—prompting her to tell stories of trail rides at cocktail hour, refilling her water glass at the dinner table. Lois is grateful to Bailey for this caretaking; it's obvious Mary Elizabeth needs it.

When Bailey positions the easel in the sun, the creak of the wood is so loud that it startles several swallows, who take flight from the lone sycamore by the pasture. Lois gathers her towel and book. Greer will never come out now.

"Sorry, Lois, are we disturbing you?" Bailey asks.

"No, you're fine," she says, but Bailey has already turned from her, chasing after the sun hat that's been blown from Mary Elizabeth's head.

During cocktail hour, Rita asks Vera to play the piano, and she begins with Debussy, stumbling over the notes. For once, everyone encourages her to go on when she covers her face with her hands, and soon she's jangling out Cole Porter, with June singing along in a steady soprano.

At dinner, the girls tease Dorothy over Charlie. He gave her an arrowhead he found in the dirt, which he polished until it shone like glass. When she thanked him, he stammered out a short history of the Washoe Tribe, trying and failing to recall certain dates and the names of chiefs as the other girls stifled their laughter.

"Charlie is harmless," Rita says. "He practically grew up on this ranch—his father worked for me until he threw his back out. He knows the rules about fraternizing with guests."

Everyone settles, lapsing into the contented silence of a meal's beginning. The pork chops are toothsome, slightly sweet. When Lois looks up to pass the butter dish, she sees Dorothy's eyes widen, staring at something over Lois's shoulder.

"*Oh!*" Dorothy says, and Lois turns to find Greer in the doorway.

She wears a finely knit gray sweater, bunched up slightly so that you can see her forearms, and dark trousers belted at the waist, loose and relaxed, not narrowing at the ankle. Her bright hair falls over her right collarbone. She doesn't wear any makeup, her bruise marbling the side of her face, softer in the table's candlelight. Lois can sense the girls staring at it. Forks still in their hands.

"Miss Lang," Rita says, dabbing a napkin at the corners of her mouth.

"Hello," Greer says, pulling out a chair between Vera and Mary Elizabeth. "Sorry I'm late."

"We're just happy you finally joined us," Rita says.

"Yes, well, I thought it was time."

Several of the girls murmur at this; gentle, polite notes of agreement. Lois sees Vera and June exchange looks, silently acknowledging the bruise with quick flares of their eyelids. Bailey summons Anna, asking her to pour Greer water. Lois wishes the chair beside her had been open.

"I'm Greer. Rita keeps calling me Miss Lang, but I don't expect anyone else to."

Rita gives her a compressed smile as Greer spears a pork chop onto her plate. She takes several spoonfuls from the casserole dish, scraping the fried onions off the top so that she's left with only the naked green beans. No one else eats.

"Do you want any mashed potatoes?" Mary Elizabeth asks, offering her the large silver spoon.

"No, thank you."

"I'm on a diet too," Dorothy says, leaning over Mary Elizabeth's left arm. "But Anna's potatoes are something else. I think there's some sort of witchcraft involved in making them."

"I'm not on a diet. I just don't like rich foods."

Dorothy frowns, and Lois thinks of Greer's breakfast trays: brown bread and salmon, a cup of black coffee. She looks down at her own plate, a pat of butter leaching into her split dinner roll, and sees the other girls doing the same. Only Rita has begun to eat again, as if the new guest is nothing but a momentary disturbance, a bird that battered against the window.

"I feel as if I've interrupted," Greer says as she looks around the table, her gaze briefly pausing on Lois. A flicker of recognition that causes Lois to open her mouth, though with everyone else present she does not know what to say. "Please eat."

At these words, everyone begins to pick at their food. Lois tries to think of a question to ask Greer, something to rekindle the intimacy she felt by the pool, but each one sounds too absurd: *What did you dream of last night? What does the bruise feel like?* She can taste the heavy cream of the mashed potatoes, each bite slipping down her throat like a stone.

"Where are you from, Greer?" June asks, combing her potatoes with her fork. Lois has learned that she sees this as her role: to begin the formal interrogation. She would have made a better lawyer than Lawrence.

"New York."

June is quiet, as if waiting for her to say something else, but Greer just brings another bite of pork chop to her mouth. She eats without pause, already sawing her knife against the bone.

"You just look so familiar," June continues. "Did you go to Miss Porter's? Not that we'd be the same year, but—"

"No, I didn't. My father didn't want to send me away."

"I thought the same thing," Dorothy says. "I'm trying to put my finger on it. Were you at Landon and Judy's wedding at the New Yorker last winter?"

"Honestly, all of those weddings run together for me."

"I know what you mean," June says. "And your family, they're in hotels, aren't they?"

"Yes, they are," Greer says, and several of the girls look at one another, confirming that their suspicions were correct. "Very astute of you."

"Well, they've had some time to speculate," Rita says.

"I imagine so, yes." Greer smiles with closed lips, and though her expression is different than the one she wore by the pool, it has a similar power, suggesting some shared confidence. "Maybe I should have joined you all sooner."

The girls laugh at this, the room beginning to loosen. Lois is annoyed by the camaraderie, her flicker of recognition now consumed by their collective flame. Rita takes a sip of her water, and though Lois is not sure why, she can tell she's also displeased.

"Lang is German, isn't it?" Vera asks.

"Yes, my husband's family emigrated from Germany in the early 1800s, but lord, let's not talk about him," Greer says.

The girls nod as if they know the entire story, the fact of the bruise suspended in the air above them, as present as Rita's chandelier. Lois sees Bailey and Rita exchange looks, and Bailey begins to talk about where she thinks they'll all go that evening; Jimmy Durante is performing at the Mapes, or they can go to one of their usual bars. Greer reaches for another pork chop, paying no heed to the other girls' restraint, and Lois feels defeated. Greer will go out with the others and she will stay at the ranch, stuck staring at the stoic faces of the card deck. Perhaps there was nothing special about their exchange. It's obvious Greer makes every girl feel the way she felt by the pool: seen, chosen. Anna brings out a blackberry pie, but none of the girls eat. When she returns to clear the table, she frowns at the dish, which she usually finds empty.

"Why don't you come out with us, Greer?" Dorothy asks as they all stand.

"You should!" Vera says. "You've been cooped up at the ranch. The bartenders at the Highlands make the strongest drinks, and, well, it was the funniest thing, just the other night—"

One of Rita's dachshunds is running between Lois's legs, trying to nip at the back of her heel. She steps around it in frustration, wishing Rita would pick the dog up like she normally does, retiring to the living room with her glass of port.

"Are you going, Lois?" Greer asks.

Lois looks up. Everyone has turned to her, though it takes several moments for the question to register. The other girls are obviously also confused, lips parted as they wait for Lois to say something that helps them make sense of Greer's inquiry. Greer is looking at her, eyebrows raised, and Lois feels her attention in the pulp of her teeth.

"Lois usually stays in," June says.

"Yes, I usually do," Lois says, and coughs, spittle caught in her throat. Her answer came out rasped, as if she hadn't spoken for days.

"Well, I think I'll stay in too, then," Greer says. "Maybe some other time."

She smiles at each of them before turning down the hallway to her room. For a moment, they all watch her walk away from them, listening to the click of her loafers against the hardwood.

"Do you know her?" Dorothy asks.

"No, I don't," Lois says. "I just saw her at the pool yesterday."

"How terribly odd," June says, everyone but Lois nodding in agreement.

Twelve

· · · · · · ·

The next morning, Lois wakes with a fever. Her sheets are damp, and for a moment she thinks she's aboard the train again, the air sour, like the bread dough Ela would keep in a porcelain bowl in the pantry. When she stands, she's conscious of every hair on her forearms, each puckering at the root. She closes the curtains so that the light in the room burns a deep orange, and then finds herself sitting cross-legged on the bathroom floor just so she can finish brushing her teeth.

Anna brings her chicken broth and plain slices of bread. It hurts her teeth to chew, so she softens crustless pieces on her tongue and swallows. Bailey stands in the doorway, asking if she needs anything, but Lois just shakes her head. She tells her that it's probably a bad reaction to something she ate, though Lois worries it's something deeper, the same thing that killed her mother. She thinks this every time her appetite evaporates. Lawrence would always tell her this was nonsense, and for a brief moment she wishes he was here to reassure her, to list all the other symptoms she doesn't have, the *Physician's Desk Reference* open on his thigh.

The first day she mostly sleeps, dipping in and out of consciousness. She can never tell how long she's been out until she looks at the clock. Sometimes, it's two hours. Other times, several minutes. When she's awake, she listens to the sounds of the ranch. There are footsteps in the hallway, doors opening and closing, the idle scrape of someone's nails on the wall as they pass. She catches the middle of a hushed conversation, Vera telling someone she needs to buy some more Yardley hand cream. *My skin is practically reptilian.* Lois thinks of her lizard, who's started to appear in her room every night, its body pressed against the plaster.

Of downstairs, Lois hears very little. The sudden bark of a laugh, the table being cleared, porcelain chiming against porcelain. The muffled notes of a Teresa Brewer record float up through the ceiling. Lois can hear nothing distinctly of Greer, even when she lies on the floor and presses her ear against the knotted planks of wood. Though Lois likes to imagine Greer has disappeared again, it's most likely she's sitting with the other girls for breakfast, lunch, and dinner. They will ask her more questions, and they'll be able to see what she's wearing, to watch her as she cuts a tender, pink curve of salmon with the side of her fork, eating everything but the bones. Lois's anger at this, her absence, makes her fever burn hotter still.

The night before, Greer asked Lois if she was going out. She hadn't seemed to care which of the other girls would be joining. Lois wonders if she imagined this, if she was already ill then, and indeed, afterward she remembers walking up the staircase and falling asleep the moment her head touched her pillow, as if she were being pulled under by a short, sharp tug.

When she tries to imagine why Greer would not go out unless Lois joined, her thoughts spiral and loosen like the trail of an airplane. It seems impossible that Greer could feel that same recognition, not just as if they knew one another, but as if they were meant to know one another. Something connecting them that runs deeper than the surface similarities—the pedestrian likes and dislikes, the friendly husbands, the shared memories of grade school follies—that knit so many girls together. *It's unusual to be missing your bottom teeth and not your top,* Lois says into her pillow, opening her mouth and running her fingers along the ridges.

At night, the howl of the coyotes stirs her from sleep and she can feel their high croon in her bones. An ache radiates from her gut, and she thinks again of her mother. When she was in the hospital, Lois spent all hours of the day with her, whether she was awake or sleeping. Her father visited after the plant was closed, but even then, he and her mother barely spoke.

Lois was used to distance, to scratching like a dog at her mother's bedroom door. Even when she was young, Lois knew her mother wasn't suited to the role, and that this was a disappointment to her in a long line of so many. Her mother was temperamental and caustic, leaving Lois on her own or with Ela except for the occasional drive, their trips to the theater, the afternoons in the kitchen when Lois passed elaborate stories off as truths. This absence made Lois's hunger for attention wolfish and feral. Her stories becoming more outlandish, her behavior more absurd—conjuring an affair between her teacher and headmaster, accidentally cracking her radius when she wanted to prove she was brave enough to jump off the shed—just for the smallest scraps of her mother's love, fat and gristle.

But now that her mother was sick, she was open, softening. She would talk to Lois for hours, stories about her childhood, swollen horsefly bites and bare cupboards, a towheaded boy who kissed her and then made her swallow a clod of dirt, and how when she told her own mother, the woman snipped off six inches of her hair in punishment for being loose. As she spoke, Lois began to understand her mother's hatred for her own parents, her desire to cut herself loose and sew with a new thread. And when Lois had to leave the room, to bathe and change clothes, how panicked her mother became, kneading the stiff cotton sheets as if she were now the daughter—Lois the attendant mother neither of them had. It pleased Lois, it frightened her. She finally had her mother's attention, but she feared no longer being the child.

One morning, Lois's mother asked Ela to bring her wedding dress to the hospital. By this time, she was so thin Lois could wrap her fingers around her upper arm. Ela acquiesced, setting the large powder-pink box on the side of her bed, and when she left, Lois's mother asked her to open it, to pull back the tissue paper to reveal the ivory gown, the hospital light pooling across the gathered satin. Lois had only seen it in a photograph: her father staring stiffly at the camera and her mother holding her bouquet of roses and baby's breath up to her chin, her smile not reaching her eyes. Their marriage as much a business relationship as any her father held with local butchers. Her father needed a wife, and Lois's mother needed to escape her family's cramped home at the city's edge.

"I want you to put it on," her mother said.

"Now?" Lois asked, looking out the doorway to a nurse wheeling a cot down the hall.

"I might not get to see you in a wedding dress otherwise."

"You think it's that unlikely someone will ever propose?"

"Well, unfortunately you're an odd one, just like me, so time will tell, I suppose. It was looking pretty bleak before your father."

"Well, I'm not sure I even want to get married."

"Don't say that," her mother said sharply, pulling herself up against the metal headboard. "As awful as it is, marriage is the only way for a woman to get any freedom, trust me. Otherwise, what are you going to do, live with your father and Ela forever?"

"I don't know." Lois picked at a cuticle, sulky and annoyed.

"Well, I know. Find a husband. Anyone with money will do."

"Because that worked out so well for you?"

"Better than if I had said no," her mother said, her voice flickering on her final word, as if there were no greater weight to bear. "Now, please, indulge me. Put the dress on."

In the hospital bathroom, Lois stepped into the dress, trying to keep the satin up and away from the sickly yellow tile, the grout's jagged pebble. The neck sat close to her throat and the sleeves ended in diamond points at her wrists. It was too small for her. Her mother was always more delicately boned, so Lois had to leave the back slightly open, exposing the top band of her brassiere. In the mirror, her face appeared featureless, her nose and mouth like light pencil marks on a sheet of paper. She hadn't been wearing any makeup to the hospital and her hair fell in limp black waves around her face. She did not look like a bride.

Through the door, she heard footsteps and the doctor's baritone. She emerged to find her mother curled to the side of her bed, taking in rapid breaths as if she couldn't get enough air. The nurse was trying to get her to sit back up, her mother's dressing gown open so that Lois could see her back. Each rib was as pronounced as those of the cows that would lie stripped on her father's butcher's blocks, and it was then, at that moment, that Lois knew her mother was going to die. When the nurse and doctor became conscious that Lois was in the room, they looked at her impassively, as if there were nothing odd about her wearing a wedding dress. The nurse flicked her finger against the glass syringe as the doctor rattled off the names of medications. The needle punctured her mother's upper arm.

Lois crouched near the baseboards, her hands folded over her chest until her mother unfurled, her breath deepening. After she fell asleep, the nurse and doctor slipped back out into the hallway.

Lois returned to the bathroom. She tried to unbutton herself, but her fingers kept slipping on the silk loops. Sweat stains inked the satin above her belly, the white soiled to a rainwater-gray. She looked over her shoulder, trying to better catch the pearl buttons in the mirror, but at the sight of her soft, full back she grabbed at the sides of the fabric and pulled, the seams ripping loose, splitting and tearing. The dress fell to the floor.

She does not know how long she sat on the tile and cried. After a time, she stood up and put her own dress back on. Outside, her mother was still sleeping. Lois gingerly perched on the side of her bed and tightened the blanket so her mother's body was fully covered. The wedding dress was hers now, spoiled with the distinct, sour musk of Lois's teenage sweat. And though part of her knew what she'd eventually have to do after her mother passed, that as a girl she'd have no choice in the matter, the part of her that was still a child wanted to savagely resist it, like when she'd tried to jam one of her baby teeth back into her frayed, tender gum. She tucked the satin back into its box and carefully folded the tissue paper, walking through the glossy hallways of the hospital and out the front door, circling the building to where she'd seen the orderlies disappear to smoke their cigarettes. She found a bank of rusted green Dumpsters, one of which she lifted open, and slipped the dress box inside.

Thirteen

· · · · · · · ·

On the second day, Lois's head begins to clear. It feels as if a rainstorm has passed, sunlight falling through the window in a block of light, sharpening everything in the room. She strips her bed, conscious of the stale smell. Anna brings her food and she finds herself ravenous, draining two bowls of chicken broth and tearing at the bread's dry crust. After eating, she takes a shower, letting the hot water stream between her shoulder blades. Though she planned to go downstairs and wait for Greer by the pool, when she steps out into the steam the tile seems to shift beneath her feet. After sitting for a moment on the bathroom floor, she staggers down the hallway and collapses on her bare mattress, a towel wrapped loosely around her wet torso.

She doesn't leave the room until it's time for dinner. Her black hair has dried oddly from how she slept on it, lying flat against the side of her head and then splaying out into frizzed kinks. She ties it back and shakily draws liner along her upper lashes. As a child, she knew her mother was unwell by the absence of her foundation and lipstick, when you could see her speckle of sun spots, the waxy, mauve sheen beneath her eyes. Lois would slip into her mother's room when she was away, applying the tubes and tins of color to her own plain face. There was an intoxicating power in the process, a sense of control, and so, when the headmaster told her she had to be more active in school life to make up for her absences, doing makeup for their plays was inevitable. Her time backstage did not change what her classmates thought of her, but it gave her a sense of place and purpose, however fleeting, so that even now the sweet, dry smell of powder calms her.

When she considers Greer, all of Lois's clothes seem prudish, but she eventually zips herself into the same navy dress she wore that first morning. Below her, music from the gramophone swells. As she walks down the staircase, a lightness prickles the crown of her head, like the stirring of a limb that's fallen asleep—nerves or the lingering sickness, she's not sure.

In the living room, Dorothy is trying to teach Vera jive steps, holding hands as they tap their feet against the carpet. The others are gathered on the couch, empty coupes scattered across the coffee table. When Lois enters, several of the girls look up at her briefly, and she feels something is different—disdain rather than indifference in the narrowing of their mouths, so minute a man would never see it. Is it her sickness? Do they fear catching it? In the corner of the room, Greer reads a book on the velvet fainting couch, wearing the same sweater and trousers from the last evening Lois saw her, her bare feet tucked beneath her. Surprisingly, one of the dachshunds is stretched beside her slender calf. The dogs have never cared for anyone but Rita.

"How are you feeling?" Bailey asks, lifting her hands as she takes a few steps toward Lois, as if worried that she might fall.

"I'm much better," Lois says.

"You're sure you're well enough to join us?"

"Yes, I'm fine. Really."

Lois steals another glance at Greer. She does not look up from her book—a slim western with ocher-colored pages, which surprises Lois, who imagined her reading something sophisticated like Evelyn Waugh or Somerset Maugham. Greer's indifference to her return disappoints Lois, but before she can even figure out where to sit, Rita calls everyone in to dinner.

On the table a latticed ham glistens, drips of orange fat dotting the Delftware platter. The girls weave between one another. Before, they would dip past anyone dawdling to sit in one of the prized chairs closest to Rita, but now everyone tries to predict where Greer will go. Lois is too slow. She finds herself trapped between Mary Elizabeth and Vera, who is already asking Dorothy about the new gold chain looped around her neck, her back presented to Lois like a sloped wall.

As dinner begins, it's obvious everything is different. There is intention in how the girls ignore Lois now—dropping dishes at her elbow with a clatter, reaching over her full plate for the salt—and she feels a sputter of panic, trying to imagine what she could have done from her sickbed. Even Mary Elizabeth is quiet. It's part of a new rhythm to the entire table, every word and gesture orchestrated around Greer. The girls turn to her when they're telling stories, constantly soliciting opinions and small attentions. Mary Elizabeth airily asks her whether or not she should cut her hair. June spoons diced carrots onto Greer's plate. At first Rita doesn't acknowledge it, deep in conversation with Bailey, but Lois catches her eyes flitting to the other end of the table. Greer pays Lois no particular attention, though, unlike with the rest of the girls, there seems to be no malice behind it. Sullen and confused, Lois eats a slice of ham the size of her dinner plate, feeling free to match Greer's hunger.

"Now, what are you all laughing about?" Rita asks.

Greer had said something low in her throat that Lois didn't catch. The girls sitting close to her are still tittering, wiping their mouths with their napkins, and Lois desperately wishes she'd gotten a closer seat. The ham lies heavy in her stomach, stretching against her dress's stiff cotton.

"Nothing, Rita," Greer says, tucking a lock of silver-blond hair behind her ear. "Just a little joke."

"Well, that much I knew," Rita says.

It's unusual for anything to be withheld from Rita, and the air is pulled taut. Lois becomes conscious of the sounds lifted by the silence: bottoms shifting on wooden chairs, Mary Elizabeth setting her glass on the table, a bristle scratching at a pan in the next room. Greer's mouth curves in that same close-lipped smile from the other evening, and the other girls stare at her face, as if they're studying her to see how they themselves should feel and act. Her bruise has softened to a warm dark yellow.

"Well, I've had some requests to go back to the Highlands tonight," Bailey announces. "Are we all feeling up for it?"

"We have to go back to see if that same man is asleep on the bar," June says to Greer, and everyone at the table turns to her, except for Rita, who feeds one of her dachshunds a stub of carrot.

"Well, I don't think we have a choice," Greer says. "Let's start taking bets."

The girls burst into conversation and Lois waits, wondering if Greer will invite her, but she doesn't even look in her direction. Anna clears the table to no applause.

Rita leaves to tuck her daughters into bed, her face unreadable. Bailey excuses herself to find her keys, and Lois imagines watching the car pull out of the lot from the living room window, the headlights casting out onto the downy blue pasture, knowing that Greer is in the backseat. How she'll turn back to a meaningless flutter of cards, a room as airless and cloying as any she'd known in Lake Forest.

"I'd like to come too, if that's all right," Lois says.

Her voice comes out too loud, as if she were yelling to someone in the other room. It silences the table.

"But what about your father?" Dorothy asks, frowning.

"Oh, come on, girls. Your father's not in Reno, is he?" Greer asks, looking Lois right in the eye.

"No, he's not," Lois says.

"Well, then, it's none of his business."

At that, Greer gives her a wink, so brief that none of the other girls see it.

Fourteen

. . . .

When Lois walks into the Highlands, she can feel grit beneath her heels. The long, narrow building rises like a beacon in the desert, miles from downtown Reno. Its walls are studded with bleached cattle skulls. A small crystal chandelier dips from the ceiling and a speckled mirror hangs behind the bar, reflecting the low heads of liquor bottles, and a smattering of men gather near the bar's slab of curved wood. The place is nearly empty, the opposite of the dizzying, drunken clamor Lois imagined when she listened to the girls leave every evening. Everything is old and unvarnished, a bar none of them would go to if it were anywhere else. But in Nevada, the dirt feels novel.

Dorothy insists on buying everyone their first drink as long as she can pick the liquor. Her soon-to-be ex-husband owns a distillery in the Hudson Valley, and she believes that she knows more about alcohol than everyone else. She orders gin and tonics, leaning over the bar to select the gleaming green bottle, which allows the bartender to look down her shirt, unbuttoned so everyone can see the lace edge of her bra. His pours are heavy, and when he pushes the glasses toward the girls and announces that the bar is out of ice, they all laugh.

"Their ice machine has been broken for three years," Bailey says, as an aside to Lois.

Lois nods as she takes a small sip of the drink, the warm gin leaping down her throat. She still doesn't feel well, was close to fainting in the car's backseat, which was so full Mary Elizabeth had to sit on Dorothy's lap. She survived by leaning her head out the window like a dog and breathing in the cool air. The desert was a silent blue, the stars sharp as diamonds. Greer sat in front with Bailey, her long arm trailing out the window.

A man in a cowboy hat knocks into her elbow, spilling some of her gin onto the floor. "Sorry, darling," he says, not even looking her in the eye as he passes. Lois tucks herself tighter into the corner, watching as the group is cleaved by men. Several have surrounded Dorothy and another is leaning over Mary Elizabeth, who rests like a bird at the edge of a pool table. June is talking to Greer and Vera at the bar, her back facing the others, so that it's difficult for anyone else to approach.

Even though she'd summoned the gall to invite herself, Lois is somehow already separate and adrift from the rest of the girls, the music from the Wurlitzer so loud that she can't even hear words, only the gashes of consonants and piano keys.

The only other bar Lois has been to was with Lawrence. She drove downtown to meet him after work, dressed like Rosalind Russell in *His Girl Friday* for the occasion, imagining herself strutting through the bar and ordering a martini that would be placed on a crisp cocktail napkin. Instead, the room was overstuffed with men. She had to push through them to get to the counter, where Lawrence had already purchased her a beer in a glass rippled with water stains.

As the night goes on, she feels more and more frustrated, alone in her corner. The girls are getting drunker. June drops a glass on the floor, cackling as if the shatter is a punch line to a joke. Lois sees different paths before her, like dance steps painted on the floor: she could walk around June and insist she buy Greer her next drink, or sit next to Mary Elizabeth at the pool table. She imagines different lines of dialogue, entire conversations in which she is graceful and witty, not standing by herself with a tepid glass of gin.

The music clamors, a cymbal crashing through her head. It's been days since she's stood this long. Her calves tremor.

"This is real local nightlife," Bailey says, suddenly appearing at Lois's elbow. "Not quite as glamorous as the casinos."

"I wouldn't really know," Lois says.

"Oh yes, this is your first night out."

"Maybe my last. I don't know what my father will do when Rita calls."

"She won't call."

"Really? Why not?"

"She has to pay some lip service to what men want, but she won't let them run the ranch. At the end of the day, she just wants you to follow the rules that she sets."

"And what are those?"

"She wants you to enjoy yourself, but also to act like a lady. She's known so many girls who overindulge in a way that becomes impossible to recover from. When they return home, they continue to drink too much, spend too much, make foolish marriages, and wind up back at the ranch, and she feels responsible. She's stricter than I might be, but it's obvious she has her reasons. So, just behave yourself, and we'll make sure your father's none the wiser. Deal?"

"Deal." A hitch in Lois's chest loosens. "Did she tell you to say all that?"

"Not those exact words, but I'm happy to be the messenger." Bailey smiles. "Anyway, if you do want to go to a casino tonight, you'll have to extract Dorothy from the jaws of those men in order to leave. I think one of them works at the Washoe Pines Ranch, a few miles west of ours. Not a tightly run ship. A lot of guest and ranch hand fraternization, as Rita calls it."

Bailey is drinking a tall glass of water, and Lois tries to remember if Dorothy passed her a gin. As their chaperone, she undoubtedly has to stay sober.

"Rita does run a tight ship," Lois says.

"She has to, or, well, *we* have to. Our sterling reputation is how we attract our clientele. She'd probably shoot Charlie if he tried anything. Not that he ever would."

Lois laughs, quickly stifling it with a cough, and Bailey wipes her mouth dry with her shirtsleeve. She tells Lois about the time one of the horses gave birth to a new foal, slippery and bowlegged. The mare was in labor for longer than anyone expected, circling her stall for hours and battering her head against the wooden gate. They all waited in the stable, dragging dining chairs across the hay-covered floors and eating cold ham sandwiches Anna had made, but Charlie couldn't take it. After the seventh hour he left, unable to return until Bailey pulled the foal free.

"Maybe that's why he gets along with Mary Elizabeth," Lois says. "They're both like children."

"I imagine you know enough not to say that about Mary Elizabeth," Bailey says, and Lois feels a flush of guilt, though she's unsure what Bailey is alluding to. She notices how Bailey's eyes hover on Mary Elizabeth, as if she too is waiting for a path to open.

"You know, you can go talk to someone else."

"I don't want you standing here alone."

"I don't need anyone to babysit me." Lois's voice is harder than she intended, a clot of a cough forming in her chest.

"All right." Bailey lifts her water glass from the counter. "Understood."

Before Lois can form an apology, Bailey slips between the men standing in front of them, walking toward the pool table. Two stools open to Lois's right, and she collapses onto one of the split leather seats.

Men and women come and go around her. The bar has grown more crowded, and she's lost Greer in the thicket of people. She overhears an older man tell the bartender that he saw an explosion farther south in a dry lake bed, a towering mushroom of white smoke, slurring that he thinks the government is going to bomb North Korea into the sea.

Lois wishes she were in her bed, exhausted by her lingering sickness, by her disappointment. It's not an unfamiliar feeling. She closes her eyes and sees the bar where she joined Lawrence, silver tinsel wrapped around the room's wooden columns. One of Lawrence's coworkers at the law firm, the one with the neck as thin as a bowling pin, is telling a story about one of their clients. Every time she tries to speak, Lawrence talks over her, explaining who Stevie is, what *prima facie* means, how Mrs. Walker always burns the coffee. The beer tastes like flat soda and vinegar. Her forced smile makes her cheeks ache.

"Now, I've been watching you for the whole night, and I just can't fathom how no one has talked to you yet," a man's voice says, interrupting her thoughts.

She opens her eyes to find the same man who rambled to the bartender about Korea sinking into the open stool next to her. A stretch of thin black cord loops around his neck, clasped with a silver snake's head at the level of his collar. He looks as old as her father, his eyes sunken and small.

"I'm actually not feeling very well," Lois says.

"Nothing the Reno cure won't fix, and you look plenty healthy to me," he slurs, leaning so close that she can see the sludge of tobacco coating his front teeth. "Healthy as a horse."

"Excuse me, I think you've stolen my seat."

Greer has appeared at his side. Her hands are deep in her pockets, and she's looking at the man as if he's a waiter who brought her the wrong plate; not as if he were someone worthy of true disdain, just a shallow annoyance.

"Oh, well, pardon me," he says, standing up.

"Thank you." Greer slides onto the stool.

"So, where are you two—" he begins.

"That's enough," Greer says, holding up her hand.

The man opens his mouth and closes it, like a fish. He looks to the bartender, as if he could do something, but he's pouring another drink for Dorothy. He stares at the back of Greer's head for another moment and then, remarkably, walks away.

"Thank you," Lois says.

"You know, only real drinkers sit alone at bars," Greer says. "And you don't seem like a real drinker."

"I'm not."

Greer is angled toward her, so that their knees are nearly touching. Though Lois isn't short, Greer is several inches taller, and she feels this imbalance even when they're sitting. At this distance, she sees a faint crease between Greer's eyebrows, suggesting that she's a few years older than Lois thought, perhaps twenty-seven or twenty-eight. Her skin is almost translucent in its paleness, so that the bruise rests above it, as if on a pane of glass.

"And you're still a little sick, aren't you?" Greer asks.

"I'm fine," Lois protests.

Greer pulls a silver cigarette case out of her front pocket, and Lois is distracted by her fingernails, bitten down so severely that the skin above them is puffed and pink, incongruous with every other part of her. Lois remembers the brightness of her blood that afternoon at the pool. She offers Lois a cigarette, but Lois refuses, certain she would vomit at the first inhalation. She rarely smokes.

"You know, I've been hearing some stories about you," Greer says.

"What do you mean?"

"That you're a bit of a liar."

Lois tries to think of everything she told the girls, in the same way she'd try to recall the details of imagined conversations and lunch dates, what she'd conjured of her shadow life for her mother or Lawrence, each thread woven so tightly with her own that often she forgot what was real and what was just a story.

"Apparently one of the girls—June or Dorothy, I can't keep them straight . . . ," Greer continues, turning so she's looking out toward the open room, her elbows on the bar's end. "Anyway, one of them found out from Bailey that your father owns a meatpacking plant in Chicago."

"So?"

"So, you told everyone that your family's in real estate. That your father lunches with the McCormicks."

Greer has shifted back toward her, studying Lois like she did by the pool, waiting to see if she'd emerge from the turquoise water. Sweat prickles Lois's upper lip.

"It's not a lie, exactly," Lois says slowly.

"How so?"

"Well, he owns the plant. I never said what sort of real estate he's in."

Greer's mouth widens, and suddenly she is laughing. For a moment Lois worries she's laughing at her, but it's clear that this is different, as if Lois had told a very good joke. Greer sputters out a small ribbon of cigarette smoke and then offers it conspiratorially to Lois, who takes the cigarette between her fingers and inhales, letting the smoke fill her lungs. She does not feel ill any longer.

"Was that story you told me a lie? The one about you almost drowning?" Greer asks.

"No. I wouldn't lie to you."

"Good." Greer takes her cigarette back. She doesn't look away from Lois as she ashes it onto the floor. The silence that follows is comfortable, almost familiar, and for the first time all night Lois feels as if she can take a full breath.

Behind them, singing has begun. Greer turns to look at the girls, who are all perched on the other end of the bar, their legs dangling next to empty stools. They've started to sing "Goodnight, Irene," swaying back and forth. Mary Elizabeth has spilled beer down the front of her shirt, so you can see the outline of her bra through the cotton, and Lois realizes this is the first time she's seen her drink. Men watch, leaning against their painted pool cues.

"My mother used to sing this to herself," Greer says as she hands Lois the cigarette.

Lois opens her mouth to ask a question, but Greer is already leaving to stand in front of the girls, pushing aside several bystanders with a brisk shove. Each turns to complain, but says nothing once they see her bruise. Before the girls, she shakes her hair back from her shoulders and raises her hands as if she's a conductor, directing each note.

"Stop rambling and stop gambling, quit staying out late at night," they sing even louder, laughing as Greer thrusts her arms upward. It's clear some of them don't know all of the lyrics, waiting a beat to join in on certain words, so that the song undulates through the air.

Greer turns back to Lois and beckons her near with a flick of her wrist, but as much as she wants to be close to Greer again, Lois stays still, knowing the other girls wouldn't want her to join. She looks for the damp line of Greer's lips on the cigarette, but it's spoiled with the smudged red of her own lipstick. After another moment, Greer turns around again, waving her closer until Lois has no choice but to go to her. She hops onto the bar next to June, who is lifting a glass of liquor aloft as if she's toasting the chandelier. The wood is sticky beneath Lois's hands.

At first she feels foolish, but then June drunkenly makes her take a sip of her whiskey as if she's any other girl, and when they start another verse, Lois begins to sing—softly at first, until Greer yells at them all to be louder still, and the girls look at one another in challenge, raising their voices to meet her demand. The men shake their heads and Lois feels light as air, sitting a foot above everyone else in the bar, together with the girls in their separateness.

When they finish, they begin the song all over again.

They stay another hour. Even though it's June, they sing several Christmas carols, the only other songs all of them know, and some of the men join, one handing out shot glasses of peppermint schnapps during their rendition of "Winter Wonderland." At Vera's suggestion of a hymn, Greer tells them to get off the bar. She has them play several rounds of pool, and when Lois miraculously gets two balls in with one shot, the room erupts into cheers, Dorothy lifting her hand into the air as if she's won a prizefight. Greer convinces Mary Elizabeth to steal one of the patrons' cowboy hats, which she does with a dreamy confidence. "*Luminal*," June whispers to Lois at some point. "The only way that girl stays upright is Luminal." The schnapps numbs Lois's tongue, but the rest of her feels loose, unrestricted, as if the boning has been removed from her brassiere.

As they leave, several men throng the doorway outside. The moonlight defines the desert's rubble and squat, furred shrubs—a landscape that still looks alien to Lois, the terrain of another country. Bailey is starting the car. At the sight of Greer, one man steps forward and takes off his hat. His profile is like a cliff face, with a strong, straight nose and a cleft at his chin.

"Now, who did that to you, darling?" the man asks, reaching out and briefly cupping Greer's cheek. She bats his hand away so forcefully that he stumbles backward into a flowering of rabbitbrush.

"Don't touch me," she says, and spits on his cowboy boots, splattering the worn leather. Her upper lip spikes to an animal's snarl, her incisors wet in the moonlight.

The other girls stop near the doorway in shock, but Greer simply slips her hands back into her trouser pockets and continues out to the car.

When the man rises with the help of one of his friends, a trickle of blood winds around his palm from the plant's dried nettles. Lois feels pressed to apologize, but then Dorothy starts to laugh and it catches like wildfire between them, fast and light. The more ruffled the men look, the harder the girls laugh, so that by the time they pile into the car, their bodies nearly feverish in the frigid night air, Lois's cheeks are wet with tears.

Fifteen

· · · · · · ·

Greer still does not join them at breakfast. Anna brings her tray to her room, a daily reminder of Greer's wealth. Lois knows it bothers Rita, noting how she takes in a short, pointed breath through her nose, though it could not happen without her consent. The girls are ravenous, nearly swallowing the hard-boiled eggs and strips of bacon whole. Rita murmurs that they're eating like ranch hands. Below the table, one of the dachshunds whines.

"I missed you at cards, Lois. Did you enjoy your evening?" Rita asks.

"Yes, I did," Lois says.

"Lovely. Bailey told me you had a good talk."

Lois nods, laying her fork across her plate, not wanting to eat under Rita's attention, though Rita's quickly distracted by Anna asking whether she should bake a pie for dinner. Lois remembers that Bailey was the one who exposed the lie about her father, but there has never been any maliciousness from her; it was undoubtedly an accident.

In the sober light of day, the girls are not as friendly as they were the night before. They wordlessly pass Lois the carafe of coffee, mumbling to one another as they wipe the gray of old mascara from beneath their eyelids. Mary Elizabeth's husband called again last night, and this morning her face is blank, reminding Lois of what June told her: Luminal. The rest have remembered themselves, and Lois recalls a moment backstage in high school when Doris Spanger spilled her fears about the play—how everyone would think she wasn't pretty enough to be Juliet, how they would stare at her long torso and flat nose—until two other girls entered and her face shifted, looking through Lois as if she were a ghost. But when June begins to hum "Goodnight, Irene," drawing quiet hiccups of laughter, Lois feels as if she's now part of some unspoken conversation. She smiles into her black coffee.

"Is everything all right?" Rita asks.

"Sorry. Something in my throat," June says, and they all exchange glances as Rita's cup slips against its saucer, nearly chipping the porcelain.

That afternoon, Lois pulls on her bathing suit, desperate for sun after so many hours in her room when she was sick. Outside, the air smells like ash, as if someone has been gathering sagebrush and lighting it on fire. There is a drowned beetle in the pool. Insects are larger in Nevada, and Lois is surprised that she doesn't mind them. She likes that they make themselves known, unlike the delicate cobwebs and speck-sized ants back home. She fishes the beetle out with her sandal heel and feels stronger, the last of the sickness burning away at her edges.

As she takes slow, steady laps, she plays moments from the night before in the reel of her head, in the same way she imagines favorite scenes from films: the appreciative rise of Bailey's eyebrows when Lois's pool balls rolled into the net sockets; Dorothy stumbling toward her with two glasses of gin; Greer handing Lois her lit cigarette, smoke unfurling from her mouth like a swath of silk.

In high school, girls would gossip about their weekends in the dining hall while Lois sat nearby with an open book. Over barely touched trays of creamed chipped beef and cornmeal pudding, everything soft and over-salted since the start of the war, they would mercilessly tear apart other girls' dresses and figures, recount what they said to boys they liked and boys they hated. Someone would always have been so drunk that she couldn't recall any detail, aghast at her friends' recounting of who she danced with, incensed by how no one woke her when she fell asleep in a car's cold back-seat. Lois would listen as she pretended to read the same page, imagining how it would feel to have Eric Shepherd's hand tug at the waistband of her underwear. Their lives brighter, sharper, a vein of lemon opening the throat.

Now, after having been at the ranch for two weeks, it feels miraculous to have stories of her own, even though she has no one to tell them to. She dives to the bottom of the pool and remembers the shape of Greer's foot that first day. A perfect arc. A bird's wing.

After an hour, Greer opens the screen door, wearing the same oversized oxford and sunglasses as the other afternoon. She walks across the concrete in bare feet, holding a coffee cup by its rim. Lois is wrapped in a towel, having just emerged from the water, and offers her a weak "Hello." Greer takes the seat next to her and picks up the book Lois left on the side table's mottled glass: her mother's well-worn copy of *Rebecca*.

"Is this any good?" Greer asks, as if they are already in the middle of a conversation.

"It's one of my favorites."

"Hm. I've never heard of it." She opens it flippantly. Lois flinches at the stretched spine.

"You've never seen the film?"

"No. Should I have?"

"Oh yes," Lois begins tentatively. "Laurence Olivier—he's the perfect Maxim, so much so that now I think of him whenever I read it, which rarely happens, because those characters, you know those sorts of shadowy images you have when you first read a book, they're so hard to get rid of. Joan Fontaine's a little too beautiful. I think she should be plainer, not dazzling, because Rebecca's the dazzling one, but she's still marvelous and it's so much better than her *Jane Eyre*. My mother hated that film, and once she made me read the book I agreed. That casting made no sense, but then it's nearly impossible to cast any star in that role, they really ought to have found someone unknown—"

Lois twitches, remembering how Lawrence would press her thigh underneath the table when they had guests over, old classmates she thought she'd never have to see again, letting her know she was talking too much after she had a few drinks. And how the morning after she'd find a violet bruise mottling the skin just below her hip. The size of his thumbprint.

"Anyway," she finishes in a rush, "it's very good."

"The girls told me you're rather quiet," Greer says. "But you're not, around me, are you?"

"I suppose not." Lois's earlobes warm.

"Well, I'll take that as a compliment. Read me a little." Greer hands Lois the book and closes her eyes.

Lois looks down at its cover, her fingertips leaving small, wet smudges on the hard cloth. She hasn't read a book aloud since school.

"You can read, can't you?" Greer teases, opening one eye.

"Yes, of course." Lois laughs. "Should I start at the beginning?"

"From wherever you like."

Lois returns to page one. She loves the first line and says it slowly, "Last night I dreamt I went to Manderley again," thrilling at Greer's small smile. Lois continues, drawing her heels closer to her bottom. In her excitement, she begins to trip over words, pausing in the middle of sentences, adjectives split from nouns. When Greer says they should leave it there for today, she's disappointed. She'd just begun to find a rhythm, and it was such a release to speak, even if she was saying someone else's words. Florence hovers near the window, faintly singing some Irish song about cockles and mussels as she dusts.

"It doesn't sound like a happy marriage," Greer says, turning her head toward Lois, though Lois can barely see her eyes through the dark amber of her sunglasses.

"What do you mean?" Lois asks.

"In the book. Max and . . . whoever."

"She says they're happy. That even though they don't have much, they're at peace."

"They're poor and bored. Would you be happy if you were poor and bored?"

"I suppose not."

"Exactly." Greer smiles. "She sounds like those sad, sniffling girls who fill boardinghouses."

"Oh?" Lois says, remembering Ela's letter—the building she had meant to call.

"Yes, you know the type. I like to listen to you read, though. It makes me feel like a little girl before bedtime, safe and warm." Greer arcs her arms above her head and yawns, and Lois remembers how she looked after she pushed the man last night, the wetness of her teeth.

"My mother gave me books, but she never read to me," Lois says.

"Well, mine didn't either, to be honest." Greer laughs at this admission, and Lois joins her, an ease in this shared absence. "Maybe that's why it's so nice to listen to you. And there's an energy to your voice that I like. It's obvious when you care about something."

"I'm sorry I kept stumbling over words."

"Don't apologize. It's rare in life to have something to truly apologize for. No apologizing to one another, and no lying to one another. All right?"

"All right."

"Good."

Lois rubs the book's spine, trying not to show how much Greer's words flatter her.

That night, a storm churns across the desert, soaking the sand until it becomes clay. Rain rustles the maples and the girls all stay indoors. Rita's daughters bring the dachshunds into their beds. The girls retire to the living room after dinner, lighting candles, telling their own stories of tornadoes and floods. Though the others seem surprised that Lois doesn't retreat to her room after dinner, no one says anything of it, and she does her best to stay quiet, hoping to linger among them as long as possible. Greer tells them about an August morning in Maine (*Maine*, Lois can almost hear each of the girls thinking, *she summers in Maine*) when the rain was so heavy that a skin of water coated their first floor, and how their rugs never smelled the same after, like moss and wet leaves. When Bailey nods off in her armchair, Greer goads Dorothy into finding Rita's port, and though it feels more sacred than altar wine, everyone takes a small sip from the bottle. And for the first time, when everyone goes to sleep, Lois feels the emptiness of her bedroom.

Sixteen

· · · · · · ·

The days Lois was sick feel like blank pages in the middle of a book. She needs to know if the other girls learned anything new about Greer. She follows Mary Elizabeth to the stables the next morning, though both are briefly distracted by the new litter of kittens in one of the empty stalls, their mother licking their matted fur with her pink, stippled tongue. When they begin to talk, all Mary Elizabeth shares is that Dorothy's convinced she's an Astor. Her cigarette case has a curling *A* etched into the silver.

"Do you think her husband did that to her?" Mary Elizabeth whispers, even though they're alone.

"I don't know," Lois says.

"I think it must have been."

"Well, I suppose it's always the husband, really." Mary Elizabeth picks at a bent piece of hay. Her eyes are more focused in the morning, her fingers more assured. "Yours has been calling the ranch pretty often, hasn't he?"

"Oh yes. He can get a bit . . . upset. I'm sorry if it's woken you."

"You don't need to apologize. It's his fault."

"That's not what he thinks."

Lois watches as Mary Elizabeth continues to pluck at the hay, and she thinks briefly of asking her if she wants to scream. To open her mouth and howl. Only after Lois was married did she understand why her mother drove them to that lonely curve of trees. A valve releasing a torrent of steam so the vessel itself didn't combust. But she can't imagine Mary Elizabeth would do something so improper, and so instead they sit beside one another in silence.

In the next stall, a horse rises from sleep. One of the kittens rolls away from its mother, offering up its delicate swell of belly, so vulnerable it hurts Lois's teeth.

At the Highlands that evening, Lois keeps bringing the same glass of gin to her mouth out of a nervous desire to do something with her hands, barely wetting her lips. After dinner, Greer did not ask Lois if she wanted to join them—it was assumed in the way she looked at her from across the table. Greer had enveloped her in the ranch's collective "we." *We're all ready to go? We'll take Bailey's car?* And now here Lois is, quietly pulling at her dress collar.

It doesn't feel like the end of the night before. Everyone is too sober. There's another group of divorcées by the bar, though they're obviously less well-off. A blond one's roots show, and their blush is an acidic pink. The air between the two groups is strained with an unspoken competition: who the men prefer, who is laughing loudest. Lois can tell June and Dorothy don't particularly want her there, befuddled by Greer's interest in her, asking and answering questions about Lois's presence in the way they purse their lips or flare their eyelids. It dries her mouth.

Bailey and Mary Elizabeth hover by the pool table, and the others press against the bar, watching a man in a waistcoat try to fix the Wurlitzer. Though men approach, Greer dismisses each of them with a cold glare. Dorothy is describing what she wants to wear to her second wedding: an ivory, ermine-lined suit, obviously trying to impress Greer with her taste.

"But he still hasn't left his wife yet, has he?" June asks.

"Well, no, but he will. He's paying for me to be out here. She's just not terribly stable, so he wants to wait until his business is done in Chicago and he's back home."

"Chicago," June repeats, and takes a sip of her drink. "No doubt he's rubbing shoulders with Lois's father. A real titan of industry."

Lois opens her mouth, but Greer interrupts before she can begin her apology.

"Oh come on, June, who cares?" Greer says. "As if you've never lied about anything?"

"I haven't. Not like that—not about my own family."

"So your husband knows all about your cousin?" Greer asks, her voice sharp. Lois has to chew on the fatty muscle of her cheek to stop from smiling.

"Well, no, but—"

"You know, I have an idea for how you can all make amends," Greer interrupts. "Each of you gets to ask Lois a question, and Lois has to respond honestly. Then, no more snide comments, no more looks like the ones I see you all giving one another. The hatchet will be buried. Do we all agree?"

Vera and Dorothy nod, but June just stares at the bottom of her glass, obviously ruffled by Greer's chastisement. She's used to being in the driver's seat. Sometimes Lois wonders if this is why she left her elderly husband—he became too unmalleable, gears rusted into place.

"June?" Greer asks. Her voice is lighter, as if her harsh words seconds before were all a part of this new game. "We can't play without you."

June laughs, eager to forgive. "All right, yes, I agree."

Lois swallows a mouthful of gin. She knows she can't refuse Greer, but the thought of having to respond truthfully to their questions about her life—revealing its dull details, or, worse, being forced to spill out her frenzied thoughts—makes her jaw clench.

"All right, Vera first," Greer says.

"Oh, well, um—let me see. Well, where—where does your family come from?" Vera asks, prickles of mascara dotting the bags under her eyes. She excels at monologues, not actual conversation, and June and Dorothy let out annoyed huffs at the question's innocence.

"Poland," Lois says. "My mother's family are from Lublin and my father's family lived in Warsaw. He was born in Chicago, but my mother wasn't, though she never liked to talk about Lublin. She said there wasn't much to tell, that she was American now. And then my parents moved to Lake Forest soon after they were married."

"Lake Forest is such a funny name, now that I think of it: Lake. Forest," Vera begins.

"Did you tell the truth about your husband and why you left? Or was that a lie too?" June interrupts.

The man in the waistcoat slams his palm against the Wurlitzer's domed top, cursing under his breath. He is handsome, like a gaunt William Holden. Lois wonders if he's listening.

"Some of it was true," Lois says.

"Come on, Lois," Greer says softly. "You're earning true forgiveness here."

"Well, I lied when I said he was impotent. He wanted children."

"And you didn't," Greer says, like they are telling the story together. Lois wonders how she knew.

"No, but it was more than that. Before I met Lawrence, I didn't know what to do. My mother died of cancer when I was seventeen, and I'd been so distracted that I hadn't applied to any colleges, probably didn't have good enough grades to go anyway, to be honest. And then he appeared so soon after she passed—almost like I conjured him."

"You fell in love," Greer says. Behind her, the Wurlitzer has begun to glow its warm egg-yolk yellow, the attractive man pulled away by another divorcée with a gap between her two front teeth.

"Yes. Or I thought I did. He was from this old Lake Forest family, and I was so surprised when he talked to me at the theater. He told me a girl shouldn't be going to movies on her own, so he'd take me every week. It was such a relief, to talk to someone. To have someone listen to me. So when he asked, even though we'd only known one another for a few months—"

"You said yes," Greer says.

"But after we were married, he began to act so differently." Lois's throat constricts, and she begins to talk faster, as if she's running out of air. "Criticized how I sat and dressed. Told me I shouldn't go to the movies so often. Whenever he was in the house, I was scared to breathe. And then, in May, I thought I was pregnant. I was late and terrified at the thought that I'd be truly stuck and—and helpless. I'd take my children to the doctor that I hated, to the school where girls hated me. But then I got my period at the theater, and I was just sitting there, about to watch *Royal Wedding,* and I realized that I had to leave. And I know that may seem absurd, no felonies or desertion, no new husband lined up, but I just felt that—if I stayed with him—I'd, not explode, exactly, that sounds too violent or exciting even, but collapse in on myself. That I'd disappear."

Lois stops and takes a breath—her lungs nearly emptied. Greer is smiling at her as if she's passed some test, and Lois is comforted, until she looks at the others. Vera and June wear concerned, pained looks, and Dorothy is tugging at her gold chain, as if she doesn't know what to say.

"Well, that one's a little difficult to follow," Dorothy says. "Let me think."

June turns to put on an Ink Spots record, and Lois finishes the last of her warm gin. She feels as if she's removed an item of clothing, that she's standing in only her stiff lace brassiere.

"I think maybe Lois has had enough truths," Greer says, and Lois flushes with gratitude. "How about we give her a dare?"

"Oooh yes," Dorothy says, clasping her hands together. The girls look to Greer, awaiting further orders.

"Lois," Greer says. "I want you to plant a lipstick kiss on Roger's prized bison skull."

Greer points to the bleached skull hanging over the front doorway, its curved form like that of a mammoth petrified insect. In lowered voices, the girls explain how Roger, the bartender, shot the bison fifteen years ago after it lumbered onto the stretch of desert behind the Highlands. It was the first bison anyone had seen in the area in years. He shot it directly between the eyes—Lois can see now the bullet mark pocking the bone—and made a rug from its gnarled hide that he offers to show girls as a way to lure them to his bedroom upstairs.

Goose bumps needle Lois's forearms in something close to pleasure. The challenge reminds her of thrusting her hand out for the highest tree branch as a child, yodeling like Herman Brix's Tarzan. Her mother's laughter at Lois's recounting, a lit match behind her irises. The same flame she sees in Greer's eyes now.

"But there's no way she can do that," June says. "It's twelve feet or so above the floor."

"Well, if Lois thinks she can't do it—" Greer begins.

"I can do it," Lois says.

There's a new giddiness to the girls. Greer has opened a window, kindled a shared sense that anything can happen. Dorothy orders another round of drinks, and Lois uncaps and twists open her matte-red lipstick, caking it against her already painted mouth. She spent longer on her makeup than usual that evening, powdering a scabbed blemish to oblivion, redrawing her eyeliner until it was a perfect slope. The gin has begun to buzz at her fingertips, and as she walks toward the entryway, she thinks of how she'd approach this when she was younger: swift and unthinking, as if every bone were unbreakable. She drags a wooden chair from a table, waking an old man with a friar-like ring of white hair, and steps onto its seat. Next to the entrance there are two rickety shelves lined with plump ceramic statues of horses, and she tests the wood's strength in the lower one with the tip of her shoe. The shelf winces under her weight when she lifts herself onto it, the dry pine splintering. She tamps down her fear. Greer is watching.

"What are you doing over there?" a voice bellows, and Lois knows she has to move.

Gripping the doorframe with one hand, she lifts herself onto the next shelf, putting her nearly level with the skull. She wishes she were barefoot. That there was less crinoline beneath her dress, making her feel wide as a bell. To close the final inches, she pushes herself up onto the pointed toes of her shoes and just reaches the window ledge with her other hand, her finger bones close to snapping as she pulls her body upward. Behind her, there is a roar of chatter and cheering as she leans over and presses her lips against the cool, dusty bone.

Beneath her feet, she feels the shelf shudder, and without another thought she drops to the floor. A young man in a ten-gallon hat rushes to help her up, and when she rises—both knees stinging so sharply she's sure there must be blood, so much of it rushing through her with the current of a rapid—she feels stronger than she has in years. The whole bar erupts in thunderous applause. Greer raises her clapping hands above her head.

"Now, how am I going to even get up there to clean it?" Roger asks.

Seventeen

. . . .

They return to the bar for the next several nights. Lois slips into the car's backseat without a word, her hips thumping against June's or Dorothy's. She holds her breath every time, as if someone will suddenly remember that she's not wanted, but once the engine starts she settles into the pleasure of the car: the warm, overlapping bodies, the girls' breath against her cheek, peppermint and the faint, feral ghost of whatever they had for dinner; how they treat her limbs like anyone else's, like their own.

At the Highlands, the regulars greet her as "bison girl." Lois maintains a one-drink limit—not wanting to make a fool out of herself and lose whatever affection she's gained—and, luckily for her thin envelope of bills, there's always a man willing to buy a round. Often, these men split them, herding half the girls by the pool table or toward the bar's curve, but Greer has a rule every one of the girls follows: men are to be limited to thirty minutes. "Decide what you want from them, take it, and then leave," she instructs. These words tilt Lois's axis. The idea of seeing every interaction with a man as a transaction, an exchange where they are in complete control.

As the hours pass, the girls' eyes become glassy and heavy-lidded, their lipstick rubbed away to reveal the pale, tender shades of their mouths. To Lois's shock, sometimes the others briefly disappear into a back office with one of the cowboys—even Vera, who emerges pink as a newborn—and she realizes this is in line with Greer's rule, that they can decide they want something more than just a free drink. She thinks of this in her bedroom dark: the weight of a loosened belt buckle, a hot mouth on her neck, more lurid than any film. Her eyes follow the William Holden look-alike, who comes often, but he expresses no interest. It's been like this with everyone but Lawrence, as if they sense something's off about her, a dog's ear pitched to a whine no one else can hear.

Late in the evening, the girls often dance with one another, nearly falling asleep while shuffling their feet to Bing Crosby. At some point, Dorothy rhapsodizes about each girl's beauty. Vera asks Lois to draw eyeliner on just like her own. She loves the intimacy of these moments, how one of the girls will sometimes rest their cheek against her shoulder at the bar, as if she expects it, as if she is no different from them.

One night, Mary Elizabeth defaces a section of the bar top with drawings of dahlias, which no one realizes until a man lifts his forearms and finds his skin smeared with pen ink. Bailey apologizes profusely as Roger yells about the age of the wood.

"You have to watch how much you drink," Bailey says to Mary Elizabeth on the drive back. "I know it feels different to be on your own, but some rules from back home still apply here."

"Don't listen to her," Greer interrupts. "You can do whatever you want."

"You know what it's mixing with," Bailey whispers to Greer in the front seat, though everyone else can hear. Greer sighs and turns around to the other girls, her face as stern as her voice.

"You can do whatever you want," she repeats.

They all nod, eager as students, desperate to believe her.

In the mornings, the girls have to excuse themselves to vomit in the downstairs bathroom, the strained sounds of retching audible from the breakfast table. Rita, exasperated, tells Anna to keep the first-floor bathroom window open.

One morning, after the plates are cleared, Rita finally invites Lois into her study. Lois feels a ripple of pleasure at the request, remembering how desperately she desired this privilege when she first arrived. It was different than the sleepy hours Rita had to spend with her at the card table in the living room—the shut door evidence of some confidence, of Rita's interest and care.

"I've heard that some of the girls are spending more time with local gentlemen," Rita begins.

Lois says nothing. On the car rides, the girls speak frankly about diaphragms tucked next to their lipstick, laughing about how some of the men are prepared and others will try to convince them it doesn't matter, that they'll just pull out. Though she's new to these sorts of friendships, she knows to repeat none of this.

"I've talked to them, but I worry they still don't really know what they're risking," Rita continues. "I don't think anyone wants to marry a ranch hand. And, well, I think you could be a good influence on them."

Lois smiles and shakes her head. "I don't know about that."

"I do. I think it's good you're not rushing right into another marriage like some of the other girls, and that you're not indulging the attentions of Reno's gentlemen. You have a level head on your shoulders. That's rarer than you think for girls your age."

Though before Lois wanted so deeply for Rita to think she was as strong as her, all she can think of now is that her head has never felt level. It's a balloon one moment and an anchor in the next, but she does not want to explain this to Rita. It's something she thinks only Greer would understand.

"Thank you. But I really don't think anyone will listen to me."

"Well, promise me you'll at least try."

It's odd, to realize Rita wants something from her. That she needs Lois to help rebalance the scales that have tottered and dipped since Greer arrived. Lois has felt it like the drop in pressure before a storm—Rita losing her sway. Anna cooking roast beef two nights in a row because Greer said she liked it. Florence wearing her hair down because Greer told her it looked more fetching that way. Even Bailey occasionally laughs at Greer's remarks, though she catches herself in the act, looking at Rita in apology.

"I will," Lois says, though she plans to do no such thing.

Lois begins to notice that every time they visit the Highlands, Greer asks something of them. It happens whenever there's a lull—a conversation sloping downward, the bar thinning, as if she knows they all need a jolt of her electricity. She opens her mouth and Lois can sense what's coming with a new, muscled focus in her body, like a racehorse before the pistol is fired. Vera is told to steal a bottle of rye, Dorothy to carve a heart into the wall with Greer's pocketknife. It's always when Bailey's in the restroom or talking to someone from a nearby ranch. They all have affection for Bailey, and don't want her to struggle over what to disclose to Rita.

The other girls resist at first, but then Greer's voice whets to a whisper, sharp and delicate as a single razor blade on their skin. Their eyes widen, suddenly aware of how close their blood flows to the surface. They remember how Greer pushed that cowboy into the rabbitbrush, or the other evening, how when she thought another divorcée had stolen her drink she told the girl that if she did it again, she'd slip crushed glass into her gin, and they relent. Afterward, they're each treated like heroes—glasses raised in laughter—their small misdeeds sparking the air so something catches between them all, drawing them close like a flame. These are the moments Lois waits for. The moments Greer is sun-bright with joy. She does not appear to take pleasure from food or alcohol, only these acts of deviance.

Greer always saves the most dramatic dares for Lois. This is its own compliment, greater than anything Dorothy says about her painted face.

By the pool, Lois and Greer find another routine. Though they never agree on it, Greer appears a little before two and Lois reads to her for an hour as she lies in the sun, her skin soon darkening to a honeyed brown so her bruise becomes almost invisible. She always wears the same shirt, though Lois knows she owns several, as she's seen them strung out on the clothesline, gleaming like abalone shells. One morning, Lois tries to scrunch up her own shirtsleeves in imitation of how Greer wears them, but the cotton balloons at her biceps, making her look broad and ungainly, every attempt overwrought with effort.

Lois tries to soften her makeup to look more natural: lighter blush, fainter liner. Her skin has become tawny, and though she likes this new color, how it makes her feel healthy and vigorous, it's impossible to imagine going barefaced. She's not Greer, whose beauty is its own orbit.

"That's enough," Greer says when she wants Lois to stop reading, in a tone that shows she's used to giving orders. Sometimes it's at the end of a chapter. Other times Lois is midsentence.

"You're not going to remember what's going on with the characters," Lois protests.

"Yes, I will."

"I should give you daily quizzes, then." Greer laughs at this, and the next day, when Lois brings her a handwritten series of questions, she laughs harder still. Lois quickly realizes that she doesn't have to censor herself around Greer. They have a shared humor, and even the sound of Greer's laugh—the pure, loud cackle—melts into harmony with her own, so that they start to seem indistinguishable.

When they stop reading, Greer naps and Lois swims. Lois imagines that Greer didn't pack a bathing suit, as she's always in her underwear beneath her cover-up, and she pictures her hastily throwing whatever was clean into her suitcase and arriving at the airport to purchase the first flight headed west. Lois wonders if Greer's husband even knows where she is; if it's too dangerous for him to have the ranch's address. She is not physical like the other girls. She does not dance or clasp hands or kiss others on the cheek, and Lois wonders if this is because of him. If he has colored all touch.

In the bathroom's oval mirror, she practices asking Greer questions.

Had he done it before?

Does he know you're here?

Greer asks Lois about her father's meatpacking plant, about Ela, and about what she would have studied in college. She comments on the idiocy of Lois's classmates, the harshness of her father, each word making Lois feel validated, as if her feelings have been those of a girl who sees the world as it is. Greer is more interested in learning about Lois's life than talking about her own, which is its own flattery, and so, in turn, each fact Lois learns about her becomes precious. Greer has four siblings and broke her arm falling off a horse when she was seven. When she was younger, she lived in France for several months and believes all of its museums are mausoleums. She thinks President Truman is as corrupt as Al Capone. If the girls ask her what music she wants to listen to, she'll always choose Billie Holiday's record with Eddie Heywood. When June prods her, asking if she's new home or old home, she says that she prefers hotel rooms. She has no children.

They speak with the casual intensity of sisters, but Lois never asks Greer the questions about her husband she's rehearsed. She does not want to bring any pain back to the surface, and their time together has become so essential that it feels fragile, like the houses she would build out of small pine blocks as a child. She worries the wrong word will be too heavy a weight, sending everything toppling to the floor.

Eighteen

. . . .

G reer decides that Lois needs new clothes. At cocktail hour, Lois picks at a seam running along her bicep, which presses into her skin like a lashing. Her dress sleeves have felt tighter in recent days. Greer lays her open paperback against her knee, looking Lois up and down.

"What?" Lois asks.

"We'll go shopping tomorrow," Greer says, and resumes reading.

Lois knows the other girls heard, though they pretend not to. Dorothy smiles faintly as she runs her finger along the rim of her glass, undoubtedly remembering that she made the same pronouncement over two weeks ago, when Lois first arrived. Mary Elizabeth fumbles with the record needle, the room briefly filled with scratched air. Greer says nothing else about it for the entire evening, and Lois assumes she's forgotten, that it was just a passing whim, until the next day at lunch when she tells Bailey that they'll all need a ride into town.

L ois has never liked shopping. When she was young, she was drawn to the voluminous satin dresses actresses wore in *Pride and Prejudice* and *Gone with the Wind*, their sleeves the size of a Christmas ham. She wanted to fill a room, her mother buying her wine-colored dresses that fell to the floor. When the girls at school became conscious of what clothing signified, no longer wriggling in protest as their mothers stamped shoes onto their feet, they began to tease Lois relentlessly. But even when she'd go to the stores her classmates went to, purchasing identical stiff plaid skirts and shirts with slim, drooping bows at the collar, she never looked right.

On the drive, they pass a wild horse nosing through the dirt and whiskers of desert grass. The sky is a dry blue. Lois hasn't returned to downtown Reno since she visited her lawyer, and as they approach, the sounds of the city swell, as if someone is turning the knob of a radio. They motor beneath the arch she'd seen from the train station, R-E-N-O spelled out in white block letters, and pass unlit neon signs advertising jewelry and cafés, saddles and night-clubs. One casino has an enormous mural painted on its front, uninspired in everything but scale, with settlers circling their wagons by an impossibly blue waterfall. The side streets are unremarkable, the brick buildings mundane and familiar, but there's a frisson in the air, the luxurious sense of potential that comes from so many people being on holiday in the same place.

Parker's is heady with the smell of leather. When they arrive, Greer strides purposefully among the racks of clothes, appearing to forget every-one else. Dorothy insists that Lois try on a western shirt stitched with a sweep of blue fringe, and though she feels ridiculous in it, the other girls are so adamant that she places it on the counter, bullied by their praise.

"You'll be ready to head back out on the trail with us," Dorothy says.

"I don't know if clothing was the issue there," June says.

"June," Dorothy scolds.

"No." Lois laughs. "She's right."

She has just under a hundred dollars from her father—with men always picking up their tab at the Highlands, she's spent almost nothing—and so she told herself she could spend ten at the store, though even that amount makes her anxious. Whenever she emerges from the dressing room, Lois is surprised that Greer is nowhere to be found. She tries on pairs of Levi's, finally finding a size that doesn't gape or cut off her circulation, though she feels like they flatten her backside. This is how all shopping goes: eventually she purchases something because it fits, because it's inoffensive. She tamped down any desire she felt for a color or neckline years ago, knowing she can't be trusted, so that now she's not even sure what she likes.

By the back wall, she joins the other girls, who are trying on brightly stitched cowboy boots. Mary Elizabeth runs her hand along their square leather toes as if she's skimming fence posts, humming to herself. Lois won-ders how much Luminal she's taken today. Her husband's calls are becoming more and more frequent. A boot is suctioned to Vera's foot, and June is trying to pry it off, her spine curving into a C.

"What would your husbands say if they saw you in cowboy boots?" Dorothy asks.

"I'd be shocked if he looked up from his newspaper long enough to notice," June chokes out. Vera shifts her bottom on the chair, as if that will help.

"Joe always liked for me to look a certain way," Vera says. "Same for the children. He's called all clothing 'uniforms' since the war. He'd say, 'That uniform hasn't been properly ironed,' or 'That uniform is fitting a little tight,' like he was doing a Patton impression. Our maid actually wore a uniform, now that I think of it. This stiff blue dress. Maybe that's part of why he liked her, part of why, well, you know. It was always so well starched."

Mary Elizabeth has picked one of the boots up off the shelf and holds it like a baby, cradling the shaft. They all watch her for a moment, unsure what to say to Vera. Her loss feels greater than the rest: middle-aged, three children, her body shaped like a sack of flour. The others can convince themselves that being a divorcée won't be a black mark, that their youth or beauty will keep them above water, but with Vera, it will pull her under.

"George likes me to look a certain way as well. No black or plaids. No pants. No updos. He'd probably hate how these boots hide my calves," Dorothy says to break the silence.

"Why are you marrying him, again?" Greer has appeared behind them. A braided leather belt with a silver buckle is looped around her waist, and Lois can't recall if she was wearing it when they arrived.

Dorothy laughs. "Well, I love him."

"Well, if he loves you, he shouldn't care whether you shear off your hair or wear a pin-striped suit. Make sure he knows that before you're wed. You'll have less power after."

"I don't know if that's true. Then I'll be his wife—"

"And that gives you power? Over what? The type of flowers in the entryway?" Greer hands Lois three shirts, all pale linen. "Now, then, try these on. With the jeans."

"Aren't these men's shirts?" Lois asks.

"I don't know, maybe. Does that matter?"

"You're Katharine Hepburn, Lois," June says, her face locked in a pained grimace as Vera's boot finally comes loose.

"Right," she says.

In the dressing room, the shirt billows down the tops of her thighs, the collar wide around her neck. She looks not like Katharine Hepburn, but instead like a woman who stole one of her overweight husband's shirts. When she comes out, Greer lets out a short, harsh laugh.

"Well, that's not how you wear it," she says, and kneels by Lois's side, flipping the cuffs and rolling the sleeves up her arm, quick and efficient. She tucks the hem into Lois's waistband, Lois's stomach clenching at the dip of her hands, the brief snag of Greer's fingernail on her underwear. It's the first time Greer has touched her.

"There," Greer says, and rises. The other girls have gathered to assess her work. Vera's in bare feet, as if she's frightened to put even her own shoes back on.

Lois turns to the mirror. She doesn't see herself looking back, instead finding a girl who owns her own apartment in the city, rising in the morning to put a copper kettle on the stove, a cat rubbing against her bare calf. Like the girls she's seen waiting for a bus in Chicago, the set of their mouths always suggesting an impatience, a desire to be in motion. She looks like someone who paints, who understands how to play with light and shadow, hinted at in the way the cream shirt is open to a low bone of her chest, the accordion of the bunched-up sleeves, a body suggested rather than known. Her shoulders looser, her torso no longer constricted by a dress's stiff poplin. She doesn't look like herself, but like someone she'd rather be—even the color of her hair is somehow different beneath the store lights, a glimmer of blue in the black.

The only thing that doesn't look right is the flare of her lipstick. She wipes the back of her hand across her mouth, dulling the color.

"Much more Reno," Dorothy says.

"Much more Lois, I think," Greer says. They find one another's eyes in the mirror and grin, as if Lois has completed another dare.

Afterward, Greer briskly walks outside as the others pay. The shirts tip Lois over what she hoped to spend, but it's impossible not to purchase them. She does not put her own clothes back on, stuffing her dress in the paper bag as if it were refuse, something to be thrown out on the side of the road.

Nineteen

. . . .

era is leaving. It's Lois's first real reminder that their time together is brief, and that in less than four weeks everyone, including her, will be gone. At breakfast, Bailey tells everyone that it's tradition for divorcées to go to the Virginia Street Bridge after the courthouse hearing and throw their wedding rings into the river. Vera sharply inhales at the thought, cocooning her finger with her other hand, as if Bailey were demanding her ring at that moment. June says she'll be happy to get rid of it, and Dorothy just mumbles about how she hates the word *divorcée*, that it's nearly as bad as *old maid*.

"I felt the same way when I first came here," Bailey says. "But then I realized there's nothing wrong with the word. It has whatever meaning you give it."

"That's true, in some ways, though everyone will have their opinions," Rita says. "That's why it's so important to behave well. It shows everyone that we're not who they expect us to be."

Lois looks down at her band. Their names and wedding date are engraved along the inner curve: *Lawrence and Lois, August 3rd, 1947.* The ring never felt linked to Lawrence—it was simply proof that she was a wife, that she was no longer just a shadow in the corner of the school's dressing room.

She still does not have a place to live after her father's home. Since Greer arrived, she's made little progress, her plans amounting to nothing more than a penciled tally of imagined figures. The boardinghouse excised after Greer's dismissal. At the pool that afternoon she struggles to focus on the book, clumsily pausing at the ends of paragraphs after realizing she has no recollection of what she's just said. Greer turns to her. A strand of hair shimmers like a silverfish at her throat. Lois begins to apologize, bites her tongue.

She wonders where Greer's ring is—if she threw it out the window of her taxi that first night, letting the desert swallow it whole.

At dinner, Anna serves Vera's favorite, roast chicken, the whole first floor perfumed with rosemary and butter. Everyone applauds when Vera enters, and there's a card on her plate where each girl wrote little notes of encouragement, with even a line from Patty in purple colored pencil, thanking Vera for teaching her how to French braid her hair.

Throughout dinner Vera speaks of her children and the different gifts she's bought for them: a leather wallet, a silver bracelet, a stuffed pony made with real horsehair. Mary Elizabeth cries, telling Vera she'll miss her terribly. June rolls her eyes, but Lois is moved by the sincerity of her emotion; it's better for her to be overly sentimental than numb. Near the end of the meal, Vera and Rita begin to have a quiet conversation, speaking in the private language of mothers.

"Well, Vera, how would you like to celebrate your last night?" Greer asks when Anna begins to clear the plates.

"She has a big day tomorrow, what with the courthouse and a morning flight right after," Rita says.

"I'm sure, but it's your last night with all of us, your last night in Reno, and I think . . . ," Greer says, pausing for a moment, "that we should go to a casino."

The girls sound out their agreement, erupting into chatter about where they should go. Bailey attempts to corral everyone, loudly announcing that they should go to Harrah's—a true Reno institution. Vera protests at first, nervously pulling at her curls, but after the other girls beg her to go, she relents. Through it all, Rita sits silently in her chair, and Lois feels an odd sense of guilt. *Promise me you'll at least try,* Rita had asked her in the study. The others pay her no attention, leaping from the table to change into their cocktail dresses.

"I promise we won't be out very late," Bailey says later as they file past the living room, and Rita nods, her mouth a hard line.

Reno is a different city at night, teetering on the knife's edge between garishness and glamour. Virginia Street is shocked to life by neon, the rows of signs making Lois's eyes smart, everything mammoth and bright. Women wearing cheap, oversized pearls throng the doorways of casinos and clubs, though Harrah's clientele is obviously wealthier, with fox furs nested at their throats. Bailey parks, and the girls open the overfull car's doors and tumble out onto the street. Unlike the others, Greer hadn't changed into a cocktail dress. Her trousers and sweater would be shocking on anyone else, but looking at her, Lois misses the looseness of her own linen shirts, the warmth of her new denim.

In the marquee's glow, Lois pauses, the casino's massive form looming over her like a threat. There's a familiar tremor in her fingers. It's the same feeling she got standing on Promontory Point as a child. Pulled to jump, even with the rocks below cresting jagged as teeth. A terrifying sense that she could not trust her own body, that the deep impulses of her primal self jerked toward destruction.

The others stride inside as if it's just another bar, but Greer turns back for her. She picks a piece of lint from Lois's shoulder, in the way Lois's mother would occasionally brush a wisp of hair from her forehead before they got out of the car, and tilts her head toward the doorway. Lois follows her inside.

A haze of smoke rests over the green felt card tables, each patterned with roulette circles or tiles of playing cards. The lights cast a warm yellow halo around the gamblers. They all look slightly unkempt, ties loosened, a dress strap falling off the shoulder, which makes everyone seem more intimate, as if it's late in the evening at a small New Year's Eve party, the girls minutes away from slipping off their shoes. It's more people than Lois has ever seen in a single space, larger than her wedding or the endless, sweltering assemblies they'd hold at the start of the school year. It makes the Highlands look like a waiting room. And then there's the noise: the clack of chips, the drone of the roulette ball, a man yelling out numbers and colors, someone yelping in pain or excitement, Lois can't see them to tell. She feels as if she's at her first film again, awed and overwhelmed, a kernel of popcorn softening on her small, pink tongue. Sometimes Lois felt that this was why her mother took her to the movies, even if she could not articulate it. To show Lois that there were other ways to live.

"Where do we . . . go?" she asks.

"To the bar," Greer says. "Always the bar."

Dorothy is there already, with a martini glass filled to the brim. Vera nervously powders her nose. Bailey finds Mary Elizabeth a seat, and June waves at a young man in a boxy suit a dozen yards away. Lois has never seen him before. He begins to wind his way through the blackjack tables, pressing his hand against his wide gold tie as he squeezes between the crowds.

"It's Harry," June says, turning to Greer. "I'm so glad you'll get to meet him."

"The cousin," Dorothy mumbles to Lois, the rim of her glass pressed against her bottom lip.

June introduces him to everyone as just Harry, grinning as he snakes his arm around her waist. He has small, narrowly set eyes and is an inch shorter than June, which only makes their age difference more apparent. He kisses Lois's hand when they're introduced, and she instantly dislikes him. A smear of his spit wets her skin.

"Harry's in town for a meeting. He's an incredibly talented screenwriter." June perches her hands on his shoulder.

"Well, I don't know about that," Harry says.

"What movies have you written?" Lois asks.

"You probably haven't seen them. They're tough, crime stuff, not appropriate for ladies like yourselves."

"Lois has seen every movie ever made," Greer says.

"Is that so?" he asks, his eyes fixed on Greer's bruise. "And, sorry, what was your name again?"

"Ava Gardner."

Lois laughs and June follows, slightly too loud, leaving Harry no choice but to do the same. Greer lifts her hand to get the bartender's attention. Her displeasure is obvious. It crimps the air, causing the other girls to finish their first drinks in rapid gulps, unsure how to appease her. Lois is annoyed—June should have known not to invite him. Greer's rule is clear: no more than thirty minutes.

"Well, we need to go get some chips." June pats Harry's lapel, her smile strained.

"Yes, good idea. Nice to meet all of you," he says.

They disappear into the din. Lois is disappointed that June is abandoning them, that they won't move through the casino as a flock. Once Lois and Greer both have a martini in hand, they all decide to go to the cashier as well, passing table after bustling table. She waits in line beside Greer, but when the man at the horseshoe desk asks how much money she wants in chips, she has no idea what to do. She didn't realize she'd have to surrender one of the precious bills folded in her purse pocket.

"You're not gambling?" Greer asks.

"I—I don't know."

"You have to play with me. We'll be one another's good-luck charms."

"Well, how much do I need to spend?"

"That's simple. However much you're willing to lose." Greer hands the man a fifty.

"Start with ten," Bailey says quietly.

Lois's hand lightly shakes when she hands over the bills—everything she'd brought with her that evening. The cashier counts out a neat stack of colored chips, and Lois is frightened by how suddenly the smooth plastic doesn't seem like money anymore, only tokens for a game.

For the next hour, the girls rush from roulette tables to slot machines, pulled along by the casino's current. Bailey appears to know everyone, greeting other divorcées—girls who serve drinks, girls who the casinos pay to gamble and take photographs. It was something Lois hadn't considered: all of the girls who can't afford to waste their days napping on deck chairs, who spend their six weeks mending clothes and pouring coffee. Bailey kisses them on their rouged cheeks as if they're no different than the guests at the ranch.

Men ask Dorothy and Mary Elizabeth to blow on dice and pull their slot's silver levers. "You know, they used to do this with a mouse over at Harold's," an older man tells Lois, as everyone lays their chips on the roulette table. "You'd place bets on which numbered hole he'd scurry into." She turns to tell the other girls and they all laugh at the absurdity of it: a little, finely boned mouse amid all of this.

The rooms churn with an endless number of people—nothing like the

Highlands' set cast of characters. Lois searches for movie stars, familiar jaw-lines and cheekbones, but finds only strangers. There's a freedom to it, the giddy rush of anonymity. When a waitress in a short fluted skirt asks if Lois wants another drink, she orders a gin and tonic, even though she's already had her self-imposed limit.

Greer is their guide. She's comfortable in the casino in the way Lois imagines she's comfortable anywhere, never wondering whether or not she'll be welcome. When she gambles, she doesn't hesitate, briskly picking a num-ber or pulling the slot lever. She impresses the girls with details about Monte Carlo; the sharp salt smell of it, even inside the casino. Lois can't distinguish any pattern to her choices, but as she slowly loses her chips, making foolish, uncalculated bets, Greer builds a small tower. The disks bulge in her trouser pockets.

Men try to flirt with Lois, leering down the neck of her satin cocktail dress, and she thinks of how all it takes to get something is to not want it so badly. She considers leading one of them—tall and thin, with eye-brows thick as a brush—to the empty coat check or the alley outside, but it wouldn't be worth leaving Greer's side. They do not separate, though the other girls come and go, bees floating from flower to flower. Though this dispersing disappoints Lois at first, she cares less as the hours pass, as she loses count of which number of drink is in her hand.

L et's go find Bailey and Vera," Greer says after another round of roulette. "I think they're playing blackjack."

Lois can't find a waitress, so she places her empty glass on the carpet, and Greer laughs and does the same even though her tumbler is full. The casino has begun to warm and blur. They ascend to the second floor, where Bailey and Vera's table is presided over by a stout woman with glasses, her silk shirt busy with a pattern of playing cards. This floor is for high rollers, evident in the fabric of everyone's clothes and the state of their teeth. The dealer shuffles and places several cards on the felt with a clean *thwick* of her thumb. Lois hasn't seen a female dealer at any of the other tables.

Bailey's dealt an eight of hearts and a seven of diamonds, giving her fifteen to the dealer's twelve. Lois is entranced by the woman's hands, her nails painted a glossy burgundy so dark they're nearly black, like the shell of a scorpion. Vera gently shakes her head.

"I never know what to do. Though I suppose it's all random," Vera says.

She holds up her lone one-dollar chip. The circle doubles and Lois has to blink to bring it back into focus. She grins at this as if it's a party trick, blinking again and again.

"Luck isn't random," Greer says. "You just have to know if you're lucky or not."

"Yes. *Yes,*" Lois says, and Greer laughs.

Bailey hits and receives a nine, giving the dealer the game. Lois looks for a waitress to order another drink. One by one, each of the other players loses, and Bailey braces herself against the table and stands. The dealer sweeps the cards back into the deck. Her face is older but completely unlined, as if she's never smiled or grimaced. Lois imagines tugging at the sides of her mouth.

"I don't know how, but I always lose at Peg's table," Bailey says.

"I didn't know there were female dealers here," Greer says, looking at Peg approvingly, and Lois feels a surge of jealousy.

"She was one of the first in Reno, and she's an incredible poker player. She plays in some private games with absurd limits. You all should meet her." Bailey turns back to Peg, who's shuffling for the next round. "Peg, I'd like you to meet two of our other guests, Greer Lang and Lois Gorski. Girls, this is Peg, my favorite and least favorite dealer in Reno. I can't frequent her table, or I'd be penniless."

"Welcome," Peg says, giving them a curt nod. "Would you like to play a hand?"

"Sure," Greer says, and takes a seat.

Lois has nothing left to play, so she has to sit out as Peg deals cards for Greer and two rumpled, tuxedo-clad men who have sidled up to the table. The shapes of the room have begun to slither, and when Lois blinks again Vera is at her side, talking in the way she always does, as if she's hosting her own dull radio show. She prattles on about her mother's house, how the only thing she allows anyone to listen to is *Mystery Theater,* and how Vera is going to have to go into the garden to smoke, even in the winter. Lois is able to find balance by focusing on a speck of lipstick on her front tooth.

"I don't think I ever really thought what my days were going to be like," Vera says. "I thought about getting the children to my mother's, about the train ride and the ranch. But I didn't think about what I'm going to tell their teachers or whether I'll still have dinner with Barbara and Kate, because their husbands will be there, and that will be odd, won't it, to just have me be there alone?"

"It might," Lois says, remembering dinner parties with Lawrence's colleagues, how all their wives wanted to talk about were other wives who weren't there, gossip as thin as powdered milk. "But really, do you even want to have dinner with Barbara and Kate?"

"Yes, I do."

"I don't think you do. I think we should stay at this casino and never have dinner with anyone ever again. We'll survive off of cocktail olives. That's what I plan to do."

"You know I can't do that, with my children."

They are closer together now, so that Lois can see the lipstick mark's dark pit. "Oh right. You have children. I'm so sorry."

"And there are so many things like, well, for Christmas, will I just go to all of the parties by myself, when everyone is there with their husbands? Joe would always get so drunk at the Millers' party. Last year, he fell asleep in their guest room, under the covers and everything, as if it were his bed. But isn't that better than showing up by myself, with some sad bottle of sherry?"

Lois feels a weight at her shoulders and worries that Vera's sadness is catching.

"Listen." Lois clasps Vera's forearm. "Do you want to run through the casino with me right now? I mean really run, until we're breathless?"

"No. Of course not." Vera begins to blink. "I'm in a cocktail dress."

"Oh right. How about we just yell, then?"

"Indoors?"

Bailey returns with another round of drinks and Lois turns her attention to the alcohol, which she finishes in one messy swallow. After losing twice, Greer decides she's had enough, and Lois is relieved to have her back at her side.

"Well, that was something," Greer says. "Vera, are you crying?"

To cheer Vera up, they spend the next hour playing penny slots, amassing small piles of copper on the counters. The coins remind Lois of the delicious heft of her childhood piggy bank, making her feel richer than any fold of bills could, and she thinks maybe she'll be able to earn her ten dollars back penny by penny. Greer takes Vera aside at some point. Lois watches them from the corner of her eye. Their faces are serious, but when they return, the mood lightens, Greer cheering Vera on whenever a coin dings the metal tray. Vera blooms under her attention, laughing and ordering another martini from one of the roving waitresses. Mary Elizabeth and Dorothy join them, breathless and tipsy, and Lois is deliriously happy that nearly all of them are together again. She tells them about her piggy bank's long, painted lashes and how she'd talk to it as she counted her dimes and nickels, promising she'd never let it be slaughtered like the pigs at her father's plant. They laugh and talk about childhood bedrooms not so different from her own, herds of porcelain dolls and beds tall enough to shimmy beneath, and Lois starts to believe they would have been her friends if they'd known her then, no longer even tasting the gin washing her throat, and then she is outside, staring at the lights of the marquee until everything burns black.

Twenty

· · · · · · ·

Everyone is late to breakfast. The toast is cold and the eggs have started to congeal. Lois is so hungover that everything is at a slight remove, as if cotton balls are tamped in her ears. She could have slept through the afternoon if it wasn't for the sounds of other girls in the hallway, slow footsteps and moans. When June shook her awake in the car, the birds were beginning to call out to one another, a line of lavender on the horizon. In her bedroom, she hovered so close to the lizard that she could trace its scales.

Rita doesn't look up when the girls enter. She cuts a sausage link in half with her knife, her elbows bobbing as her dull blade grinds into the china. They try to make as little noise as possible as they take their seats, as if perhaps Rita will look up and think they've always been there. Bailey gives them a pained smile—there's nothing she can do.

"Is there any way we could get a fresh pot of coffee?" June asks.

"A fresh pot?" Rita says, finally looking up to the table.

"Yes. It's just gotten a little cold."

"Well, it was piping hot when we sat down to breakfast over half an hour ago, but of course, since you're all here now, we'll have Anna boil more water. Anna!" Rita turns to the door.

The girls squirm under the weight of Rita's obvious disapproval. Anna opens the door. Greer's tray is in her hand, the lily in full bloom this morning, its petals a riotous orange. Rita tells her to make everyone another pot of coffee once she's returned from Miss Lang's room, and Anna nods before tottering down the hallway. Lois wishes she were as wealthy as Greer, so she could at least have the luxury of eating her piece of cold toast in bed.

"You all missed Vera," Rita says. "I know she would have loved to have everyone there to say their goodbyes, but Bailey and I saw her off."

The girls murmur words of remorse, fumbling through their hangovers, though it obviously hadn't occurred to any of them until that moment that

Vera isn't here. Lois has a vague memory of Vera drunkenly telling everyone to visit her in Boston, how they could ride the Swan Boats with her children in the Public Garden.

"I think we gave her a pretty good send-off last night," Dorothy says.

"Well, I'm not sure she felt the same, by the way she was looking up the staircase before she left," Rita says, and the girls swallow their smiles.

"Greer thought that—" June begins.

"Miss Lang is not here right now. What did *you* think?"

The girls are all silent, even June.

"Now, I know you all love Miss Lang, but don't let that blind you to making the right decisions for yourselves," Rita continues. "I want you all to enjoy your time here, of course I do, but many girls have stayed with us, and those who went on to have happy, fulfilling lives didn't see this time as a reprieve or a recess, but the start of something new."

Lois considers how little thought she's given to life after the ranch, and regret rests between her shoulder blades like the rounded edge of an anchor. The other girls look solemnly at Rita, except for Mary Elizabeth, who looks like she might vomit onto her breakfast plate. Lois realizes it's been several days since her husband called.

"I'm sorry, Rita," Lois says. "About Vera."

The others follow, mimicking her words like a chorus of errant school-girls.

"Well, you don't have to apologize to me. All I ask is that you think of what I said, and perhaps stay in a few nights a week, turn in early. It would do Bailey some good too," Rita says. "Now, who's going out on the trail?"

By the pool, the heat is cleansing. Lois feels calmer for the punishment of it, the light so urgent she can barely open her eyes. She's grateful when Greer tells her to stop reading to her after only a few paragraphs, lifting her shirt up and down by one of its glazed buttons to fan herself.

"Rita was not happy with us this morning," Lois says, pressing her cheek against the rungs of the deck chair.

"Why?" Greer asks.

"We slept in late and all missed saying goodbye to Vera."

Greer snorts. "Well, we're not her children. We're paying guests. And what does it matter to her? She pretends she cares about us, but she's practically another husband, trying to control our every thought and move. We all said goodbye to Vera last night. Lining up in the hallway and making false promises to write would have been so much worse."

"I think I promised to visit her in Boston. . . ."

"Drunkenly. That's different. It's not a lie when you're drunk."

Lois thinks of how Rita addressed each of them, her sense of propriety that now feels archaic, brittle as Lois's great-grandmother's christening bonnet. Even Bailey sometimes chafes against it. Sometimes she forgets that they've all paid Rita to stay here, and that any day they could pick up and go to another ranch. Though Lois's father had sent the check to Rita in advance, so she has less free will than the other girls. Still, she feels frustrated thinking of how remorseful she felt hours before, desperate for Rita's forgiveness. The rhythms learned from school, even when she hated her teachers, imagining them floating up to the sky and popping like balloons.

"What did you talk to Vera about? When you left the slots?" Lois asks.

"Oh, several things. We've been talking about her life after the divorce. I think there are ways she can get more money from her husband, so she doesn't have to live with her awful mother. I was trying to spare her from another marriage. I could already see it, that she'd throw herself at the first man who patted her son on the head."

"I didn't know you spoke about those things."

"Of course. With all the girls. You're not jealous, are you?" Greer teases.

"No. No, of course not. I just didn't know."

"Yes, well, someone has to, and Bailey and Rita are a bit worthless. They coddle Mary Elizabeth, when she's stronger than both of them, given the abuse she's suffered."

"The abuse?"

"Haven't you noticed?" Greer lowers her voice. "The long sleeves? They cover a welt along her left forearm. Her husband took a poker from the fireplace and pressed it against her skin. Perfectly down the center too. There's even a hook at the end."

Lois crosses her arms, her fingers reflexively touching the smooth skin below her elbow. She thinks of Mary Elizabeth and her prim shirts, buttoned at the wrist. Anna rushing in from the kitchen with her scalded palm, and how Mary Elizabeth's face drained of all color.

"How did you see it?"

"She showed it to me the other day when she wouldn't stop asking about my bruise."

The screen door opens, and Carol and Patty appear. Florence accompanies them, holding Carol's hand until she wriggles away from her toward the water. They're in matching bathing suits again, both a flat, medicinal pink, and Patty, the oldest, lunges into the pool ahead of Carol.

"Is it already Friday?" Greer asks Florence.

"Yes, I'm sorry, ma'am, it is," Florence says.

"Don't be sorry. If I was them, I'd insist on swimming every day."

The girls watch Greer as they begin to paddle. The handful of times they've roamed through cocktail hour they've acted as if she's a strange wild animal presiding atop their mother's fainting sofa, full of fear or awe, Lois can't tell. Carol fumbles in the water, pitching forward so only her head stays dry, and Patty laughs, ducking beneath the pool's skin and emerging several feet away.

Lois turns to Greer, who's leaned back in her armchair with her eyes closed. The bruise is still there in an ache of yellows. Lois has more questions to ask, but it feels impossible with the children there.

"Should I start reading again?" Lois asks.

"No, I won't be able to hear anything."

The girls begin to race. It's clearly Patty's idea, who glides from one end of the pool to the other, with Carol thrashing behind, beating her little feet. When Carol complains it's not fair after the third race, they see who can hold their breath the longest. The girls sink to the pool's bottom, giving Greer and Lois half a minute of silence until Carol finally floats to the top to see if she's won, gasping and wiping the water from her eyes.

Florence disappears inside the house. Lois tries to relax, banishing flashes of Mary Elizabeth's tight, puckered scar, instead imagining what Anna will serve for dinner. Given the girl's new abstinence, she's begun to bring slices of pie only to Rita and Bailey, keeping the rest covered with a dish towel on the kitchen counter, to be served again the next night. Lois doesn't miss it. Even jam has begun to taste too sweet. The girls all mirror Greer's eating habits, wolfing down fried eggs and cuts of meat, leaving only stripped bones, the glistening rib cage of a roast chicken. Lois's body feels stronger for it, a small ridge of muscle finning each upper arm. Even her hair is thicker. Its brush-like ends need a trim, but she refuses to cut it, as if it's become some life force.

She turns on her side so that the sunlight warms her back, and then suddenly a wave of water summits the pool's edge, crashing onto the concrete. Greer rises to inspect the pearls of water on her feet. The girls crouch in the shallow end, looking at her as if she might drown them.

"We're sorry," Patty says, so quietly it's nearly a whisper.

Greer looks at them and smiles, pushing her sunglasses up into her hair.

"It's just water," Greer says, wiping her feet and then holding up her hands. "And I'm not a witch, so I think I'll be all right. Are you a witch, Lois?"

"I don't think so."

"Thank god. Well, then, see, nothing to be sorry about. I'm Greer and this is my friend Lois. Tell me, what are your names again?"

The girls look at one another, trying to see if the other thinks it's safe to talk. Greer is at ease with them, and Lois realizes she's never asked her if she wants children.

"I'm Patty and this is Carol," Patty finally says.

"Of course, Patty and Carol. And you're my little night owl, aren't you, Carol?" Greer asks, and Carol's face flushes.

Lois isn't sure what Greer means by this, as both girls are sent to bed by eight in the evening. Patty turns to her sister, her mouth inquisitive and half open, and without saying a word the girls swim to the other corner of the pool. They put their heads together and whisper, their hair two slick halves of a heart. Greer reclines and bites at the puffed skin circling her thumbnail, her incisor pointed as an arrowhead. Lois senses a quiver of anxiety in the air.

"What was that about?" she asks.

"Oh, nothing," Greer says, tearing a hangnail loose. "Just a funny nickname."

After a few minutes, the girls kick toward where Lois and Greer are sitting and lift their bodies so they can fold their arms on the concrete lip. Greer cocks her head and folds her arms as well, inviting them in.

"Can we ask you a question?" Patty asks.

"Depends on the question," Greer says, and when the girls look at one another, their lips twisted shut, she laughs, relaxed again. "I'm just kidding, of course you can."

"Are you very famous?" Patty asks.

"Oh god, no. Why would you think that?"

"Because our mother told us not to talk to you, and she always does that when someone's famous," Patty says.

"Hm." Greer frowns. "Well, your mother must have just been trying to give me a little peace my first couple of days, but don't listen to her. You can talk to me all you want. Lois talks to me all the time, don't you, Lois?"

"All the time," Lois says after a moment, stuttering on the first word. The girls have introduced some distance—Greer feels suddenly opaque, a shape with new angles.

"But she's old," Carol says.

Greer laughs again. Carol has started to strain to stay upright on the ledge, and after speaking she drops her head into her arms, her legs dangling in the water. Though Lois knows how young the girls are, the word *old* smarts.

"How old do you think I am?" Lois asks.

"Thirty-eight," Carol says, languidly rocking her feet back and forth, like the clapper of a bell.

"Thirty-eight. She must think Anna is nearly dead," Greer says, causing Lois to snort.

"Do you have any siblings?" Carol asks Greer.

"I have four, actually. Two brothers and two sisters."

"Do you like them?"

"Of course, though I haven't spoken to them for a little while. I'm the oldest, so I took care of them growing up after my mother passed away, and, well, I needed time away after all of that. Time for myself."

Lois is shocked to learn that Greer's mother has also passed. That Greer wouldn't say something after Lois mentioned her own mother's death. An absence of an absence. She sees Greer with a black bow in her hair, Greer processing down a cathedral's central aisle, four blond children trailing close behind her like ducklings.

"Can I ask another question?" Patty says.

"Why not?" Greer says, following the trail of a loose thread at her sleeve.

"What happened to your face?"

Greer's fingers grip the clean white thread and yank it out at the root. She brings her hand to the concrete, letting the cotton flutter to the ground. Lois looks at the girls' plain, expressionless faces, holding her breath. A dragonfly skims the pool. It's such a simple question, one they would ask any other child on the playground, one that even Mary Elizabeth was able to ask in her hazy innocence.

"A man hurt me," Greer says. "But don't worry, he's very far away from here."

"How far?" Carol asks.

"Hundreds of miles. And he won't be coming any closer."

"Why?"

"Because when I was done with him, he looked a lot worse than I do."

Florence opens the door, towels folded over her forearm, and the girls plunge to the bottom of the pool. Lois does not move, fixed by a new image: Greer rising from the penthouse carpet, cracking the porcelain table lamp against her husband's skull. Blood soaking the carpet like oil. Greer lifting a grinning, phosphorescent poker from the fireplace just like Mary Elizabeth's husband and pressing the iron against bare skin.

Greer puts her sunglasses back on and asks Florence if she thinks it will rain again this evening. The girls bob up and down, thrashing their arms as they slowly make their way to the shallow end. Carol has begun to sing a song about Old Mother Hubbard. "*When she came there, the cupboard was bare, and so the poor dog had none,*" she sings in circles, never returning to the first verse, her voice high as a train whistle. The heat feels suddenly oppressive. For the first time in days, Lois wants to be alone in her room.

Twenty-One

. . . .

There was one moment when Lois thought Lawrence might hit her. They were talking about children. He came up behind her as she was washing her face, laying his large, warm palm against her stomach, and she nudged him away with her elbows, her hands slippery with soap. He asked her when, and then he asked her why not now, and before she knew it she was speaking about the war and how it seemed unfathomable to bring a baby into a world where children were led into gas chambers, where men murdered men and bombs leveled cities, talking past the one fear thudding at her sternum, which was that if she had a child she would never be able to leave Lawrence—that she would die like her mother, in so many ways alone and unknown. And then Lawrence was pressing his knuckles against the doorframe, asking her if she thought he was a murderer, if she thought what he did in the war was murder, and though she knew what she ought to say, instead she said that she didn't know. And when he turned to her, his eyes open so wide that his irises were ringed with white, she became conscious of the potential of his body for the first time—the weight of his muscles against her muscles, his bones against her bones. She hated how frail she suddenly felt, seized with a memory of her father grabbing her by the wrist, and how she had flinched at the hot cuff of his fingers before he flung her into her room as if she were something to be disposed of, as if she weighed less than air.

A week later, her diaphragm disappeared. A gap in the dark wood of her drawer that seemed to fall through to the floor, to the house's foundation, bottomless as a crack in the earth.

That evening, Charlie organizes a jackrabbit shoot. On the eastern side of Washoe Lake, thousands roam. Bailey explains they're not the kind of rabbit anyone eats—not like plump, docile Florida Whites or Palominos.

Jackrabbits are lean, with long, wide ears. After they shoot them, they leave their bodies in the dirt for the coyotes, though even they sometimes leave the jackrabbits alone, knowing they're little more than hair and bone.

"We won't get in any trouble?" Dorothy asks, flicking a clod of dirt from her bootheel on the front porch.

"No, no. Cattlemen never have enough grass for their livestock around here, so they're grateful for any kills you can make," Charlie says.

Lois hadn't wanted to join them. At dinner, Lois watched Greer's hands—how they slid under a platter and gripped a butter knife—and imagined what they'd done.

But the others insisted she come, and she didn't know how to refuse this desire for her presence, still so unfamiliar to her. She piles into the bed of the truck with Greer, June, and Mary Elizabeth, a .22 rifle loose at their feet in the pickup's belly. Dorothy sits next to Charlie in the front seat. They packed beers in one of Anna's cloth grocery bags, the brown bottles loudly clinking against one another. Lois's jeans are too tight after a washing, the waistband cutting into her stomach unless she sits upright, which is difficult to do when the truck takes off, rumbling over clumps of desert grass.

Though it's already July, the evenings remain cold. Sometimes the desert feels more itself at this time of day. Lois can almost hear it breathing. The rocks glitter, the dry grass softens to silk.

The girls grip the truck's sides, swaying back and forth. Greer sits on the floor, cupping her hands over her mouth as she tries to light the end of her cigarette, and Lois watches Dorothy's red hair flame out from the open window. Dorothy hasn't received any gifts for the past two days, and after dinner June whispered that she drunkenly telephoned her beau after they returned from the casino, telling him she would wear whatever she liked, just like Greer said, and that he called the next day to tell her she'd woken up his wife and that he and Dorothy were done, simple as blowing out a candle. Now she's left with no money of her own. Her family is unable to help—last week she had let slip to Lois that her father is just a car mechanic in Utah. If Dorothy is angry at Greer, she does not show it, but then of course Greer did not tell her to call George at three in the morning. Lois wishes there were something she could do, but she has so little to give; she has only fifty-seven dollars left. She'd counted that afternoon.

Mary Elizabeth is trying to rid June of her hiccups. Her body seizes every minute, no matter how long she holds her breath or how many times she stretches her tongue to the tip of her nose, a remedy that Mary Elizabeth swears has cured her since she was a little girl. Lois jerks away after staring too long at her covered forearms. It's still light, but at the mountain's edges the sky is tinged a molten orange. A faint sliver of moon hangs to the south.

Greer kicks Lois's boot, pointing to a hawk circling above their heads, and Lois gives her an uneasy smile. From a distance, you can't even see her bruise. Lois wonders how her husband looks. Gnarled ropes of stitches lacing his cheek. An eye still swollen shut, round as an egg.

To Lois's surprise, Mary Elizabeth asks to shoot first, gracefully loading and aiming in one clean movement. For the first time, she sees who Mary Elizabeth must have been before the Luminal, before her husband, a girl raised on a former plantation in Kentucky surrounded by five brothers. Fierce and clear-eyed, bounding off to the stables every morning in polished boots. Who they all were before their men. Mary Elizabeth pulls the trigger, killing the first jackrabbit she targets. The loud pop makes the other girls jump.

Lois doesn't want to hold the gun. Her father keeps a pistol in his study, which she found in a desk drawer one rainy afternoon when she was six. She doesn't remember taking it, only Ela finding it in her bedroom, another toy scattered across the carpet alongside building blocks and peeling puzzle pieces, and how Ela yelled at Lois's father for the first and only time, a torrent of borderless Polish words that Lois heard from behind a closed door. *This can kill you if you touch it,* Ela told her after.

Dorothy goes next, leaning out of the truck window with a lit cigarette at the corner of her mouth. Her hands are unsteady, dipping and rising in small circles. At dinner, she left the table several times to fill her coupe to the brim with what Lois suspected was straight gin, the clear liquid heavy and viscous. She misses, but loads the rifle again, until it becomes obvious she's not aiming at the animals. She just wants to shoot. When she finally lowers the barrel, Lois is relieved.

"All right, Lois, your turn," Dorothy says, extending the rifle to her.

"I don't know if I want to," Lois says.

"Come on, everyone takes a turn," Greer says, a bottle of beer loose in her hand.

"You can go next, then."

Though she tries to sound nonchalant, she can hear the whinny of fear in her own voice. She knows Greer can hear it too, and Greer refuses to let Lois break her gaze. Her eyes are hard and bright in the evening air, and Lois feels them boring deeper into her, tight as screws, as if she's unearthing everything Lois has been thinking for the past several hours. For once, Lois resents their closeness. Greer's ability to see through her.

"I need to finish my beer first. You go."

Lois takes the gun. It's another dare, and she has no choice but to prove she can do it. The other girls clear to her sides, leaving her an open view of the lake. When each had loaded the rifle, Lois watched how they raised the bolt, pulling it back as far as it would go, and then placed the bullet in the chamber, locking it. She grabs a bullet from the box, nestling the butt of the rifle between her shoulder and collarbone and crooking her finger around the smooth metal trigger.

"Don't put your finger on the trigger until you're ready," Greer says, lightly touching her wrist.

Lois flinches, and Greer—obviously surprised by this—withdraws her hand. Lois raises the barrel, trying to find a jackrabbit. There are several banded together, crouched close to the ground, the inside of their large ears warmed to a soft pink by the setting sun. Swallowing the saliva that's pooled under her tongue, she pulls the trigger. The gunshot cracks her eardrum.

The jackrabbits scatter, the bullet having done nothing but kick up dust. Lois is shocked by how the shot ricocheted through her with something close to pleasure, realigning her bones. In the burning black after she fired, she saw Greer rising from the penthouse carpet, coiling her fingers around the lamp base. There was a slant of violence in her eyes, and Lois feels herself slipping toward it.

"You need to focus on your breathing," Greer says, gentler than before. "Breathe in when you're aiming, breathe out when you shoot."

Lois huffs through her nose and raises the rifle again. She finds another cluster of jackrabbits and fires, once again hitting nothing but dirt. Greer frowns. Mary Elizabeth is too distracted by June's hiccups to care. Charlie says something from the driver's seat that she can't parse, though she imagines it's some form of encouragement. The night air is becoming colder.

"I think you're missing on purpose," Greer says.

"Why would I do that?" Lois snaps.

Greer says nothing, tipping the neck of her beer against her lips, and Lois feels bullied by her silence, as if her fear is so obvious that it doesn't need to be explained. For the first time, Lois feels an anger toward Greer, dark coal pushed away to unearth the embers, a part of her she's been taught to hide. *Sometimes you get so hysterical, it's impossible to talk to you,* Lawrence said that evening in the bathroom, even though she hadn't spoken for several minutes. She'd wanted to hit him then, when she no longer worried that he would hit her, but then he'd stalked away to his study and she'd been left alone, the powdery scent of cold cream turning her stomach.

She lifts the rifle, finding a jackrabbit paused over a flowering of desert grass. Its jaw churns, its round black eyes unassuming. There's a thrumming in her chest and she holds her breath, finding the frame, and then with an exhalation she fires.

Charlie whistles from the front seat, and the other girls erupt in applause. He starts the engine, and as they swerve to the west, Lois sees the receding body of the jackrabbit limp on its side, dark, sticky blood trickling from its haunches. She feels even more powerful and elated than she had after kissing the bison skull, as if her foot could burst through the truck's steel bottom.

"I think my hiccups are gone," June says, touching the hollow of her collarbone.

They all laugh, and Greer smiles at Lois proudly, handing her the beer bottle.

Twenty-Two

Lois writes Ela a letter. She feels sorry that she hadn't responded earlier—they've been apart for over three weeks, the longest amount of time they haven't spoken in Lois's entire life. Though she only planned to reassure her there was nothing to worry about with Lawrence and her father talking, she fills several pages before breakfast. She tells her about the ranch and the horses, Anna's cooking, and the swimming pool. In the margins, she draws a mountain range. She writes about each of the girls: June's poor taste in men, Dorothy's gifts, Mary Elizabeth's early morning telephone calls. But after writing Greer's name, she pauses, a drop of ink ballooning on the paper. There is too much to say. She looks up to the ceiling, the sentences spooling out into the room's dry heat. She could tell Ela about the night she arrived, the bruise and the economical suitcase; or she could attempt to describe her clothes, though she knows that would come across as trivial. There's no way to describe this second skin, how Greer's wealth is everything and nothing. How, when they're together, Lois feels like herself, like the person she wants to be. She knows if she told Ela that Greer had fought back against her husband she would nod her head approvingly, and Lois feels calmed by this, sure that her initial, fearful reaction was outsized. Leaning back over her desk, she writes two sentences. *And I've made a real friend—a girl named Greer from Manhattan. You'd like her.* She says nothing of the boardinghouse or her plans for after, finishing by telling Ela she'll bring her back a pair of cowboy boots, though after she closes the envelope she realizes she doesn't know the size of her feet.

That morning, she keeps thinking of Ela opening the letter and turning over the pieces of paper by the kitchen window. She imagines her smiling, to know that Lois is capable of being happy, on this ranch near the edge of the country. To know that Lois is no longer alone.

"It's Annie Oakley," Greer says when she finds Lois waiting by the pool.

From her chair, Lois pretends to raise a rifle, lifting the barrel and taking aim at the bright, static sun.

That night, they return to the casino. At first the other girls express some hesitation, to appease Rita, but when it becomes obvious Greer wants nothing else, they relent. "Why go to a bar in Nevada? There are bars everywhere," she says, and no one argues.

It's clear Bailey continues to report on them. In the morning, Rita pulls Dorothy aside to speak to her after she passed out at a blackjack table; she talks to June after she called a divorcée from the Lazy Me a painted heifer when the girl stole June's seat at the bar.

It's difficult to truly resent Bailey for this—each of them knows she is simply doing her job, her sense of loyalty as much a part of her as her tanned skin. She tries to intervene whenever she witnesses a particularly egregious offense, though her words fall largely on deaf ears. Her kindness starts to seem quaint. Her trust in others naive. "Other women are not your enemies," she said after June insulted the divorcée, and Greer had muttered, "Until they steal your seat." Regardless of what's shared, Rita's concern matters less as the days pass. The girls miss breakfast, and drink too much during cocktail hour, playing records so loudly that Rita's daughters come in to complain they can't hear *The Cisco Kid* on the radio.

"We missed hearing what the sheriff said," Carol whines.

She practically crawls into Rita's lap, her voice clotted with tears. Greer and Lois are perched a yard away on the settee, able to hear every word. Patty rests her chin on the chair back.

"Well, come on, then, yell at us," Greer says over Glenn Miller's brass horns. "Your mother's not the one playing the music."

"I don't tell my children to yell," Rita says.

"Fine. You don't need to yell at us, Carol, but don't just moan and sulk and wait for your mother to take control. I'd rather you come over here and snap the record in half."

Patty and Carol turn to Rita, waiting to see what she'll do. Her jaw shifts, and she rises, taking several steps toward the sofa. That evening, the handkerchief knotted at her throat is a brown burgundy, the color of dried blood, and Lois suddenly fears her in the way she sometimes fears Greer, seized with the realization that she has no idea what Rita will do. She crouches down as if Greer and Lois are also her children—two little girls she has to stoop to meet eye to eye.

"I can't stop you from being a bad influence on the other girls here, but if you speak to my daughters like that again, you'll have to find another ranch. I've never sent anyone away before, but I will." Her voice is a forceful whisper. "Now come on, girls, let's go to your room." Panic tightens Lois's shoulders, but when they leave, Greer just rolls her eyes. The record continues to spin.

There are new people at Harrah's every night, but some things remain the same. At the slots, someone buys them drinks—men in Italian wool suits, men with tobacco-stained teeth, men old enough to be their fathers—and to Lois's annoyance Dorothy indulges their attentions for too long. Every evening, Lois scans the crowds for celebrities. They travel to Reno not just for divorces, but for the lush clubs and casinos—not like Las Vegas, where everything is seedier. In Reno, gambling isn't vice, it's industry. One night, they see Clark Gable playing poker, his carefully clipped mustache unmistakable. Lois nearly screams his name. His eyes such a familiar pastel-blue, his skin a ruddy umber. Greer dares Lois to find out if he has a good hand, and she has to swallow a fresh glass of gin to work up the nerve. When she returns, they laugh at his poor cards, which make him seem almost human.

"Has Harry met any movie stars?" Lois asks June.

"He was once at a lunch with Thomas Mitchell," June says.

"I still think you should be the screenwriter," Greer tells her.

"Well, since we talked, I've thought of it, but you haven't heard some of his ideas. There's one he has about a woman who can't see, but her sense of smell—"

"Then steal the ideas. It appears they're all he has to offer."

"What do you think, Lois?" June asks. "You like Harry, don't you?"

"You're much more clever," Lois says.

"I don't know about that."

"Oh come on, June," Greer says. "Your cleverness is the one thing you've known about yourself since kindergarten. You just need to figure out how to truly use it to your advantage."

June laughs, her cheeks pinkening. Afterward, she no longer invites Harry to the casino.

After eleven, Bailey usually has to find a chair for Mary Elizabeth, her Luminal and alcohol mixing to the point that it's difficult for her to stand, though in the frenzy of the casino even this feels normal. Around the same hour, they go to Peg's table, the only place where Greer loses. Peg looks the same every evening, another lost marker of time: the silk shirt patterned with playing cards, her hair pulled into a low, tight chignon. When Greer has had enough, she shakes Peg's hand, and Peg begins to acknowledge Greer in her own way, briefly nodding whenever she takes a seat. No one else plays, too drunk for arithmetic. Lois parses out a few dollars for every evening. Opening the envelope is nearly painful, but then there's the tug of wanting to play beside Greer, the feverish possibility of winning money of her very own.

At the casino, Greer's reins tighten, her instructions for the dares more specific. When Dorothy attempts to steal a bottle of vodka, Greer grips her wrist. "Not yet. They're watching," she says, jerking her head toward two men planted between blackjack tables. "You need to learn when they're not." Lois grins, the lightness of the gin making the men appear as threatening as surly older brothers. Greer stops making asks of Mary Elizabeth, who can't pay attention for long enough to follow instructions. Even Dorothy and June sometimes falter, missing the beats when they could steal another divorcée's French 75 or deface the men's restroom door with lipstick, but Lois never does. Even in the haze of alcohol, Greer's attention makes the motion of the roulette wheel click into focus. She feels as purposeful as she does cutting through the pool's cold water, and Greer's smile widens with every escalation: the nipped bottle of champagne, the tangle of maraschino cherry stems Lois slips into a man's chest pocket.

At Harrah's, Lois feels herself opening. It's partially the alcohol, she knows, and how after the third drink she feels as if she's shaken off a heavy coat, but it's also that she feels stronger after the bison skull, after the jackrabbit. The space between her and everyone else slips away, and Lois really begins to talk to the other girls, able to find the pauses in the conversation, the beats of breath where she can burrow in. Though Lawrence isn't there to pinch her thigh, often the next morning she returns to her old self, worrying that she talked over someone or cut someone off, only able to calm down by remembering the girls laughing at her impression of Joan Davis, or how June rested her hand on her upper arm as Lois told a story about the night one of the members of the Onwentsia Club got so drunk that he went golfing in the dark, shattering several of the clubhouse windows. She warms herself with these small blushes of approval.

She feels them all becoming closer. Mary Elizabeth sits next to her at each meal. June solicits her opinions about a possible screenplay, and they spend an entire cocktail hour casting every role. One morning, Dorothy tells her about how she's worried she can't have children, fibroids lining her uterus like soft, wet pearls.

Sometimes they ask her questions about Greer. "What do you all even talk about at the pool?" June asks her late one night, but as dear as each of them have become to her, Lois refuses to share what she knows: Greer's mother, her violence, how she hated her teachers at school just like Lois had, calling them all *wizened old virgins.* How Lois feels different ever since Greer handed her the beer bottle in the back of Charlie's pickup. Their closeness deepening to something elemental. "Oh, lots of things," Lois says.

At the end of the night, the girls migrate to the Riverside or the Mapes' Sky Room to listen to whoever's performing that evening, velvety crooners and big brass bands, audience members wrapped in silk and brocade. They're suddenly so tired they can barely stay upright, loopy and drunk. Every other night, someone tells them Sinatra is coming into town, but like some glittering messiah, he never arrives. They make each other laugh with no more than a word, everyone inhabiting the same sacred space, back atop the scarred wood of the Highlands bar. In these moments, Lois feels as if they've entered a world Greer has willed into existence, where they can do whatever pleases them. Lois stops wearing any lipstick, focusing instead on her hazel eyes, the liner thick as Cleopatra's. Her envelope of bills dwindles to twenty dollars, her father's livid face looming like a memory and a premonition. The cashier learns her name.

Twenty-Three

· · · · · · · · · · · · ·

When Mary Elizabeth's husband comes to the ranch, Lois is not downstairs to see him. In the water earlier in the day, she felt the deep burn of her muscles growing, having eaten two omelets that morning to fuel her laps, and she'd taken a nap after the pool, her damp, chlorinated hair wetting her pillow as she curled into herself like an ammonite. Since the girls have accepted her as one of their own, she's able to fall asleep within minutes no matter the time of day, snapping into unconsciousness as if someone has turned off a light.

At cocktail hour, June tells Lois he arrived late in the afternoon. Rita met him on the front porch and he'd removed his gray fedora, their conversation inaudible from the girls' position at the living room window. All they could report was that he was handsome, with a strong Roman nose, and that he'd plucked each of the speckled feathers from his hat ribbon as they spoke. After a few minutes, Rita fetched Mary Elizabeth from her bedroom, and when they saw her pass in the hallway, her skin was the pale yellow of buttermilk. When Rita came back inside, she told the girls to give them some privacy, and so they flitted up to Dorothy's bedroom to watch them from the second floor. Mary Elizabeth and her husband's voices became louder and louder until finally they heard the front door swing open, footsteps quick as rain patter on the wood floor, and then he drove off, his car wavering into the brown grass when he turned down the long, narrow road.

"He called her a whore," June says. "That was one word that was easy to make out."

"Why did he come, though?" Lois asks.

"To win her back, I gather."

That night at the casino, Mary Elizabeth says very little. She's taken so much Luminal she can barely form words, absent articles and consonants. Everyone is attuned to the threat of her husband, looking over one another's shoulders to see if he'll emerge from a knot of gamblers.

"Do you think he'll try to hurt her?" Lois whispers to Greer.

"Not in the casino, at least," Greer says.

Mary Elizabeth hadn't joined them at cocktail hour, but she sat down to dinner as if nothing had happened and ate an entire skirt steak, more food than Lois had seen her consume over the course of a day, her hands moving as slowly as if she were underwater. Fat and butter pooled on her plate.

"Why is a raven like a writing desk?" June asks after losing ten dollars in less than ten minutes at roulette. The others stare at the table's white grid, distracted by their own bets.

"What?" Dorothy looks confused.

"Remember, that's a riddle that Alice asks. Why is a raven like a writing desk?"

On the car ride earlier, the girls tried to distract Mary Elizabeth by talking about how *Alice in Wonderland* was premiering at the end of July, which Lois realized is just a few weeks away, counting the days left at the ranch: *eighteen, nineteen*. Time has begun to race and skip. Mary Elizabeth didn't listen, breathing on the window glass and drawing flowers in the wet fog.

"I don't think she asks it. The Mad Hatter asks it," Lois says.

"But what's the answer?" Dorothy asks.

"There is no answer," Greer says. "They're both bad at roulette."

Lois laughs, but the sound dies quickly in her throat. She is anxious tonight, unable to stop rolling the word *whore* around in her mouth, tonguing its sharp edges. It's not a word her father or Lawrence used, instead favoring *disappointment* or *fool*.

She gets too drunk. Her hand sways in the air like a reed to call the waitress over. As the hours pass, she gives every man who approaches her a different name and makes up elaborate stories about the men and women at different tables. She decides who is sleeping with whom, who just lost their last cent, talking loudly enough that they can hear, the girls' laughter something she consumes desperately, like another glass of gin.

Bailey tells her to eat the olives at the bottom of her glass, their brine stinging a cut on the roof of her mouth. In the bathroom mirror, she slowly reapplies her mascara, her reflection wavering as if she's standing over unsteady water.

"That man's been watching you most of the night," Greer says when she returns to the roulette table. Lois turns toward the bar to find a face she recognizes: a broad jaw, eyes pale as the lake frozen in winter. The gaunt William Holden from the Highlands. He is watching her in a way he never did at the bar, unabashed, his lips slightly pursed, as if a toothpick should be settled between them.

"You should go put him out of his misery. Or, well, put you both out of your misery."

"What do you mean?" Lois asks.

"I've seen how you look at him."

Even in her drunkenness, Lois feels the tight throttle of shame. As if Greer could see her arching in the darkness of her bedroom. She briefly lifts her tumbler to her mouth, but finds it empty. The melting ice clinks against her front teeth.

"I don't know what—" she begins.

"Oh come on, now," Greer says. "Don't be a meek little mouse."

It's another dare, she realizes. A test to see if she'll take what she wants without hesitation. In the looseness of the alcohol, the room and her body softening, the decision suddenly feels simple. She nods and places her drink on the table's rim, but before she leaves, Greer grabs her wrist. Her grip is firm as a leather strap.

"Just remember. Thirty minutes."

When Lois sits atop the stool next to him, he is not surprised.

"You're that girl that kissed Roger's bison skull, aren't you?" he asks.

"Yes." She smiles. "I am."

She learns he is a ranch hand at Washoe Pines. He's here shepherding some of their divorcées, but he tries to leave them alone, as they always end up squabbling or weeping, and tending to them makes him feel like a babysitter. He buys her another gin martini. There is something crude about the shape of his mouth. She asks him about horses, about desert trails, thinking of how it will feel to kiss him, her want beginning to take a distinct shape. He asks her very little. When she finishes her drink, she realizes he's placed his hand on her knee, stroking the bone with his thumb.

She tells him she needs to breathe some of the night air, and he follows. It's surprising to her how simple this is; there is no other instruction that she needs to give him. In the shadowed gap between Harrah's building and the next, he reaches for the nape of her neck. He presses her against the brick wall, quick to slip his tongue into her mouth, licking the back of her teeth. Her body responds, hungry for him in the way she's become hungry for the blood of a steak, the jelly of bone marrow. She scrapes her fingernails against his scalp, his hair longer than Lawrence's, oily with pomade. He smells like oil and rum, like the faint, fermented musk of a horse stable.

At first there is a thrill to his desire, a shared rhythm. His hands grip her waist and then slide up to her chest, and this frees her to dip her fingers into his rear jeans pockets, pulling him even closer. She does not need to imagine that he is someone else or that she is not herself. The pleasure is enough.

But then she senses a new urgency. He abandons her mouth and begins to lift her dress up, skating the clips of her pantyhose. She pushes his hand down, which deters him for a moment, but then his fingers are hooking the top of her silk underwear, trying to roll them loose with his thumb. His knee pinning her in place, the jut of his hip bones pressing against her to the point of pain, so that he will be free to take what he wants. Fear overwhelms everything else. She spreads her palms against his chest and shoves.

He's startled by the force of it, and for a moment she opens her mouth to apologize, but then stops herself. She pulls down her dress, and they stare at one another, breathing heavily. He glances briefly at the stream of casino-goers bathed in yellow light several yards away. If she yelled, they would hear her.

"Tease," he spits.

She finds the other girls at the bar. Bailey is not with them. Greer gives her a closemouthed smile, though Lois struggles to return it. In the restroom, she flattened her hair and straightened the straps of her satin dress, but there are other signs she cannot smooth away: swollen lips, a crease at her hem.

Dorothy is the only one sitting, propping herself up at the elbows. Her sadness has sanded off her edges, and for the past three nights she's gotten so drunk that she's vomited in the ladies' room—the other evening she didn't even make it to the toilet bowl, splashing the sink with a sulfurous rinse of bile. Lois held her red hair back as she talked of Utah between retches—of frigid lakes and frigid women who hate her, and how in her father's house even drinking coffee is a sin. Bailey gently suggests she drink a glass of water, but they do little more. It's impossible to tell her not to drink, or, worse, to stay home.

"We're ordering another round," Greer says.

Greer told Lois she shouldn't mix her colors of alcohol—choose brown or clear—so she asks for another gin martini, wanting the slur of more liquor. A puffed man in a loose tie watches them, and after they've each placed their orders, he signals that he'll pick up the tab.

"It's the divorcée special," he says as he turns toward them, pulling on a phantom train whistle.

This is the dance. The amount of time owed for a five-dollar tab. They all raise their glasses to him as he crunches an ice cube between his teeth, even Mary Elizabeth following suit. Lois drains her glass.

"Tell me, where are you ladies residing?"

"Now, why would we tell you that?" Dorothy says, her dimples thimble-deep.

"Well, from the looks of you all, I don't think you're Olinghouse or Stevenson types. I'm guessing you're resting your pretty aristocratic heads at the Golden Yarrow?"

The other girls laugh in response, except for Greer, who's speaking to the bartender. She leaves the others to do the work of placation. Lois pictures a maid in a starched apron picking Greer's stockings up from the floor, turning off the faucet she'd left on in the bathroom, her existence forever frictionless. She would never let a man put her in a vulnerable position, Lois briefly thinks, though, of course, she must have.

"I'll take that as a yes?" he asks.

Though he's trying to disguise it, his earnestness cuts through Lois's fog.

Men don't usually care that much about where they're staying, always more interested in whether or not one of the girls will go home with them. *Beware any men that start asking you too many questions about the place,* Rita had said.

"Are you a reporter? A stringer?" Lois asks, louder than she'd intended.

"I'm no such thing. Hate stringers, scum of the earth." He rotates his empty glass on the bar top. "I'm just interested in where you all are from."

"Well, we're not at the Golden Yarrow. We sleep out in the desert. Just circled our wagons and set up camp," Lois says, but then she feels it— Greer's hand on the small of her back, turning her away from the man.

"I don't think this one's ever slept under the stars. Though she's not dressed for an evening at a casino either," the man says, looking at Greer. "What's your name?"

"Agnes," Greer says. "Have we earned our drinks yet? Because if not, I'd rather just pay the tab myself."

"Hey, now. I'm just trying to have a polite conversation. I think you all are being a little ungrateful, all things considered."

The other girls shift uncomfortably as Greer turns back to the bar, nodding at Lois to follow, but Lois can't let his insult linger. Her hatred for him swells sudden as a flood. The man gnaws at his bottom lip, and she sees that the tooth next to his canine is graying, nearly dead.

"You think you can just buy—" Lois begins.

"Thank you for the drinks," June interrupts, but the man holds up his hand.

"Listen, just remember what the good Lord says in Matthew about what you all have done: 'What therefore God has joined together, let not man separate.' Hope you whores sleep well tonight in your wagon thinking about that."

The girls fold back in on themselves. Dorothy murmurs consolations to Mary Elizabeth, wiping her cheeks with her thumbs even though the girl isn't crying yet. Lois grips her glass, wondering if she could shatter it with just a flex of her fingers. She can't look away from the man's broad back.

"I wish I had some scripture memorized about all men being cads," June says.

Lois's eyes travel to his skull, a thumbprint of balding skin near its crown. The bartender places a fresh whiskey at his elbow.

"Someone should have slapped him, or at least spat in his drink," Lois says.

"Why don't you?" Greer asks.

Lois looks behind her to find that Greer has rejoined them. She is watching Lois—perhaps she's been watching her this whole time—and though she says nothing else, Lois can sense words gathering just beneath the surface. A heavier weight to them than she's felt before, a tipping of Greer's cards to reveal some larger plan.

"You want me to?"

"I don't want you to do anything. I think you want to."

Lois licks her lips, though she can barely feel them. Everything is numbed except for the tight throb of her pulse at her wrist. She places her drink on the bar top and clears her throat. The girls watch her in anticipation, and even though Mary Elizabeth drops her forehead to June's shoulder, Lois knows that she wants her to punish him. He's swallowed the sadness and anger ripening in the air around them, using the same words to insult them as Mary Elizabeth's husband, the same snide tone as the ranch hand.

A pool of spit collects beneath her tongue. Greer is smiling, and Lois is back at the Highlands, back in the bed of Charlie's truck nestling the butt of the rifle in her shoulder's dip. Fury tightening like a coil, desperate for release. *Breathe in when you're aiming, breathe out when you shoot.*

In three swift steps, her face is hovering over the glass's rim. The sleeve of his blazer gently grazes her cheek, and she jerks back before she can spit. His mouth roars open, and before she's conscious of what she's doing, Lois knocks his tumbler to the floor and hawks the glob of phlegm onto his face. Someone's fingers wrap around her wrist, and she is pulled back, running beside the others as if they're a herd of horses, breathless from laughter as their heels thud against the casino floor.

Twenty-Four

Lois misses breakfast again. Not even the sounds of the house wake her from her heavy, numbed sleep. She opens her eyes after ten, her head an egg cracking open. Her mouth tastes like spoiled milk. In the bathroom, she finds blood slicking her underwear, the inside of her thighs rusted brown. Lawrence would sigh whenever she'd tell him it was that time, as if he always expected a child, even when they weren't trying. She remembers the one morning when she forgot to flush, his ashen face after seeing toilet paper bloated with red. But at the ranch, it doesn't matter.

"You were particularly funny last night," Greer says by the water. "You almost made Peg laugh."

Lois smiles, not wanting to reveal that she doesn't remember being at Peg's table; that one moment she's marveling at how perfectly the penny fits into its silver slot, and the next she's in the windy car, fumbling with how to tie a scarf over Dorothy's hair, helpless and giggling.

"And how was your ranch hand? Everything you dreamed?"

"Not exactly," Lois says slowly. "For now, I think I'll stay away from men."

"I'm sorry to hear that."

Lois is surprised that Greer doesn't probe further. A part of her wants to purge how weak she felt after the alley, but she decides against it. She is Annie Oakley—not Betty Hutton's saccharine impersonation, but Barbara Stanwyck's, her spine like the cold, straight steel of a gun.

They finish *Rebecca*. When Lois reads the final sentences aloud, Manderley burning, *And the ashes blew toward us with the salt wind from the sea,* Greer finds some dark delight. She never liked Maxim, an older man and always so superior, more like a father than a husband, or his young, deferential wife. And so when their house burns, she lets out a "Ha!"—the sound like a crow call. It startles Lois. She always finds such a deep sadness in the idea of Manderley falling, and even though she knows on the first page it's lost to them, the final sentences are always a fresh horror. Manderley wasn't property. It felt to Lois like forest or coastline, something innocent and alive, and how heavy to have the weight of that death hung around your neck. It would pull her under.

She assumed Greer would feel the same, but she feels foolish explaining this to her now, overly sentimental. Instead, she closes the book and rests it against her thighs. Lois suggests they begin *The Age of Innocence* next, trying to offer it up as simply as a dish at the dinner table, when she'd actually planned it for days. Though Greer laughs at the title, she agrees. They have just two and a half weeks to finish it. Lois shivers off the thought.

"Is there a movie of that one?" Greer asks.

"Not yet, but there should be. Lauren Bacall could be Ellen Olenska. She'd be perfect," Lois says. "Though they may cast one of those awful, sickeningly sweet new girls, like Doris Day. They're weightless, nothing like Hepburn or Bergman. They all look like porcelain dolls."

"Ellen O-len-ska. That's a good name."

"It is. Better than Lois Gorski."

"There's nothing wrong with Lois Gorski."

"In fourth grade, Lenora Heller said it sounded like a sneeze, and I think she's right. Like an angry sneeze."

"Change it, then, if you don't like it. Lois Olenska."

"Maybe." Lois laughs, though it's obvious Greer isn't joking.

She slips into the pool, resting her feet against the cement wall and springing her body forward. The thrust forces her eyes shut, so all she can sense is the pressure of water, which wants her to sink and rise all at once. Earlier, in the empty kitchen, she sawed off a slice of roast beef as thick as her thumb, gobbling it over the sink. Her body has shed the last of its girlish softness, her muscles solid as a fist. As she kicks her feet, she pushes away any thoughts of the ranch hand, of Mary Elizabeth's husband, and pictures the stringer's shocked face, her spit on his cheek, glossy as an egg white. At the pool's other end, she emerges triumphant. She wishes Greer would swim.

When she returns to her seat, Greer is frowning at the bottom of her shirt, holding it above her stomach so that it's taut.

"I lost a button this morning," Greer says.

"Do you know how to sew it back on?" Lois asks, pressing her towel to her face.

"I have no idea," Greer says, and Lois feels foolish for asking, for assuming Greer would ever sit with someone like Ela in her kitchen, patiently learning how to mend a ripped seam.

"I can do it, if you want," Lois offers.

"Really? I would ask Florence, but, well, I bet you'll take better care of it," Greer says.

"I'll do my best," Lois says, pleased to be trusted, even with something as small as a button.

When they retire from the sun, Greer asks Lois to her room. Though they've spent so many hours together, she's never seen where Greer sleeps. Greer leads her down a hallway she's never passed through on the eastern side of the house, which runs parallel to the dining room and ends in a closed door. On the walls are Japanese block prints of mountains and chrysanthemums, women kneeling on the floor, and Lois's sandals smack against the wood, no matter how much she tries to quiet them by arching her feet. They leave smudges of water behind her.

Greer opens the door to her room, to a rush of light. It's no bigger than Lois's own, but lusher and more beautifully appointed. She hadn't realized the rooms were any different, but here is a blue velvet armchair, a bureau painted with an English hunting scene on four drawers, foxhounds sprinting across the polished mahogany, and a tall glass vase on the windowsill, marbled yellow and white. Lois thinks of her squat marigolds, a small, pebbled chip at the vase's mouth. But as she takes a few tentative steps inside, she realizes how dirty the room is. There are tangles of hair nesting by the baseboards and a fine powder of dust on the window ledges. Empty water glasses ringed with stains. The faint rot of mildew, like a damp dish towel. No flowers. She doesn't know how to ask without insulting the room, but it's obvious that for some reason Greer does not allow Florence inside.

With her back to Lois, Greer pulls her shirt over her head, as casually as if they were sisters. Lois is surprised by how slim she actually is beneath her loose clothes, her vertebrae a line of small white stones. When she shifts,

Lois sees a narrow, puffed scar winding beneath her ribs, as if the skin had been gashed open. She winces and turns toward the window as Greer plucks at a navy sweater hanging from her closet doorknob, pulling it over her naked torso. She does not bother with pants, rummaging through a dish of coins on her dresser, and Lois pretends to be consumed by a gold ink pot on the sill, opening and closing it with her thumb.

"Here it is." Greer holds a pearlescent circle up to the window light.

"Oh good," Lois says, opening her palm to receive it.

"Thanks for doing that. I didn't pack many clothes."

She sits cross-legged on top of her blanket, resting against her wrinkled satin pillows. Lois leans down to pick up her shirt from the floor like a maid, folding it over her forearm.

"Can I ask you something?" Lois asks.

"You can ask me anything."

"Did your husband do that to you?"

Greer's lips part, and she looks down at the bare tops of her feet as she wriggles her toes. Lois is alert to any sign she's made a mistake, but there's no tic or pull of anger in Greer's face.

"We're so similar, you and I," Greer says. "I remember thinking it, that night at the Highlands, when you talked about your mother dying. Mine passed when I was twelve. Tuberculosis."

"You mentioned that, by the pool. I've wanted to ask, but—I worried you didn't want to talk about her."

"Again, you can ask me anything. You know that, don't you?"

"I do. I do, but it's hard for me to talk about my own mother, and I thought you might feel the same. I wanted to respect that."

With an open palm Greer gestures for her to sit, and Lois perches at the edge of the mattress. She hasn't been in another girl's room since elementary school.

"Why is it hard for you?" Greer asks.

"Well, there's a part of me that misses her. Outside of Ela, she was all I had. But there's another part of me that's so . . . angry with her. It's not just that she abandoned me, but that she was never really there in the first place. I left school to go with her to the movies, told stories to entertain her, to make my life seem like some film she would love, but none of it made a difference. I was always left alone."

"From what you've told me, so was she, I imagine. Alone."

"I suppose. My father wasn't great company."

"When my mother died, my father never even shed a tear, said hardly more than a word to me or my siblings," Greer says, rubbing her thumb against the bone of her big toe. "I'm the oldest, so afterward I had to keep everyone together. I made sure my siblings got out of bed and went to school, comforted them when they cried in the night, and they were always crying, it was . . . too much. I barely consider him a father, to be honest. And so I left."

"You got married."

Greer looks up at her, her eyes refocusing, as if she were lost in reverie.

"Yes. Just like you, I wanted to start a new life, but then it became obvious it wasn't what I thought it would be. He was cruel and selfish—mercurial, really. He'd be a completely different person from one moment to the next. There was no . . . center."

"Had he hurt you before?"

"No, but there were others." She folds her arms over her ribs, lightly stroking where the scar rests beneath her sweater. "It won't happen again, though. That's a promise I made to myself. You know, you've never really spoken to me about what you want to do after Reno. The other girls prattle on the second you ask them a question or two, but you've been quiet."

"I don't know." Lois looks down at the shirt on her lap. "I want to live alone, but the other girls made that sound so absurd. As if I was being foolish or naive."

"They're the naive ones. I keep trying to help them see how their lives could be different, not so constrained and dependent, but they're like baby lambs," Greer says, and Lois laughs, relief filling her chest like helium. "Where do you want to live?"

"My father won't allow me to stay in his house for more than half a year, and I don't—I don't have a trust or anything. There will be alimony, which I'll have to take, but I don't know how much."

"But if you could live anywhere, where would you go?"

"California. Los Angeles." Lois is surprised by how easily this comes to her.

"You want to live among the movie stars."

"No. Yes. I want to live thousands of miles from home."

Greer lets the words hover in the air, looking at Lois very intently, so that she feels as if she cannot move.

"Well, I want the same. And I don't want to be dependent on my husband or my family's money anymore," Greer says. "To really start over, I can't be tied to them in any way. I don't want to be tied to any man."

Lois feels herself nodding, remembering her father's face as he handed her the brown paper envelope of money for Reno, as solemn as if she'd asked him to cut off a limb. She knows Lawrence will simply be taking her father's place. Every month a new envelope.

"I think you'd like that as well," Greer says.

"Yes," Lois breathes, more exhalation than word.

They continue to stare at one another, Lois waiting for an answer, though she has asked no question. In the hallway, another door creaks open. Lois jumps at the sound, nearly dropping Greer's stray button. When she looks up, Greer has turned from her, lifting a gold wristwatch from her bedside table to tell the time. As if her focus on Lois has broken.

"Well, I think I'm going to take a nap before dinner," Greer says.

"Oh, all right."

"Thanks again for the button," Greer says, slipping her long legs beneath her sheets, waiting for Lois to close her door.

n the living room, Rita's daughters are piecing together a puzzle. It's spread across the carpet, but Lois begins to see the shape of a castle nestled in a forest. The girls' heads are bowed together, their French braids sloppier since Vera left, unraveling at their shoulders. Carol snaps two pieces together and Patty reaches for them to form a tower, showing Carol her work as if she played no part in it. When they hear Lois approaching, they look up briefly and then turn back to the puzzle. Their interest in the guests changes day by day. Adults are some other life-form, birds flying above their ocean. Lois can almost remember the feeling.

Outside the front door, she hears voices. As she approaches, she can see Bailey on the porch speaking to a young man in a gray linen suit standing at the bottom of the stairs. His arms are folded over a narrow chest.

"Emme?" he says, peering into the darkness of the entryway.

"I told you: Mary Elizabeth's not here," Bailey says. "I can show you her empty room if I have to—it's just off the hallway on the first floor."

"She's right there—I see her. I'm not as drugged as she is." He points at Lois, so that Bailey turns her head.

Lois steps closer to the open door, to prove she's not the man's wife. He's different than the girls described—his left cheek is pocked with several mites of blood from where he'd cut himself shaving, and his eyes are slit like a snake's. There's a vertigo to his presence, a sense that if Lois fell, she'd keep falling. She decides to stay inside the entryway.

Bailey sighs. "That's another guest."

"Is Emme in there?"

"She's not here," Lois says. "She went into town."

"Well, when is she going to be back?"

"I'm not sure, but I don't believe she wants to see you," Lois says.

The man laughs and drops his head, scratching at the nape of his neck so furiously Lois can feel the friction of his fingernails against her own skin. She wishes she were wearing more than her thin striped cover-up, and pulls at its belt, tightening it around her waist.

"She doesn't want to see her husband," he says. "Of course, of course. Why would any of you want to see your husbands? How absurd of me to ask, to impose upon my wife again after I flew two thousand miles to this plot of hell in the middle of the desert."

"I think—" Bailey begins.

"I've had enough of what you all think. Just tell Emme that our conversation isn't over, that I still have things to say and that I have a right to say them."

When he turns on the ignition, the engine roars. Bailey retreats inside after he is out of sight, smoothing out the front of her shirt. She clicks the door shut, and they walk toward the staircase.

"He'll be back," Bailey says.

"Should we call the police?" Lois asks.

"Well, he hasn't committed any crime, has he? At least not in Reno."

"It doesn't seem right."

"I know, but there's not much we can do about that. Speaking of diffi-cult men, are you doing all right? I thought I saw you talking to one of the hands from Washoe Pines, but when I made my way toward the bar, you were gone. I told Greer they were trouble a while ago."

"I'm fine." Unease slithers around Lois's belly, a dark, slippery eel. She thinks of Greer pushing her toward him. *You should go put him out of his misery.*

"You're sure? You can always talk to me—"

"I can take care of myself."

"All right, understood. I was just . . . worried." Lois needs a glass of wa-ter, something to help her rinse and cleanse. She turns to retreat to her room, but Bailey calls out to her. "Mr. Tarleton called for you again. Said you should come into his office tomorrow to discuss some things. You can call his secretary to make an appointment."

"Thank you."

She thinks of her lawyer's cloistered office, the paperwork resting on his desk, pages of text that she probably won't even read.

"You know where the phone is, yes?"

"I do." Lois rubs the sash of her cover-up, pulling it even tighter. "I'll call back later."

Lois mends the shirt before dinner, smoothing the rich cotton out over the end of her bed. The fabric is heavier than she imagined. Unlatch-ing the stiff leather sewing kit Ela had given her one Christmas, she cuts a length of white thread. She loops the needle through the shirt's placket and tries to unspool everything she felt that afternoon. She hates how much Mary Elizabeth's husband had scared her. Another man sensing some weak-ness within her, something he can exploit or take advantage of, like a shark smelling blood. When she's finished, she holds the shirt in front of her, and before she can question what she's doing, she strips off her bathing suit and pulls it over her head. It's longer on her than on Greer, the front hem kissing her knees, but she likes the way she feels in it, stronger and unrestricted, as if the fabric has its own power, potent as the rolled cigarettes she'd steal from Ela's coat pockets. If Greer knew who she was pushing her toward last night, it must have been done with intention, to make it clear that she shouldn't waste any more of her time on men. She must have known that Lois would be strong enough to protect herself. To be wholly on her own. *I think you'd like that as well,* Greer had said in her bedroom. "Yes," Lois repeats in the mirror and still after, when she folds the shirt into a neat square and washes her hands for dinner, the word its own rosary.

Twenty-Five

Lois approaches the end of her fourth week, the time after the ranch beginning to crest on the horizon. After their conversation in Greer's bedroom, she waits for guidance, but Greer offers nothing. In the mornings, she returns to her notebook, looking at her soft pencil marks. "Don't be a meek little mouse," she says to herself. She writes down jobs she thinks she could do—telephone operator, English tutor—frustration tightening her rib cage, the ideas as half formed as her sums and lists.

It's unfathomable that new guests will arrive at the ranch and sleep in Lois's bed, that Greer will remain after she's gone. The thought of this, of Greer sitting out by the pool while Lois boards a train back to Lake Forest, makes Lois feel unbalanced, her mind stuttering like a looping record. She thinks of Vera and how completely everyone has forgotten her—not as if she'd passed, but as if she'd never existed.

The evening appears to be the furthest point in time anyone can consider, except for Rita, who Lois imagines is counting down the days until their departure. She and Greer barely speak. The ranch has become unwieldy as a ship in a storm. Dorothy starts to drink in the mornings. Mary Elizabeth accidentally shatters Rita's grandmother's butter dish, her pupils dilated to the width of a pencil. One afternoon, they return to find a letter from her husband on the front porch with half a dozen dahlias, dirt clinging to their gossamer roots as if they were stripped from someone's garden. Florence buries the flowers in nearby soil, and Mary Elizabeth rips the envelope in two. That evening, her tremor becomes so severe that she has Lois put on her makeup. Lois tries to revive the steady-handed girl she glimpsed in the pickup truck: hiding her bruised sleeplessness with a pot of concealer, brushing life into her cheeks with a blush palette. "He can't hurt you here," Lois says. When Mary Elizabeth doesn't respond, Lois isn't sure if she didn't hear her, or if she simply doesn't believe it.

One evening at the Riverside, they lose Dorothy. In the early morning, Bailey begins to round them up to return home. Charlie drove them, as Bailey's car refused to start, and Lois assumes he's sleeping off his buzz in the truck, having told them he'd wait outside after stopping by the Corner Bar for a few drinks. Dorothy disappeared earlier in the evening. After they watched the Riverside Starlets, the hotel's chorus line, sweep across the stage in their white tulle skirts, she was lured away by a man in a charcoal silk suit, his mustache thin as a line of pen. If she's still with him, their time together is much longer than thirty minutes. She'd gotten soused before they even arrived and insisted on wearing every piece of jewelry she was given, clipping mismatched earrings to each lobe like an exiled princess. In the car, she told Lois the order in which she'd been given each piece, as if that meant something.

After several loops, Bailey can find no trace of her. They all join the search, circling the wood-paneled lobby and politely knocking on the stalls of the women's restroom, even visiting the hotel's placid, dimly lit pool. They pass one another as they canvass different floors, shrugging their shoulders and shaking their heads, annoyed at how their drunkenness is beginning to lift. Everyone wants to be in their beds.

To Lois's surprise, June is the first to panic.

"Do you think she could have been kidnapped? Should we call the police?" she asks.

"She's been missing for a few hours," Bailey says. "Let's not get ahead of ourselves."

"I'm sure if we went home she'd find her way back," Greer says. "She clearly wants to be lost for a little while."

"You know we have to find her," Bailey says to Greer, lower in her throat. "Rita'll blame you for this as much as me."

Lois splinters off to ask one of the bartenders if he's seen Dorothy. He sneers at her, saying he can't keep track of all the girls he's served. That first afternoon, Rita explained the Golden Yarrow's staff had to see the girls every day in order to testify, and Lois wonders if Dorothy's six weeks will reset if she disappears for too long. She ascends to the third floor, which appears to be nothing but an empty hallway of hotel room doors, the carpet richer than downstairs, thick as lamb's wool. But as she begins to turn back, the air rustles with movement.

She finds Dorothy backed against a recessed wall near the end of the hallway, nearly hidden by the body of a man, her fingers gripping his winged shoulder blades. Lois knows she should look away, that she should tell Bailey to discreetly extract Dorothy from the man's embrace, but she stays rooted to the carpet. A heat fizzes within her, like the foam of a Coca-Cola bristling against the neck of its glass bottle. They are not kissing in the way she's used to watching: Cary Grant dryly pressing his lips against Ingrid Bergman's. And she can't imagine this is how she appeared in Harrah's alleyway—an act which felt hurried and brutal. There is something slow and sensual in how Dorothy opens her mouth and pulls the man deeper inside of her, in how he runs his thumb beneath her breast.

The man's leather jacket lies in a heap at their feet—tossed off as if they're in his bedroom—and Lois recognizes its copper hue. She knows his blond hair. It's Charlie.

Dorothy opens her eyes, locking with Lois's own before Lois can turn away. Lois crosses the hallway, leaping down the stairs two at a time, nearly twisting her ankle in her kitten heels. The girls have all congregated by the hotel's front doors.

"Any luck?" Greer asks, stamping out a cigarette on the carpet.

"No. I—" Lois begins.

"Well, thank Moses," June interrupts, lifting her hand to her forehead.

Dorothy emerges from behind Lois. Her mouth is wiped clean, though Lois can see the rub of lipstick on her lower right cheek. She's unsteady on her feet, slurring an apology, explaining that one of the musicians invited her backstage and that she lost track of the time. June reprimands her like a mother. One of her earrings is missing, and Lois blushes at how naked her lobe appears beneath the lobby lights.

Charlie joins them a moment later, his keys hooked to his thumb. His presence is barely worthy of comment. The girls file out into the cool night, ready to be driven home.

Dorothy falls asleep in the truck bed, her cheek flattening against its lip. Lois looks out across the desert, seeing Dorothy and Charlie's shapes in the darkness, the shifting muscles of his back. She had foolishly done the same thing three nights ago, but she had learned her lesson, and there is some even greater betrayal in doing it with Charlie. He sleeps twenty yards away from the house, in a room by the stables. Close enough that everyone will sense what they've done, like when Lois once left the stove on after boiling water for coffee; that low thrum of danger, an acrid note of gas worming through the air. He's become another man on the front porch, threatening to come inside. All because Dorothy needed to feel wanted herself. It's pathetic, Lois thinks, remembering the Washoe Pines ranch hand's dry fingers nearly ripping the seam of her underwear. To need a man so desperately.

But in her bed, she thinks of their wet, open mouths illuminated by the soft overhead lights and touches herself, startled by how easily she comes.

Twenty-Six

T he next morning, Dorothy doesn't look at Lois as they file into the cars for church. Her eyes pointedly linger in the air above Lois's head, and when their knees bump against one another in the backseat, Dorothy blushes. This self-consciousness, this modesty, surprises Lois, and she thinks of Dorothy's years raised under the threat of her father's open palm in Utah. She obviously doesn't want Lois to tell anyone what happened. The car starts, and Lois sits with the power she's been given, like several chips dropped into her hand.

As the collection plate is passed, Lois thinks of her envelope. She has only singles left. Though she doesn't want to sit on the sidelines at the casino, soon she may not even have enough to pay for meals on her train ride home. In the pew, Dorothy reminisces about her soon-to-be-ex-husband's cousin who always gave her long looks at holiday parties. She asks the other girls whether it would be awful if she gave him a call.

"If he's not married, who cares?" June whispers.

There is some new warmth between June and Dorothy that Lois doesn't understand. Dorothy smiles, pulling her chain bracelet in circles around her wrist, becoming herself again. Lois is surprised she's already considering her next conquest, and she thinks of Charlie preparing the horses for the afternoon ride, brushing their dry, matted hair.

"Well, I think there are certain people you shouldn't get involved with," Lois says.

She's surprised by her own reprimand, her cadence matching Greer's. She's never said anything of the sort to the girls before. Dorothy looks at her for the first time that morning, her pupils narrowing to a pinhead. A knot tightens in Lois's chest but she holds her ground, thinking of how Greer would act. She opens her mouth, ready to sing the morning's last hymn.

After days of not returning his calls, Lois has an appointment with Mr. Tarleton. She could only put it off for so long without risking an angry telegram from her father. Mary Elizabeth joins her for a meeting with her own lawyer, and in the car's backseat she keeps arching her back as if she can't take in a real breath in her shot silk suit. Lois remembers how shallow her own breathing became that day at the beach. The storm-green of Lake Michigan, dragging her out to its deep, shoreless center.

"Will your husband be there?" Lois asks.

"No. I don't know where he is. I wonder what will happen, if they can't find him. If I won't be able to . . ." Mary Elizabeth can't finish the thought.

"Your lawyer will sort it out. It will all be fine," Lois says.

Mary Elizabeth nods, clasping and unclasping Lois's hand. Her ring casts wavering pins of light onto the car roof. Lois is not sure if what she said is accurate, but these are the lies she still allows herself, the ones she wishes were true. She looks down at her own band, imagining it sinking to the river's bottom.

"Are you going to throw it in the river? Your ring?" Lois asks.

"Yes," Mary Elizabeth says, her voice clearer than Lois has ever heard, firm as a horse bit. "I don't ever want to think about him again."

Mr. Tarleton had left four messages at the house. Lois imagines there's papers to sign or perhaps some words from her father, as she can't imagine him ever calling her directly. She's never heard his voice on the telephone.

At first Mr. Tarleton wants to speak about anything other than her divorce. He talks about how Senator McCarthy is the only politician with any sense of urgency and asks how her body is faring in the heat, looking her up and down in a way that makes her lunch's mashed bread and ham steak creep back up her throat. Only when she makes up an appointment at the hair salon does he pull out her file, his fingers brushing up and down his tie.

"Now, I've heard from Mr. Saunders's attorney," he begins. "And I'm afraid they're counter-filing."

"What does that mean?" Lois asks.

"Well, to have the record officially state he did nothing wrong, he's claiming you deserted him."

"What?"

"Desertion means you haven't shared a home for two years, and that you were the one to leave. Obviously, we know that's not true, but as neither of you have evidence for much of anything, it's just testimony, and this way he has a reason to not give you a cent."

"But he—he promised me."

She immediately regrets her words, how her voice has quieted to a whisper. It feels as if someone's swiftly punched her in the stomach.

"Well, unfortunately we don't have that in writing. It would be different if he cheated or abused you, and it would obviously be different if you had children, but you don't. I tried my best, but—"

"So, what does this mean? What about the house?"

"It's his house. It was paid for with his money. It's in his name."

Lois sees Lawrence in her father's study. The light is cool and pale, dust motes floating in the air. They're speaking about what is to be done with her, how she is to live. Lawrence hasn't shaved for several days and the crop of gold stubble on his cheeks makes him look older—his birthday is at the end of the month, she remembers, though she no longer has to buy him a present, to try to imagine what he would even want. Her father is trying to convince him to leave her with something for the years they had together, that it's the duty of a husband, and Lawrence is asking him why, when she no longer wants to be his wife. It's not as difficult as Lawrence thought, to be this cruel. It was the same when Lois decided to leave, so surprisingly simple, as she sat in the movie theater watching the credits cut through the dark.

"I just can't really believe—" she begins, and stops. "I thought that he would have to—after almost four years—"

"I have everything here, typed out. There's been no mistake. We can fight it, but even in Nevada judges haven't been friendly to women who leave their husbands when there's no real sob story to tell. And the fact that your father is rather well-off won't help either."

"Did he say anything? My father?"

"He wants this taken care of as quietly and quickly as possible."

Lois nods, knotting her fingers together. Mr. Tarleton has received his orders. Her father thinks this is a fitting punishment. He is siding with Lawrence, even though he never liked him, just to teach her a lesson. She sees them rising in the study and shaking hands. Her father wincing at the creak of Lawrence's shoes on the carpet. Lawrence's car gliding beneath the branches of pin oaks, and the relief both must have felt, to be done with it all.

"So I'm entitled to nothing," Lois says. "I have nothing."

"He said you can keep the rings. The jewelry he's bought you."

"The jewelry," she repeats.

He'd bought her a frail gold locket she hated, a pair of diamond studs that never looked right in her ears, and a short strand of pearls she sometimes wore, rolling them against her lips in the darkness of the movie theater. They are all still in her long velvet jewelry box, atop their dresser—his dresser, in his home.

"That's something, isn't it? It breaks my heart to tell a girl she can't keep her jewelry."

Lois nods and looks down at the sloping muscle of her forearms, lean from her hours in the pool. She flexes her fingers and imagines them grabbing the back of Mr. Tarleton's large, soft head, and slamming it against the desk.

Twenty-Seven

T he next morning, she wakes early and throws the sheets off her body. No breeze combs through the window screen. The air is stifling. She slept poorly, waking up several times in a sweat, assuming she was ill again, but her forehead is cool. As the room lightens, she thinks of the lizard that she watched last night until her eyes ached, now no doubt burrowed deep in the house's walls. She wanted to understand how it could be so still, displaying no fear of her. How to have ice fleck her blood.

Looking across the floor, she realizes Florence must have cleaned the room the day before. Her shoes are lined up neatly along the baseboards. The wood is polished, no longer clouded with dust and strands of hair. She sees Florence smelling her perfume, opening her drawers, and she sits upright, hopping from her bed and padding to the dresser. She counts the remaining bills, her breath slowing as she tallies them over and over, suddenly conscious of how tied she is to what her father will give her. Of course Florence hadn't stolen a cent.

Her father hid money all over their house. She realized this when she was seven, finding a roll of bills in the belly of a cow-shaped milk pitcher, tied together with a length of twine. Since the Depression, he's never trusted banks, and she's never seen him write a check if he didn't have to. She told no one what she found, though it became a game to find the money. It was hidden in old hatboxes and porcelain vases above the mantel, tucked into a pair of his stiff dress shoes. She never took any of it, fearful her father would know immediately, that he'd crack a cane across her backside.

She sits near the window, folding her legs. Though nothing was taken, she decides to start locking her bedroom door. The sun hangs just above the violet line of the mountains.

Beneath the maple, she notices the swing is swaying back and forth, as if someone has just jumped from it. Scanning the blond grass, she finds no one. It must have been the wind, she thinks, though the air is turgid.

Downstairs, she hears the clang of Anna's cast-iron skillet, announcing that the day has begun.

That afternoon, they abandon the pool for the desert. Greer says that she needs to stretch her legs.

Lois hadn't told her anything about what Mr. Tarleton said. At the casino last night, all she wanted was to forget, and Greer also slipped off at some point to speak to one of the dealers about a new card game, leaving Lois to sulk at the bar alone. Bailey found Lois and the other girls after midnight, concerned about their well-being, as a man smoking in the alley had been robbed after the thief shattered a tumbler against the back of his skull. He woke to blood caked in his hair. But then Greer appeared safe and sound, oblivious to any disturbance.

They walk out past the horse pasture. Grit crackles beneath their heels. The sagebrush is blooming, its stalks tipped with small yellow flowers.

As they circle the ranch's grounds, all Lois can think of is Lawrence assessing each explanation for a divorce, as she had over four weeks before, and deciding there's no word more fitting than *desertion*. She sees him passing through her in their upstairs hallway, at the bathroom sink, her outline petal soft. She sees herself staring at her reflection in the mirror, drawing on her mouth with lipstick even though she would see no one for hours. Lying about her afternoons with such clarity it frightened her. He is telling her: *You are right*. He is telling her: *You were never even here*.

"Dorothy is leaving soon," Lois says.

"I suppose you're right." Greer says nothing else, but Lois can't stay quiet. There's a churning in her chest.

"What do you think will happen to her?" she asks.

"Well, I've hoped for more for all of them." Greer sighs. "I've done what I could, but sometimes people prefer to stay where it's safe, to stick to what they know, even when what they know is a prison. So, for Dorothy, I think she'll probably live with some man who she thinks will marry her, and then she'll eventually realize that he has no reason to, given she's already sleeping with him. Then she'll float from cocktail party to cocktail party until she becomes terrified her looks are fading, at which point she'll meet some homely widower with two children who will never like her, and remarry."

Lois is surprised by the brutality of this prediction, though it has the ring of truth. "What do you think I'll do?"

Greer cocks her head toward Lois, her long clavicle cresting against her skin. Clouds rush over them, dipping their bodies in and out of shadow.

"What do you want to do?"

Lois thumbs her denim belt loops. She's stopped walking, and she stares at the ground beneath her, at the sparse grass threading the sand and dirt.

"Lawrence counter-filed yesterday. Or, I found out about it yesterday. He says I deserted him, and so he's not going to give me any alimony, and my father doesn't want me to fight it because he's so ashamed of what I've done, so all I'll be left with is a pearl necklace and an ugly locket. I'll have to ask for money just to go see a film, and then, in six months, I'm not sure what will happen."

She grinds her heel into the earth, ripping the grass from its roots.

"You're angry," Greer says.

"No, I'm not."

"Look at me." Lois stiffens when she meets her eyes, which are sharp as colored glass. "You're angry."

"Yes, I am."

"And that's good. Anger is powerful. Have you thought that perhaps this is a gift? Did you really want to have to take his money?"

"I don't know what other choice I have, and he promised that he'd . . . take care of me."

"Never trust a man who says something like that. Ever. No one will ever give you anything if they can help it. Even your own father won't let you stay in his house. All they'll do is take, which is why we have to do the same."

Another bank of clouds muffles the sun. Lois nods and closes her eyes, furious now at the tears tightening her throat. She doesn't want to cry in front of Greer.

"Take a breath, Lois."

She feels a hand graze the side of her head, and looks up to find Greer tucking a lock of hair behind her ear, staring into the cartilage's dark whorl. Her face is passive, as if she's caressing her own skin. At first Lois is startled. The other girls loop their arms through her own, rest their cheeks against her shoulder, but Greer's touches are always instructive and brisk. Now her fingers trail the line of Lois's hair. It's nothing like when Lawrence would caress her. There's nothing of her mother's occasional tenderness either, Greer briefly tugging at her split ends in the way you'd only touch your own strands, a little too sharply, knowing the pain you can handle. As if the two of them are one and the same. As if nothing separates them. Nerves spark across Lois's skull, and she wants to tell Greer she's wrong. That this is something being given, and that without her, Lois will return to Lake Forest and all the muscle she's developed at the ranch will wither away again. It will be another thing they take from her.

"I want to scream," Lois says.

"Screaming is useless." Greer withdraws her hand. "A waste of anger. Hold it in."

Twenty-Eight

T hat night, Lois is pulled from sleep. Later, she'll decide it was the sound of broken glass that woke her, but when she first opens her eyes, all she hears is the formless movement of a body. There are no voices, just the house bending to someone's weight, moaning under its foreignness. Lois lifts her head, which is heavy as a paint can. She is still drunk from the casino. Outside her window, the sky is pitch-black and powdered with stars.

She lies still on her bed and listens as footsteps move through the rooms downstairs. Though she has no reason to believe it isn't Bailey or June, a part of her knows that it isn't. A voice low in the inner shell of her ear whispering that it's someone else: Charlie, slipping into Dorothy's room. Like when she'd hear a teacher mouth her name seconds before it was uttered or know which tree branch was about to snap—tapping into some deeper current, nothing of magic or God in it, just her innermost animal.

Lois rises from her bed and opens the door, listening for the motion of anyone else waking. Several measured footsteps fall near the stairwell and then creak in retreat. They must have decided it's safer to meet on the first floor. She imagines them stretched along the fainting sofa. Sprawled naked on the carpet. Dorothy's hair a damp rope of red. Lois wants them to be caught, for Dorothy to learn that all men, even Charlie, are not to be trusted. She thinks of what Greer would dare her to do.

At the bottom of the stairs, there is dirt beneath her feet, stamps of grit dragged in from the driveway. Lois tries to tread lightly, lifting herself up on her toes like a ballet dancer, but pitches forward, clamping her hand over her mouth to stop herself from laughing. She's drunker than she thought. Stopping at the doorway of the living room, she peers inside.

The pale green sewing stool is tipped over. She follows its line to the moonlight and finds shards of glass scattered before a window ledge. Her skin chills at the jagged remnants of a rock or a fist, her heels dropping to the carpet. Air whistles through the broken window. The person in the house is not Charlie.

Lois wipes her cold hands on her nightgown. She suddenly wishes she were sober, struggling to parse what could be happening. She thinks of the ranch hand bringing his palm to his chest after she pushed him, and the reporter trying to guess where the girls slept, his thick, pink fingers snapping for the check. His face when she spat at him. An anger strong as a storm. She imagines each of them wrapping their jackets around their fist and forearm and punching through the glass.

She hears a low grunt near the hallway and walks on the balls of her feet across the floor. In the narrow corridor, shadows gather to form a tall figure consuming a doorframe. Though he's turned from her, Lois knows who it is without seeing his face.

"Emme," he whispers, pawing at the door. "Emme."

She pulls herself back into the living room, her body lit with the same fear she felt the afternoon he'd mistaken her for his wife. The same day Lois had seen the scar carved into Greer's back, as brutal as Mary Elizabeth's brand. The marks of men. Lois inhales deeply, holding the air in her chest, and tries to think of what Greer would do.

Breathe in when you're aiming, breathe out when you shoot.

After taking a few quiet steps, she is in Rita's study, unhooking the antique rifle from the wall. It is cold in her hands, grainy with dust, and the eyes in each of the photographs follow her. She tells herself it is too old to actually fire, as the briny gin she swallowed hours before laps the back of her throat. It is not so different from spitting in the reporter's face.

At the entrance to the hallway, she lifts the barrel and aims it at his back, the rifle unsteady in her hands. He is wearing the same gray linen suit.

"Step away from her door," she says, and he turns his head to look at her, jerking back at the shoulder when he sees the gun, as if he's already been shot.

"What in God's name?" he asks.

"I won't let you hurt her."

"I can't believe—" He laughs, and then stops himself. "You need to put that down."

Lois keeps the barrel raised, furious at his laughter. Light floods from beneath two doorways, the girls clicking on their bedside lamps one by one. Bailey is the first to open her door, her hair knotted in pin curls and her face still slack with sleep.

"He broke in," Lois calls to her. "Through the living room window."

"Jesus Christ," Greer says, emerging from her room at the end of the hallway.

When Mary Elizabeth opens her door and screams, her husband is already walking toward Lois, his hands knocking against his side in tight fists. Above them, the others are waking, angles of light tessellating the high ceiling. He keeps licking his chapped lips, obviously drunker than her, drunker than he was the other afternoon, his eyes a veined pink. The air is acrid with the smell of piss. Though he's not as large as Lawrence, his leanness is menacing, and even intoxicated there's a confidence to his movements, in his strength, that Lois did not expect. She thought he would kneel on the floor and lift his hands in supplication, ready to be bound.

"Put the gun down."

He is nearly close enough to grab the barrel. Lois hooks her finger around the trigger.

"What's going on down there?" Rita asks at the top of the stairs, and then Carol calls for her, a confused cry.

Lois waits for someone to tell her what to do, but they simply hold their breath. The gun is heavy. Her arms have begun to shake, even with her new slopes of muscles, even after her hours in the pool. He is wearing his wedding ring, a throb of gold in the dark, and watches her in the way Lawrence would when she became upset. Eyes open too wide. As if she were the one who was raving and incoherent. She remembers the smell of their bathroom that week before he hid her diaphragm, its faint tang of mold. The sudden cognizance of her own vulnerability. Greer and Mary Elizabeth must have each had similar moments, perhaps just seconds before the fireworks of burst blood vessels, the scald of metal against skin. He takes another step and tears of anger begin to blur Lois's sight. She wants to be back in the pickup, for him to sprint off into the night like one of the jackrabbits, but instead he is stalking toward her as if he is the one holding the rifle. He can't feel what they have felt. The girls, whose bodies are so familiar with danger.

"Lois, I think—" Bailey begins.

"Just put the goddamn gun down," he says, thrusting his hand out and gripping the barrel.

She pulls the trigger, her heart stopping at the sound of the dull, impotent click just as Greer cracks a vase against the crown of his head.

Twenty-Nine

· · · · · · · · · · · ·

n the dining room, Anna brings everyone black coffee so bitter it hurts
Lois's cheeks. Every lamp has been turned on, as if that will cast out any
lingering darkness, so the room is bright as a stage set. Mary Elizabeth's
mouth is limp with shock, and she keeps tucking a phantom curl of hair
behind her ear. Charlie lifted her husband into his dry bathtub out by the
stables after they'd bandaged his head, angling a chair beneath the doorknob
to lock him in. In the living room, Anna is taping Christmas wrapping
paper over the broken window, and Lois keeps thinking how odd it looks,
mistletoe in July.

Greer took the rifle from her after he collapsed on the carpet. She nodded at Lois like a proud general after some terrible battle, as if she understood and there was nothing else that could be said. Lois barely felt the gun
leave her hands, light-headed with a sense of her own power—that she had
stood her ground, that they had kept the girls safe.

With her buzzing limbs, she needs water, not coffee. Looking down at
her lap in the dining room, her finger is still bent in the shape of a crook.
She straightens it.

"Well, now we need to decide what to do," Rita says, tapping a ring
against her cup.

"We call the police," Bailey says.

"Is that what you want, Mary Elizabeth?" Rita asks.

"I—I just assumed we had to. What else would we do with him?" Mary
Elizabeth asks, looking from Bailey to Rita.

Though she's more lucid than Lois has seen her in weeks, Mary Elizabeth's voice is small and strangled, like she's been dropped to the bottom of
a well. Bailey sits next to her. Her hand is pressed against Mary Elizabeth's
lower back, as if to keep her upright.

"We could drive him to the airport to ensure he takes the next flight home. If we call the police, it will find its way into the papers. And your family . . . ," Rita says.

"It will follow you as well. Not just him," Bailey says solemnly.

"I don't even know how he got out here, with his debts," Mary Elizabeth says, shutting her eyes. "And I can't ask my father to buy him a plane ticket. I can't . . . I can't . . ."

Bailey rubs her back in circles, trying to calm her, but after another moment it's obvious Mary Elizabeth needs to return to her room. As the two of them get up to leave, the others sit in silence. June refills Dorothy's empty coffee. Their relationship had shifted at some point, perhaps when George abandoned Dorothy; their hatred burning off, leaving only a devout sense of kinship. Lois realizes no one besides Greer has looked her in the eye. Not like after the jackrabbit or the stringer, when they all pressed close to her in adulation. It's almost as if they're scared of her, even though Greer had cut the bright crescent of blood at the back of the man's head.

"Think I should probably stick to jackrabbits," Lois offers, but no one laughs, not even Greer, who is biting at the skin around her thumb with a ferocious intensity. Like she wants to hit bone. Her chest rises and falls in quick waves. If Lois didn't know any better, she'd say she looked frightened as well.

"What about his family?" Rita asks when Bailey returns.

"Mary Elizabeth told me they want nothing to do with him. His father's dead and he's lost contact with his brothers."

"I'll pay for the ticket," Greer says. "Then we'll all be done with this."

Everyone looks to Greer and then to Rita, as if to gather if this is allowed.

"That's very generous of you, but I don't think we could accept that. That Mary Elizabeth could accept that," Rita says.

"It's nothing, really." Greer stirs her coffee, the gentle clink of the spoon the only noise in the room. Blood seeps from her thumb's cuticle bed, and Rita and Bailey exchange heavy looks.

"Greer, I'm not sure—" Bailey begins.

"It's clear we don't want to bring the police into it and see him thrown in jail, but we can't have him anywhere nearby either. I also imagine Rita doesn't want the Golden Yarrow in any of the papers for something like this. No police, no journalists."

"I just want what's best for Mary Elizabeth," Rita says.

"Well, fine." Greer's jaw tightens, and Lois flashes to how her face looked when she cracked the vase against the man's skull, her eyes black as pitch. For a fleeting moment, Lois had been more scared of her than of Mary Elizabeth's husband. "But even without taking the ranch's reputation into consideration, this is the best option."

One of Rita's dachshunds is whining near the kitchen door, its nails scraping at the wood. Rita signals to Anna, who goes to let it outside.

"I could take him to the airport," Charlie offers. "When he's dried out, that is."

"All right, then." Greer rises from the table without taking a sip of her coffee. "It's settled."

Everyone unfurls from their seats. The relief among the girls is palpable, Greer's generosity warming the air. Some look at the clock pulsing on the wall to gauge the hours remaining before morning, though it feels impossible to sleep, and Rita, Charlie, and Bailey excuse themselves to the office. Greer is still distracted, and no one else looks at Lois as they slip out into the hallway.

Before she goes back up to her room, Lois sees that someone removed the rifle from the place Greer left it, undoubtedly just to return it to its rightful place on the wall. A simple act, she tells herself, signifying nothing. They must know she did not want to truly kill him. She knew that the gun wouldn't fire, and she had to do whatever she could to scare him. To keep them all safe. In the morning, they will thank her.

Upstairs, her mattress does not feel right, soft and forgiving. She lies in the bathtub, too cold to sleep.

Thirty

· · · · · ·

A t the breakfast table, the girls hush themselves into silence with the languid beating of their fans. No one slept enough and the day is drowsy with heat. Afterward, Mary Elizabeth goes to Charlie's room out by the stables to speak to her husband. The others watch as Charlie walks him to his car. Though he's wearing freshly laundered jeans and a button-up, clothes undoubtedly lent from Charlie's closet, he looks near death, his skin tinged a sickly, jaundiced yellow, just like his wife's when he first arrived. He reminds Lois of the stray dogs she'd see in Chicago, eyes milk-white and hair matted. Before he gets into his car, he looks up to the house's roof as if the whole structure might collapse on him.

Though no one says a word to Lois about the night before, she can tell that the girls still think she went too far. There is a stiffness in their shoulders, a hesitancy before they ask her to pass the carafe of water, as if she might suddenly flip the table over. Mary Elizabeth says nothing, having turned inward. She spends the rest of the day in her room.

In the afternoon, no one wants to do anything but float in the shallow end of the pool and nap in the deck chairs, their limbs splayed like cats. Lois wants to speak to Greer about the prior evening, but the others are too near, so she laps from edge to edge until she can barely breathe. The silence makes her doubt the steps she took, and she wants Greer to clear the air, to assure the others that Lois simply did what was necessary. She doesn't know how to insist she knew the rifle wasn't loaded—and did she? She has no memory of checking the chamber—without sounding hysterical. Suddenly she is back at the dinner parties in Lake Forest, having spoken far too loudly and for far too long, and how impossible to take it all back, when like a glass of spilled wine it's soaked and stained the floor.

In the evening, no one ventures beyond the ranch's living room. Anna warms milk on the stove, darkening it with honey and whiskey, and they all go to sleep early. Lois dreams that her teeth are popping from her gums one by one, dropped into her coffee like pearls from a broken string. She wakes in a nest of damp sheets.

The next afternoon, they go to the rodeo. Charlie talked of it all week, and so everyone but Rita and her daughters makes the drive to Glenbrook, their cars winding along the steep, narrow Kingsbury Grade. "It will be a welcome distraction, I'm sure," Rita says at breakfast, and the girls all nod their heads. Even Mary Elizabeth joins them—her eyes less clouded, her body taut. Lois wonders if she's stopped taking her pills.

The rodeo grounds are in a wide, verdant meadow next to an apple orchard. Mountains circle the land, sharp with pine trees. It's remarkable to her how much Nevada can shift, from city to desert to forest. The event has attracted a smattering of tourists like themselves, divorcées who look like they've never been within ten miles of a cow, as well as locals with shining red faces, as if a layer of their skin has been stripped. The men inspect the penned mustangs and broncos while their wives try to find seats, wrestling with freckled children in thin cotton shirts. But it's the teenagers Lois can't take her eyes from. They're indolent in their youth, leaning against the metal horse pen; boys with skinny arms and girls with full cheeks, their faces brazenly speckled with blemishes. Watching them, Lois feels a nostalgia for something she never had.

While Charlie leads them to a row of seats, Lois's eyes follow one of the girls who has just hopped onto the fence's top rail. She lifts up her skirt so that the boy she's with catches a brief glimpse of tanned thigh.

"That girl'll be on the nest within a week," Greer says.

Lois turns to her, grateful for the gesture of levity. Though the girls chatted in the car, no one spoke directly to her. Greer was quiet in the passenger's seat.

"I don't know, maybe she's all show," Lois says. "Maybe she's the editor of her school's newspaper and goes home every night to care for her sick grandmother before she does her homework."

"Maybe she's been with every boy in her class."

"Maybe she just got accepted to Barnard, and she's going to study Russian literature and then come back here to teach afterward. Become count-less students' favorite teacher. She'll weep every year at graduation."

"You think someone who came from here could get into Barnard?"

"I don't know, why not?"

"You've watched too many films."

Lois smiles, feeling as if she's been thrown a rope after thrashing in open water; she'd missed Greer fiercely, even though it had been just a day since they were alone. They turn their heads at Charlie's whistle. It's time to take their seats.

Before the rodeo begins, everyone rises to a tinny recording of "The Star-Spangled Banner," the men cupping their cowboy hats against their chests. During the war, people became so somber during this song that Lois could barely breathe, but now everyone has begun to stir again, anxious for it to be over, just like in the years before. Sometimes Lois misses the intensity of that feeling, in the same way she misses the first time Lawrence kissed her, not like the hundreds of times after, each a fainter and fainter impression, the briefest flutter of warmth. No different than when she'd press her own lips together to even out her lipstick.

The first event is calf roping. Charlie attempts to explain how it works, but only Mary Elizabeth listens—after the other night, Lois struggles to look at him. When the men lead their horses to the edge of the grounds, Greer takes a deep inhale of her cigarette and then stubs it out beneath her front heel, quickly patting Lois's thigh as if she weren't already paying attention. The calf is set loose, the man stampeding after it on his horse, lassoing the calf and then, after dismounting in one fluid leap, flipping its body over and tying the calf's feet together. This happens relentlessly, the crowd whooping from the moment the rope gets tangled around the calf's body until it's lying helpless, tipped over onto the dirt.

The fastest cowboy has the calf trussed in seventeen seconds. The applause is thunderous. He waves to the crowd as his winning time is announced, and an older man with a broom-like silver mustache hands him an envelope.

"How much do they get for winning?" Greer asks.

"Probably about fifty dollars, but at big rodeos they can win hundreds," Bailey says.

Afterward, large barrels are wheeled out across the pen while several girls lead their horses toward the gates. They begin to race one at a time, mounting their saddles and taking off at a trot once the flag is waved, circling the barrels. They go so fast that Lois is amazed every time a horse turns and does not fall on its side. She holds her breath as the girls grip the reins, their arms tightly angled and their backs straight as a plank of wood. They are in complete control of the animal, and Lois finds herself wishing they'd abandon the route and break through the metal fence, losing themselves in the orchard's leaves.

When it's over, Greer grips her hand briefly, and from that one touch Lois knows she felt the same thing, that same desperate urge for them to keep running.

After a few painful minutes when a bull bucks at a rodeo clown caged in a barrel, a line of cows is led into the pen. Men with steel pails in the crook of their arms follow. The brims of their cowboy hats shadow their faces.

"From this distance they all look so attractive, but I feel like up close they'll have yellow teeth and smell like manure," June says, fanning herself with her pocketbook.

She and Dorothy are growing bored. They've asked how much longer the rodeo will go on for and whether there's any big finale that's worth the wait.

"I don't think they *all* smell like manure," Mary Elizabeth says, chewing her bottom lip.

"They're cowboys," June interjects. "And not like Gary Cooper playing a cowboy, real cowboys who grew up in Oklahoma or Wyoming. Emphasis on the *cow*."

"Did you ever see *The Fountainhead*?" Lois asks June.

"Oh yes, do you know, I heard they told Barbara Stanwyck she was too old—"

"There's nothing wrong with growing up in Oklahoma," Greer interrupts, lighting a new cigarette. Lois winces at her tone, which is pointed as a knife's edge.

"No one's saying there is. They just have different ways of living," June says. She is in her debate mode, assured and commanding. In moments like this, Lois understands how she married someone so much older. She must have never really been a little girl.

"Cowboys brush their teeth and bathe just like everyone else. I know it's hard to believe, but civilized life exists outside of Connecticut," Greer says.

"I know that," June says. "I didn't mean it like that."

Greer hands Lois her cigarette, a small gesture that defines a circle, bringing Lois closer and pushing everyone else further away. Lois takes a drag.

"Well, bath or no bath, I'd let them lasso me just like those baby calves," Dorothy says, and the other girls laugh—even Mary Elizabeth.

"Yes, thatta girl, Dorothy." Greer takes her cigarette back and gestures it toward Charlie. "Though it's probably a good idea to stay away from ranch hands from now on, no matter how desperate you've become for some attention."

Dorothy's head snaps from Greer to Lois, eyes widening with hurt. Bailey and Charlie are talking off to the side about horse breeds, but Mary Elizabeth and June exchange glances. Lois spasms with guilt, but then she remembers she hadn't told Greer anything about what she'd seen.

"Dorothy, did you—" Mary Elizabeth begins.

"Of course she did. Now, time for the cows," Greer announces.

Lois looks toward the pen. Even from their raised seats, she can hear the sear of milk against metal. Men in the stands yell at the ones pumping, urging them to go faster, and Lois remembers the men at her father's plant, bellowing at one another over a cow just like this one, stripped and quartered. When they're finished, a judge comes around with a measuring stick. Lois wishes she and the others would go back to the ranch. The rodeo has become too absurd, and the air between the girls has curdled.

"Bailey, what do you think about going to the casino?" Greer asks.

"You want to leave?" Charlie asks.

"I'm having a good time," Mary Elizabeth says.

"Yes, we're just fine here," June says, drawing herself up to her full height.

Lois and Dorothy lock eyes before Dorothy quickly pulls into herself, and Lois realizes just how frightened of her Dorothy has become. She leans against June, who cups one of her knees in a way that feels almost protective, and Greer passes Lois the cigarette. It hangs limply between her fingers.

"Well, why don't we split up, then? I know Charlie wanted to show some of you the inn—Mark Twain stayed there, I believe—and I'm happy to take anyone wherever they'd like to go," Bailey says, leaning forward almost as if to separate the two sides of the bench.

"Fine by me," Greer says.

Greer stands to take her leave, and Lois thinks for a moment of how if she stayed, she could catch Dorothy on their walk back to Charlie's truck and explain that she hadn't said anything. That she regrets her words at church, that Dorothy could call whomever she liked. She could tell her that all she wanted was to protect each of them, and that no one at the ranch has any reason to fear her.

"Come on," Greer says, and Lois rises.

Thirty-One

. . . .

N o one joins them at the casino. It's the first time Lois can remember the girls not following Greer.

When they arrive, Bailey gracefully extricates herself, sensing she's not welcome. They order gin fizzes at the bar. The bartender winks at Greer, telling her it's on the house, which she accepts with a brief, cold smile. She begins to talk to Lois about which tables they should go to first, but Lois only nods, distracted. She's considering how to make amends, how to let the others know she's still the same girl who made them laugh with impressions of W. C. Fields, who held their hair back in the restroom, who listened as they whispered their small griefs.

"All right, fine, I'll give," Greer says, turning to her. "What's the matter?"

"Nothing," Lois says.

"Oh come on, spit it out. You were pouting the whole car ride."

"You knew about Dorothy and Charlie?"

"Of course." Greer licks her lips, her tongue a fine point, and Lois thinks of her lizard. "I saw them at the bar—he was buying her yet another gin and tonic, and they were both swaying like they were on a ship. I figured it was just a matter of time until they sort of fell into each other."

"You didn't say anything when we were looking for her."

"Neither did you. I thought you'd tell me if you saw something like that."

"Well, I didn't think—"

"You said you'd never lie."

"I'm—I'm sorry. I really didn't mean—"

"Again with the apologizing. It's bad luck to apologize in a casino." Greer's voice softens as she straightens the cuff of Lois's right sleeve, and Lois exhales. "But if you see anything else like that, you should tell me."

"I will."

The bartender measures ounces of lemon juice and gin, ice clinking against the silver cocktail shaker. The sound irritates her. Her body feels raw.

"I think the other girls are frightened of me, after the other night," Lois says. "Even though they're the ones I was protecting."

"Of course you were. You kept us all safe."

"But I'm worried they don't know that I could never—would never—hurt them, like I wanted to hurt him."

"Lois, you did the right thing. He left you with no other choice."

Greer looks at her with such understanding that Lois feels light-headed, her emotions so close to the surface, as near and tender as veins. Had Lawrence ever understood her? Sometimes she felt he knew she was lying, his eyes stilling as she talked about the nonexistent rosebushes the ladies wanted to have planted along the park or her phantom friend Lucille's complaints about her maid. A torrent of words as weightless as breath. And how he looked at her sometimes, a glance over the edge of his newspaper, a cock of his head as she slipped beneath their sheets, as if she were a stranger he'd suddenly found in his home.

"You all right, Annie?" Greer says. "I need my sharpshooter sharp."

Lois nods and mirrors Greer's smile. She takes a small sip of her drink, the alcohol and lemon singeing her throat.

"Now," Greer says, turning to scan the floor. "Let's go get some chips."

A t the cashier, Greer lays out another fifty-dollar bill on the counter. Lois wonders how many of these she has in her wallet, unimportant as old grocery lists.

"You need to risk a little more than that," Greer says, looking at the crumpled single in Lois's palm. "You're always playing it too safe."

"I can't. I have just over ten dollars left for the train," Lois says.

Greer nods, biting the inside of her cheek as if considering something. The cashier begins to count out their chips. As she taps her nails on the lacquered wood, Greer's brow furrows, and she tells the man that there's someone yelling in the backroom. Lois can't hear a thing. The casino is a roar of chatter. After straining to listen, the cashier turns to open the door, and Greer quickly leans over the counter and grabs two chips, whisking them into Lois's purse.

Lois is struck dumb. She does not move, hearing Ela's voice tell her she should put them back, in the same tone she'd use when Lois stole a faworki from the china plate on the kitchen counter, its powdered sugar smeared across her shirtsleeves. She stares into her purse's open mouth. Each chip is twenty dollars. When she looks up, Greer winks at her—just like she did that first evening before they left for the Highlands, another secret between them, and Lois smiles, her blood crackling like oil in a pan. Looking quickly behind them to make sure no one else has seen, she latches her purse shut.

"There's no one in the office," the man says, his eyebrow raised.

"Must have been coming from somewhere else," Greer says, shrugging and taking the stack of chips from his hands.

Thirty-Two

Greer does not make amends with the others. They wait for it the next day, expectant. At cocktail hour she reads on the fainting sofa, and at dinner she speaks only to Lois. Lois is surprised by how seamlessly she ignores the other girls, sensing their eagerness to forgive her—a pattern learned from errant husbands. They mumble to one another about the errands they have to run and complain about how long the drive was back from the rodeo. Their faces look older, parched and thin, as if their evenings have finally caught up with them. The absence of Greer's attention some draining force.

The girls continue to tread lightly around Lois, keeping her at a safe distance. Dorothy refuses to look at her. *Stay sharp,* Lois repeats to herself, though it is difficult not to call out to them. Not to ask June about her screenplay or check on how Mary Elizabeth slept.

The dinner table is cleared. Dorothy ate two slices of pineapple cake, and no one tells her there's a blond crumb on her bottom lip.

"Bailey, can you drive Lois and me to Harrah's tonight?" Greer says.

"Just you and Lois?" Bailey asks.

"The rest of us want to go to the Highlands," June says, as if they'd already planned it.

Lois wants them all in the car again, singing along to Patti Page on the radio and checking each other's straight white teeth, but she has to follow Greer's lead. She wants Lois and only Lois to join her—the holy oil smeared on her forehead, so warm it hums.

"Charlie will drive the others, Bailey," Rita says, smiling as she lifts one of her twitchy dachshunds onto her lap. "The Highlands sounds like a nice change of scenery. A bit quieter. I know that after a while the casinos can lose their charm."

They form a new pattern. Over the next few days, as Lois comes to the end of her fifth week, she and Greer go to the casino alone. After that first evening, it's no longer discussed—the others pile into the back of Charlie's pickup, slapping its side like a horse when they're all inside and laughing too loudly, as if they're trying to show how little they care that Greer is not with them. After rumbling down the driveway the two cars split in the darkness, their lights casting across separate stretches of desert.

At Harrah's, their loop tightens. They no longer go to the slots, instead immediately ascending to the floors with higher limits. They return to Peg's table and Lois learns her regulars: a pink-skinned man in an ivory cowboy hat who breathes as if he's just run across the casino floor; an older woman who carries her chips around in a velvet satchel; and a young man who obviously comes for Greer, giving her more attention than any hand of cards, though she barely looks at him.

There is a new impatience in Greer. She doesn't want to linger at the bar or make small talk with the waitresses—it's as if by no longer inviting the other girls she's decided to sliver the fat off their evenings, desiring only the lean exchange of bets and chips. *I don't want to be dependent on my husband or my family's money anymore,* she said, and Lois wonders if she's trying to earn enough to strike out on her own, though that feels impossible.

Greer doesn't steal for Lois again, but on their second evening alone she introduces a new dare. Lois has to pocket a chip from a particularly soused gambler, a man who keeps sneezing without covering his mouth.

"Now, he'll be easy," Greer says. They stand at the opposite edge of the roulette table, her voice a careful whisper. "It's everyone else you need to watch for. I'd palm it when eyes will be drawn elsewhere, like when the dealer slips the ball along the running rail."

"All right," Lois says. Sweat dampens the cups of her bra. She wishes she'd had one more drink.

"And then just be sure to stay there. It'll draw attention if you immediately move away."

Lois nods and takes her place beside the man. He smells oddly sweet, like honeycomb. Greer is placing her bet on the green felt, and before Lois has time to think, the dealer is pinching the silver sphere between his fingers. Everyone's eyes shift in unison, and when the man cranes forward to watch the ball spin, Lois's hand coasts over his fallen tower of chips. She grips the plastic so tightly that when she opens her palm in the ladies' room twenty minutes later, it's bit a circle of red into her skin.

At the bar, she opens her purse, the chip slipped in beside her compact. Greer slaps it on the counter with a grin.

"Look at you," she says.

"I might just keep it," Lois says, pushing it in small circles.

"No." Greer laughs. "This is a symbol of luck. You have to play."

Afterward, this petty theft becomes the dare for every evening. Lois is surprised by how little guilt she feels. She only takes from men rich enough not to notice, and she loses the chips within an hour, the plastic circles cycled back into the same wooden racks they came from. They feel like something the casino owes her, as simple as dice.

There are moments when she misses the other girls. The warm tumult of their bodies in the backseat; the way Dorothy would frantically scan her face in her pocket mirror before they got out of the car, as if to assure herself she was still pretty; June's acerbic remarks on her husband's senility; how Mary Elizabeth would coach her to always leave a little bit of her gin in her glass, telling her a real lady never finishes her drink. The feeling of being one of many. But then Greer flushes with pride after Lois palms three chips at once, or they collapse into one another in laughter after taunting their least favorite bartender, and she's reminded that this is all that matters.

During certain beats when she is alone, Bailey finds her. Her face barely disguising her concern, she asks how Lois is doing. "Fine," Lois says, smiling. "Never better."

Thirty-Three

· · · · · · · · · · ·

t's Dorothy's second-to-last day at the ranch. At breakfast, she's oddly cheerful. The air in the dining room has been strained since the rodeo, but this morning she distracts everyone by talking about Palm Springs, about a house she's going to owned by a man named Leroy, whom Lois has never heard of before but everyone else seems to know of. It has a swimming pool and lemon trees in the front yard; a blue Jaguar in the garage that she can drive, as long as she's careful. Mary Elizabeth will remain until Lois's last day, just eight days away, and June will stay for a little longer than planned, as Harry has another meeting with a producer in the city. If there was ever a time when she considered leaving him, or actually stealing his ideas and becoming a screenwriter herself, there is no trace of it now. Lois thinks of all their side conversations with Greer, the rules and the dares. How quickly the girls have given up on them.

Mary Elizabeth enthuses over the prospect of not living out of a suitcase. There's a slight tremor in her hands as she lifts her coffee cup to her mouth, and though Lois hates herself for thinking this, she wishes she would take a Luminal; her frailness has become too brittle, unpleasant in its severity. She smiled at Lois when she sat down at the table, but Lois caught it too late, her head turning toward Anna emerging from the kitchen. When she jerked back, Mary Elizabeth was already speaking to Bailey, so that Lois wondered if she imagined it. There's been no word of her husband.

Lois wishes Greer were with them. With her absence, breakfast is when Lois feels most alone. Rita talks about two other girls who will be arriving— one from Ohio, another from New York.

"I can't imagine I'll like them as much as you all. We've really become our own little family here," Rita says. Ever since the rodeo, she has relaxed, obviously relieved at the girls' division.

Lois feels nauseous and takes only small bites of bread.

After breakfast, Rita finds her.

She invites Lois into her study, and Lois remembers the last time she crossed its worn floorboards—the room lush with shadow, the cold sweat that beaded her skin. Now the study is warm as butter, the wooden chair Lois sits in baked from a shaft of sun. Rita opens and closes a desk drawer, and there is the faint whiff of fermented sugar. Lois remembers her Tootsie Rolls.

"How have you been faring?" Rita asks. "We never really got to speak, just you and I, after the incident with Mary Elizabeth's husband. That must have been traumatic, finding him the way you did."

"I imagine it was more traumatic for Mary Elizabeth," Lois says.

"Yes, well, Bailey's been looking after her."

"That's good."

Lois isn't sure what Rita is hoping for from this exchange. The rifle rests on the wall, potent as a question mark. It's been over two weeks since Lois was last invited into her study, and their card games feel as distant as childhood memories—a time when the world was seen from a different height, a different angle.

"I haven't said anything about the incident to your father, in case you were worried about that," Rita says.

"I honestly hadn't thought of it."

"Well, if there's another incident, or any other reason for us to be concerned, it may be appropriate for me to call."

A dry laugh of surprise strains Lois's throat. She thought for a brief moment that Rita may just be checking in on her. That she was concerned how Lois was recovering after finding wind whispering through a broken window, a man stalking toward her in the dark. Instead, all she cares about is that the Golden Yarrow's reputation remain as gleaming as the girls' wedding rings. Her voice rich with its old, unshakable sense of authority.

"There won't be any other incidents," Lois says.

"I'm glad to hear it." Rita breathes out. "Please know that—"

"Unless you allow some other drunken husband to break into your house."

Rita closes her mouth. They study one another, almost as if they're playing gin rummy again, trying to glean the other's hand by the taut angle of an elbow, whether a smile is ghosting a bottom lip.

"If anything like that were to happen again, you should find me, find Bailey, not take a rifle off the wall," Rita begins. "I worry that Miss Lang has convinced you that there are no consequences to your actions. That you could shoot a man and just bury him out back."

"I knew the rifle wasn't loaded."

"Fine. Fine. But you have a week left here, until you're back in Lake Forest, and I'm concerned that—is this how you'll behave there? When you're completely and utterly on your own? I feel as if you're setting yourself up for a rude awakening. Your father told me your mother passed when you were in school, and I worry—"

"I don't need a mother anymore."

Lois's tone is sharp, cutting Rita silent. After a heavy pause, Rita nods as if she's decided something, running her tongue across her front teeth. If Lois didn't know better, she'd say there's a sadness weighting her eyes.

"Very well, then," Rita says. "Well, I don't want to keep you." Lois rises, but before she can turn the door handle, Rita's voice reaches out, like an unwanted hand brushing the nape of Lois's neck. "I know you can't see it now, but I just want what's best for you. I hope you remember that."

That night at the casino, Lois is manic. The anger that she felt in control of during her conversation with Rita grows and becomes wild, humming like bees in her chest. She can't stop talking—meandering ruminations on their fellow gamblers, snide remarks about the sort of girl Lawrence might now marry, small, simple—almost as if she's trying to empty herself, to say everything she can possibly think of while Greer is still there to listen. The hours whip past, and it is impossible not to think of how few evenings like this she has left, a small enough number to count on her fingers.

"Rita gave me a lecture today," Lois says as they sit down to play roulette. She removes a fresh cigarette from her carton but fumbles with the lighter, the metal wheel nipping her thumb.

"She still has hope for you, then, unfortunately. She gave up on me long ago." Greer takes the lighter from Lois's hands and clicks on the flame in one clean grind. Lois inhales, holding the smoke in her mouth.

"No, no, I'm fairly hopeless," Lois says as she exhales, and then repeats the word, savoring the skipping stone jump of the *l,* the deflation of the *s.* Perhaps she's drunker than she thought. Greer laughs, snapping her fingers to bring Lois back to attention. It's time to place their bets. Lois has one chip left, stolen from a man with half-moon glasses, something sinister in his thinness, or at least that's what Lois told herself to justify the five dollars pressed against her thumb.

She places her chip on the felt—on number seventeen, her birth date—and watches the wheel whir and slow to a click. The motion of the dealer's hands echoes a memory of the theater. Her mother's body pressed beside her. A man on the screen, some unknown actor with a face blunt as a hammer, counting out cards beneath a bare light bulb. The winning number is called out, and both her and Greer's chips are raked away from them. Sometimes she wants to insist that she keep what she steals, but she knows it would amount to so little—a few dollars every evening. Not worthy of Greer's disappointment during this final skein of days.

A moving image lingers like an aftertaste as they sit at the bar. The audience's delighted cackle as the man left a casino just like this one, thousands of dollars lining his suit jacket, and slipped into a stream of people, anonymous and untraceable as a single fish in a shimmering school of mackerel. She can't remember thinking it was anything more than clever as a child, but after her small thefts, she understands the immense power of stealing that amount of money. She wants to share it with Greer, and takes a sip of her sidecar.

"There's this film, I can't remember the name, about a pair of men who steal from a casino. Not like, well, you know," Lois says, placing her tumbler on the counter. "But a real theft."

"You always remember the names of films."

Greer barely seems to be listening to her, her eyes following the churn of the crowd in the way she sometimes does, as if she can sense how luck is surging or draining from particular tables.

"Yes, I know, but that's not the point. In the film, it wasn't some big heist," Lois continues. "They don't break into a basement safe with machine guns. It was really just about timing, stealing chips when the dealers weren't looking, almost like a ballet."

A man at a blackjack table jumps up from his seat, fisting his hair as if he wants to rip it out from the roots. Greer shakes her head.

"I wish we could do that," Lois finishes.

"What?"

"That sort of a theft. To be able to lift enough money to start a new life, like you said a while back, untied to anyone else. To be able to just leave the ranch, to tell Rita we're going off on our own. I'd love to see her face—"

"So why not do it?"

Lois laughs. "You need to—to know things. I'm not capable of something like that."

"You're capable of anything. All those men have is a little bit of knowledge. Information. And obviously, the confidence they can do it and not get caught."

"I suppose," Lois says, imagining herself navigating the casino floor with a choreographed precision. Greer idling the engine of a Cadillac outside. She feels the bees stir again, and she presses a palm to the warm skin of her sternum.

"But you'd need to steal a lot of chips, to make that risk worth it," Greer says.

Greer's spine has straightened, and her voice has a low, careful cadence, as if trying to guide Lois toward or away from something. Lois looks down at the lining of her bust, certain she's made a mistake.

"You're right, it was a foolish thing to say."

"It's not foolish. I just said it would have to be worth it."

Lois opens her mouth, though no words come to her. Greer must know there's no way Lois could steal enough for even a plane ticket, especially with just a week left, but there's no humor in her expression, no sense of indulgence. Lois thinks of those rash, exhilarating propositions from childhood, the ones she'd whisper to herself in the quiet of her bedroom—*I'll jump off the shed, I'll run away from home*—and those moments after, when everything feels suspended in a moment between what was and what could be. *What if. What if.*

"Should we go upstairs?" Greer picks up her drink from the counter, and the room comes back into focus. Lois gives her head a quick shake. It was a misunderstanding, that feeling of gravity. The sheen of too much alcohol.

"Lead the way," she says.

Thirty-Four

. . . .

Lois receives a letter from her father, no longer than a paragraph. He writes that he's talked to Mr. Tarleton about Lawrence, and that he does not think she should go to court. *It's an ungenerous decision, but as you are the one who left him, not an unjust one,* he writes in his thick block lettering, the period a large circle, as if to emphasize the finality of his point. After crumpling up the letter, Lois throws it in her wastebasket, and when it begins to open, she pulls the basket near and slams her heel against its bottom, so that the paper flattens.

The money does not matter to him. He wants her to remarry, to never have to see her again.

The night before, she struggled to fall asleep. Late in the evening, Greer had disappeared. She said she needed to use the restroom and was gone for an hour. After knocking on each stall and circling the first floor several times, Lois finally found her at Peg's table. They were alone, their heads bowed together in a way that reminded Lois of Patty and Carol at the lip of the pool. When they looked up at her approach, their faces altered, and Peg began to shuffle again.

"What were you talking about?" Lois asked as they walked to the Riverside.

"The rules of blackjack," Greer said.

At cocktail hour, a new girl appears. She is older, in her late thirties or early forties, and wears a pressed gray suit, her ring finger weighted with a large emerald. Her face is severe, each curl lacquered like a basket weave. Lois is given her name and immediately forgets it. Normally she would eavesdrop and wait for someone else to say it, repeating the name to herself, but she realizes now it does not matter—there's under a week left.

Lois sits near Greer, who is reading another cheap paperback, a man on a black stallion firing a pistol, the explosion a static orange star. Dorothy drops the needle onto a record. She is leaving tomorrow morning, and the others sit in silence, their listlessness making Lois feel even more restless. The new guest asks for a glass of sherry, the same drink Lawrence's mother would always take before dinner. She may be older than Lois thought. Bailey brings it to her in one of the crystal glasses that opens like a flower.

"I don't know how you kept your suit like that in transit. It's like you had a personal steamer following you around," Rita says to the new guest.

One of Rita's dachshunds is curled on her lap, gnawing at her finger with blunted teeth.

"It's all in how you sit, really. Just good posture," the new guest says.

"And you've had such a long journey. She comes to us from Manhattan," Rita says, looking at the other girls.

"Greer is from Manhattan as well," June says.

"Really? Where in the city do you live?" the new guest asks.

Everyone looks to Greer, whose eyes remain fixed on her book. Lois sees the annoyed shift of her jaw. It carries the weight of a fault line. She looks to the clock, to see if Anna will save them, but it's still half an hour until dinner.

"Upper East Side." Greer glances up briefly from the page.

"Of course," the new guest says, as if there were no other answer. "But what cross streets?"

"Well, do you want the address of my husband's apartment that I won't go back to, or that of my father's that I won't go back to?"

Greer takes a long sip of her drink, and Lois follows to demonstrate her alliance. The cocktail is so tart it makes her insides pucker.

"I'm sorry, I didn't mean—" the new guest begins.

"Don't pay any attention to Greer," Rita says. "She doesn't like to talk about herself. Isn't that right, girls?"

The girls look to one another, seeing if anyone will be brave enough to make a sound. Even though they've split down the middle, it's obvious the girls all still revere Greer.

"She wants to project a real air of mystery to keep us all interested," Rita continues. "Sometimes I think that's why I love my dogs so much. There's nothing mysterious about them. You know when they're hungry, you know when they want to go for a walk. Their tails and ears tell you just about everything. It makes them more human, I think, or at the very least more tolerable to be around."

"As if you—" Greer begins.

"As if I what?"

Greer breathes in deeply and turns back to her book, though Lois can tell she is not reading, her eyes bored into a fixed spot. No one knows what to say as Rita smiles at her dachshund, raking her nails across the slope of its leonine head. Lois is surprised by Greer's silence. She's never held her tongue. Bailey stands, holding up her empty tumbler.

"Who needs a fresh drink?" she asks.

Late in the evening, there's a knock on Lois's door. She's in her night-gown, getting ready for sleep after having just listened to the girls pile into Bailey's car. When the front door opened Dorothy screamed, and Bailey said, "Just leave it alone, and it'll leave you alone." A desert mouse, or a scorpion.

Greer hadn't wanted to go out. After dinner, where she ate nothing but a small chicken breast, she complained of a headache and withdrew to her bedroom. But when Lois opens the door, she finds Greer in the hallway.

"Oh."

"Can I come in?" Greer asks.

Greer steps across the floor, running her fingers along the bed frame's iron curls. Greer has never been in Lois's room before, and probably hasn't realized how the other rooms differ from her own. Lois is painfully conscious of how it all looks. Everything is just a little bit plainer: the carpet more worn, the curtains thinner. Greer picks up one of the lipsticks on her dresser and turns it over to read the color. She rotates Lois's vase of fresh marigolds.

"That new guest is awful," Lois offers.

Greer nods as she looks out the window. She's clearly uninterested in talking about anything that happened that evening, taking a seat on Lois's loosely made bed and crossing her legs. She pats the blanket, inviting Lois to join her. Lois wishes she were wearing a different nightgown, conscious of the brown stain on its hem, a remnant of her last period.

"I think I know how we can do it."

"Do what?"

"You know." Greer shifts on the mattress so that they're even closer, mirrored like two queens in a deck of cards. "The theft."

"The theft," Lois repeats, as if the word is foreign. She'd convinced herself she imagined Greer's seriousness the evening before—that it was obviously all a joke.

"When we talked last night, I thought about a conversation I had with Peg about how the casino works. People watch the tables, you know. Pit bosses check the chip counts, supervisors stop by to observe. You've noticed those men that stop by every once in a while in shiny suits, like the one that brought us Sambuca for some reason?"

"Yes, I figured as much. But what—"

"But no one's checking every hand but the dealer—that would be impossible." Greer speaks slowly, as if this were a lesson. "And so when someone comes in and makes a big bet and wins, the only one who can confirm the cards they were dealt is the dealer."

"Well, and the other people at the table."

"But there are stretches where there's no one else at Peg's table but me. Well, and you."

"I'm sorry." Lois is suddenly hot, uncomfortable. "What are we talking about?"

"What if I make a few big bets at the table, and Peg keeps dealing me winning hands?"

"Why would she do that?"

"Well, we'll give her a cut, of course. She apparently made a catastrophic bet at a poker game last week, so she's willing to take the risk."

"I don't think I understand. You told her—how did you think—"

"It's so obvious, really. And listen, you and I both know we can't palm enough chips to get us much of anything. This is what we have to do if we really want to start out on our own. We'll take all the money both of us have—how much do you have, again?"

"Almost nothing."

"You father won't wire you more?"

"No. Never."

"Well, then we'll have to take a couple hundred from Rita's safe in her study."

"You want to steal from Rita?"

"It's a key safe, so we just need to find the key, and we'll pay her back with our earnings when we get back to the ranch. She won't even realize it's gone. At the casino, you'll be our lookout, and afterward, you'll cash out a quarter of the chips and pay Peg's sister outside the casino. We can't risk someone following me."

Lois nods, her heartbeat heavy and insistent, like the sound of Ela kneading a wet sheet in the wash. She feels as if the room has contracted. Although she introduced the idea, she hadn't thought through what she was saying. The clock is frantically ticking, the walls now the span of her arms. Greer's hand stills her own, and she realizes she's been scratching furiously at a spider bite, an inflamed button of skin at her ankle.

"I need this, Lois. I have nowhere to go back to, really, just like you. We want the same thing. I sensed it that first day I saw you in the pool, how easily you could hold your breath and plunge to the bottom. It was almost like you didn't care if you ever came to the surface."

Lois presses her thumb against the raised bite. Her skin is warm, and she can feel the tears begin to gather at her eyelids. She can't refute what Greer has said, even if that wasn't exactly what she felt that day. It's a feeling she's known, and there's such a relief in hearing someone else say it, in having someone else see her desperate, unwavering loneliness.

"And what if . . . ," Greer continues, her voice softer, "what if we started our new lives together? We could move to California. I know you mentioned Los Angeles, but you don't want to be like all of those other girls, moving there to become a movie star or marry a movie star. What about San Francisco? We'd get a break from this heat. You could swim in the bay. And we could stay at a hotel for a bit and then see, maybe find something a little more permanent."

"Together? Live together, you and me?"

"Why not?"

Lois sees an apartment in California, the neck of a palm tree craning over their balcony. Waking in the morning in her own room, in her own bed. Greer waiting for her in the kitchen, her calves resting against a chair, the day before them both open and full. How much clearer this comes to her than any apartment in Chicago. She wants to look down to her chest, imagining her pulse visible near the neck of her nightgown.

"But we'd—we'd really be stealing that much?"

"We'd be taking. In the same way I took those chips for you the other night, or the chips you've taken each night since. And who are we taking from, aside from Rita, who won't even notice? Men who own the casino, rich men who have more than they'll ever need and pay Peg and the other dealers a tiny fraction of what they make? They won't miss it."

"They won't miss it," Lois repeats.

"And I know you can do it. I trust you to do it. Only you. You're my Annie Oakley."

Lois feels herself nodding, wanting to be the person who Greer sees. *Marriage is the only way for a woman to get any freedom,* her mother had said. But this was another way, and she'd never have to see her father or Lawrence again. And Greer is right, Lois has taken from the casino before and felt nothing. Only a tremble of pride, of vindication. That wasn't so different from what Greer is proposing. It's the same, actually, just on a different scale.

"I think," Lois begins, "I may know where Rita's key is."

"Well," Greer says, a new light in her eyes. "Look at you."

Thirty-Five

．．．．．．．．．．．．

From her room, Lois sees Dorothy get into Charlie's truck. She is wearing a skirt suit and white gloves, a circle hat pinned to her red curls. The wind rips across the lawn. Desert sand lifts in a clean wave, each speck visible in the morning sun. Crowns of heads appear below Lois, the other girls stepping out from the porch shade. She counts. Only she and Greer aren't there. Carol and Patty run toward the swing. Charlie and Bailey hoist Dorothy's trunks onto the truck bed, placing them atop a folded blanket.

Lois woke hungry. She went downstairs before everyone was awake and asked Anna for a piece of toast with a runny egg. Anna clucked her tongue but did as she asked, pouring Lois a cup of coffee from her own pot, already cold. She drank it in her bed and ate the toast while looking out her window, watching the world take shape under the rising sun. When she began to hear footsteps, the motions of Dorothy leaving and everyone drawn to the stairwell, she felt the pull to join. Everyone would expect her to say goodbye. But then she realized it didn't matter. Dorothy hadn't spoken to her in a week. She had told Lois nothing of Leroy, of the Jaguar or swimming pool. Each girl would leave, new ones would arrive, and Lois didn't owe them anything.

Below her window, the new guest lingers off to the side, holding the ends of her thin silk scarf up to her nose and lips to stop the grit from getting in. Lois shakes her head. She briefly wishes she was down there just so she could stand beside her, sticking out her tongue and letting the desert sand coat her mouth.

The engine starts with a dull roar and Mary Elizabeth sneezes into a handkerchief. June wipes her tears away with the back of her wrist, and Dorothy rolls down the car window, smiling and waving goodbye like a new bride.

Mr. Tarleton has a new secretary, a girl with cheeks so full Lois imagines she's hiding cotton balls next to her rows of teeth. Lois takes a seat in the waiting room, crossing her legs. It's her last appointment before the courthouse. A marble of dirt is clumped to the bottom of her boot, and she flicks it off, wiping her fingers clean on the chair's leather. *No one ever puts on a dress during the day unless they're seeing their lawyer,* June had told her at breakfast nearly six weeks before. She looks down at her jeans and loose linen shirt, realizing she hadn't thought for a moment that she should wear anything else.

The door opens and Mr. Tarleton emerges, wiping his forehead with a handkerchief.

"Miss Gorski," he says. "The time has come."

As usual, he talks for too long. He complains about the heat, how hot his car seat is in the morning, and how busy he is, as girls just can't seem to stay married these days, and how sometimes it makes him miss the war. Lois watches his lips move, thinking of how she and Greer will go to the casino tonight, the secret of what they're doing like a toffee on her tongue, the sugar flaming her blood.

". . . and then she said it was a jackrabbit, not a dog," Mr. Tarleton says, and looks at Lois expectantly.

"Ah," she says, raising her eyebrows.

"Yes, well, anyways, a very funny girl. Should we get to the paperwork?"

There are pages and pages of it, block text on white. Nothing has changed since the last time she came. There will be no alimony, the house will be Lawrence's, as it was always in his name. She will have her jewelry and some wedding gifts, glassware and the china, the pattern of which she hated the second she unwrapped it, tree branches and cool blue blossoms, a color that made all food unappetizing. She'll find a way to ship her mother's books. The rest no longer matters. The rooms are like those of her childhood doll house, filled with pieces she can only imagine holding in her hand for a brief moment, to try to conjure some emotion. She and Greer will buy what they need in California. They talked about finding a building with a pool, ivory walls and pale wood furniture, philodendrons in terra-cotta planters. Greer proposed a bar cart stocked with only what they liked to drink: no sherry or port. Lois suggested a parakeet.

As she sees her name printed again and again, she thinks of how she'll have to remember to write *Gorski* in her signature. Her mother's maiden name was Ostrow. Perhaps she'll go by that, or, like Greer said, choose a new name that is only hers.

"I'll be at the courthouse with you, and it shouldn't take much time if they aren't running behind schedule. Which also means you shouldn't be late. Judges hate when you're late. And wear that red dress you came in the first day." Mr. Tarleton looks at Lois's jeans.

"I don't own a red dress."

"Well, wear *a* dress, all right?"

Lois glances at the clock hanging above his head. Bailey said to find her at the Riverside when she was ready to go back to the ranch. The other girls went out on a trail ride with Charlie.

"So, will you be moving back home with your father? Or is there some *cousin* you'll be staying with?"

He is leaning forward on his desk, his folded hands pressed against his chest. His smile is suggestive, the grin of the boys who would linger outside the drugstore, asking girls if they'd ever seen a trouser snake. She thinks of how Greer would treat him.

"No, neither."

Mr. Tarleton waits for her to say something else. "So, where will you go?"

"Is that something you need to know, as my lawyer?"

"Well, not exactly. Technically, you're supposed to say you'll stay in Nevada, so—"

"Good. So we're finished here?" Lois asks, standing.

He walks her to the front door but does not say another word, wiping fresh sweat from his brow.

At the casino that night, Greer and Lois decide how they will do it. Lois is loose with alcohol after having too much to drink during cocktail hour. In the early evening, her nerves began to fizz at the thought of going to the casino, and June's attempts at a Tom Collins were heavy with gin. She picked at her plate, lifting the stiff slice of roast with her fork and dropping it again. All she could eat were the mashed potatoes, velvety against her tongue.

In hushed tones at the bar, they decide that they will arrive as if it's a night like any other and go to Peg's table a little after eleven. One of Peg's regulars, the man in an ivory cowboy hat, will be there, but he'll leave after a couple of hands like he always does. Then, before the other regulars join and the pit bosses circle, Greer will win several hands. Everything will be doubled and then doubled, again and again. Lois will watch for anyone coming. Afterward, Greer will meet Lois in the bathroom and then Lois will slip an envelope to Peg's sister—who apparently looks like another Peg, really, and will be wearing a thin checked coat—who will be waiting in the gap between Harrah's and the club next door. Then they'll return to the ranch and leave the afternoon after Lois has gone to court.

"But wait—your divorce. Won't you have to be at the Golden Yarrow for another week?"

"Don't worry about that. I'm working something out with my lawyer," Greer says, her eyes flitting over the heads of nearby gamblers.

"But won't you need Bailey to testify? To say that you've been here for six weeks?"

"I've been talking to Peg, and she said I can pay someone to do that."

Greer turns to face the casino floor, leaning against the bar's edge. Lois wonders if Greer will think differently when they're on their own. Money won't continue to open door after door, though when Lois asked Greer what they'll do when they've spent everything they stole, if they'll find jobs, Greer just laughed. "We'll steal again," she said. This image of herself as a thief has begun to entrance Lois: how they could select marks who are groping girls' thighs or cussing at waitresses, how she could learn to unclasp Rolexes and pluck wallets from suit pockets. Acts that don't feel like crimes, but corrections to a larger imbalance.

Lois brings her tumbler to her lips. The gin tastes different tonight, floral and stale, like the smell of pressed flowers.

"Steady," Greer says. "You'll want to remember all of this."

"I know." Lois obediently sets the glass down. Greer has never commented on her drinking before.

They lap the casino. They go to the restroom to decide which stall she should wait in with an empty purse. The restroom is too full for them to talk inside. Girls lean toward the mirror, one picking mint from her teeth. At the slot machines, Greer says the number of the stall several times, telling Lois to count outward from the restroom's door.

"You've got it?"

"Yes, I do. I'll be in the third stall. You'll be in the fourth from the door."

"All right, and then what will you do?"

"I'll go to the alley on the right as I leave. Peg's sister will be wearing a plaid coat."

Greer looks at her, as if she's considering whether or not to say something, but then shakes her head. They ascend to Peg's floor, bantering over what they'll name their parakeet. "Hedy," Lois proposes. "Screech," Greer counters. Looking out over the carpet, they find Bailey at Peg's table, a rare sight. Nerves flutter in Lois's chest.

"Do we think—" Lois begins.

"I think we need fresh drinks." Greer snaps her fingers at an approaching waitress.

At the bar's end, Greer tells her she is to do her best not to be noticed that evening. She should attract no attention. It reminds Lois of a game she played with her favorite stuffed animal, a bear made from oilcloth. The game was for no one to see them as they moved throughout the house. She would tiptoe past doorways and shuffle behind curtain ruffles, the bear's neck tight in the crook of her arm. The fear of being seen became so great that her body quaked, though it was so long before anyone came looking, and how much greater the fear was that no one would find her, gratitude spilling out at the sound of Ela's steps on the stairwell, Lois's small body bursting for the door of the closet she was hiding in to swing open.

"And remember, if anyone stops to ask you anything, just don't talk too much. You can always tell someone's lying when they talk too much, or when they won't look you in the eye," Greer says.

Lois opens her lids wide, dipping her head to try to catch Greer's eye. She wants to make her laugh, but Greer is distracted. Bailey snags her attention like a thorn.

Thirty-Six

· · · · · · · · · ·

The next afternoon, another guest arrives. Lois is dressed for the pool and it feels odd greeting her in nothing but a bathing suit and a linen shirt. She's mousy-haired and anemic-looking, as if she's never eaten a steak, and has just taken a plane from Cleveland. Bailey escorts her to her room, leaving Mary Elizabeth and Lois alone with Rita. For a moment, Lois thinks Mary Elizabeth wants to speak with her—the girl takes a breath in preparation, a finger tracing a shape on her covered forearm—but then Rita interjects.

"And just a few more days for you two."

"I know, I can't believe it," Mary Elizabeth says. "It feels like we just arrived, and the thought of—" The words catch in her throat. She grips the bridge of her nose and then excuses herself, scuttling up the stairs.

"Poor girl. Sometimes people get so attached to the ranch, it feels like a new home. A better home, in so many ways, than any they've known." Rita's eyes rest on the stairwell.

"I'm sure that's true." Lois shifts on her feet. She doesn't like being alone with Rita. It's impossible not to feel the warm coals of anger from their last conversation, and even polite chatter feels like a betrayal of Greer.

"But you're ready to leave," Rita says, turning to Lois.

"Well, we all have to at some point. Even Carol and Patty." She had meant this as a joke, but Rita doesn't smile. A sadness softens her features, this time unmistakable.

"Of course, even Carol and Patty. I just wish you'd gotten more out of your stay."

Behind her, Lois hears a door open. The brush of bare feet on the hallway floor. Rita looks beyond Lois and her expression cools.

"And you've barely gone out on the trails," Rita continues, the pitch of her voice changing so that she sounds like an exaggerated version of herself.

"There's so much of Nevada to see, and on horseback is really the only way to see it."

Greer appears in the doorway. At first Lois thinks her hair is tucked into the collar of her shirt, but then she realizes she's cut it to just below her chin. Rita smiles at her entrance, a lift of the mouth that does not reach her eyes.

"What a striking haircut."

"Thank you," Greer says.

"Well, don't let me get in your way." Rita extends her arm to the hallway. "Enjoy the pool."

By the water, Lois watches Greer stretch along the deck chair. Though at first the cut seemed fine, the longer Lois stares she finds uneven angles, the lines of unsteady scissors. It makes Greer look older. Lois tries to imagine her with no hair at all, wearing none of her beautiful clothes, her face marbled with a fresh bruise. She thinks of the women who sit on wooden crates outside Marshall Field's with dirty teeth, the soles of their shoes untacking. An air of menace about them.

"Your hair," Lois says.

"What?" Greer brings a hand to the blunted tips. "Oh yes. I got bored, thought I'd try something new."

"Did you cut it yourself?"

"Is it that obvious?" Greer laughs.

"No, I—well. There *is* a bit at the back that's longer."

"Really? I tried to hold a mirror up, but it was hard to do that and cut at the same time. Do you have scissors?"

"Sewing scissors. I'm not sure—"

"They should work fine."

When Lois returns, Greer tells her she can cut her hair on the deck chair. She insists Rita won't mind, though Lois has no doubt that she will. She asks Greer to turn her head so she can find the shortest point and then work from there. Eventually she realizes it would be easier if the hair were wet, and Greer dunks her head in the pool water, the strands darkening to ash. She hangs Lois's towel around her shoulders, and Lois wonders how it smells. She makes the strands taut, mimicking what she's seen in the mirror at salons. Shiny mites of hair fall to the concrete.

"It's so much shorter," Lois says. "Did you cut this because—"

"No, lord, don't be so dramatic. You've seen too many films. It's just getting so hot, and it felt like this huge weight I could just snip off."

Lois imagines Florence finding a ropy nest of Greer's hair in the wastebasket. The thought repulses her, Greer's hair as much a part of her as an ear or finger.

"But speaking of, do you remember everything?" Greer asks, and Lois drops her hand, the scissor blades yawning open. She turns to check if anyone's in the sunroom, but all she sees through the screen are the dark forms of furniture.

"Yes. I mean, everything important."

"Well, we'll go again tomorrow, so I can talk to Peg for a bit, and then I'll come to your room the day after so we can go over everything one last time."

"All right. Should I talk to Peg as well?"

"No, you don't need to."

Lois nods. She thinks of Greer and Peg watching her approach the other evening, when Greer said all they were discussing was blackjack. How their faces shifted.

"And you know, you can't drink as much as you have been. I know you drink when you're nervous and fluttery, but it's childish."

"Childish," Lois repeats.

"You end up talking far too much. Droning on and on. And if you do that the night of, you'll risk everything, and then where will I be."

Greer says this flatly, barely moving her body, the reprimand—the cut of the *I* rather than *we*—pointed and stinging. Lawrence's phantom pinch twinges Lois's thigh, a feeling she'd forgotten, Greer always pushing her to speak more, to talk louder. A dragonfly hovers over the pool. The water is still, and she thinks of the story of the girl vomiting into it.

"I'm sorry. You know I wouldn't do anything to—to ruin this."

Greer says nothing, and Lois remembers the rodeo, how Greer left Dorothy wounded in the stands. She never spoke to her again. She hasn't said another word to Mary Elizabeth or June either, even after all their hours together. But then Lois had done the same to Dorothy. She hadn't even said goodbye. Her palms are suddenly moist, the threat of Greer's cruelty like the cold metal of the scissors against her own neck. She tries to focus on the line of Greer's hair.

When she finishes, she stands in front of Greer to see if both sides are even. The cleanness of the cut calms her. Greer is her beautiful self again, and she feels absurd for thinking of the women on State Street. The dragonfly lands on the concrete by her feet, its wings shimmering.

"How do I look?"

"Perfect."

"Good. Will you read for a bit?" Greer smiles, and Lois thinks of the weight of what they are planning. How it must be throwing Greer off balance, so that she is not fully herself.

"Of course."

She takes a seat and opens the book, its pages stark white in the sun.

Thirty-Seven

. . . .

The next morning, Lois asks Mary Elizabeth if she can join her on the trail. Rita's words echo in her head, and she wants to see the desert up close one last time. She had trouble sleeping. Whenever she woke the sheets were wrapped around her body, the lizard in its same place by the window ledge, static as a crack in the plaster. Mary Elizabeth agrees without a moment's hesitation, and Lois blisters with guilt at how quickly she abandoned her. She can't stomach much more than toast.

"You're sure you don't want anything else? It's a long trail ride," Bailey says.

"They'll be back in time for lunch," Rita says. "I feel like there was a time when all of you were eating like wolves. Sometimes the body needs lighter fare. And I'm glad you're finally going out on another trail ride, Lois."

"Making the most of my time here," Lois says.

"Good," Rita says after a moment's hesitation, and then turns to the new guest from New York, complimenting this morning's stiff chartreuse suit.

Charlie takes them on a route out toward Washoe Lake. Lois is still uneasy with him, conscious of his hands as he helps her onto her horse. They are joined by one of the new guests, the younger one, who came to the stables dressed for the English countryside, with jodhpurs and tall polished boots. On the trail, she and Mary Elizabeth lapse into an easy conversation about horseback riding, dotted with the names of breeds and competitions that make Lois feel as if they're speaking another language. The desert stretches before them, and as the ranch begins to recede in the distance, Lois notices that everything has become drier. The patches of grass have stiffened, the blades a pale gray. Sweeps of dirt as white as chalk coat the ground.

After nearly an hour, the lake still appears as if it's miles away, a thumbprint of blue beneath a wave of mountains. Charlie points out the distant frame of the Washoe Pines ranch house. *I told Greer they were trouble,* Bailey had said, and Lois wonders how Greer could have known that Lois would be able to protect herself from the ranch hand. That he wouldn't pin her down, press a blade to her skin. They stop to take a drink of water, and Lois worries they haven't brought enough in their canteens. The desert appears dead in a way it hasn't before. In the baked heat, the air feels difficult to breathe.

Mary Elizabeth and the new guest ask Lois about Chicago summers. She struggles to answer them, saying something about how long the lake water stays cold, the bite of it, and when she looks up, she finds Charlie watching her.

"We should turn back now, before the sun gets too fierce," Charlie says.

"So soon?" the new guest asks. "We haven't even made it to the lake."

"I think we should." Charlie gathers his reins in his hands. "At this time of the year, it's not good to be out for too long."

Back in the stables, Lois realizes she's sweated through her shirt, the white darkening at her belly. When Charlie helps her off the horse, she tries to thank him in a way that he'll understand is for more than just the dismount.

"Not a problem," he says, his cheeks briefly reddening before he leads the horse by its bridle, disappearing into the stall.

They don't read that day. Lois doesn't want to and Greer does not ask. The book remains on the wrought-iron side table, the ribbon marking their place sticking out like the tongue of a snake. At a certain point, Lois wonders if Greer has fallen asleep, but there are small movements: a scratch of her upper lip, a rolling of her ankle.

Lois gets in the pool. At first she laps back and forth, beating her arms through the water, but she tires easily. She floats in the deep end, watching as Greer crosses her legs. When she takes a big inhalation, she curls her body so that she sinks to the pool's stippled bottom, opening her eyes to the cool blue. She remembers the attention Greer paid her that first afternoon and wonders how long it would take for her to begin to worry, to peer over the ledge to see if Lois is all right and not truly willing herself to drown. Her fingers brush against the concrete, her lungs tightening. She slowly releases her breath. The sky stretches above her, uninterrupted by even a passing bird. Her diaphragm begins to spasm. Strands of hair sway above her head.

Greer does not appear. Lois can't see even her ankle, only black spots singeing the blue. *He looked a lot worse than I do,* Greer had said, and Lois sees her own body splayed out on the concrete, her belly swollen and her skin the color of a boy's nursery. Greer standing over her, her eyes darkened to that same black, oily sheen as when she'd cracked the vase against the skull of Mary Elizabeth's husband. Lois closes her eyes and kicks herself upward to the air.

Thirty-Eight

· · · · · · · · · · ·

When they arrive for Greer's final conversation with Peg, the casino feels different, overfull. It's too loud, the bright pings of the slot machines jolting Lois's body, voices and laughter an overwhelming din. Countless men and women swarm the bar and clot the doors to the entrance and restrooms. This is what Lois loved about the casino, but now in every person she sees someone who could be watching them. Someone who could notice the different way Peg will shuffle the cards; someone who could wonder at her and Greer arriving together and then splitting in a way they never had before.

June and the new guests decided to join them that evening—the younger one had never been to a casino and asked to come along, oblivious to everything that had come before. Though Lois had panicked, Greer's coldness made it obvious they wouldn't be staying together. They cleaved apart at the front door.

"It's busy tonight," Lois says.

"Seems the same to me," Greer says.

They pass the time by sliding coins into slots. Bailey chaperones the others at the bar, and Lois watches Harry join them. From a distance, she's able to see how much more relaxed June is beside him, her eyes softer, their hands effortlessly clasped. Perhaps Greer was wrong, and he makes June feel like the light, blithe girl she never got to be. At breakfast, she talked of a small ceremony in Santa Barbara, a lunch of oysters and crab legs.

Lois takes another coin from her cup and tips it into the slot. Two older women in floor-length evening dresses park at neighboring machines, pulling the levers so slowly that around them the casino seems to speed up, whirring like an animatronic band Lois once saw at a lounge in Chicago, painted men jerkily hitting drums and playing the trombone.

"What do you think about getting a cat?" Greer asks. "A California cat."

"What about Screech?"

"They'll become friends." Greer smiles at her, and the thrum in Lois's chest quiets.

"As long as he stays in his cage, I suppose."

"Well, yes, until we know we can trust the cat."

"All right, you'll let me know when that day comes. I don't need Screech's final screech on my conscience." Lois laughs. "Do you want to go listen to the band for a bit at the Mapes?"

"No, I'll need to leave soon," Greer says, pulling the lever.

Lois nods, her anxiety returning. Behind them, a spike of applause makes her jump. A man has just won at roulette. He kisses a woman on the neck, his mouth opening in a way that makes Lois think he's going to bite her soft, creamy skin.

After eleven, they go upstairs to find Peg alone, mechanically shuffling a deck of cards. Though they say nothing of it, there's a palpable relief at Bailey not being there. Greer chats about San Francisco neighborhoods, but Lois becomes distracted, watching men hunch over the edge of roulette tables, gnawing at their knuckles as the ball drones. Girls sway behind them, impatiently patting them on the shoulder and telling them it's time to go home. A man loops his tie around a waitress's neck. A girl's necklace breaks, cheap bronze beads scattering across the carpet. All of it makes Lois's skin itch, scenes she can't follow.

Greer tells Lois to go to the bar to wait, and for once Lois is relieved to be alone. She orders a glass of water, though she'd like nothing more than gin. Next to her, two overly made-up girls paw at the counter, trying to get the bartender to drink with them.

Lois takes a sip of water to wet her throat. She watches Peg's painted mouth, how small it remains even when she speaks. She always knew Peg held some fascination for Greer—one of the first female dealers, and how indifferent she seems to everyone, even someone like Greer, who's never ignored. Watching them now, Lois wonders why she can't be at the table. If there's something they don't want her to know.

She raises her hand. The bartender is quick to bring her a gin and tonic. She watches him uncork the green bottle and press the lime, calmed by his graceful movements. She's in the kitchen again, watching Ela make a pot of tea.

When Greer approaches the bar she is smiling, and Lois decides to ignore the worry gathering at her edges. Everything hinges on this theft, and she trusts Greer, just as Greer trusts her. Greer orders a whiskey on the rocks, and a man a few seats down signals for her tab. He is handsome in the way Lois remembers some of the fathers at school being handsome, black threads of arm hair peeking out from his shirt cuffs, his muscles like thick fillets of meat. A silk tie is loosened at his neck. Greer looks at him and then quickly turns away.

"Everything all right?" Lois asks.

"What do you mean?"

"With Peg, is everything all right?"

"Oh, of course. We'll talk about it tomorrow night, but everything's as we planned."

The bartender places the whiskey in front of Greer and she looks at it as if she's searching for something in the tumbler—a gnat thumbed against the ice, a sliver of glass.

"You said on the rocks, right?" the bartender asks.

"Yes, I did."

She blinks away whatever was amiss, lifting the glass and draining it like a shot. Rolling her shoulders back, she looks at Lois, her smile returning.

"Everything's all right," she repeats, patting Lois on the knee. Over her shoulder, Lois sees Bailey moving toward them, the other girls trailing behind her. The new guest stumbles like she's had too much to drink.

"We need to cut out," Bailey says.

"To the Golden Yarrow!" the new guest yells, throwing her hands in the air.

"Now," she says, and Greer and Lois nod, rising from their seats.

Lois notices that the man who bought Greer's whiskey has twisted toward them on his stool—undoubtedly annoyed he's already lost his chance to talk to her. His elbow rests on the bar, his mouth slightly open, like he's trying to remember something. As they begin to depart, he stands.

"Hey, I *do* know you," he says, pointing his finger at Greer's back.

The others turn to him, though Greer keeps walking as if she hadn't heard a word. Bailey looks to Lois, but she just shakes her head, unable to offer any explanation, and soon they're all distracted by the new guest taking off her shoes. She tells everyone she wants to feel the meadow grass between her toes.

As they descend the staircase, Lois looks over her shoulder. The man is still standing where they left him, his brow creased, watching them leave.

At the house, the new guest falls into one of the porch's columns. Maude, Lois learned in the car, when Bailey kept asking whether or not she was going to vomit on the leather seats. They left her standing alone as Bailey turned the lock in the front door, and then there was a thud, a sound that Lois associates only with children in a tantrum, small bodies flinging themselves across wooden floors.

They help her up, and Lois is surprised by the weight of her at barely over five feet. She struggles to lift her even with Bailey's help.

"I need . . . I need to call my husband," Maude says, brushing her hair away from her face.

"No, you don't," Bailey says, throwing one of Maude's arms over her shoulders. Lois takes the other, so that she's propped up between them.

"I forgot to tell him how much to pay the gardener, and he comes tomorrow, he comes on Wednesdays."

"Tomorrow's Thursday," Greer says. "Or, well, today's Thursday."

At this, Maude begins to cry. Lois is surprised by the ferocity of it, her body spasming with each sob. June takes a handkerchief out of her clutch to wipe Maude's cheeks and chin.

"I'm going to bed," Greer says.

"Of course you are," Bailey mutters under her breath.

The words surprise Lois, as Bailey never criticizes the girls like Rita sometimes does, only advises or encourages, but Greer does not hear her. She disappears down the hallway without even a look for Lois.

They lift Maude up the stairs to her room, a herculean effort that for the first time makes Lois conscious of the number of stairs. It's three doors down from Lois's and about the same size, the first room she sees inside that is not hers or Greer's. Clothes are strewn across the armchair, and on the dresser rests an open box of Junior Mints and tissues blotted with lipstick. The minutiae of Maude's life, not meant to be seen. As they lower her onto the bed, Lois wonders if they would have become friends if Maude had arrived weeks before. Or if she and the other girls would have been even closer if Lois had seen their rooms in this way, with the same unwashed windows and marigolds, this tender detritus of curling magazines and loose powder. Paths at the ranch cracking open to her like different branches of a tree.

Maude appears to already be asleep, and Lois lifts her head, tucking a pillow beneath her hair. Without the weight of her, Lois suddenly feels very alone, and she tries to think of another reason to touch her. The older new guest stands off to the side as Bailey slips off Maude's shoes and lays them on the floor. June fills a glass of water in the bathroom sink and places it by the bed. They close the door quietly behind them, and when it clicks shut, they say nothing, nodding to one another in the darkness before retreating to their separate rooms.

Thirty-Nine

· · · · · · · · · · · ·

T he day before the theft, Lois decides to go to the movies. When Bailey asks, she's vague about her plans, saying she has to run errands. Only when she's in the car does she realize she didn't tell Greer not to expect her by the pool.

"Your appointment at the courthouse is in just a few days, isn't it?" Bailey asks.

"Oh yes," Lois says.

"How are you feeling? Some girls get anxious, but there's nothing to be anxious about. I just felt enormous relief afterward, and it'll be over in a blink."

"I don't feel anxious."

"Good." Bailey looks over at her, as if to assess whether she's lying. "Well, just be sure to wear a dress. Jeans aren't appropriate for the courthouse, even in Reno. And you'll be leaving the day after? I'll be the one to drive you to the train station."

"I'm leaving that same day, actually. You can drop me at the station after the courthouse."

"Oh, all right. Rita said—well, she must have gotten the wrong time from your father."

"She must have." Lois looks out the window.

There is a movie theater several blocks from Harrah's called the Granada. They've passed it every time they've driven to town. In the daylight the neon is off, STRANGERS ON A TRAIN spelled out beneath it in large black letters. The man behind the glass is sweating so much that Lois has to wipe her hands on her skirt when she takes the paper stub. The change rattles in her purse.

The ambient bubbling of the popcorn machine calms her. A reminder that all movie theaters are the same. The film is not starting for another hour, but when she asks, they let her sit in the empty theater. She buys popcorn and eats all of it within minutes, her tongue stinging with salt.

Though she told herself she was just going to get a refill, at the concession stand the boxes of candy pop beneath the glass. It's been weeks since she's eaten sugar. Greer never told her not to, Lois had just followed her lead, so she asks for M&M's and Junior Mints, brushing past the thin-necked teenager's "Both?"

Back in her seat, she begins consuming the M&M's piece by piece and then starts to pour them into her hand, the candy shells giving her palms an oily sheen that she licks off, wiping her hand on the seat cushion. She thinks of the man from the casino last night, how he said he knew Greer. A mistake, undoubtedly, or just a desperate attempt to talk to her. Lois opens the Junior Mints. It feels good to be hungry. To satisfy that hunger with something as empty as candy.

When she's finished, she gingerly places the boxes beneath her seat. Sugar rushes through her blood, tightening her heartbeat.

The movie theater is the only place she ever saw her mother cry, as if the darkness gave her permission. It frightened Lois at first, seeing rivulets of mascara weep down her mother's face, and how even after she cleaned herself up in the restroom, her skin would have the dull rub of gray. Her unhappiness finally made visible. But then Lois began to tell herself that her mother was not a lonely, ill woman, she was just upset by noble Myra walking in front of a truck at the end of *Waterloo Bridge*. And so Lois allowed herself to cry as well. To laugh louder than she would at home or school. It was a release and also a returning to her body, a feeling similar to when she'd suddenly remember why she'd gone to another room after hovering on the threshold for several moments, her life outside of the theater muddy and blank. As a child, she imagined this would be different when she was older. Her life would not be her mother's. It would become its own film, and she'd no longer need an escape.

At the Granada, all she feels is the sugar. She stays still, counting every beat in her chest until other moviegoers step into the cool dark and find their seats.

When she returns to the ranch, Florence stops her on her way up the stairs. She has a phone call. Lois pads to Rita's office to find the receiver facedown on the side table. It's undoubtedly Mr. Tarleton's secretary. He said she'd call to remind Lois of the time she'd need to be in court, as if she couldn't manage to remember on her own.

"Hello?" she says.

"*Hello?* Do you always sound so rude when you pick up the telephone?"

Lois exhales. It's Ela. Her voice floods Lois like a familiar scent—the sweet, stained velvet of her mother's jewelry box, the vegetal tea Ela would simmer on the stove—and Lois has the sudden urge to weep.

"Ela, I—"

"I'm calling because I was cleaning your sheets yesterday to get your room ready, and your father tells me you're not coming home."

"How does he know that?"

"Mr. Tarleton told him, and he ordered me to call you. Where do you think you are going to?"

Ela is angry, and Lois steels herself, wrapping the phone cord tightly around her thumb.

"I'm going to California. There's another girl here who I'm going to go with. I wrote you about her, remember? We'll find an apartment out there. I'm so sorry I didn't tell you."

"To California? Why would you go to California? You know no one in California."

"That's a little bit of the appeal."

"To be a young girl alone in a strange city? You know, he won't actually make you leave in six months. I will speak to him."

"I'll send you the address when I have it," Lois continues, pretending not to have heard her. "We can write. You could even visit. We could go to the beach and see the ocean."

"You don't sound like yourself," Ela says.

"What do you mean?"

"You sound . . . *wyniosły*."

"I don't know what that means, Ela."

"That's not my fault."

Lois rolls her incisor over her lip. She knows Ela is upset with her for not writing, for having to learn all of this from Lois's father, but she also wonders if Ela can sense how she's changing—if she knows what Lois is planning to do tomorrow evening, what she's already done. If she intuits some danger. At the edge of Lois's vision, Rita's safe looms like a shadow. Greer said she'll open it tonight when everyone is in their beds.

"How's my father?" Lois asks.

"Same as ever. Always at the plant, so no one is ever home. And he barely eats anymore. I keep throwing away pots of stew. I can't eat them all by myself. Raccoons keep tearing through the trash. It's a waste."

"You just need to cook less."

"I don't know how to cook less."

"Well, that's unfortunate."

"Yes, well. We've all been through worse misfortune. You know that."

A strange homesickness rolls through her. She sees the house's rooms: the dark, cluttered parlor with the Persian rug her mother loved, asking guests to take off their shoes before they walked across its thick pile. The upstairs hallway tiled with photographs of stoic relatives she never met. Her parents' bedroom, with its heavy curtains so her mother could sleep at all hours of the day, and her own bedroom, so much of which was still the same: the notebooks and dollhouse, the movie posters and tins of face paint. When she married, she'd left so much behind, as if by doing so the lonely child who lived there would be left behind as well.

She dries her nose, dampening the cuff of her linen shirt.

"You know, if you ever want to leave, Ela, just look in the cow pitcher," Lois says.

"You think I don't know about that?" Ela snaps.

Both ends of the line are quiet. Lois feels the distance between them, hundreds of miles of telephone wire stretching across plains and rivers, over gabled house roofs and fields of uncut grass. There is no one to go back to but Ela, and Lois is not sure when she will see her again.

"Well, I have to get going," Ela says.

"I should too, I suppose. I'll call when I have my new phone number, though don't give it to my father."

"I won't. *Uważaj na siebie*," Ela says. The same phrase she'd say every morning when Lois would open the front door, wiping her hands on her apron.

"I will."

n her room, Lois slips off both of her wedding rings. They leave a band of white above her knuckle, the same color as every part of her that hasn't seen the sun. She waves her hand up and down to see if it feels lighter, but there is no real difference. She knew she wouldn't wear them for much longer, but a small voice inside her had said she could slip them on when she wanted to be left alone at a bar or treated well at a department store, tapping the gold against a glass counter. That Lawrence's wife would still be a role she could play.

When she first wore the engagement ring, she wished she could show her mother. Ela had no patience for it. *Very . . . large,* she said as she dried a glass. *Your hands are too small for it.*

Lois does not have a box for them, so she drops the rings into the toe of a stocking, knotting the nylon and stowing it toward the back of her drawer. Seeing the velvet box, she takes out her mother's necklace, loosening the clasp. The heavy lattice of black opals is cold against her breastbone.

In the mirror, the necklace doesn't look right. Lois doesn't have her mother's long neck, and when she unbuttons her shirt the black draws attention to several dark freckles on her chest. She twists open a tube of lipstick and paints her lips burgundy, smudging two dots on her cheeks and rubbing them outward to give her face more color. A lesson learned from her drama teacher, that lipstick stains longer than blush. Opening her closet, she takes out a black velvet dress trimmed with ivory silk and slips it over her head. Still, the necklace looks inelegant. A piece of costume jewelry on a child.

She looks at her empty purse, which lies flat on her dresser. She sees herself perched on the lip of a toilet, the bag hung between her legs, wearing a cocktail dress pulled from a headless mannequin or a pale linen shirt she hadn't chosen, her jeans folded in the way Greer had told her to, the hems flipped up so the bones of her ankles show. She sees herself at the cashier being handed an envelope of money that's not her own.

That first afternoon by the pool, she hadn't told Greer the entirety of the day she'd nearly drowned. It was the summer after her mother died, and she had gone to the beach alone. Lois had not visited the lake since her death. It was late in the day and the other beachgoers were shaking sand from the beach blankets, ready to go home, but Lois wanted to go out one last time, remembering how she'd show off for her mother in the water as a child, fiercely paddling toward an invisible shore. She swam out farther and farther until there were no swimmers in sight, only lines of water. The lake below her was like an open mouth, a cold, dark chasm, and then suddenly there were blooms of sand and a rush of current pulling her toward the horizon line, and a new fear unlike any she'd known took hold. Behind her, she could hear hoarse cries from the beach, and then a woman's head rose from the water like a seal's, and Lois was in the crook of her arm, her legs slackening as they swam parallel to and then toward the shore.

After the woman spilled her onto the sand, she collapsed onto her knees and dry-retched, her mouth open so that Lois could see her missing teeth. Someone wrapped Lois in a towel, rubbing her thighs and belly until she began to warm, her body coming back to her as if pulled from sleep, and she knew then she would never swim that far again; that the brave, fearless version of herself would never make it back to the shore. In her room at the ranch, Lois is not sure if she has found that girl. Or if she is still flailing in the frigid waters of the lake, the waves crashing over her head.

Cocktail hour is almost beginning. She takes off the dress and goes to the bathroom, scrubbing her face until her skin is pink.

Forty

· · · · ·

That night, there is a gentle rapping on her door. Lois has been waiting for Greer to arrive for over an hour. They're supposed to go over everything one last time. Greer hadn't come to cocktail hour or dinner and Lois began to feel the low, electric hum of panic. Rita asked after her, and when Bailey went to see if Greer would join them, she said that no one answered her knocks. The room's lights were off, a band of black beneath the door.

"I wasn't sure if you were still coming," Lois says.

Before she closes the door behind them, Lois peers into the hallway, but the house is quiet. The girls are out at the Highlands with Bailey. Greer looks like she hasn't slept, her hair unwashed. When she sits in the armchair, Lois notices that she's bitten her ring finger so severely that it's bled onto her thumb, brown blood caked at both cuticles.

"Why wouldn't I come?" Greer asks.

"You weren't at dinner," Lois says, taking a seat on her bed.

"You weren't at the pool."

"I had a last-minute appointment with my lawyer."

"Ah."

Greer is wearing the same sweater she wore that first night she joined everyone at dinner, the front tucked into her trousers in a way that Lois has spent hours trying to mimic, though now the wool is netted with wrinkles. Her face is still but stretched, a tic tightening her mouth as she leans toward Lois, her hands clasped between her knees.

"So, do you remember exactly what you need to do?" Greer asks.

"Yes."

"Tell me."

Greer picks at her thumb's rim of dried blood. She doesn't meet Lois's eyes, and Lois feels desperate for her to.

"Is everything all right?" Lois asks.

"Of course it is, I'm just tired. Now, tell me."

"Well, first, I'll keep watch at the bar when you go to the table. If one of the pit bosses approaches early, I'll—I'll alert you by shattering my glass on the floor."

Lois sees the men in their expensive suits shaking hands with whoever is hemorrhaging chips onto the tables, gold rings weighting their fingers. One evening, they ejected a man with a flick of their wrists, and he'd yelled as security pulled him by the collar of his jacket, disappearing through an unmarked door.

"And . . . ?"

"I don't think I can do this."

Greer's head snaps up. "What do you mean? This was your idea."

"But I've never done anything like this before. I've lied, but this—"

"And you think I have?" Greer pulls back in her chair.

"No, I'm not saying that. But I've been thinking—what if we didn't do any of it?" The idea seizes her, as if she's discovered a trapdoor. "I'll beg my father for more money, and I know you don't want to, but you can use your trust fund, just for a little bit, and then we can get work somewhere—"

"No, no." Greer shakes her head. "We both know this is the only way."

"I know I thought that before, but maybe it's not, and we can still start—"

"Why can't you just do this for me?"

Greer's desperation comes swiftly. Her pupils swell, the cut on her finger newly open, and Lois is surprised by this aching need, the suddenness of the blood.

"I would do anything for you, you know that." Lois kneels in front of her on the floor.

"You won't, though. You're saying you won't. After all the other girls disappointed me, after everything I told you."

"Greer, I—"

"I trusted you. I thought you understood."

"I'm sorry, I'm sorry, I do understand, it's just—is it your husband? Are you worried about him finding you if you use the trust, or—"

Greer begins to knead the bones of her temple, and Lois knows she's once again said the wrong thing, that something is slipping away from her.

A coyote croons in the distance. Greer takes a deep breath in through her nose and lifts her head.

"Can I have a glass of water?"

Lois goes to the bathroom to fill her cup. Her hands tremor as she turns on the faucet, the water briefly running a noxious, rusted orange.

Looking in the mirror, she sees Greer's face instead of her own—how the bruise had inked it like a map: rivers of broken blood vessels, swollen mountains of purple and green. She sees Greer urging her onto the counter to sing with the other girls, mouthing, *Sometimes I have a great notion, to jump in the river and drown,* as everyone laughed. Greer handing her the rifle in the bed of Charlie's truck. Greer leaning over the counter to palm two chips and stash them in Lois's purse. She turns off the faucet and presses her forehead against the glass, her own familiar features emerging, her dull skin marked by nothing more than the ghost of a blemish, and she remembers the way Greer had looked at her when she emerged from the pool. As if she were also worth studying, her face its own country, and how afterward, everything had changed.

"All right, all right," she whispers to the mirror, her breath fogging the glass.

When she returns, Greer is standing by her dresser. There is a new sense of calm about her, and Lois feels a sweep of relief.

"I'm sorry. I'll do it. I don't know what I was thinking," Lois says.

"Are you sure?" Greer takes the glass from Lois's hand.

"Yes. You're right, it's the only way."

Greer takes a sip of water, her eyes alighting on the lipsticks and bobby pins scattered across the glossed wood. She picks up *The Age of Innocence* and turns it over as if she'd never really looked at it before.

"We never finished the book," Greer says.

"Well, we can finish it in San Francisco."

"I don't know, I think we need a new book." Greer sets it back down. "New state, new city, new book."

"All right."

"How does it end, though? Does May push Ellen in front of a train?"

Lois laughs, though the rattle is dry in her throat. "Ellen goes to New York for some reason, to care for her grandmother, if I'm remembering right. And then at some point she and Archer agree to be together, but then abruptly she leaves. For somewhere in Europe, I think, and we learn later that it's because she found out May is pregnant. And so, then they just have separate lives."

"That's how it ends? She just up and disappears?"

"Well, there's a final scene where, years and years later, Archer is about to visit Ellen, but then he decides not to. That he just wants the memory of what they had."

"Kind of a boring book."

"I think you're right, now that I'm describing it. Probably why it hasn't been made into a movie."

"No houses burning down."

"No fires whatsoever."

Greer finishes her water and hands Lois the empty glass. They say good night and Lois hovers by the open door, listening to the distance soften and swallow the creak of Greer's feet, knowing that soon she'll slip into Rita's study. At the final footstep, a thought throbs in Lois's head. Guilt heavy as a stone. When pressed to tell Greer how she'd spent her day, she lied.

It's impossible to sleep. At first Lois watches the clock, finding comfort in the hours she has left until morning: eight, seven, six. She pictures the casino, not as the glittering neon palace it was when she first walked through its doors a month before, but as a series of rooms with tired people and tired carpets, only pulsing to life at the possibility of money, or sex, or some other release. She goes to her closet to choose what she'll wear the next day, hooking a green dress she's never worn over the door. At the casino, jeans would be too noticeable, and it feels right to wear something with no history, no lingering ghost of the person she was before.

At 2:12 the car sweeps onto the gravel, though the girls don't speak, the only sounds the car doors closing and the front door opening. There are just a few of them left from that first day, less than the hours until morning, and she finds herself desperately missing Dorothy and Vera; wanting to hear their laughter tumbling out of the car windows, the staccato of their boots in the hallway.

She wishes she could stop unraveling everything that might go wrong: missed signals, an arrest, or, worse, a train ticket home to her father's house. The fear of each crests at her throat. It's the fear she felt at the fair's Ferris wheel when she was eight, its steel skeleton looming over the evening grass. The operator told her she'd be fine once she got in, laughing as the bar lowered over her stomach, as she felt the lift and the weightless swinging, as if she could be tipped out like sugar from a measuring cup, the fear not diminishing but building until it was its own living thing. Afterward, she ran to the row of mulberry bushes in the parking lot and vomited until she felt hollow.

Somewhere in the house a pipe groans, and Lois thinks of slipping downstairs to Greer's room for comfort, for reassurance. But she can't admit this fear to her, especially after their last conversation. It would be too much weakness, weakness she wishes she could purge from her body, just like at the fair.

To calm herself, she tries to conjure the apartment they'll have in San Francisco. The white iron of their balcony and the books stacked next to her bed. Greer filling an ice tray in the basin of the kitchen sink. But she can't seem to hold on to any of it, the rooms fading to soft shapes and blurs of color, in the same way she sometimes thinks of her mother's face and can't define her features. Instead, she sees the men from the casino, watching her as she watches Peg's table. The light streaming through the pool water. The eyes of Mary Elizabeth's husband, wolfish and bloodshot. Greer's bruise, pulsing as if it were some living thing, as alive as the fear in Lois's body, spreading to her forehead, her chin, and her cheeks.

Lois curls onto her side. At the place where two walls meet, she sees the lizard. It's oddly bent, so that its mouth touches its tail, nearly a circle. She watches, waiting for it to unfurl and skitter across the wall, but it stays still. Even as her body tires in its desperation for sleep, she does not close her eyes, refusing even to blink. Her irises strain and stiffen. A tear runs down the slope of her nose, wetting her cheek.

At some point she thinks she hears the muffled swing of a door opening below her, but then there is nothing, the sounds dissolving into the current between her ears.

Eventually she rises, throwing her sheets off her body in a sudden fury.

She steps closer to the lizard, wanting it to scurry away from her, a large, looming shape in the dark. But as she draws closer it disappears as suddenly as a candle flame being snuffed out. It doesn't make sense. She moves, letting in the light from the moon, and it reappears. Nothing but a shadow from the windowsill. An empty vase, hollow at its center, casting a circle onto the wall.

Forty-One

. . . .

On the drive to the casino, the night is colder than usual, the air stripped of its humidity. In the backseat, Lois's eyes are grainy with exhaustion—she can't have slept for more than two hours. Her mouth is so dry that at dinner she drank two carafes of water. Now she's desperate to pee, the pressure as severe as a hand on her belly. Charlie is driving—there's some friend he wants to see, in from Arizona. Only June has joined them tonight. She's talking to Bailey about some new script Harry is working on about a long-in-the-tooth gangster who tries to rob five banks in one day. How, to make the sound of gunfire, they use blanks filled with black powder or a hammer cracking against steel.

Lois hangs her head out the window, the cold air battering her awake. Greer's long arm brushes the car door, just like that first evening they went to the Highlands. There is no going back now.

At the bar, Lois tries to soothe her nerves with routine. The familiarity of the bartender's hands gripping the silver ice scoop and stirring the gin and tonic. Chips clicking together at a nearby table. Smoke so dense and heavy she can taste the ash on her tongue. Greer is as beautiful as ever in one of her crisp, gleaming oxfords, the lines of which Lois knows so well, how it puffs at her shoulders and opens to a particular toffee-colored freckle on her chest. She briskly orders their drinks and scans the crowds. Though there's no sign of the raw desperation Lois experienced last night, she can sense something is different. There is a sharper edge to Greer, her spine a brittle wire.

"Are you all right?" Lois asks her.

"Of course I am."

"So there was no issue with Rita's—"

"No issue at all. No one saw."

The bartender sets their tumblers on two cream napkins. June and Bailey have already disappeared into the crowd, and Lois briefly wishes she'd just ordered water, though she knows Greer wouldn't have allowed it. Everything has to be as it always is.

"How about we start with roulette?" Greer asks.

"All right."

When she slides her stack of bills onto the cashier's desk, Greer gets chips in a color Lois has never seen before: a shiny, un-scuffed black. "It's our last night in Reno, wish us luck," Greer tells the cashier, but he just shakes his head. Lois is shocked at how unfazed he is at such a sum of money. He must see more foolish decisions being made every evening.

At roulette, Greer loses twenty dollars and wins twenty back again. Lois stands beside her, uncomfortable in her dark silk dress; the bodice is too stiff, one of the seams puckering under her armpits and rubbing the skin raw. She watches Greer place chips onto the table and tries to remember how she normally acts at the casino. If she holds her drink up to her chest or lets her hand dangle at her side, the glass's smudged rim pressed against her fingertips. Every motion is jerky and mechanical, and she feels as if the other gamblers are watching her more closely than usual. A man in a navy suit stares at the dip of skin below her bottom lip. Two waifs who can't be more than eighteen scan her body from her ankles to her shoulders, hands cupping their mouths. Lois nervously rubs her wrist.

"I forgot my watch," she whispers to Greer.

"What?" Greer asks, tucking several more chips into her overfull pockets.

"My watch—I . . . I must not have put it on, and I need it to keep track of when—"

"Yes, Jesus Christ, I know."

Greer pulls away from the table, a muscle knotting at her jaw. Lois has already made a mistake. Greer shakes her head with a nanny's brusque annoyance and begins to unlatch her gold watch.

"Take mine."

"No, no, how will you—"

"I just need to know when to go to her table, and I'm surrounded by men with watches. I'll be fine."

They migrate to the slots, and Lois finishes her drink. For a brief while the alcohol's syrupy warmth soothes her, but a headache follows, swifter than usual. She knows she'd feel better if she could talk, but Greer doesn't invite conversation. And even if she was warmer, more like her usual self, Lois can't speak about their fellow gamblers like she normally does; if she does, they'll start to watch her like those at the roulette table, following her route from the slots to the bar to the third stall from the door. They'll tell the bartender, who will summon one of the pit bosses. *I don't know why exactly,* they'll say, *but I just sense something's wrong.*

Greer lifts her hand to summon a waitress, ordering them two gin and tonics.

"I thought I wouldn't have another drink tonight," Lois says.

"You need to. You look like you're at a wake. Especially in that dress," Greer says.

"It's green."

"It's black."

They smile at one another, buoyed by the lightness of the spat, its lack of consequence.

The drinks arrive, and Lois drains the glass in the same way she'd swallow castor oil as a child, opening her throat so as not to taste its rancid fishiness. As if the alcohol will keep her on this cloud of levity. But when she places the tumbler on the slot's counter, she realizes that Greer has become very still, staring out across the cacophonous crowd. Lois follows her gaze, but she's unsure what she's looking at—a girl clumsily adjusting a pale pink shoulder strap, an older, overweight man nudging a tower of chips forward. Greer rises from her seat.

"Is it time?" Lois asks.

Greer looks back at her, and for a moment her eyes have a frightened wildness, like the cows Lois and her mother saw herded into the back of a rusted gray truck one spring morning, as if they knew they'd be cleaved and drained within hours. But then she blinks and lifts her chin slightly, breathing out through her nose. Her face smooths to a placid calm just like it had the evening before.

"Are you really all right?" Lois asks.

"Yes, of course," Greer says. "I just need to use the restroom. I'll meet you upstairs."

"You don't want me to come with you?"

"To the restroom?" she asks, and even amid all of this, Lois feels a small, girlish curl of embarrassment.

"No, I'm sorry."

"Lois, for the last time, don't apologize," Greer says. "I'll see you soon."

Upstairs, Lois orders a French 75—a drink that should be sipped, the champagne's prickling bubbles ensuring she won't swallow it in one gulp. Her heartbeats have become rapid as a rabbit's. At Peg's table, the man in the ivory cowboy hat is rubbing the back of his neck and staring down at his meager pile of chips. It's 11:15, nearly time for him to leave.

She scans the neighboring tables, holding a teaspoon of sugared champagne under her tongue, and tugs at the hem of her dress. In the bar top's shadow, it does look black, not the color she thought it was under the bright lights of the department store in Chicago. Even the shopgirl hadn't seemed to want to sell it to her, plucking dresses in red satin and chartreuse chiffon from nearby racks, insistently hanging them over her dressing room door, but for once Lois could not be persuaded. She holds the gold watch against the fabric, to see if that will change the color.

The watch is familiar, she realizes. And not because Greer has worn it before. She sees a flash of the ranch house's dining room table, everyone's faces unknown to her, a flock of strangers. The air heavy with butter and pork fat. Dorothy, then just the redhead, lifting her thin white wrist.

Did everyone see what George sent today? He even had it engraved.

It is difficult to unlatch, Lois's fingers suddenly numb, almost as if she's wearing skin-colored gloves. She is telling herself it is a coincidence, but when she finally turns the watch face over, there it is: *For Dorothy, whose love is worth more than gold.*

A glass shatters, and she jumps. The bartender is apologizing and fumbling for a dustpan. A trickle of blood wets his thumb. Though she doesn't remember drinking, Lois's flute is nearly empty. The people sitting across from her at the bar have changed. Turning, she finds that the man in the cowboy hat has left Peg's table, but Greer is nowhere to be found. She turns the watch over—11:32, one minute after Greer should have taken her seat.

Peg looks out across the crowd. Lois tries to catch her eye, but Peg passes over her as if she were anyone else.

They are up to something, Ela would cluck at a brace of crows outside the kitchen window, and Lois feels this now, a chill constricting her rib cage. The instinct to run. She stands, and then sits again. Possibilities pulse: Greer given the wrong time by a drunken gambler; the watch a gift, Dorothy unable to look at it after George left her. One of the supervisors will sweep Peg's table at 11:55, and so Lois waits for another ten minutes before she abandons her seat, stashing the watch in her purse.

She laps the floor, her breath stopping at any strand of blond hair, moving so quickly that she nicks several gamblers with her shoulder and elbows, knocking someone's tumbler to the carpet.

"Excuse you!" they yell, but she keeps moving, thudding down the stairs in her heels.

It's then that she sees him. The handsome older man from the other evening who claimed to know Greer. He is wearing the same finely tailored suit and speaking to one of the pit bosses by the roulette tables, the one with the narrow eyes who gifted them two glasses of Sambuca. Lois's mouth sours at the memory of it, at the sight of them scanning the crowds in the same way she is. As if they are looking for someone.

She retreats to the ladies' room, taking a seat in the third stall from the door. Different girls enter the fourth stall, different knobby ankles and unfamiliar shoes, red suede pumps and scuffed spectators, none of them Greer's polished loafers. She tries to think of what could be happening, but the alcohol dulls her thoughts, not allowing them to take shape. She rubs her eyes, the heavy liner smearing onto her fingertips. A girl's fist is insistently rapping at the stall door.

She returns to the second floor and finds Peg's small, manicured hands shuffling and reshuffling cards, an older couple pulling out two chairs to take a seat at her table. It's 12:05, and the window for their theft has shut. Lois's breaths become shallower, and she finds herself walking toward the arc of green.

"Please place your chips on the table," Peg says without looking up.

"I don't have any," Lois says.

The older couple stare at her. The woman's ruby lipstick is dry and cracked.

"If you want to sit at the table, you need to play. If you want to play, you need chips." There is a blankness to Peg's gaze, which makes Lois want to knock off her glasses and tear at the collar of her silk shirt. Instead, she leans forward over the cards, her forearms pressing into the hard felt.

"Do you know where she is?"

"Where who is?"

This close, Lois can tell Peg is biting at the flesh of her cheek, noting a soft dip in the skin.

"What did she tell you about tonight?"

The older man stands, touching the woman's shoulder so she knows to follow. Lois hears the click of chips as they're swept into his palm. They don't want a part of any scene.

"I don't know what you're talking about," Peg says.

"Should I go ask your sister, then?"

"I don't have a sister."

"Excuse me, ma'am." Lois looks up to find the pit boss standing behind her, too close, almost as if he's about to pull out her chair and ask her to dance. Each grain of his black stubble is thick as a pin. "Will you come with me?"

It would not be difficult for her to run. He does not grab her like the man they dragged down the hallway by his jacket collar. Instead, he presses his hand firmly against her lower back, guiding her down the stairs so as not to draw comment. When they left, Peg turned back to her deck, though Lois noticed a tremor in her hands. The pit boss said they would speak after her shift.

"Where are we going?" she asks.

"Just to our back office for a bit. But don't worry, you'll be back at the bar ordering a cocktail in no time."

His voice is pitched to the false tenor of advertisements, men on the radio promising thinner waists and whiter smiles. She tries to think of what he may know and what, if anything, she should say. Whether Greer will be waiting for them in the windowless room. They wind through the crowd, faces rushing past her like a cascade of shuffled cards, until her eyes catch at familiar tanned skin, a forehead creased in concern.

Bailey steps in front of them, solid as a shield. The man's stride stutters to a halt.

"I'm sorry, what is this about, Roy?" Bailey asks.

"Nothing. We're just looking for one of the guests at your ranch, the tall blond girl, and we believe this young woman may be able to help."

"I don't know where she is," Lois says, to Bailey more than him.

"As you well know, I don't think Rita would want any of her guests brought into your back room."

"That may be the case, but this is a necessity."

"To you, not to the Golden Yarrow."

"I don't want to have to call the police." His voice is quieter, sharpening to a threat. Lois's pulse quickens. The watch is a lead weight in her purse.

"If it's actually that important, call the police. You can find us back at the ranch."

Bailey turns to Lois, and Lois knows to follow, though it's difficult to move. She wishes Bailey would take her hand. As they walk across the carpet, its ivy pattern coiling and tightening, Lois realizes she'll never return to the casino again. When she turns back for one last look, she finds more men in dark suits by the bar, gathering like storm clouds.

They emerge onto the street, the night air even colder. Bailey finds Charlie parked on the curb. He is asleep in the driver's seat, his head bowed over the steering wheel. She pounds her fist against the window glass.

"You need to drive Lois and June home. I'll send her out in a moment."

Charlie nods, leaning over to open the door for Lois.

"What about Greer?" she asks.

"I'll go talk to some of the staff and look around myself. It's going to be just like when we found Dorothy. When you wake up, she'll be in her bed."

Forty-Two

. . . .

n the backseat, Lois drops her head between her legs, digging her fingernails into her stockings. They aren't even strong enough to rip the nylon. She tries to imagine Greer at the police station or Greer returning to the Golden Yarrow, but neither scene coalesces. Greer had sensed danger. Perhaps the man is tied to her husband: a business associate, a college friend she met briefly at their wedding, another face in a procession line trailing down a wood-paneled, candlelit hallway, here to drag her back home. The watch a gift from Dorothy, and Peg merely a talented liar, adept at bluffs. Perhaps Greer will be in Lois's room, sitting cross-legged on the bed, ready to explain everything to her. Lois can almost convince herself.

The car slows, rumbling over the familiar gravel road. She lifts her head.

Too many lights are on at the ranch for the time of day it is, the night still a dark blue. "That's odd," Charlie says, and Lois feels the blood drain from her face.

Coming into the foyer, they find the whole house awake and crowded around Carol. They are all still in their nightgowns, their faces puffy from sleep. Carol's nightgown is a little too young for her, white cotton checked with woven cherries, the hem falling well above her knees and for some reason licked with dirt, as if she'd just run in from the yard. Patty is in the corner by the stand of walking canes, knocking them with her knuckles.

"Oh good, you're all back," Rita says when they walk in the door. "Is Bailey—"

"She's still there looking for her," Charlie says.

"Well, Greer's been back here. We were all asleep, but then I woke up when Bailey called, everyone woke up, really, and Carol was just telling us she left in a cab. Carol, well, she gets up in the night. She knows she's not supposed to, but—"

"She left?" Lois asks, her stomach tightening as if she swallowed a shock of ice water.

"She's coming back," Carol says.

Everyone turns to Carol, who is wiping her nose with her forearm. Mary Elizabeth pulls at one of her soft ringlets of hair.

"Why do you say that?" Rita asks.

"She told me she'd bring me a rabbit."

"A rabbit? What are you talking about?" Rita crouches so she's level with Carol's eyes.

"Miss Greer saw me in the yard and said there was a burrow of rabbits, a mama and a lot of little babies, and she had to go get in the cab to check on them to make sure they had enough to eat. And that if I stayed quiet on the porch she'd bring me back one of the babies so that I could have it as a pet."

It sounds like a fairy tale. Carol conjuring Greer as a princess in a puff-sleeved dress, a ribbon in her hair. Lois presses her hand against the doorframe to steady herself.

"That's why you didn't wake me?" Rita asks.

Carol looks to Patty, and Lois can almost see the thread between them, tight as a violin bow. The air in the entryway shifts.

"What else are you not telling me?" Rita asks.

"She's been going into different rooms. Mostly during the day, but once I saw her do it at night, when everyone was asleep. But that time she told me it was just to check on everyone, to make sure everyone stayed in their rooms just like you sometimes check on us."

There is sound and movement: inhalations of breath, hands lifted to cover mouths, and Lois can't distinguish who is near her any longer. All of the girls are out of focus except for Rita and Carol. She blinks to sharpen the room, a drone in her ear like rushing water, clutching her purse to her belly, terrified of the watch spilling out of its stiff satin. It has to be a dream—it's a scene in a film, one that she cannot place. A chorus of women. A little girl asleep in the woods. Greer dressed in black tights and a black turtleneck, slipping into darkened rooms.

"She's been going into people's rooms, their bedrooms? When did this first happen?" Rita asks, her fingers tightening around Carol's arm.

"I don't know. A while ago. She gave me a gift so I wouldn't tell anyone."

"What do you mean, a gift?"

"A silver locket with a rose on it, but she said I couldn't wear it until my birthday and that if I wore it before, she'd take it back."

"Wait, with a rose engraved?" June asks, stepping into the small, narrowing frame. "That's mine. I thought I lost it. How did she . . ."

Faces float past Lois—she is beneath the water, waves sloshing over her head. June rushes up the stairs and the older guest follows. Lois remembers the woman's large emerald ring, how it caught the light like an ember. Florence draws the sign of the cross against her chest and Lois catches the words *grandmother's brooch, strand of pearls.* Rita is saying something, yelling toward the kitchen, and the water's current becomes louder until it drowns out all other sound. She looks down at her feet, which have separated from her body. Pig feet on the counter, waxy and peach-pale, Ela taking out the silver stock pot, filling it until it's almost too heavy to lift, and Lois begins to walk slowly toward the living room, stumbling on the lip of the carpet.

Forty-Three

I n the morning, two policemen come to the ranch. They wear ill-fitting suits and smoke cigarettes on the front porch, asking Charlie about the horses. They're not like the policemen from films. Their voices have the patience of a schoolteacher and neither looks to be much older than thirty. When Lois comes into the living room after changing her clothes, one is giving Carol a toy sheriff's star, and they thank Anna profusely when she brings them iced tea, rising as she teeters toward them with an overfull tray. Though they may be suspicious of Lois, they do not show it, and interrogate her gently as if she is another child.

They ask her many questions. Where Greer might have gone. Where she has family, where she has friends. If Lois has names or addresses. How she got the bruise. Lois tells them everything she knows, a collection of facts so small she can hold them in the palm of one hand. Two sisters and two brothers. A mother dead. Though she knows what she can't tell them to protect herself, she is too numb to withhold anything else, to weigh and measure her words. Every time she finishes speaking, they sit in silence for several moments as if waiting for her to continue.

"So, you don't know anything else about her husband?" one asks at some point, his pen poised above a bare notebook page.

"No. I don't even know his name."

"All right. Anything else about her, though, that we haven't already discussed? Doesn't matter how unimportant you think it might be."

Lois tells them about how Greer never seemed to like any character from either book they read. A story about a house in Maine, the floor coated with rainwater. They begin writing, and Lois wonders if she should be saying any of this, if this is a betrayal worse than what Greer has done.

"And she never—she never told you to call her another name?"

"No. Why would she do that?"

"Well . . . ," he says, seeming to decide something after looking at his partner. "After talking to some of the staff at the casino and a colleague in Vegas, we think Miss Lang might not be who she said she was."

He tells Lois of reports of missing hotel room keys and missing clips of money from bedside tables. A girl who wore the same silk dress night after night at a casino. In Las Vegas, two days before Greer arrived at the Golden Yarrow, a man named Greg Lennon lost his room key, and after passing out in the bathtub he woke to find a girl going through his drawers. He came to the station with a deep gash on his forehead and a sutured slit in his stomach, a ripple of bruised knuckles at his side. Though he wouldn't admit to fighting the girl, saying he'd gotten into a brawl with a man armed with a switchblade earlier in the evening, the police did not believe him. In his description, the girl was nearly his height with light blond hair. She'd run off with his wallet and a slim leather bag of clothes.

"Greg Lennon?" Lois repeats, seeing the initials knotted at Greer's cuffs.

"Yes, probably not a coincidence. A man at Harrah's identified her, said he recognized her from another casino in Vegas and remembered the reports," the other policeman says.

Lois remembers what it felt like when the doctor told her that her mother had passed. She'd gone home to change her dress. Her mother was declining but not at the cliff's edge, or so they said before Lois left, before she chose to linger in the shower and stand naked in front of her closet, trying to remember which dress her mother had said made her look like a young Rosalind Russell. When the doctor met her in the hallway, sweat shimmering on his upper lip, she thought it was a mistake—so confident in the error that even when he said her mother's name she felt as if she were hovering several feet above her body, still watching it happen to someone else.

"And obviously the jewelry theft is serious, but she also emptied the ranch's safe."

"She emptied it?"

"Yes. Stole nearly two thousand dollars. And the maid told us she heard some banging and scraping the night before last, as if maybe the girl was packing up. But you never saw her take anything, or were asked to help her steal something?"

She looks at the policeman's hands, a smudge of ink on his thumb. In the kitchen, Anna has turned on the faucet, and above them the floorboards creak under the weight of someone's feet. *You can always tell someone's lying when they talk too much, or when they won't look you in the eye.* She hopes the sounds of the ranch are loud enough that neither of the men can hear her heart.

"No," she says, lifting her head.

When they dismiss Lois, she goes out to the pool. She has not eaten breakfast and in the morning sun she feels like a husk, one of the drying cicada shells that littered Lake Forest one summer, clasped to porch railings and tree bark. Sitting in Greer's chair, she runs her hands along the bottom rungs, as if there might be some cylinder of paper tied with string, a note passed beneath a desk. There's nothing, and she thinks of Peg at the casino—how she looked at Lois not as a conspirator, but as a threat. What plan had Greer shared with her? Was Lois always meant to be abandoned—a lookout, and then a fool waiting in a bathroom stall as Greer took a cab back to the ranch, where her bags were packed and ready for her to slip back into the night?

She takes off her jeans, the back of her knees and tailbone damp with sweat. She pulls at her shirttails to hide her underwear, conscious that the men may be able to see, and sits at the pool's edge. The policemen said they thought Greer had ridden east, away from the city. They told other neighboring stations to look out for a woman with light blond hair cut to the chin.

Dipping her feet into the water, she sees Greer in a pair of sunglasses that Lois thought looked like the ones Mary Elizabeth wore on the first couple of trail rides, the same honeyed tortoiseshell. Had she ever worn them when Mary Elizabeth was near?

There are brown leaves at the pool's bottom. A dead dragonfly floats by her calves, and she leans closer to see its veined wings. In the water's glass, her face begins to take shape. The small waves caused by her feet make her reflection unsteady, as if she's being swung back and forth. She tries to think of what she knows that is true, who Greer is if she is not from Manhattan, not an abused wife or a girl so wealthy that she walks into the men's section of a clothing store as if everything were already her own. Why she would push the girls in the way she did, unless it was just a test that only Lois passed, her only reward to be a jilted accomplice. She thinks of Greer's clothes: the soft, thin cashmere and finely spun cotton, crisp at the cuffs and collar; the tailored trousers cinched in place by a wide leather belt; and how all of the shoulder seams hit at the top of her biceps, hints that the clothes were not in fact made for her. And would she wear any of the jewelry she stole? The grainy strand of pearls or the emerald ring that always looked too bright, the color of poison?

Lois remembers how Greer had asked her for a glass of water the night before the planned theft, and how Lois found her by her dresser, and there is a spasm in her stomach, a sudden, pulsing contraction. Her knees jerk open so that her face is lost in the thrash of water, her throat thrusting forward as she vomits into the pool.

H ours later, she returns to her room. Anna made her a turkey sandwich which she ate without taste, swallowing it in three bites. The older guest, whose name Lois will never know, left for a hotel after saying she couldn't sleep in a room where she'd been violated in such a way, even if it meant staying in Reno an extra week. Rita gathered the remaining guests in the living room and apologized, her voice raw and strained, asking them not to speak to any reporters, that once they found out about the story they'd circle like vultures and it would be difficult for the Golden Yarrow to recover. They all nodded obediently. The sounds of Charlie sucking water out of the pool droned in the background.

Lois knows she has to call her father. A painful request for more money for the train. Ela will have to pick her up at Union Station and then there will be the quiet drive home, the skyscrapers giving way to oaks and elms. But she can't bring herself to do it. He won't say anything, but in his silence she'll hear that this is all as he'd expected. She's once again the disappointment, the child, the fool.

In her room, her sheets and blanket are still tightly tucked into her mattress. She has to pack her things—her printed poplin dresses and low heels, her western shirts and turquoise belt buckles, the linen shirts Greer had picked out for her, all of which suddenly feel absurd, garments pulled from a costume trunk. She approaches the bureau and runs her fingers along the wooden ledge, avoiding the oval mirror.

Can I have a glass of water?

Lois tries to think of how long she'd been in the bathroom. One minute, maybe two. It can't have been after—she'd been locking her door.

She slowly opens the drawer and unfolds the pale pink slip, uncovering her velvet jewelry box. She takes a breath and opens it quickly, as if that will lessen the pain of what's to come. Her mother's necklace, gone.

Forty-Four

. . . .

Lois rises early the next morning. She'd fallen into a dreamless sleep, though she does not feel rested, her forehead heavy as if she had too much to drink. Lying in bed, she calculates the day with a cool detachment. She will call her father before the courthouse hearing—they'd been able to delay it by a day, given everything that had happened—and stay another night at the ranch. The watch stowed beneath her mattress she'll bury in the damp soil of one of Rita's ferns. It's impossible to think beyond that. That in a few days, she'll be back in her narrow bed in Lake Forest.

Downstairs, she hears voices on the porch, and finds Bailey, Rita, June, and Charlie with Mary Elizabeth, sliding her suitcases into the truck's flatbed. Carol and Patty stand in front of Rita, fidgeting beneath her arms—one of Rita's hands rests on each of their shoulders, as if to pin them in place. Lois had forgotten Mary Elizabeth was leaving that day.

"I thought I'd miss you," Mary Elizabeth says.

"I'm sorry we won't be riding the train together," Lois says, and realizes how much she means it. They could have shared meals in the dining car. She wouldn't have to be so suddenly on her own.

"I'm flying, actually."

"Really? I thought you were scared of planes."

"I am, but after all of this—well, how can I let myself be scared of something like that?"

She looks to Bailey, whose face has the strain of false cheer, and Lois realizes how difficult it must be for both her and Rita, to have so many relationships be so transient, their home a way station. Mary Elizabeth hugs June, Rita, and each of her daughters, and then reaches out to Lois. They hold one another in a tight embrace, as if each is trying to tell the other something.

"I'm sorry that I never thanked you," she says into Lois's hair. "For what you did. I didn't know how—"

"Please, don't apologize."

Mary Elizabeth pulls away, taking Lois's hand and pressing it between her palms. "Come visit me if you ever want to get a little more comfortable riding horses."

Lois laughs. "I'll do that."

Charlie starts the engine and Bailey gets into the truck next to Mary Elizabeth, who waves goodbye. Several flies begin to loop overhead, and as they pull away, Rita shushes Carol, who is asking if she can have a slice of the pound cake Anna baked yesterday. Lois does not want to watch the car disappear, so she retreats inside, slipping into the kitchen. Anna is cracking eggs into a bowl, their brown shells littering the counter. The curtains hold the morning light so the room softly glows. Though she resists, insisting that she serve Lois at the table, eventually Anna lets her sit in a chair by the window to drink her cup of coffee. She watches as Anna clicks the stove to life and peels the potatoes, trying to think only of Ela, an apron looped around her neck, picking at a thread of thyme.

I n the afternoon, Lois puts on the navy dress she first wore to see her lawyer. She brushes blush on her cheeks and paints her mouth with lipstick. In the bathroom mirror, she feels as if she's looking at a photograph, a different version of herself tucked into a frame. Her lips feel gummy and dry. She considers trying on another dress, but she's already packed her things and doesn't want to sift through her suitcase. Her train ticket will be waiting for her at the station tomorrow morning and her father is wiring her twenty-five dollars. *Nothing more,* he said, though she would never have asked for it. She unknots her nylons and puts her wedding and engagement rings in her pocket—wondering briefly if Greer had seen them.

Bailey is waiting for her in the stairwell and Rita is on the front porch, watching Patty and Carol run in circles by the swing, war paint on their faces, gashes of blue and red. Rita jumps at the sound of the door opening. Her palm had been covering her mouth, as if trying to hold something in.

"You're off, then?" Rita asks.

When she smiles, Lois notices that her lips are chapped and her eyeliner smeared, small notes of disarray, and she thinks of the key to the safe, shame drying her throat. There are purple crescents beneath Rita's lower lashes.

"Should be back in a few hours," Bailey responds when Lois says nothing.

"Good, good. You'll return to the Golden Yarrow an unmarried woman, how about that?" Rita says, placing her hands on her hips.

Lois nods and tries to smile as well, though the effort hurts her cheeks. She knows she should apologize to Rita for so many things, but she doesn't know how to begin. Carol lets out a warbling battle cry. Both girls have picked up fallen tree branches and are breaking them against the trunk, shards of bark splintering into the air. Rita shouts at them to be careful, walking down the steps with Lois, the girls pretending not to hear until all that remains of the branches are nubs no bigger than their hands.

Rita looks back to Lois, shaking her head. Behind her, the leaves rustle in a rush of wind and Lois pictures clouds of red earth rising across the desert, twisting toward the house so that later Charlie will have to wash the painted wood until it gleams white in the sun. That first day, it appeared like such a simple structure as his truck crested the hill. A large house with green shutters resting in the shade of two maple trees. Not very different than several others they passed, a handful of other ranches her father must have considered, that Greer must have considered. Though of course she'd choose the Golden Yarrow, with its foolish, wealthy girls.

"What is a golden yarrow? I always meant to ask," Lois says.

"Oh, it's just a common desert flower. You've probably seen dozens of them, almost like weeds, really. They're nothing special."

"Then why did you name your ranch after them?"

"Well, it sounds much grander than that, doesn't it?"

Behind her, the engine sputters to life. Lois waves goodbye to Rita and slides across the leather seat, warm from the sun.

Forty-Five

· · · · · · · · · · ·

They drive in silence to the courthouse. Bailey clicks the radio on and off, her hands restless on the steering wheel. Lois can tell that she wants to say something. They haven't spoken since she brought Lois a glass of water the morning before, when she'd sat on the fainting sofa for what may have been twenty minutes or two hours, the wall in front of her shifting in the light.

There is too much between them. Greer's secrets and Lois's closeness to her, which everyone at the ranch must find suspicious, no matter what the policemen said. It sits beside them like another passenger. The city has begun to take shape before them, familiar brick buildings rising from the desert.

"Are you all right?" Lois asks.

"Yes. Well, as all right as I can be," Bailey says. "Angry at myself, more than anything."

"Why?"

"Looking back over everything, it's just, I don't know. There were all these signs I chose to ignore. Rita feels the same."

"What do you mean?"

"Well, she said she'd arrange her own transport to the ranch, which so few girls do, and she arrived so oddly late that first night, but she said it was because her flight was delayed into San Francisco. We never spoke to her in New York—a friend of hers called us to make the reservation, and there was so much noise in the background, as if she was in the kitchen of a restaurant. And then her face—but, well, we're not really strangers to that. Last October a woman showed up with broken ribs, could barely stand from the pain. That's why we gave her extra time as well, to pay us in full. It was obvious she was in danger."

"I'm surprised Rita allowed that. She seemed to hate her from the start."

"She didn't hate her, exactly. She just sensed trouble, but we'd never forced a girl to leave before, and I—I stupidly insisted—"

"It's impossible to imagine something like this. You can't be angry at yourself."

In Reno, they park the car and sit in silence. The domed courthouse rests in front of them, its facade lined by six stone columns. Bailey presses her thumbprints against the steering wheel.

"I overheard you on the telephone. Talking about moving to California with Greer."

"Oh?" Fear grips her.

"In Rita's study. I didn't mean to be listening—I was just passing by."

"Well, I was—we were. I didn't want to go back to Lake Forest and Greer didn't want to go home either, so she suggested we move there, but really, I had no idea—"

"No, no, I know. Rita told the police how your father arranged your stay, the check she has from your home in Lake Forest. And obviously you're still here, aren't you? I have a good sense for people, and I know you wouldn't have done what she did."

Lois nods and looks out the car window, bile creeping up her throat again, and she wonders if she'll vomit in the parking lot. Outside the car she can hear the sounds of a group of young girls nearby, grinding sticks of chalk across the sidewalk.

"She stole my mother's necklace," Lois says.

Bailey shakes her head in dismay, and Lois hates herself for soliciting this pity, for trying to emphasize her innocence, given what she planned to take. What she allowed Greer to steal.

"Did you tell the police?"

"No."

In front of them, the courthouse doors open and an older woman emerges, a flat black hat pinned to her hair. She pauses at the top stair to look out to the buildings and streets as if she'd never seen them before, and Lois remembers why she herself is here. A man appears behind the woman and they shake hands before she slips a pair of sunglasses over her eyes, descending to the city below.

"We're going to be late," Bailey says, looking at her watch, and Lois opens the car door, stepping out into the harsh afternoon light.

She's not in the courthouse for long. The proceedings take less than ten minutes. Lawrence is represented by a lawyer wearing horn-rimmed glasses who never once looks at her face, and Bailey's called as a witness to swear that Lois has resided at the Golden Yarrow every day for the last six weeks. When Lois takes the stand, they ask her to confirm the same facts, the judge speaking so fast Lois has to watch his lips to make sure she understands his questions.

"When you arrived, was it your intention to make Nevada your home?" he asks.

"Yes," Lois says.

"Is this still your intention?"

"Yes."

The moment she is pronounced legally divorced, Mr. Tarleton invites her to a nearby bar for a drink. She looks at his face as if he's a stranger, a man who'd just stopped her to ask for the time, the judge's words still echoing: *This marriage is declared at an end.* When the courtroom begins to transition, Lawrence's lawyer's briefcase latching shut, a new set of heels clacking against the tile, she comes back to herself and shakes her head. He doesn't persist, looking beyond her to a face he recognizes and clapping Lois quickly on the shoulder before scuttering away to someone more promising. With relief, she realizes she'll never see him again.

When she emerges in the daylight, she takes her rings out of her dress pocket and holds the weight of them in her palm. Bailey asks her if she wants to go to the bridge, telling her she doesn't have to if she'd rather keep them. Most of the girls throw away fake rings.

"I kept mine," she says, but Lois says she wants to go. Bailey will wait for her at the Riverside.

After crossing the street, she turns the corner to find the bridge looming before her, as much a part of the earth as the mountains. There are few people milling about, the dry heat particularly brutal at this time of the afternoon, and as she walks toward the railing she swishes her skirt back and forth to rustle the air around her thighs. She'd forgotten the pleasantness of bare legs.

Below the bridge, the river is a cold dark blue. She thought she'd feel lighter after the courthouse, but instead the weight on her shoulders seems to have gotten heavier. She wishes there was somewhere to sit. There is nothing to do but lean against the stone wall of the bridge, resting on her forearms. Looking down at her hand, she slips on her wedding band and engagement ring. The diamond holds the sun, so searing and bright that she looks away.

There's a part of Lois that always knew she would go back to her father's house. Though it had not felt like her home since her mother passed—besides some moments in the kitchen with Ela when she could almost imagine that her mother was just out on an errand, about to walk through the door with a bushel of peonies in her arms—she always felt her true self was locked inside it. That she would always be the little girl alone in her room dreaming of the movie theater, and that, try as she might to change, everything else could be peeled away like petals and that strange, lonely girl would be the dark heart of pollen. And perhaps, just like the others, Greer had seen her as little else. The perfect accomplice. An easy mark. Someone not easily remembered who was desperate to begin again.

Lois closes her eyes and twists off both rings, the gold catching at her knuckle. She imagines pulling her arm back and feeling the weight of them leave her palm, watching them arc through the air until finally they disappear beneath the river's skin with one clean swallow. In the water's blue, she sees the stones of her mother's necklace. It's difficult to know how much Greer could sell it for. How much she could get for a strand of pearls or an emerald ring.

Opening her eyes, Lois slips the rings into her pocket.

There is a bell latched to the door of the pawnshop, announcing her entrance. Inside, a man with a large white mustache is rolling a cigarette on the glass counter, tobacco flecking his fingers. He lifts his head as if he's been expecting her, licking the paper's edge.

Even though they'd only been in her palm for a few minutes, they are already wet and warm. Her fingers had tightened around them, her grip so fierce that Lois wondered if they would somehow slip into her body. But when she loosens her hand, they're both there, the gold gleaming under the store's lights.

"How much could I get for these?" she asks, placing the rings in front of him.

Forty-Six

· · · · · · · · · ·

Six Weeks Later

Lizards quiver through Lois's apartment. She finds one the first morning, pressed against a window screen. Another in the bathtub. Then, a week later, one stretched along a wall in her bedroom, nearly hidden by early evening shadows. It might be the same lizard, skittering between rooms. Sometimes she tells herself it's the lizard from the ranch, though she knows its body is different, darker and striated.

The apartment is in a white box of a building, and old men in undershirts smoke on the concrete walkway outside her front door. The unit itself is small and cheaply constructed. The walls are thin, the hinges of the kitchen cabinets are loose, and there are drizzles of hard blue paint on the living room floor. It always smells of exhaust and there is no balcony, though from her bedroom the skinny necks of several palm trees spike above the window ledge. Even within the apartment, she feels outside of it, which sometimes makes her feel connected to Los Angeles in an exhilarating, dizzying way, and other times makes her feel exposed and afraid. Every morning, she walks to a rotating handful of motels to use their pool, lapping from edge to edge. She's only been yelled at once. A woman in a housecoat demanded she pay for a night's stay until she realized Lois had nothing but a striped cover-up and a single apartment key, and so she turned from her, cursing in a language Lois did not understand. She knows she should experience the ocean, but its immensity, its wildness, frightens her.

She has a roommate, a girl from Oregon whose prettiness is as uncomplicated as a tulip's. Her name is Faye, and she's lived in the apartment for nearly a year. A friend of a friend of Bailey's—a waitress at Landrum's—connected them. Faye's roommate had just decided to move back home to Berkeley, leaving her stranded with two girls' rent to pay. Within the week,

Lois was moving into an abandoned room. In the middle of the floor stood a fish-shaped lamp with no light bulb. The windowsill was dirty with empty matchbooks and strands of dark hair. "She left a bottle of shampoo too," Faye said, which Lois used to wash every part of herself.

Faye moved to Los Angeles to be an actress. She is disinterested in Lois, rather vain and self-absorbed, which Lois thinks is probably for the best. She spends most of her time at auditions or her job as a cigarette girl at a nightclub in Hollywood, though Lois is never to tell Faye's mother this if she calls. Every day, she practices falling, her body thudding against the wooden floor. Sometimes she asks Lois to watch her, to make sure it looks natural enough. Lois tells her it does, though Faye never fully surrenders. Her knees bend too soon and her arm rises to protect her torso, the jerky reflexes of self-preservation. One morning when Faye is out on an audition, Lois attempts this herself, and her head knocks against the floor so severely that she tastes metal on her tongue.

After Lois pawned her rings for two hundred dollars, Rita allowed her to stay at the ranch for another week at no cost. The only condition was that Lois call her father to explain she wasn't coming home. Lois was at first surprised by this generosity, sick with guilt over everything that had happened, but it was obvious Rita felt guilty as well. That she felt she had failed to protect Lois in some way, and Lois had no choice but to accept this redress. She was a foal, wet-eyed and unsteady on new legs. The only thing she felt confident in was her compass, which pointed south, to Los Angeles. Though Rita tried to convince Lois that it was in her best interest to return to Lake Forest, Bailey found her Faye.

When Lois first moves in to the apartment, all she can afford is a mattress, but after getting a job at a makeup counter she begins to buy small things from flea markets: a bedside table with violets painted on its drawers, a square mirror she hangs on the wall. Lawrence sends her books and she asks Ela to ship items from her room: the lace curtains her father's mother brought over from Poland; a jar of sea glass; some of her notebooks, filled with drawings of faces and rabbits, ideas for different endings for films.

Rhett Butler reappearing at the front door and telling Scarlett he loved her, that he'd been a fool minutes before.

This is what she'd wanted of love, she realizes while reading it. A man on a doorstep. Nothing of the moments after, when you somehow find yourself alone again.

Faye brings a man back to their apartment every once in a while, and Lois can hear them through the walls. A palm slapping the plaster; high-pitched, rolling moans. The first night it happens, she imagines the guest as a dark, handsome stranger, a loose bow tie strung around his neck, and begins to touch herself, a heat building and cresting. But then in the morning the man emerges from the bathroom potbellied and pale, a wedding ring on his finger, and Lois feels queasy. She dumps out her coffee in the kitchen sink.

She has not told Faye she was married. Only that she is from a town outside of Chicago and decided to leave after her mother passed. Lois can only imagine what Faye's mother would say if she learned her daughter was living with a divorcée, and she does not want to be another thing the girl has to lie about. She keeps this from the girls at the makeup counter as well, though they are friendlier and more curious. She has not lied to any of them, which she claims as some small victory. When they ask more questions about home, the years before, she just changes the subject to the movie she saw the day before or their shared dislike of every customer, the myriad ways women are awful to women who serve them, as if this dynamic, contained and anonymous, excuses all sins.

Though she tells herself this is for her own protection, Lois knows she is keeping her cards close to her chest in the way she imagines Greer did, trying to decide which ones she wants to play. She wants to hold on to this power, this ability to create a new life unencumbered by everything that's come before, though she can already tell this is causing some of the girls to pull away from her. When she leaves her counter, Cynthia does not squeeze her hand in the way she does Abigail's. Though they go out for drinks, Lois has not seen any of their homes.

"Do you want to be set up with anybody? I know this producer. Television, not films yet, but I think you'd really like him," Cynthia says, trying on a new shade of lipstick.

"No, not right now," Lois says, turning to look for a customer who is not there.

After a month in the city, Lois begins to bring men home from bars or Sunday matinees. She keeps a paring knife beneath her mattress in case they become too aggressive, but if anything, they seem frightened of her. She tells them what to do to her body—how to position themselves on top of her, where on her neck to kiss—until she's learned exactly what she needs to come. After they've finished, she waits ten minutes and then slowly rises to put on her dressing gown, a cue they all seem to understand, fumbling for their socks and wrinkled underwear. Greer's words echo in her head. *Decide what you want from them, take it, and then leave.*

One afternoon at the makeup counter, Lois thinks she sees Greer. There's a glint of silver hair. A long arm plucking a beret from a faceless mannequin, the person's body half-hidden by a display of cascading silk scarves. The room narrows, a high ringing in Lois's ear, but then a stranger steps into the aisle—a woman in her fifties with a mouth like a crater. Afterward, a girl in a Chanel jacket calls Lois simple after she counts out the wrong change, and on the bus ride home every red light and car horn puts her further on edge. In her kitchen, she remembers how easily Greer composed herself after Lois brought her that glass of water, and she lifts the plate she was washing and shatters it against the drain.

Lois tries to push Greer out of her thoughts, but the anger is a constant drone. She sees her at bus stops, on park benches. She has dreams where they are sitting out by the pool. In the Golden Yarrow's shadow, her mother's bookcase stands next to her lawn chair, but every time she opens one of the books the words spiral into unreadable serpentine shapes. She wakes up sweating.

On certain nights, she misses the girls from the ranch, wanting to feel their bodies in the pressed heat of Bailey's backseat, the intimacy sprung from all taking the same blind leap. How innocent she was with them, how trusting. Some mornings, she wakes with throbbing aches in her calves, the same ones that made her whimper when she shot up by several inches at the age of thirteen. She does not know how to control how she is changing, alone in this city. She feels like a tree unknotting itself in the soil and also someone tending to it, trying to buckle its roots and train its branches to grow upward in clean, graceful lines.

Forty-Seven

B riefly, Lois tries to act. Everyone asks her if she wants to be an actress. It's assumed, if you've come to Los Angeles, that you want to act or sing, or marry an actor or singer, or a producer if you're smarter and want a house in the hills with a kidney-shaped pool. "Everyone here wants to be someone else," an older man tells her at a bar off Vine Street. "Waitresses want to be actresses, actors want to be producers, writers want to be directors, mistresses want to be wives, and the wives all want to be painters, for some reason."

Though she did makeup for countless school plays, it's never occurred to Lois that any of her classmates onstage could actually have become actors, that Bette Davis would have crossed the scratched floorboards of a humid high school auditorium. The actors she loves in films aren't really people. They're born on studio lots, a few inches taller than everyone else, their skin unblemished and their hair never unwashed. It feels impossible for anyone she knows, or Lois herself, to become one. But then, here is Faye saying a line on *The Lone Ranger,* their living room filled to watch it even though Faye is on set filming, everything in their apartment consumed by people Lois has never met, the sleeves of saltines, the shards of potato chips at the bottom of the bag, even the rind on a block of cheese. Faye is on the square screen with her face painted and altered, a mole dotting her upper lip, but still undeniably the girl who leaves her toenail clippings littered on the ledge of the bathtub.

This might be it, Lois thinks. What everything has built toward, even the afternoons with her mother. Perhaps this is what she would have wanted for Lois, if she had known it was possible: for Lois to be one of the strong, complicated women on-screen they felt they knew so well. As she falls asleep that evening, she says the word *actress* again and again, as if trying to conjure something physical she can hold in her hands and examine the next morning in the light of day.

But when she goes on an audition, she hates everything about it. How she feels during the hours before, as if someone is digging their fingers into her belly. The lines she is given for some clichéd western, words no girl would ever say. The way the casting directors look her over like one of her father's butchers swiftly sizing up a cut of meat.

"Do it again, but not so much like you're doing a Katharine Hepburn impression," one of them says, mustard crusted at the corner of his mouth.

In the hallway, she walks toward a tall wastebasket to throw away the script, only to find it's already filled with paper, the same lines repeating on page after page. She felt a flare of anger when they dismissed her, a sudden, fiery desire to prove them all wrong and become so famous she could blacklist each of their names, but now all she feels is relief. This is not what she wants: to pretend to be someone else, to recite dialogue written by faceless men. On the bus, she wipes off her lipstick with the back of her hand.

T hough she has to wear makeup at work, on her off hours she applies nothing more than mascara. It feels odd to put on anything in her cheap apartment. She likes the freedom she has to rub her nose and not worry about foundation coating her fingers, but she loves to apply it to her customers, to watch how they light up when she tilts her hand mirror toward their faces. The girls at the counter tease her for being old-fashioned in her application, as now they're being told to use liner to exaggerate the shape of the lips, to soften jawlines and cheekbones so that older women look plump as a teenager, but Lois pays little attention. When Faye goes on auditions, Lois does her makeup, covering her freckles with foundation and powder. She does not know if this is good, to make people look like different versions of themselves, but she is still good at it, and finds peace in the process: the erasure of features and then the slow recovery of them, heightened and perfected.

"Have you ever thought of doing makeup on set?" Faye asks one afternoon, admiring her reflection in their bathroom mirror, her lips a new shade from the store: French Coral.

"Do you think I could?" Lois asks.

"You should update your eye shadows, it's all pastels now, but you're better than the old tart from *The Lone Ranger*. She kept telling me about some night she spent dancing with Jimmy Cagney when she was my age, all a bunch of applesauce, I'm sure, and she drew on my mole too big. I had to wipe it off and do it myself or I'd have looked like a pen exploded on my upper lip."

Lois is flattered and intrigued by this idea of herself, standing on set wearing an apron lined with brushes, but she has no idea how to realize it. It's not an image in a mirror, but an image in a dream.

At a party that Cynthia throws in her apartment, Lois meets a girl named Tam who does makeup for Paramount. She is stylish and acerbic, wearing black pedal pushers and a short-sleeved black turtleneck. Lois approaches her, something she never would have dared before Reno. They rhapsodize over Elizabeth Taylor's eyebrows and complain about the new saccharine palettes, and Tam tells her how all of the actresses filing into her trailer look the same, candy-sweet and vacant, and what she would give for more faces like Marlene Dietrich's or even Claudette Colbert's. "Actual, real women who weren't just cast because the director assumed they'd sleep with them," she says, and Lois laughs. As the party disassembles, she takes Lois's phone number and says she'll call with a job for her, if she wants it. Lois lies in bed that night, imagining what she'll tell everyone at the store, though days pass and the only times the phone rings it's Faye's mother, asking when she's going to move back home.

n early September, Ela mails Lois a check for one hundred dollars. *The living room vase,* she writes, and Lois remembers the fall morning she discovered that hiding place, when she faked a stomachache and everyone else went to church. Another theft, though one she can live with. She knows her mother would want her to have it, how she'd cluck her tongue at Lois's new poverty but be proud of her independence, the freedom she's found hundreds of miles away—something she herself never had. Lois hasn't spoken to her father since their brief phone call at the ranch, when she explained she wasn't returning to Lake Forest. His anger was cold, resolute, as if he were receiving news of some investment that had plummeted. He did not plead for her to come home. She worried that he'd unleash his fury at Rita, but he never called, at least during the extra week she was there. Like Lawrence, there was undoubtedly part of him that was relieved to be done with her.

Dollar by dollar, Lois is sending Rita money in envelopes. *To pay for that extra week,* she writes, though truly it is for what was robbed from the safe. Though she knows Greer was the one who turned the key and pocketed the bills, she's the one who truly opened the metal door. This guilt is another thing she struggles to leave behind, like the memories of Greer laughing at Lois's stories or the way she'd snap her fingers when ordering Lois a gin and tonic, hooks that her blouse snags on as she tries to walk out the front door.

One afternoon at the counter, she remembers the name of the heist film that surfaced to her at the casino, *The Last Sting,* and she turns to tell Greer, somehow expecting her to be waiting by her side.

Forty-Eight

· · · · · · · · · · ·

When Lois receives her fourth paycheck, she goes to a discount clothing store on Ninth Street. It's nothing like the department stores she frequented in Chicago or even the small shops in Reno, staffed by older men who smiled at her as if they hadn't seen another soul in days. Here, children run under the clothing racks, their heads knocking hangers to the floor, and the employees, middle-aged women with thick calves and too much mascara, huddle at the register, rolling their eyes at any customer who interrupts them to pay. It doesn't smell like the department store where she works, floral with the perfume that girls spritz onto the wrists of housewives and husbands. It has the woozy blankness of bleach.

Lois circles the store several times, unsure what to pick up from the long rows of clothes. Since arriving in Los Angeles, she's worn her old dresses to the store and at home stays in her jeans and some of the prim cotton blouses she brought from Lake Forest, pushing the linen oxfords to the back of her closet and selling her turquoise belt buckle at a pawnshop on Alameda. Now she is overwhelmed by choice. The patterns pose endless questions: *Is this too busy? Too plain? Too much like something a child would wear? Too much like something a grandmother would wear?* Next to her, a sunburned woman with tufted orange hair lifts several skirts from the rack, folding them over her arm as if it's the simplest thing in the world.

Under the fluorescent light of the changing room, she stands in only her underwear. She'd lifted a pile of clothing from the racks, anything in her size she could find. "Are you going to put all of that back yourself?" one of the salesgirls asked, her hands on her hips, and Lois nodded, though she intends to do no such thing. She buttons a blouse with a scalloped collar over her bra, pulls on plaid capris and then a thick yellow skirt, fumbling with the zipper. It all looks cheap and garish. The colors wash out her face, which hangs hollow and pale in the mirror, even with her summer tan. She is sweating so much that she worries she'll damage the clothes, and so she picks up her own balled-up skirt from the floor and wipes her armpits dry.

After taking in several deep breaths, she tries on a simple green dress, nearly spartan in its details, the buttons lining the breast the same dark pine as the cotton. When she looks at her reflection, something shifts inside of her, the click of a key turning in a lock. The dress's sleeves fall to the dimple of her elbows and the waist is slightly loose, making her feel as if she can actually breathe. The color brightens her eyes, lifting the brushstrokes of moss in her irises. She can see herself sitting at a diner in this dress while reading a book; standing with a throng of friends at a warm, smoke-filled jazz club; or walking through an airport, a cream suitcase in her hand. She turns in the mirror to look at herself from the side, thinking she should shorten it by an inch or two, how that will reveal her calf at exactly the right curve.

Much more Lois, I think, Greer had said.

That girl at Parker's was different from the one in the green dress who looks back at her now, less familiar, but perhaps Greer had felt the same way as she folded the stiff cuffs of one of Greg Lennon's shirts. Perhaps every reflection is a lie. Lois shakes her head, refusing to let Greer ruin this, suddenly wishing someone were waiting for her outside the thin slats of the changing room door. Not Greer, or even her mother—just a friend.

At the register, she buys two of the same dress, spending all of the money she allowed herself. When she gets home, she puts one on just to lie in her bed.

At the store the next day, she tells Cynthia about Lawrence. Cynthia was complaining about her boyfriend, who still hadn't introduced her to his parents, even though they lived just a little farther north in Oxnard. Lois knows she wants to be told that this doesn't mean anything, that he still plans to marry her.

"I met my ex-husband's parents about a month in and, to be honest, I wish I hadn't, so maybe count yourself lucky—he might be sparing you," Lois says.

"Excuse me?" Cynthia sets down a compact whose hinge she was fiddling with. "You were *married?*"

There is so much she could say, the temptation to lie pulling at her like a current, to be anyone other than who she is. She married a Spaniard during a year abroad from Barnard. In Las Vegas she'd been hitched to a compulsive gambler she'd known for three weeks, the ceremony held at a little pink chapel next to a motel. She'd been cheated on or beaten, arriving at a ranch in the middle of the night with a bruise on her cheek the color of rot. Then she remembers the changing room, and she rubs her thumb against one of her dress's pine buttons.

"For almost four years, back in Lake Forest. Which kind of sounds like too long and not long enough, I'm not sure."

"Jeepers, it all—well, I was wondering, with how you always changed the subject. I thought maybe you were with some married man you didn't want to talk about."

Lois laughs. "No, definitely not."

Cynthia looks around to see if anyone is listening, her voice lowering. "I have some friends who I wish would leave their husbands."

"Really?"

"One of them spends my friend's entire paycheck on Hamm's and An-gels tickets. I have to pay for her every time we get lunch. Everyone was so happy when they got engaged, cracking open champagne like it was New Year's Eve, but I always thought she would be better off alone. Though, of course, I would never say that to her."

"I'm much better off alone. I think—I think a lot of girls would be."

"Well, I'd never leave Don, if we ever do get married, but if you needed to—if your husband was anything like that, I'm glad you did. It's very brave."

"Thank you." Lois smiles, warmth washing her cheekbones.

On her ride home, she feels lighter. When she was little, her mother showed her how if she stood in a doorway for a minute and pressed the back of her hands against the jamb, her arms would lift upward when she took a step forward, as if pulled by some invisible string. She feels this now, passing the city's streetlamps and bushy-headed palms, as if some weight she didn't know she'd been carrying had been loosened from her shoulders, her head brushing the bus's ceiling.

The next day, she asks Cynthia for Tam's phone number. Tam picks up on the sixth ring, sounding as if she's just woken up from a heavy sleep. It takes her a moment to remember who Lois is, but then her voice warms and she recalls the promise she'd made, how the job she'd thought of had actually fallen through because the director had crashed his Alfa Romeo on the Pasadena Freeway, shattering his right leg and four ribs. Lois tells her she'll take anything, and Tam promises, in a way that doesn't feel hollow, that she'll ask around. "I'm glad you called. I like your persistence," she says.

Over the next several days, Lois leaves her résumé at four studios, clipped sentences about school plays and the two months she'd been at the counter swallowed up by the paper's yawning white. Girls wearing silk scarves take them from her while never meeting her eyes, phones cradled at their ears. She glimpses the lots, buildings lined up like shoeboxes. A part of her imagined a circus. Horses clopping across the hot pavement, showgirls in feather headdresses smoking cigarettes in the alleys, men in white T-shirts pulling a replica of a sphinx through a house-sized door. Instead, there are just expensive cars preening quietly in parking lots. The buildings all shut, so she can't see what's inside.

Forty-Nine

At the start of October, Faye goes away to New Mexico to shoot a film with actors so unknown even Lois hasn't heard of them, and Lois has the apartment to herself. The first night she has Cynthia and Abigail over for drinks and they invite other friends, several of whom Lois has met, her circle slowly expanding. Though they don't have that intense, consuming closeness she felt with Greer, they're all becoming better friends, and she tells herself this is enough for now. They know about Lois's marriage and her mother, where her father works, and why Ela is the only one she writes to. A week ago, Lois finally called the number June gave her, and she had drinks with her and Harry. The conversation was stilted, accelerating around some joke or shared memory and then petering out to long sips of their cocktails, especially when Harry kept wanting to talk about Greer, no matter how sharply Lois changed the subject. Still, it's comforting to know someone else in the city.

At the apartment, the girls eat peanut butter and crackers, potato chips, a box of chocolates Abigail was gifted by a customer. There is a thoughtless joy to this consumption that Lois loves, a lack of judgment.

They drink and talk. They complain about work, about men and their mothers, until eventually someone clicks on the television and they all gather around its small, crackling screen. They watch *The Gene Autry Show*, which Lois doesn't care for, the theme song looping through her head in the shower and on her bus ride to work. Gene's horse lumbers across the screen, a woman riding next to him. She smiles so large Lois imagines she could count each of her teeth.

"Her lipstick's too dark for a cowgirl," Lois says.

"Do cowgirls and cowboys still exist?" Cynthia asks, and turns to Lois. "Were there any on the ranch?"

"There was a ranch hand, but I don't think you could call him a cowboy."

"Was he dreamy?" Abigail asks.

"No." Lois laughs. "Well, not to me, anyway."

The television is still a novelty, an extravagance. Though Faye won't say exactly how she got it, Lois assumes a man bought it for her, as it's not the sort of purchase a girl living in this apartment could afford on her own. She and Lawrence had just been talking about buying one and there was only a radio at the ranch. In the evenings, especially when she's alone, it comforts her. The sound of voices, how the screen bathes the apartment in a cool white glow.

When programming ends, the girls all go home.

The next night, Lois turns on the television after making a plate of scrambled eggs. The news is on. New York had played New York in the World Series and the Soviet Union has an atomic bomb, which makes her think of the man at the Highlands, the immense plume he saw in the desert. The eggs are oversalted. She thinks briefly of Anna's bowl of eggs, rich with cream, and how she'd sometimes spread them over a crisp cut of bacon as if they were butter. She craved a porterhouse the week before, wanting the fatty brown marrow on her tongue, but had to walk away when the butcher told her the price per pound. Outside of her cups of coffee in the kitchen, when she thinks longingly of Ela, these are the moments when she misses home.

She finishes the eggs and slumps down on the couch, lifting the waistband of her dress so it rests above her stomach. After a moment, she takes it off entirely. The blinds are open but she doesn't particularly care—it's the same as lying in her bathing suit, and the men on the balcony across the way are old enough not to be a threat. The broadcast ends, the screen momentarily dark. A commercial begins.

The first is for a television, which Lois never understands, as it's impossible to imagine someone with a television set buying a new television set. A man in a suit stands proudly in front of his purchase, his children sitting at his feet, their hair parts straight as a pencil. Lois rolls her eyes, scratching at the soft, downy hair below her belly button. The screen crackles to black again.

And then there is a clinking of piano keys, and Greer appears.

Lois is upright, her feet on the floorboards. Greer's hair is dyed brown and curled into a glossy wave, her eyebrows colored as well, and she is wearing a polka-dot shirtwaist dress, an apron tied at her waist. The shot cuts away to the blunt shape of a refrigerator and Lois slips to the floor, walking on her hands and knees until she is inches away from the screen. She blinks, pressing her fingertips against her eyelids, but when she opens them, Greer is still there. The shock rolls through Lois all over again, goose bumps sweeping across her thighs.

"You're going to be so glad you chose the Westinghouse upright freezer," Greer says, resting her slender fingers on a chrome handle. "You'll never bend down again, digging around for food. . . ."

Her voice is pitched to the tenor she uses with bartenders, amicable but cool, so they know the distance they're meant to keep. As a brunette, she's more conventionally beautiful. Her eyebrows are pronounced, mirroring the line of her cheekbones.

Lois is warm, even in her underwear, and thinks absently about getting the fan out, though she knows she can't move. She follows Greer's flat irises. It feels as if somehow Greer is watching her from the television screen, that they are locking eyes in the same way they had whenever one of them wanted to say something without a word.

The camera cuts to a close-up, and Lois notices that Greer is wearing a necklace, the chain tucked into her dress, disappearing into the long, lean shadow of her chest.

It's her mother's necklace, Lois knows and does not know. The image is furred so the chain is no more than a line, and in another moment Greer's disappeared from the screen. Replaced by a man smoking a cigarette in a fishing boat.

Lois sits in front of the television until her eyes burn. It is well after midnight when she moves to her bed. Outside her window, wind rakes the palm fronds, and her body aches as if a fever is settling into her bones, an intensity of anger radiating from her joints. For Greer to come to Los Angeles, the city Lois had desired. For her to be so flagrant as to audition for a commercial. For her to have sold Lois's mother's necklace, for her to have kept her mother's necklace.

She imagines Greer haunting parts of the city she's come to know so well: picking up her dry cleaning at the shop run by the old Jewish couple, eating a piece of rye toast at the counter of the new diner on Seventh, ordering a martini at Musso and Frank's. She imagines herself walking through the restaurant's doorway, Greer's slow smile as she sees her, tapping the shoulder of the man next to her. She says a few words to him that Lois can't hear, and he rises so Lois can take his seat.

Lois thinks of how she could hurt Greer like Greer had hurt Lois, if she found her like this. The insults she could spew, the scene she could cause: throwing the briny glassful of gin onto Greer's face and ripping the necklace from her throat. The anger that had dissipated over the past months roaring back like a fire. How she could curl her fingers into a fist, tightening the rigid muscles of her arms, the ones that she stretched every morning as she swam until her mind burned black, incinerating any thought of *Rebecca,* of white shirts, of how much she shared of herself, emptying her pockets, her purse. How before anyone could stop her, she could give Greer a fresh bruise, dark as a plum.

Fifty

· · · · ·

Lois sleeps until noon. It's a Monday, and she is without a shift. When she wakes, she feels ravenous, almost light-headed, as if everything she felt the night before had consumed some part of her. Her stomach scraped clean.

Still in her nightshirt, she turns on the television, alert for the commercial's melody. The broadcast echoes through the house as she makes herself one sandwich and then another, though neither calms the tremor in her fingers, the new hollowness in her limbs and chest. It continues as she drinks her coffee at the kitchen table, as she takes a shower, washing her hair once, twice, perhaps three times, her mind absent from her body. She is hovering near the water-stained ceiling, looking down at her dark head and shoulders, just like on the day her mother passed. This feeling its own small death. The self momentarily splitting like an atom. She does not know what she is searching for, on this calm, quiet day in her apartment. What she hopes to find by catching the commercial again, by finding Greer's image, fixed behind the glass. By finding Greer at all.

She shakes her head with the vigor of a horse and turns the faucet to cold, coming back to herself, her abs clenching. She stays under the frigid spray until she can feel every inch of her body. Each hard knuckle, each firm muscle. The callused soles of her feet.

Her bedroom is bathed in golden light. The sun in Los Angeles is different than the sun in Lake Forest or Reno. Stronger, somehow, so that she can see every angle of the city clearly, the pebbled corners of buildings and the clean lines of the parking meters, as if some camera lens she is looking through is slowly clicking into focus. Or maybe this is just something she likes to tell herself. In her closet, one of her green dresses greets her. She slips it over her head and buttons up the breast, her fingers calm and steady. Without looking in the mirror, she runs a comb through her hair.

Faye left the keys to her old Hudson, telling Lois she could drive it if she filled the tank with gas. She plucks the key from the bowl on the kitchen counter and walks out the door.

All she knows is to drive west. She hasn't been to the Pacific since arriving and does not really know how to get there, simply turning down any road she can find, boulevards and skinny lanes lined with sleepy ranch houses, until she sees signs for Venice. By the time she arrives at the ocean, it is early evening.

There are not many people left on the beach at this hour. The sun is nearly set, the sky blushing orange and violet. An old man with a long white beard sleeps in a deck chair, seagulls pecking near his toes, and a couple walks barefoot closer to the water. A young girl sprints ahead of them, crouching down and then looping back, presenting them with some prize she found on the wet sand. Lois smiles at the uncomplicated joy on her face. The ocean itself is beautiful, lapping lavender near the shoreline and then stretching out to a steely blue. Though in many ways it looks no different than Lake Michigan, Lois can sense its vastness, can see the rib cages of blue whales and the soft, rotten wood of shipwrecks littering its floor, though its power is more than that, something elemental, prehistoric. Though she thought this would terrify her, her body responds to it. It pulls any lingering anger from her like a poison.

She unzips her green dress. Kicks off her low suede heels into the sand and pulls her lace slip over her head. In nothing but her underwear, she walks toward the water. The cold shocks her ankles and then her thighs. A rope of kelp brushes against her calf as she wades deep enough so that she can let a long breath out and dive in, pushing against the current. She rises and begins to cut into the waves, pulling her body forward. There is such a relief in this motion, in the strength of her arms and the firm kicks of her feet, even in the ocean's slow, seismic roil.

She feels something frail flip against her heel. A fish, most likely, though not one she can name like those in Lake Michigan, the harmless forms of trout, perch, or bass. She does not fear it or anything else below or beyond her, the endless miles of dark water. She does not fear being pulled out in the way she was that one summer so many years ago, or during the countless days since then on shore. Now she is strong enough to withstand the current, and the ocean does not feel frigid like it had moments before. Her muscles hum with heat. She turns onto her back and takes in a deep breath, letting the waves rock her body back and forth.

Above her, the sky is hardening to a sapphire. The moon is hidden, and she thinks of Ela and how she'd comment on the moon's phase every evening, its waxing and waning, and how she should telephone her tomorrow. Some old folklore, that a new moon is a time to begin again. Lois closes her eyes, imagining herself watching the Westinghouse commercial back in Lake Forest, as if she had never known Greer. It would be another image to envy, another film promising something grander that would always seem beyond her reach—a life that no one truly knows. Without Greer, she wouldn't know what it felt like to wander a flea market alone, tasked only with pleasing herself; to have one of the girls at the counter offer her their last cigarette; to wake in the morning and lie in bed for an hour, listening to the finches flutter outside her window; to float in the belly of the ocean. She wouldn't have these quiet moments, small and bright as pearls, when she realizes that her life is finally her own.

This far from the beach, there is an incredible quiet. She can't hear the cough of revving car engines, the mewing of seagulls, or the clips of strangers' conversations. Only her strong, steady heartbeat.

As she slides her key into the lock of the apartment, Lois hears muffled voices inside. Faye is not due home until the next day, and when she opens the door, she realizes she left the television on.

On the fuzzed screen, a woman in oversized plaid pajamas rises from bed and screams at her reflection in the mirror, yelling for her husband, who looks like Lois's Cuban neighbors who are always listening to baseball games on the radio. The woman's eyebrows are a little wide-set, her nose too pronounced. "An actual, real woman," Lois murmurs to herself as she slips off her sand-glazed shoes. Her dress is still damp, her hair a tangle, but she is too tired to do anything but collapse onto the couch cushions. She thinks of the young girl from the beach that evening, now splayed on a worn Persian carpet before a television, watching this woman on a studio set of a New York apartment, the man playing her husband waiting in the wings until she calls his name. The screen flickers to a commercial for Bosco syrup: chocolate drizzled into a glass of milk, then curled atop a bowl of vanilla ice cream.

Kneeling in front of the television, Lois clicks off the set. It hums for another moment and she presses her hand against the glass, warmth blossoming across her palm.

The phone rings, and she rises to answer it.

Acknowledgments

Thank you, Caroline Bleeke, for understanding what this novel was on such an elemental level, for making it so much sharper and brighter, and for giving it a home at Flatiron. I don't know what I did to deserve you. Thank you to Sydney Jeon, Christopher Smith, Erin Kibby, Keith Hayes, Dave Cole, and everyone else at Flatiron for their work bringing this novel into the world. To Jamie Chambliss and Margaret Sutherland Brown for their unwavering belief in its potential and for their deep wells of support, patience, and kindness, especially as I navigated all of this with a newborn.

I'm grateful for every writing teacher I've ever had, those who encouraged me and those who made my skin thicker. Sherry Medwin, thank you for believing in me when I was a lost, wayward teenager. To Sergei Lobanov-Rostovsky for giving my stories shape and fire. To all my friends at Grub-Street, my first writing family. Thank you to Sewanee, Bread Loaf, and StoryStudio for their support and community. In particular, thank you to Lauren Groff for her incredible grace and guidance and to Rebecca Makkai for her invaluable insight and boundless generosity.

Thank you to Tom Houseman, Jake Mattox, and April Nauman for staying on the ranch even after our class ended. To Jessica Chiarella for her razor-sharp insights and ability to get to the beating heart of every character. Thank you to Matthew Rickart for reading innumerable pages over nearly twenty years, for countless book recommendations and mixes, and for always being a trusted reader and a trusted friend.

The Divorce Seekers by William and Sandra McGee was essential to my research. Thank you to Sandra for her additional guidance and encouragement, and to Mella Harmon and everyone else who worked on the Reno Divorce History project.

Though I've doubted myself at every turn, I'm profoundly lucky to have friends and family who have always believed in me. Thank you to Juli and Peter Dorff, Russ Resslhuber, Pamm Schroeder, and Rikke Vognsen for their support. Thank you to my Aunt PT and Uncle Chris for their love and their understanding of the power of a good cocktail.

Thank you to my brother, Alec, and my sister, Molly, for being my first and best friends. I'm still striving to be as cool as either of you but am happy just finishing in third place. Thank you to my dad, who gave me art, music, and movies and always made sure my window was open to the larger world. Thank you to my mom, who gave me novels and poetry—you taught me that I have something worth saying and have always listened. This book is yours as much as mine.

Thank you to Bob, my partner in every sense of the word. You've always understood that writing's a part of who I am, and you've pushed me to value both it and myself. I don't know where I'd be without you, and I'm honored to call you my husband.

And to my brilliant Willa. May you know every freedom.

About the Author

ROWAN BEAIRD's fiction has appeared in *The Southern Review, Plough-shares,* and *Gulf Coast.* She lives in Chicago with her husband and daughter. *The Divorcées* is her first novel.

Recommend *The Divorcées* for your next book club!
Reading Group Guide available at
www.flatironbooks.com/reading-group-guides.